Lethal Chain

Joseph Souza

For information, contact Joseph Souza via http://www.josephsouza.net.

Lethal Chain is a work of fiction. The names, characters, places, and incidents portrayed in the story are the product of the author's imagination or have been used fictionally. Any resemblance to actual persons, living or dead, businesses, companies, events, or locales is entirely coincidental.

Author photograph by Doug Bruns.

Edited by Monique Happy Editorial Services
http://www.moniquehappy.com/

ISBN: 1508945683

To Allie and Danny, who inspire me every day.

CONTENTS

Prologue
1993

Bobby felt exhausted and scared, but he tried not to show it in front of the others. He hadn't gotten a full night's sleep in weeks because of the non-stop bombardment of high-decibel noises blasting from speakers surrounding the compound. Night after night a harsh spotlight had been trained on their facility to prevent them from communicating by flashlight. During the day the men below flashed rude gestures, giving them the finger or slicing their hands across their throats. Sometime they lobbed percussion grenades in order to frighten them. For the first few days he felt as if he was losing his mind. But then he took a few deep breaths, tried to remain brave for the sake of the younger kids, and remembered that God was watching out for him and the others.

He had his books and tried to read, but found reading impossible, except for his dog-eared copy of the Bible, which he read any chance he got. Sleep came in brief increments during the day once the bright lights died and the rain drove everyone back indoors.

It seemed as if he'd just closed his eyes when he was roused back to reality. A disturbance went up outside. He raised his head up and peeked out the window, even though he'd been warned to stay out of their sight lines. A few of the men inside had been shot as they sprinted through the building, and so he was careful not to linger for too long near a window. The humidity was terrible this evening and only made the stench worse. The odor of death and decay permeated the air and there was no escaping it. He knew that his own body odor reeked, but by this point he and the others had become used to it. He couldn't remember the last time he'd bathed or showered, the water having long been shut off. But God wouldn't care what he smelled like once he reached the gates of heaven.

The blare of satanic metal music blared over the outside speakers. Sitting against the wall, with his knees tucked under his chin, he glanced up and saw the phosphorescent glow of a spotlight shimmering against the corridor wall. The wall had been repainted a few times in order to hide the vulgar words someone had scrawled in protest. He pushed himself up to a standing position, making sure to keep his spine straight. At fifteen, he knew he looked young for his age. And he'd been skinny even before the rationing of food had started.

He put his hands to his stomach and felt the jagged bones protruding from his ribcage. Since they'd cut off the electricity, the surplus food stored in the freezers had long gone bad, and they'd been forced to eat as much of it as possible before it spoiled. Fortunately, they'd stored an ample supply of canned goods for when the day of reckoning came.

God, please forgive me for hating them. Only You can render judgment over men's souls.

Darkness settled in and Bobby found he could move around more easily at night. Men hustled past him, talking in low voices and running close to the ground to keep from being spotted by the snipers. A few of the men brushed past him and down the hallway. He had no idea what they were doing or where they were running to. No one stopped to talk to him or give him instructions, knowing full well that he'd been ordered to remain nearby in case he was needed. Most of the women and children had been ordered to stay on the first floor, strictly forbidden to come upstairs. Only one woman was allowed to be on the second floor, primarily because she too had an important job to perform.

He ducked down the hallway, trying not to show any fear. Eerie shadows danced along the blood-spattered wall as the

2

spotlight darted randomly across the interior of the building. Sweat poured down his face as he thought about the possibility of dying here in this building. The humid air enveloped him and he would have given anything for the metal wings of a fan blowing cool air over his body. The rainy weather of the last few days had been a blessing. Although he felt alive and invigorated by this epic struggle, he'd also experienced a prescient dream recently that the end of times was near.

A shot rang out and ricocheted inside the building. He hit the floor and covered his ears, trying in vain to block everything out. The sounds of gunshots shouldn't have surprised him by now, but each new assault never ceased to put the fear of God into him. He'd seen many people shot and killed. Some had died instantly and had to be buried in the mass grave that they'd dug during the torrential rainstorm. Others who'd been shot lingered for days, suffering from the intense pain of their injuries. Knowing that the end was near, they'd spent their final hours on the planet praying to God for salvation.

He approached the room. The closer he got the more he could hear the great man speaking. His familiar voice was followed by the pounding of a typewriter. The cadence of his voice almost sounded like he was preaching the Gospel, and just listening to the man reassured him that everything would be fine. Dying did not scare him as much as dying a long agonizing death. Because he knew that in death he'd be set free and end up in a far better place than this short, miserable life he'd lived. Not that he wanted to die just yet, but if it happened he hoped it would be quick and painless.

One of the men in the hallway shouted; gunmen outside were approaching the building. Everyone understood that they couldn't go on like this for much longer. After all, they had agreed to surrender once their leader completed this one final piece of the puzzle. He pressed his back up against the wall and slid down until his butt rested on the littered floor. The amplified noise outside shifted to vile gangster rap. He covered his ears and pressed his eyelids shut, but it did no good. The hard cuss words rattled through his bones and pummeled his lungs. He tried to concentrate on the sound of the man's voice in the other room, but couldn't begin to comprehend the depths of the man's wisdom, especially with that Godless music blaring outside. A gunshot went off outside and he saw the blinding beam of light move across the wall.

Bobby heard the words *plague* and *pestilence* before he nodded off. Sometime later he was jolted out of his sleep by a deafening explosion. He shot up into a standing position, sleep deprivation playing tricks with his mind. Someone cried out and men began to sprint off in various directions. He peeked out the window. Tanks circled outside, the sound of their engines moving toward them. A familiar voice shouted orders to follow the others into the bunker, but he stayed put, knowing that he'd been told not to leave until ordered to do so. Surprisingly, he could still hear the man's voice followed by the woman's fingers pounding the typewriter. A loud crashing noise went up and a massive engine shifted gears. Before he knew what happened the man had come out of the room and placed his hand on his shoulder.

Bobby glanced up and realized how haggard the man looked. Despite being shot, he'd been up for days interpreting passages and had lost a significant amount of blood. His arm was wrapped in a blood-spattered sling and there was a cut along his cheek. The man leaned in and put his slim pale face next to his. His curly hair was damp with sweat and his breath was hot. Someone sprinted past them, waving his arms and shouting for them to run. The air hummed with electric currents, stirring and sparking. He could feel a wall of heat rising up from the first floor as if the flames of hell were trying to break through to the surface. After squeezing his shoulder, the man placed a rolled-up manila envelope in his hand.

"You've been chosen for this, Bobby. Take this and go now."

"But I don't want to go. I want to stay here and fight with you and the others."

4

"There'll be no victory this time, Bobby. We're sacrificial lambs being led to their slaughter."

"I don't care. I'm willing to die in the name of God."

"You're our only hope," the man said, leaning down and gazing into his eyes. "Go out there and tell our story, and make amends for this crime against our people."

"But how will I escape? They're all around us." He noticed the tall boy standing next to him. "There's nowhere for me to run."

"Samuel will show you the way. Once you get out of here, keep running and don't look back. There'll be someone waiting for you. God be with you, son." He smiled and then kissed Bobby on the cheek. His lips felt dry and clammy.

"I hate them for what they've done. Someday they'll pay for what they've done."

"You must learn to forgive, Bobby. But I hope you never forget what happened here."

"I don't want to forgive."

The man smiled. "I know you don't, Bobby, but it's God's will. Take good care, son."

Tears spilled out of his eyes and the man gently wiped them away with his calloused thumb. Then he turned away from him and walked back into the room.

Bobby looked over at the tall boy named Samuel. He was older, maybe sixteen or seventeen, and wore thick glasses that made his eyes seem much bigger than normal. The taller boy rarely spoke to anyone in the compound, especially not him. Samuel nodded and took off down the corridor and he followed behind. Gunshots went off all around them and he could hear the bullets pinging off the window frames and making a distinct *sphffft* sound in the wallboard. Covering his head, his eyes began to burn with pain the further he ran. It reminded him of the times he screwed up and had been forced to peel onions all day in the kitchen. Only this time it was a hundred times worse. Descending the stairs, he noticed that the sun was beginning to rise. He followed the thin boy down to the basement, barely able to see

5

through the tears. The stench of decay down here was much worse than upstairs, and he understood why. Against the wall were three freezers containing rotting food.

The boy led him to another room. Once inside, he and Samuel began pushing a large file cabinet across the gritty floor. A can of peas fell from the top and rolled along the cement. Samuel ran over and unlocked a small plywood door located on the wall and behind the cabinet. The burning sensation was not as bad down here as it had been upstairs. Once he'd pulled the door back Bobby saw a dark hole no larger than the ones he used to dig as a kid in the field behind their crappy little house with its crappy little chickens pecking away at the dry, crappy dirt. Samuel handed him a flashlight and then put his hand on his shoulder.

"Godspeed, Bobby."

"No way I can go down that hole." Terrified, he stared down into the black void. Crawling through there would be like descending into hell itself.

"Get out of here before it's too late." The tall boy pushed him toward the hole. "It's up to you to tell everyone how we got screwed by them. And to deliver this message." He shoved the manila envelope hard into his chest.

"What message?"

"There's no time to explain. Just go before it's too late. And make sure you hold onto that envelope as if it were your own life." The boy pushed him into the hole, despite his protests, and then closed the door behind him. Bobby pummeled the plywood and cried out to no avail. But the door was locked and he could now hear the file cabinet sliding back in place, sealing him in this tunnel.

His body began to tremble and he contemplated breaking the door down with his shoulder. But then the tunnel began to shake and dirt from above sprinkled over him. An engine above rumbled and appeared to be getting closer. Terrified, he suddenly felt as if he might get buried alive in this pitch black tunnel. He felt around in the dirt with his hand; the hole was barely large enough to accommodate him. Then he gripped the envelope and scurried forward on hands and knees. Turning on the flashlight only enhanced the endless horror of the tunnel. He had no option but to keep crawling and not look back. Using his elbows and knees, he made his way down a steep embankment, scraping his head against the dirt ceiling. The faster he crawled, he thought, the less chance he had of being buried alive in this tomb. And if that happened, no one would ever find him.

He crawled for what seemed like hours until finally he saw a pinprick of light up ahead. The stinging in his eyes had become a slight irritation now, but his knees and elbows ached, and his hands seared with pain. He wriggled over the last hundred feet until he reached the bead of light. The hole above was covered over with a metal plate allowing in only a speck of light the size of a dime. Using his shoulder, he rammed into the weighted disk until it eventually dislodged, allowing him to clamber out into the fresh air.

The sun baked his head and shoulders as he rose to his feet and squinted in the light. *Praise to God,* he thought, reveling in his miraculous crawl to freedom. He happily gulped in the fresh air, momentarily forgetting about the others. There was nothing in sight for miles. Just endless plains coming into focus. His hands burned and when he brought them up to his face he noticed a patchwork of blisters forming along the contours of his swollen palms. A thunderous explosion sounded off in the distance. Looking behind him, he saw a large plume of black smoke coiling into the sky. Then it all came back to him: the shootings, loud music, and continual harassment leading up to this slaughter. Wiping the tears from his eyes, he gripped the rolled-up manila envelope in hand, wondering what he should do with it. Upon looking up he saw a short stocky man with big ears and wearing a bolo tie walking toward him.

"Hello, Bobby. I've been waiting a long time for you to crawl out of that hole," the man said, holding his hand out to greet him. "It's about time those bastards pay for they done."

7

Chapter 1

The sky darkened and turned purple and the winds gusted violently. Tag poked his head out of the hole in the ground and scanned the small island he'd been stranded on these last few months. To his horror he saw a wall of water rushing toward the small island. Giant waves pounded the rocky shore and shot up in the air like Old Faithful. He clambered out of the hole until he was standing on the grassy knoll. Pine trees twisted and torqued in the wind. Judging from the fast-moving clouds moving in, he feared that this nor'easter would be a violent and destructive storm.

If it were up to him he'd try and erase Cooke's Island from his memory banks. But because his family was still alive and out there, waiting for him to emerge from hiding, the indelible experience of that biological attack would remain seared into his soul until his final days. His nightmares and grim flashbacks had not been merely bad dreams but symptoms of post-traumatic stress similar to the kind experienced by soldiers returning home from war. And yet how does one recover from the experience of seeing once-normal people turning into hyper-aggressive cannibals riddled with smallpox sores?

Fez scampered out of the hole and shouted out to him. He waited for the kid to catch up to him before hiking over to the rocks stacked along the shore. A sheer cliff of surf exploded against the labyrinth of rocks, sounding like a land mine going off.

They trudged across the mud-splattered island, struggling against the violent gusts, until they made their way toward a clearing located in the center of the trees. The raft they'd been working on sat on a barren patch of land. Next to it was a handsaw and a roll of twine.

"Tide rises another foot and we'll be under water," Tag shouted. "We need to finish this raft now."

"Want me to start cutting trees?" Fez asked.

"I'll take care of that," Tag said. "Where's Oggy?"

"Last I saw of that stoner he was still passed out in the hole."

"Good. We don't need him now anyways."

They got to work. Tag set about with the saw, harvesting only trees of a certain size. The wind whistled through the branches, causing the logs to bend away from the handsaw. He cut them to size and then positioned them across the base he'd previously constructed. Once the top logs had been laid perpendicular to the bottom, Fez held everything together while Tag looped the twine around the logs and secured them together.

Rain began to pepper their faces. Tag worked as quickly as possible threading the twine, his once nimble fingers used to handling the deadliest of viruses. But now they were cold, wet, and calloused from living on this island. He wished he'd built a higher work base when the weather had been nice, but then again he'd never been stranded on an island before. Nor had he ever built a raft. Once he got into the rhythm of lacing the twine around the logs he was able to move much faster, and in just over an hour the two of them had constructed a relatively sturdy vessel.

Now they had to carry it down to the surf. In their emaciated states it had taken all of their energy just to build it. He realized that they'd need Oggy's help to drag it down to the western end of the island where the protected cove facing the mainland would allow them to push off into the bay. Hopefully Oggy wasn't too stoned to help them.

He ordered Fez to go back down the hole and bring him back. Fez took off running, his long, straggly hair flapping in the

9

wind. A few minutes later he returned with Oggy, who looked not the least bit worried about the approaching storm.

"Whoa. You boys going somewhere?" Oggy asked.

"This island is going to be underwater very soon," Tag shouted. "Look how far the water level has come up already."

"And check out those purple clouds headed our way," Fez said, pointing off in the horizon. "It's going to get a lot worse, Oggy."

"The storm surge alone is going to rush over this island and inundate your hole with seawater," Tag said.

"Don't worry about me and my hole. I know how to survive out here," Oggy said.

"Will you at least help us carry it down to the water?" Tag asked.

"Damn straight I will," Oggy said.

"This is your one chance to get off this island," Fez said.

"Fuck the world, kid! Rather stay here than go back to all that other bullshit. Now grab the end of that raft and we'll carry her down."

They positioned themselves around the raft and lifted on the count of three. They carried it a short way before they had to stop and rest. Sucking in air, Tag realized that apart from losing a lot of weight, he'd also lost much of his muscle as well. It took them a good fifteen minutes before they made it down to the cove. From where he stood Tag could see the storm swell moving toward the mainland. Off in the distance, Portland appeared like a black dot on the horizon.

The rain battered them as they rested the raft on the tiny spit of beach. His back and arms ached from the exertion. Living on this island for the last month, the bulk of his calories had come primarily from the fish and rabbits they'd harvested, carbohydrates being difficult to come by.

"We have to leave now while the tide is high," Tag shouted over the roar of near-hurricane-force winds. "Hopefully we'll be able to ride the current into shore."

"Good luck, dudes," Oggy said, the rain dampening his long greasy hair.

"You'll die if you stay out here, Oggy. The winter will finish you off," Tag said, trying one last time to convince him to leave with them.

"Hell no! I'm building a fireplace in my hole with an exhaust system and everything. I got enough firewood to survive the winter. Figure I'll dry out some fish and rabbit, and as much seaweed as possible," Oggy said.

"You're going to die, you dumbass," Fez said, shaking his head. "And my dad's not going to pick you up this time when you get in trouble."

"I haven't seen your dad in a while. He alright?"

"He's dead, you dumb fucking stoner!" Fez shouted, waving his fist in the rain. "How many times I tell you that the pox got him?"

Oggy scratched his beard as if confused by the kid's words. "You guys wait here a sec before you leave. I want to give you something."

Oggy turned and ran up the hill and into the teeth of the wind. While they waited for him to return, Tag and Fez pushed the raft into the shallow cove. Tag reached down and felt the temperature of the water; the cove was relatively warm for this time of year. The storm must have pushed the jet stream closer to land. He gazed out toward Portland and saw that the waves were growing larger.

The prospect of surviving the five-mile journey unnerved him, particularly since he had to keep an eye on Fez. But the reality of his plight told him that he had little choice in the matter; if they stayed on Rabbit Island then they would both die.

The wind caused the trees to groan as it blew through their limbs. He realized that their only hope was to keep the raft afloat and let the storm surge carry them in. If the storm took a sudden turn they might find themselves being dragged out to sea where they would either die from exposure or else get picked up by the Coast Guard and arrested for treason.

The rain switched tempo and blew vertically. Tag looked up and saw Oggy running down the hill holding a pack in his right hand. He turned to Fez and saw sheets of water gushing down the kid's face and arms.

"I wanted to give you this before you guys left. Consider it my gift to you, seeing that I won't be needing it anymore," Oggy shouted.

"What is it?" Tag asked.

"Clip it around your waist. The pouch is waterproof." Oggy handed it over. "My military ID and driver's license are inside. And there's directions to my mom's house in Westbrook too. It's all yours, bro."

"Thanks," Tag said, holding the bag.

"I know you're in trouble with the law, man. Fuck 'em," Oggy said, slapping his wet shoulder. "You're now me—Robert Ogden. Once you make it to the mainland, go to my mother's house and tell her we served together in Iraq. Tell her I said you can borrow my wheels too. Keys are in the kitchen drawer. Under my mattress is a little over two thousand bucks in cash. I got no use for it here, bro. Wish there was more, but that's all I saved."

"Thanks," Tag said. "Sure you don't want to come with us, Oggy? This is your last chance."

"Why would I ever want to leave this place? I'm living the friggin' dream." Oggy gave them both quick hugs. "Now you two better get going before you miss your wave."

Tag secured the belt around his waist and then he and Fez dragged the raft deeper into the cove. Once they were standing in three feet of water they climbed atop it and lay prostrate on their stomachs. Tag used his free hand to paddle toward open water, encouraging Fez to do the same. Almost immediately the current began to pull them away. His pants instantly became soaked and the cold Atlantic seeped into his bones. But he felt fortunate now to have Oggy's ID with him. It gave the two of them at least a fighting chance to make it back to the mainland without being arrested and taken into custody.

It didn't take long for them reach open water. The waves grew in stature and the wind picked up the further they floated away from the island. He instructed Fez to wedge his hand between the logs for a tighter grip. The raft rose and fell, and he struggled to keep them facing the mainland. But the churning, swirling waters proved near impossible to maneuver through, and the raft began to spin violently in the dangerous currents.

Tag looked over and saw a wave break over Fez. The kid closed his eyes and let it wash over him, trying desperately to hold onto the raft with his left hand. Realizing the futility of paddling, he shouted for Fez to hold on with both hands and allow the current to carry them in. The kid swung his arm out over the edge and nearly got swept away, but somehow he managed to reinforce his grip. The raft spun without warning, tilting dangerously to one side like one of those tea cup rides at the Fryburg Fair, and when Tag looked over he saw Fez sailing high above him.

The raft righted itself and plummeted down a trough of black water. It felt as if they'd dropped twenty feet in less than a few seconds. Tag looked up and saw a wall of water headed toward them. It lifted them into the air, shooting the raft up at a 90-degree angle. They rode the peak and then shot down the backside as if sledding a hill. Caught in the turbulent eddies of the ocean's current, the raft twisted and turned at will, and it was all he could do to hang on. Beneath him he could hear the logs groaning and cracking, and he prayed that the raft would hold together long enough to deliver them to safety.

Tag could barely feel his hands now. He turned and saw Fez take in a mouthful of ocean as the raft corkscrewed in the shoals. At least they hadn't hit rocks—yet. If that happened the raft would shatter upon impact, sending the logs flying like surface-to-air missiles. There were a lot of rocks hidden in Casco Bay and most of the sailors in these waters used detailed navigational charts.

His foot hit a sandbar and when he looked down he saw an oily streak churning in the brackish water. He jumped back on the raft, smelling something pungent and saline. The water here bubbled over as if boiling hot. It took him a second before he realized that a school of bluefish had been feeding among some elvers. A wave pounded over them and without warning the raft jettisoned back out to sea.

"We're being pulled back out," Fez shouted, his rainswept face emerging from the sea.

"It's a rip. Hold on and the current will pull us back in!"

"This water's friggin' cold, Tag."

"I know, but if we let go we'll be swept out to sea!"

Another giant wave headed toward them and he shouted for Fez to help spin the raft around by kicking his feet. The waves were now coming in threes, each bigger than the one that preceded it. It lifted them up and over the shoal and pushed them forward as if they were body surfing. The two waves behind the first juggernaut had the same effect, and because of their momentum he figured they must have made it safely over the sand bar. Had they been sucked into the nearby whirlpool they would have gotten battered beyond repair.

A ripple of thunderheads loomed off in the distance, bruised and purple. The raft buckled and pitched, struggling against the restraints holding it together. A series of jagged rocks approached to his left and he paddled mightily to keep from crashing into them. His entire body was soaked to the core. He eyed them over the crests, not anticipating the thick, double-headed waves now pounding him from both sides. The storm worsened and the gusts increased in violent increments. His hands now felt like icy claws grasping the logs. The chop shifted and tossed the raft like a child's toy. Fez's wiry body flew in every direction but somehow the kid continued to hang on. Tag admired the tough little bastard.

"We're getting closer to land. Hang tight, kid."

"It's hard to breathe," Fez shouted, snorting seawater out of his nose. "Don't want to die out here, Tag."

"We're not gonna die!"

The storm clouds raced overhead, dark and pregnant. Tag lost track of time and thought for a moment that it might be nighttime. A jagged bolt of lightning hit nearby, electrifying the water. A weak current passed through his body as they caught a massive wave and rode the crest. At its peak he could just spot land five hundred yards away. Just as quickly they dropped like a roller coaster into a long, narrow trough. It felt like being swept into a gulley, the likes of which he and his family had hiked a few years ago in the Arizona dessert. Tag glanced over his shoulder and saw a bigger wave rolling up behind them. The raft spun unpredictably toward the incoming wave and as it did so his foot again scraped sand. *Damn!* They'd got hung up on another sandbar.

The raft took the wave head-on and Tag watched as they rose up the crest. He could just make out the smooth surface of Cooke's Island far off in the distance. Rabbit Island appeared now as a tiny speck on the horizon, barely visible to the naked eye. But rather than rolling through it like they'd been doing, the wave broke, causing the raft to flip. Fez shouted out his name as they flew upside down through the air. Tag knew they'd both be crushed if the raft landed on top of them, but his hands were so cold that he couldn't release his grip on the greasy bark.

His back slammed hard against the water and as he landed his hands came free. The water churned and he became stuck in a fast-moving whirlpool. He swallowed a mouthful of salty water and opened his eyes to the swirling green madness. For a brief second, as he rolled through thick coils of seaweed, he feared he might not surface. Then the current shot him upwards like a torpedo. His head broke the water's surface and emerged into the dim light of day. The rain pelted his face and made it hard to see. He gasped and sucked in air only to see the raft heading straight toward him, skimming the crest of another ten-foot wave. Although his energy was waning, and his lungs seared with pain, he dove back into the roiling ocean, propelling himself downward until he felt the wave's energy pass.

He popped his head out of the aftermath and saw a jagged bolt of lightning hit the surface ten yards away. A weak current of electricity zipped rough him as he searched for Fez. Where the hell was the kid? He tried to stay afloat and locate him but couldn't get his bearings in the turbulent surf. Three waves hit in rapid succession, knocking him far below the surface. He opened his eyes and saw the swirling chaos, felt the pull of death, and yet surprisingly didn't fear it. Was this how drowning victims felt before letting go? His lungs expanded like two water balloons stretched to the limits. The ocean felt as if it was gently wrapping its arms around his body and giving him a loving embrace. All he had to do was surrender to it and the pain would soon end.

But then he thought about his family, hopefully still alive somewhere and waiting for him to return. They needed him as much as he needed them. He'd survived that horrific biological attack on Cooke's Island and had miraculously come out the other side. And what about the kid? That was his immediate concern right now. He at least owed Fez a decent chance at a normal life. But after what happened to him and his family on that island, could the kid ever have a normal life?

Tag held his breath and propelled himself upwards. The raft splintered apart and the logs skated to the surface like dangerous projectiles. He felt a sudden pain in his shoulder and realized that one of the logs had just rammed into him. It spun wildly to his left after striking, nearly ripping off his face. Reaching out, he somehow managed to grab hold of it. A surge lifted his body upwards and then dropped him down again, battering his tortured shoulder. He gulped in salty air and prayed that he'd remain above the waterline for just a little bit longer.

The log rotated in the surf, sending him hurtling underwater. His grip came free and he floated off. The log's bristly bark spun inches from his nose. He was close to giving up when his feet hit a mound of sand and sent him tumbling face first into the water. He stood to his chest in the roiling surf, watching as an incoming wave bowled toward him. Turning, he saw that the beach was not a hundred yards away—he'd made it! The wave crashed over him. After it passed he noticed a grove of trees rising up over a series of sand flats. Some piping plovers flew out of the dunes. He pushed his way toward the beach, struggling against the backlash of the powerful current, waves still cascading over him. His entire body began to tremble from the cold the closer he got to the beach.

Fez was nowhere in sight.

He collapsed onto the wet sand and crawled on his hands and knees until he was far enough away from the pounding surf. The tinkle of rolling pebbles crackled in his ears. Despite the onslaught of rain and the intermittent strikes of lightning, he lay on his back, gasping for breath and trying to calm himself down. His head throbbed and his vision became blurry from the physical exertion of the journey. His body convulsed and before he passed out he thought of Fez, praying that the kid had washed safely ashore.

Chapter 2

The minivan made its last stop at the corner of Yucca and Wilton. The driver, a friendly looking man with a courteous demeanor, spoke with the individuals for a few minutes before asking them if they'd like to come back to the church and enjoy a cold drink and nice meal. The five homeless glanced thirstily at the sign on the van: The Church of Revelations. The tallest member of the group shook his head and disappeared into a nearby alley. The four others laughed, counting their blessings at such good fortune. Then they headed toward the van.

The driver stood nearby, lending a hand and guiding them safely up the stippled metal steps. One by one they made their way inside, stowing away what little possessions they had until they were seated. Despite the horrific smell now permeating the van, the driver made his way up the stairs and stood staring at his grizzled passengers. He counted fourteen heads staring back at him. Out of the group, maybe four were teen runaways. Satisfied, he passed out bags filled with cheeseburgers, fries, and drinks. Then he climbed behind the wheel.

Hollywood teemed with traffic this time of day, making the going mind-numbingly slow. Waves of shimmering heat rose off the blacktop, and a depressing patina of smog hovered over the L.A. metropolis. And yet the cool air blowing inside the van made the ride comfortable. No one complained or made a fuss. The passengers, hot and weary, unwrapped their greasy burgers and sipped from their colas, which to their delight had been spiked with rum.

After forty-five minutes the driver pulled up to an abandoned office building a few blocks off Santa Monica Boulevard. He parked in the back of the facility and announced that they'd arrived at their destination. Unlocking the back door of the building, he pointed them up toward three flights of stairs, where he promised more wine and food would be served. All but the homeless kids proceeded without hesitation, the kids still young enough to be wary of such false promises. But after some gentle coaxing, the lure of fast food and more cheap booze overcame their reservations and they dutifully climbed the stairs and made their way toward the belly of the warehouse.

"Ain't no church I know of operates out of a warehouse," one kid said as he climbed the stairs. "And they sure as hell don't give out free booze."

"The Lord doesn't care how you come to him, just that you're saved," the driver replied. "Whether on your knees or carrying forty ounces of Hurricane Malt Liquor, God welcomes all who come to Him."

"That dude's my kind of God," another kid replied, laughing.

Once they reached the top of the stairs, they were greeted by an unremarkable man with the slightest hint of adolescent acne across his face. He stepped aside and allowed them through. The large metallic door shut behind them and clicked, and in a matter of minutes, and without much resistance, the homeless found themselves surrounded by three armed men. The man with the acne ordered them to their knees. Those who refused were made to submit by force. A few protests went up, which were quickly snuffed out by a smack to the ear or a jab to the back with the barrel of a rifle. The three men strapped each of the victims to a gurney before wheeling them into a vacuumed-sealed room. A few of the kids struggled against the restraints and cried out. The older ones, having lived on L.A.'s hard streets for most of their lives, resigned themselves to their fate.

The man with the hint of acne wasted no time as the subjects were rolled into the room. He slipped on his pressurized blue suit and entered the staging area between the treatment room and office space. An ultraviolet blue light attached to the ceiling activated, killing any pathogen on contact. Not the most efficient staging process, but it would suffice until he made his way out of this dilapidated facility.

Using an industrial pair of scissors, he quickly cut away whatever clothing covered their arms. Once he'd finished, he slipped on a pair of latex gloves and produced a hypodermic needle from one of the drawers near the back of the room. He flicked the head with his middle finger until a small droplet of liquid splattered against the floor. One of his assistants, wearing a suit and mask, rushed over and poured a cup of ViralChem on the stained concrete where the droplet had landed. "A million particles of virus in one drop," he continually had to remind them. A look of satisfaction spread over the man's normally placid face as he quickly made the rounds, injecting half of his guinea pigs with the infectious agent. Only one subject was given an experimental vaccine.

With the first part of this experiment now complete, he exited the room and stood in front of the two-way mirror. He could clearly see both the control and treatment groups through the double glass window separating the two rooms. Now he just needed to sit and wait. How long it would take was anyone's guess, but by his estimation he calculated three days before the incubation period had transpired. He walked toward the desk in the center of the room and studied the monitor sitting on the surface. The armed members of his crew, relieved at having completed their assignment, collapsed on the couches behind him, resting their Uzis over their laps. The men joked and laughed among themselves while listening to the driver brag about how adept he was at enticing the homeless into his van.

Less than a day passed before the man with the acne noticed the first signs of the infection in the treatment group. He smiled; the disease was progressing just as expected. The human body seemed to be a better facilitator of the organism than did all the mice he'd experimented on. Sweat cascaded down the subjects' faces, all of which had started to turn a pale shade of blue. Their breathing became labored as they writhed in agitation, and they sneezed and coughed violently. Soon after the control group fell ill. After three days he noticed red spots developing along the exposed sections of the test group's skin, the first signs of internal hemorrhaging. Their agitated state grew increasingly violent as they clawed at the restraints in an attempt to free themselves. The control group looked on in fear as the treatment group wailed in agitation. The whites of their eyes had turned red; they had begun to progress well into the third spacing, which consisted of significant bleeding between the layers of skin.

The man with the acne stood and stretched. Glancing at his watch, he noticed that it was just after two in the morning. Perfect timing. The bright illumination from the treatment room provided the sole source of light in the otherwise dark loft space. He turned and saw that the security detail behind him had fallen asleep on the tattered couches.

He walked over to the two-way mirror and studied the two groups. It delighted him to no end to see that all but one member of the control group had become infected. This was the exact outcome he'd been expecting. The one homeless girl unaffected by the infectious agent had been given an experimental vaccine made from mouse and human antibodies that had proved successful in the primates he'd once experimented on in a previous life.

A sense of personal satisfaction came over him as he contemplated his viral masterpiece. He'd created an airborne thread virus that targeted the prefrontal cortex of the brain, resulting in hyper-aggression with only modulated body hemorrhaging similar to the rabies virus. And he'd duplicated these results in three separate experiments, meaning that the virus had passed rigorous scientific muster. In addition, he'd managed to dry out the virus and collect it in the form of dried flakes, something that had never before been done with this particular pathogen.

21

The time had come. The experimental phase of his plan was now complete. He slipped on his pressurized blue suit and entered the staging area between the treatment room and office space. The ultraviolet blue light attached to the ceiling activated.

He made his way into the room. The first sound he heard was the muffled, ear-piercing screams from the treatment group upon seeing him. Thick, clotted blood seeped from the pores of their skin. Splatters of vomit and diarrhea lay puddled on the floor, all containing billions of virus particles. He grabbed a needle and plunged it into the forearm of the closest homeless man. After a few seconds the vein collapsed on itself and blood spurted everywhere. Fortunately, he was able to draw off enough blood for future testing purposes. The test patient howled, arching his neck and struggling to break free. Ropes of hardened veins carrying clotting blood flexed along his throat. The man collected a sample from each subject to check for mutation anomalies. Then he retrieved a pair of scissors from the bench and proceeded to cut off the restraints of the most violent subject, save for the strap on one wrist, which he left dangling by a thread. It provided him with enough time to get out of the room before the strap broke.

He removed the blue suit in the staging area and waited a few seconds in order to let the ultraviolet light wash over his body, killing any residual virus that might have slipped past. Despite having administered the mouse-human vaccination to himself, he didn't want to take any unnecessary chances.

Satisfied that he'd been disinfected, he made his way in front of the one-way mirror and watched as the homeless man fought to free himself from the restraint. After a few minutes it snapped. The man opened his mouth, which was curdled with blood and saliva, and wailed at the top of his lungs. The man with the acne could not hear him scream because of the glass partition separating them, but he could just imagine. The infected autobot, now free from the restraints, raced over to one of the healthy kids and sank his teeth into the boy's face.

The man with the acne had seen enough. He pulled out his Ruger and strode purposefully over to his three henchmen, all of whom were still asleep on the couch. The driver of the van opened his eyes at the last second and looked up, but it was too late. A red spot appeared on his forehead just as he reached for his gun. The man with the acne quickly executed the two remaining men. Satisfied that they were all dead, he grabbed the gas container and poured fuel over their bodies and along the floor. The powerful smell of gas overwhelmed him and reminded him of that pungent odor from his youth. Backtracking until he arrived at the exit, he reached inside his pack, making sure the vials of blood were tucked safely inside. He pulled out a stick match and dragged it against the crumbling concrete wall. Two blue flames danced in his icy pupils. He stared at it, hesitating for a brief moment before flinging it onto the floor. The loft space quickly went up, engulfing the corpses in the inferno, and everything inside the loft.

Leaving the door open to create a vacuum, he scampered down the steps until he stood under the night sky. A residual of smoke continued to singe his nostrils as he made his way to the van. Off in the distance a chopper buzzed over the city. Good thing his driver had removed the phony denomination sign attached to the panel. Inside the cabin it reeked of cheap booze, vomit, and body odor. Fast food wrappers littered the aisle. He sat down at the wheel, turned the keys in the ignition, and sped off into the night.

The Lion will lay with the Tiger and produce an offspring, the likes of which will rise up to see God's divine plan.

Chapter 3
The Next Day

Nolette stepped out of the taxi and set forth on Portland's waterfront. Storm debris lay over the congested streets and cobblestone-paved alleys, and an inch of water lapped at her shoes. A group of protesters stood holding signs and shouting at the contingent of sailors keeping watch over the waterfront. A tall, haggard man wearing a leather cowboy hat stood on a milk crate, holding a bullhorn while reading a passage from the Bible. It took her a few seconds to realize that this was The Revelation Baptist Ministry, the most repulsive religious group in the country. They believed that the Cooke's Island plague signaled the end of times.

She tried as best she could to ignore their hateful comments as she walked briskly past them. Three petty officers stood in formation, sealing the perimeter off from the waterfront. Out in the glassy waters of the bay, Navy Patrol boats cruised around what remained of Cooke's Island, which to her eye resembled a dead zone in the middle of the ocean. A Navy destroyer sat quietly in the harbor, keeping a watchful eye on things. She thought it the most guarded five miles of real estate anywhere in the world. But what, she wondered, was there left to protect?

She slung her bag over her shoulder and strode up to the sailor holding the clipboard and controlling access to the boat ramp. The wind howled off the ocean, chilling the exposed skin on her face. She was glad that she'd dressed for the unpredictable

Maine climate. Washington D.C. was only five hundred miles away, but the difference in temperature seemed significant.

The petty officer snapped to attention as she approached, a barely detectable scowl spreading over his chiseled young face. A slice of Cooke's Island appeared over his shoulder, and just the sight of that barren spit of land made her question her decision to come here.

The young sailor asked for her name and she gave it to him. He glanced at his clipboard.

"You're late, ma'am. All guests were supposed to have arrived ten minutes ago," he said.

"But my plane got delayed because of the storm last night."

"I'm afraid I can't allow you to board," the petty officer said, looking up from his clipboard. "No exceptions."

"Look, Jensen," she said, staring at his name tag. "I received the invitation to this tour just yesterday morning. You better not hold me back for being ten minutes late or I'll raise a major stink about it in my paper."

He stared at her with a blank expression. "Hold on, ma'am, while I call my officer-on-duty."

The sailor stepped back a few paces and radioed his superior. After speaking briefly to him, he returned to the perimeter.

"It's your lucky day, ma'am. He's given you permission to join the tour. First, I need to see three pieces of identification. When you're cleared, you'll need to walk down the ramp and wait for the utility boat to transport you to the island."

Nolette showed him three IDs. Satisfied, he allowed her to pass through the checkpoint and make her way to the ramp. Two sailors escorted her and then waited wordlessly nearby. Once the utility boat pulled up to the ramp, two crew members jumped out and helped her climb through the bow door. The craft, she was informed, utilized high power suction that enabled it to make beach landings. Judging from the size of it, she thought it somewhat of an overkill to use such a large boat to transport one person. But at least it was covered and she would ride in comfort.

The engines fired up. Thick chunks of seaweed floated in the shallow depths near the dock's pillars. Water pounded the hull and the roar of powerful motors filled her ears as they moved out.

The boat accelerated into the bay. Nolette took the photograph out of her pocket and studied it. Along the bottom were the words *Tag Winters is alive!* In the picture, a man with long hair and a scraggily beard was standing on a deserted beach. It was hardly a close-up, which was why she had doubts that it was him. Behind him stood a small grove of trees. The official word from the government was that only a few people had survived the attack on Cooke's Island and that Colonel Winters had perished before they could capture him. She knew it would be a huge scoop if she could prove that he'd survived that plague and made it past the quarantine. The discovery of his existence would be the biggest story of her career.

She tucked the photograph back into her pocket and walked to the bow of the boat. The sight of Cooke's Island up ahead filled her with trepidation, and despite the military's claim of having "nuked" the entire island, she wondered if the virus might still be alive, dormant and waiting to infect another unsuspecting host.

At the age of thirty-one she'd done a lot of crazy things in her life in order to get a story: jumped out of airplanes, surfed in shark-infested waters, and spent time in war-torn countries that viewed women as second class citizens. And yet this trip to Cooke's Island, which comprised five square miles, frightened her more than any of those other assignments. Day after day she pored over those videos on her computer screen until she had practically memorized the series of events, especially the scenes in which Colonel Winters appeared with that young boy by his side.

Nolette stood at the bow, lost in thought, watching the water rush past. The notion of a quarantine island populated with homicidal victims ravaged with smallpox seemed entirely unthinkable to her. Could the one-time head of the USAMRIID actually be responsible for such a brutal biological attack? Or had he been framed as some conspiracists had suggested?

Cold foam sprayed her face and formed droplets along the vessel's windshield. She glanced back and saw the city of Portland receding from view. To the south she could see two lighthouses dotting the coast; one regal and majestic; the other short and stubby. Near Cooke's Island sat a jetty of rocks protruding out of the water. On it sat a small lighthouse bracing for the worst of Maine's weather. Nolette felt sorry for this brave little lighthouse guarding the entrance to Casco Bay. Waves rolled up and pounded against it, causing white surf to cascade in the air.

Her stomach began to roil as the ferry terminal on the deserted island approached. The words *Cooke's Island* appeared atop it like a warning to turn back. She glanced nervously over at the sailor navigating the craft, standing perfectly still like a statue, his sunglasses masking whatever emotion he might have felt. The silence grew uncomfortable and she almost wished someone would crack a joke or make a lewd remark to lighten the mood.

She felt both a sense of dread and excitement as they approached land. What would she see on that island? To familiarize herself with the terrain, she'd researched it on Google and studied every photograph and image she could find. In better times it looked lovely: sparsely populated beaches with spectacular views of both the ocean and Portland, as well as a quaint downtown with cozy taverns, inns, bookstores, and tourist shops. Would it still look the same? Or would it resemble a ghost town with a haunted past? She even wondered if Colonel Winters' summer home would still be intact.

The vessel slowed, its powerful engines downshifting as it pulled into the terminal. A horn sounded; but for what reason? Waiting for her on land were two ensigns standing guard outside a Humvee.

"We've docked, ma'am," a sailor said as the bow gate lowered onto the ramp. "You can grab your stuff now."

"I've got everything I need, thank you."

27

A member of the crew escorted her out the cabin and onto the dock. She walked to the end of the pier, trying not to stare at the various Navy personnel waiting for her on lower ground. As she took in her surroundings, she wondered how many of the victims had staggered over this very parcel of land. She took short, quick breaths, almost afraid to inhale in the event she sucked the deadly smallpox virus into her lungs. Although she knew her fears were unfounded, she couldn't help feeling terrified. It made no sense. Navy personnel had been stationed here since the outbreak, and to her knowledge not one of them had come down with the pox.

She made her way over to the two military personnel waiting for her. One of the men stuck his hand out and she took it, waiting for him to introduce himself.

"Pleasure to meet you, ma'am. My name is Lieutenant Wilcox and this is Lieutenant Calabro. Welcome to Cooke's Island."

"Nolette Swain. Thank you for inviting me today."

"You're quite fortunate we didn't start the tour without you," he said, handing her a badge with her name and photograph on it.

"My flight was delayed because of the storm. Then again, I was only informed about this tour yesterday morning," she said, examining the photograph on the badge. Had they lifted that off the Internet?

"Consider yourself fortunate that the admiral made an exception for you, ma'am. Only five reporters from around the country have been selected for this tour of Cooke's Island." He gestured with his outstretched arm. "Now if you'll kindly step aboard the van we can begin the tour. Once we're finished, Rear Admiral Starbuck will give a quick briefing and then answer any questions you might have."

"How many military personnel have been assigned to this island?" she asked.

"Not for me to comment on, ma'am. You can address all questions to Rear Admiral Starbuck in the Q&A session afterwards."

The two Naval officers guided her into the van. She made her way into the cabin, smiling politely at the other reporters staring up at her. She didn't recognize any of them, but then again she didn't pal around with other journalists in her spare time. In fact, she had very few friends at all. Her job had been her all consuming passion these past few years, leaving her little time to socialize.

She lifted her bag and made her way to the back of the van, plopping herself in the last window seat. The warm air rushing out of the heater felt inviting, and had it not been for the nervous adrenaline coursing through her system she might have closed her eyes and fallen asleep.

"If it isn't the one and only Nolette Swain," the man in the seat in front of her said, looking at her between the backrests. He climbed to his knees and smiled. "I'm quite honored to be in your presence."

"Do we know each other?" she asked, pretending not to know the most famous journalist in the country.

"If I'm not mistaken you're the current recipient of the Alfred E. Logan Award for investigative journalism." He laughed and dangled his hand over to shake. "I knew you were smart, Swain, but I had no idea you were so foxy."

Nolette tried not to look flattered by his words, although she couldn't help but feel otherwise from such a celebrated reporter as Bacon. Surprisingly, he knew who she was and it flattered her. She remembered attending a lecture given by him when she was an undergrad at Columbia; she had been riveted. She'd even waited in line afterwards to meet him and get his autograph.

James Bacon, the award-winning reporter from The New York Times: winner of a Pulitzer for investigative reporting as well as a National Literary Award for his book on the 1918 flu epidemic. He may have been a drunk, a womanizer and raconteur, but she'd read some of his work in the New Yorker ten years ago and knew he had the gift. She supposed out of professional courtesy she should be nice to him.

She shook Bacon's hand, trying not to look smitten, and plugged in one of her earbuds. Wilco began to play. Engaging in a conversation with Bacon right now was the last thing she wanted to do, especially considering that he had a well-known reputation as a drinker and philanderer.

He slumped back down in his seat.

She flipped through the notes she'd kept on her iPad, hoping to get up to speed before the tour. Most of her notes were on the subject of smallpox. She quickly perused them, and the more she read about the disease the more squeamish she became. The prospect of one's skin covered in fiery red blisters frightened the hell out of her. From the time she was a young girl she'd been terrified of being engulfed in flames, and the wounds left by smallpox looked quite similar to the injuries of people recuperating in the burn unit. In smallpox, however, the entire epidermal coat separated from the body, hardening like a suit of armor. The common perception had been that smallpox had been eradicated from modern society, but the recent outbreak on Cooke's had shattered that notion and sent the American public into a panicked frenzy.

After reading her notes, Nolette glanced up to make sure no one could see her. She clicked out of the application and began to view the videos that she'd saved on her hard drive. Her long hands cupped the tablet so only she could see what was on it. She'd downloaded these videos onto her computer before the government made it illegal to possess such footage. Merely possessing them was extremely risky. Just recently the U.S. government had begun prosecuting any group or individual caught sharing the videos on the web, and downloading them put the offender at risk. The government had made scapegoats out of the few individuals who'd tried, which was enough to scare the rest of the population into compliance. Combined with the recent crackdown on human rights, the enforcement policy had caused most citizens to fall in line.

Beck came on after Wilco and she tapped her knee. She loved Beck.

She could understand why the terrorist had chosen Cooke's Island to attack. It had more web cameras than any five square miles of real estate in the country. The intent of the experiment was to keep tabs on the migrant pattern of an endangered tern. Whoever committed this atrocity wanted the fruits of their crime to be seen by the world. With the sound muted, she viewed the short clips of the violent rampage through the streets, as well as the savage attacks on those innocents trying to escape their wrath. She watched two rare clips of Winters running through the downtown streets and fighting off the violent mobs attacking him. She kept stopping and replaying the short video over and over, completely lost in thought.

"You could get in a lot of trouble for keeping those videos on your device."

She looked over and noticed that Bacon was plopping down in the seat next to her. She quickly shut off her device and stuck it in her pocket. Removing an earplug, she noticed that he was smiling at her in an almost patronizing manner. There was no way he could have seen those videos. Although he was quite handsome for his age, there was something about him now that creeped her out.

"A few months ago he was one of the most respected infectious disease scientists in the country. Now he's considered the worst serial killer in American history. I don't know about you, Swain, but I find that hard to swallow," Bacon said.

She turned and glared at him, hoping he'd get the message to leave her alone. But instead he sat there with that dumb look over his face, refusing to budge.

"Seriously. What's the government's motive in scapegoating a fellow bureaucrat if he's dead?" Bacon asked. "The stupid bastards are damaging their own brand. No, I don't buy that a top official employed by an infectious disease institute would conduct such a blatant act of bio-terrorism."

She thought about keeping silent; she didn't like making statements until she had all the facts in hand. Then she decided to go fishing. "Some people believe he might still be alive," she said.

"And Elvis is living in a Brazilian condo with John Lennon and Jimi Hendrix." Bacon laughed, reaching into his bag and pulling out a small flask. "Care for a taste?"

"Sorry, I don't drink while I'm working."

"You're an investigative reporter and you don't drink?" He shook his head. "Shit, how things have changed with the younger generation."

"I like to think that I take my work seriously."

"But this is Cold River vodka, Swain. Distilled from organic Maine potatoes and one of the finest handcrafted vodkas in the world." He leaned into her and whispered, "And it leaves no odor."

She waved her hand. "Rumor has it that Winters made it off this island."

"Not possible. I don't see any way Winters could have done that." He poured a shot into his coffee.

The two Naval officers made their way into the van and announced that the tour would now begin. Nolette watched out the window as Casco Bay receded from view. The van climbed the hill and the first thing she noticed was that the area around the ferry terminal had been abandoned. No cars parked anywhere nor were there any power or sailboats tied up along the dock. Upon reaching the top of the ridge, seemingly the highest part of the island, she was stunned to realize that the entire island had been stripped clean of vegetation and buildings. In fact, apart from a half-dozen makeshift structures erected by the military, the entire five square miles of island had been completely leveled. Every cove and beach lay exposed to the naked eye. The destruction of Cooke's Island had been utter and complete.

"Oh my God!" Nolette said, nose pressed to the window. "I can't believe that there's nothing left."

"They say the victims became homicidal killers—zombies, for all intents and purposes. But I always suspected that they turned into something worse," Bacon whispered as the lieutenant stood at the head of the bus, ready to address them.

"What the hell could be worse than turning into a zombie?" she whispered.

"A zombie with a conscience?"

The lieutenant cleared his throat to get his passengers' attention.

"Thank you for coming to Cooke's Island today. Of all the journalists in the country, the five of you have been handpicked to go on this tour and report back to the world. We want you to see for yourself the aftermath of one of the most significant biological attacks in this country's history—in the world's history. Thanks to the brave efforts of the Navy Seals, this threat was contained in a timely and competent manner. As you can see, the island has been sterilized beyond recognition in order to ensure that this agent will never again terrorize our citizens." A few hands went up. "Sorry, but all questions will be answered by Rear Admiral Starbuck afterwards. Unless there are any other concerns, we will begin the tour."

A once inhabited island now completely leveled of all buildings, trees, and vegetation. There were no animals or wildlife except a few seagulls soaring above the desolate landscape. The only vestiges of civilization remaining were the labyrinth of dirt roads that separated the island into its respective grids. A low-level fog hovered along the barren beach. The van traveled on the only paved road that circled the island. Nolette wondered if Colonel Winters had traveled this same route during his stay here.

Bacon returned to his seat and settled next to the window. After taking a few photographs, Nolette lifted her tablet and began to dictate into it what she was seeing. She had so many questions now that she wasn't sure she'd be able to get them all in. The biggest question she had was how Colonel Winters had not come down with smallpox after everything he'd been exposed to. Was it coincidence or just sheer luck?

Much of the cove was covered with dreadlocks of seaweed bobbing in the surf. Naval vessels cruised the island just off shore. She wondered if this place would ever return to normal. A powerful emotion overcame her as the van turned north and traveled parallel to the beach. She felt the haunting presence of the diseased calling out to her; she envisioned their mutilated bodies walking about and practically smelled the fetid odor of their decaying flesh. The combination of jet lag and lack of sleep made this apocalyptic nightmare seem all too real.

"You know this is all bullshit," Bacon whispered through the seats.

"What are you talking about?"

"They're trying to put a spin on this. Good thing the bastards were smart enough to get rid of all the incriminating evidence so that they can rewrite the history of this event. Probably shredded all the documents related to it too. Cover their fucking ass."

"If you think the government is behind this attack then you're crazier than I thought." She returned to her dictating.

"I'm convinced this is a conspiracy."

"I think the vodka's affecting your mind."

"Hell no, it's the only thing keeping me sane."

Staring out at this vast nothingness, she felt as if she should have taken that drink now. No way this was the final chapter. Not only did she believe that Colonel Winters was still alive, but that he'd rise up and do it again. She reflected on all the men, women, and children who had come down with the smallpox or succumbed to the violent gangs. She had no idea what Winters' motive was for committing this crime against humanity, but he certainly had the means and know-how to do it.

"I'll tell you one thing, Swain, smallpox by itself doesn't cause people to exhibit such aggressive behavior. Something stinks here worse than a crate full of rotting halibut, and I doubt they'll ever tell us the truth."

She'd done a lot of research on smallpox and knew a good deal about the disease, but didn't feel like responding to Bacon for fear of having to listen to more of his theories. For all his fame and renown, he didn't come across as a judicious and open-minded reporter.

"In fact, smallpox usually has the opposite effect," he continued. "The victim remains passive while the virus runs its course, and they experience everything that's happening to them. Their expressions tend to freeze into a look of sheer terror."

"I see you've done your homework, Bacon. Are you trying to add another Pulitzer to your shelf?"

Bacon laughed. "I'd love to add another dozen to my pile and keep the rest of you ingrates away," he said. "You know, Swain, you're pretty hot when you're talking about infectious diseases."

"No pun intended, of course."

"That level four hot lab was made specifically for you."

"Your pick-up lines need a lot of work, Bacon. Now why don't you go quarantine your libido somewhere else."

"If love was a contagious disease, babe, I'd be ravished right about now."

She rolled her eyes, desperate to get rid of him.

"Why have you been ignoring me ever since we got on this love boat, Swain?"

"Look, I can't talk to you right now, Bacon. Besides, you're acting like a complete ass and have been drinking before noon."

"Guilty as charged. And in my day, drinking was a prerequisite to being a good reporter."

"Maybe back in the stone ages it was, but not in this day and age."

The van lumbered up the hill toward the northern tip of the island. The further west they traveled the higher they ascended. Nolette wondered how much it must have cost the government to level this island. She took the photograph out of her pocket and stared at it. Could it really be him? Could Colonel Tag Winters, miraculously, still be alive? She certainly hoped so—it would make one helluva story.

Chapter 4

Tag woke to a booming crack of thunder. He opened his eyes only to be blinded by the pounding rain. *How long have I been out?* His body shook from the cold, damp permeating his clothes. A wave splashed under his legs before rushing back out to sea and carrying with it an avalanche of rolling pebbles. He sat up in pain, his shoulder aching, and saw that the tide had risen. Dark skies passed overhead as the wind continued to blow in intermittent gusts. A jagged bolt of lightning struck out in the bay, illuminating the buoys and nearby islands.

He thought of his family, momentarily believing that his wife and kids were back at the cottage waiting for him to start barbecuing steaks and burgers. Time had lost all meaning and he now thought he was back on Cooke's Island. But after sitting up and taking in his surroundings, and experiencing the torrential rain beating down on his head, he realized his mistake.

He crawled to a standing position and brushed the sand off his damp pants. Limping along the shoreline, he watched as the sea continued to churn, the green waves piling on top of one another in angry fashion. Beyond the clouds he saw a slice of blue sky, indicating that the worst of the storm had passed. To his left he noticed a dense grove of trees, and just off the coast a thick fog had begun to move inland.

But where was Fez? He stumbled along the beach, wrapping his arms around his body for warmth. The winds began to taper off as he walked along the sand, clam shells, and rocks. A series of logs had washed up along the beach, forming an odd pattern. These logs had once comprised the raft that had saved his life, even if it had split apart near the end of the journey.

He walked until he came to the mouth of a fast-flowing river, which emptied into the ocean. The two bodies of water swirled in violent eddies upon meeting. He walked down the bank, keeping his eyes and ears open for any sign of Fez. After a few minutes he saw a small body lying in a fetal position on a weedy section of the bank. *Fez!* He jogged toward it, praying that the kid was still alive. Above it stood a massive pine tree swaying in the breeze. Despite his aches and pains, he squatted down next to Fez and turned him over. Thankfully, the kid was still breathing, although his face felt cold to the touch. Tag cupped the kid's hands in his own and vigorously rubbed them. He felt incredibly grateful that the two of them had made it off Rabbit Island alive. But what would be next for them? And where would they go from here?

Beneath him Fez stirred. The kid lifted his head and began to thrash as if still struggling to stay afloat. Tag wrapped his arms around his torso, trying to reassure him that he was now safe. He caught an elbow to the mouth and his upper lip split. Warm blood trickled onto his gums and tongue.

"Take it easy, kid. It's just me, Tag. You're okay now."

"Wha... What happened?" Fez said after he'd finally stopped moving.

"We did it. We made it ashore."

He lifted his head and looked around as if confused. "I'm f-f-freezing."

"We need to get moving. Help keep us warm."

"My stomach hurts."

"You swallowed a lot of seawater out on that raft. Lucky it didn't get into your lungs."

Fez sat up and coughed up foamy water. "What do we do now, Tag?"

"We're going to find a way off this beach. Oggy gave me directions to his mother's house. Once we get there we can rest up."

"But we don't even know where we are. Heck, that storm could have dropped us off in Canada for all we know."

Tag laughed. "I doubt we made it as far as Canada. We're most likely in a suburb somewhere north of Portland."

Fez crawled to his knees and stood. "Might as well get going before it gets dark. Looks like fog is moving in too."

"You sure you're good to go?"

"Not doing me a lotta good laying out here in the rain and freezing my ass off."

Tag started down the beach with the kid in tow. His upper lip stung and his shoulder hurt from getting struck by that errant log. The last six weeks on Rabbit Island had been hard, but at least it had given him ample time to heal and try and make sense about what had happened on Cooke's Island. The mysterious terrorist had given every indication that he would strike again, and just the idea of revisiting that nightmare scenario had caused him many a sleepless nights.

A thick fog descended over them as they made their way along the bank of the river. They searched for any opening in the woods. Through the brume he thought he saw the outline of a large house. They pushed through the thick vegetation in order to make their way to it, and the further they walked the more he could see that this was not just any old house. A long private road led to a circular driveway and a few expensive cars sat in the roundabout. Candles flickered in a few of the windows, most likely the result of a power outage caused by the storm. Maybe he could hot wire one of the cars, he thought. But with his hands frozen into claws there was no way he could manipulate the wires.

He crouched low, the limbs of the brush providing ample cover. Night would soon descend upon them. Five cars sat parked in the circular driveway. Starting with the Mercedes, he made his way down the line, checking to see if any of them had their keys still in the ignition. From the house he could hear the sound of voices and music. A party of some sort was taking place up there. He thought of the food they must be eating: golden corn chips and soft cheeses, creamy dips and trays of salty meats with crusty baguettes and spicy mustards. Months of eating fish, rabbit, and seaweed had left him in a perpetual state of hunger, dreaming constantly about the foods he craved. He snapped out of his daydream only to realize that someone was making their way down to the cars. He and Fez crawled under the chassis of a Porsche SUV, hoping that whoever was on their way down wouldn't be the owners of this vehicle. Two doors slammed in front of them, and when Tag looked through the front end, he saw the Mercedes pulling away. He and Fez slid out from under the SUV and waited patiently by the driver's side.

"That was close," Fez said.

"We have to figure out how to get out of here before we get noticed."

"Try and hurry, Tag, because I'm freezing my butt off."

"Hang in there, kid. I'll figure something out."

Tag heard a distinct clicking sound followed by the rumble of an engine. It took him a second to realize that the white Hummer parked two cars down had been remotely started. What a stroke of luck! Glancing over the hood, he saw two couples conversing on the front porch. The two women embraced while the men shook hands. He knew he needed to move fast. The inside of that Hummer would be nice and warm by the time they climbed inside. It was a modern convenience that now seemed completely foreign to him.

He crept over to the running vehicle. Broken limbs and tree branches littered the driveway, some of which had fallen over the parked vehicles. The stereo blared inside the Hummer and he recognized the familiar voice of Bono. How long had it been since he'd listened to music?

He pulled on the handle and opened the door, letting Fez climb in first. The tinted windows provided a modicum of cover. After Fez entered, Tag moved inside, holding the door so as not to make any noise. Gripping the steering wheel, he punched the gas and the Hummer rocketed forward, clipping the Prius in front of them.

He gunned it down the private road. In the rearview mirror he saw the two couples running out onto the driveway and waving their arms for him to stop. It was the first time in his life he'd ever stolen anything significant, and he felt a pang of guilt as he sped away. Up ahead a large tree lay sprawled across the road. He swerved hard to the left to keep from hitting it as Bono belted out 'Where the Streets Have No Name.' He hooked a right back onto the main road and then turned right on one of the leafy side streets, knowing that the cops would soon be on the lookout for this Hummer. It didn't leave him much driving time knowing that he'd need to ditch this vehicle as soon as possible. The only problem he had right now was that he had no idea how to get to Westbrook.

Then he noticed something that made him smile. Keeping his eyes on the road, he unzipped the pouch around his waist and pulled out the slip with the address written on it. He monitored the GPS system and realized they had landed in Freeport, located seventeen miles due north of Portland.

"L.L. Bean country," Fez said as he turned up the heat. "That was one of our big trips to the mainland every year. L.L. Bean and the Cumberland Fair."

"Plug in this address," Tag ordered, passing over the directions.

"Look what I found!" Fez said, reaching into the backseat. "A bag of barbecue chips!"

Tag snatched the bag out of his hands. "You can have it right after you put in the address. You're not getting orange fingerprints all over this GPS."

"Yes, sir!"

Fez configured in the address and seconds later a woman's voice came over the speaker, telling them which way to turn. Tag handed back the bag of chips and watched as Fez shoved a handful in his mouth.

"Don't eat too fast, kid, or you'll end up with a bad belly ache," Tag said, reaching in the bag and pulling out a few orange chips for himself.

"You sound like my mother."

"Sorry."

"She used to say stuff like that to me all the time. Don't run with scissors. Wait an hour to go in the water after you eat. Make sure you flush."

"She must have been a real good lady."

"Yeah, she was the best." He shoved a handful into his mouth and stared wistfully out the window. "Okay if we don't talk about her right now?"

"Sure."

He patted Fez's knee as he took a sharp left onto Route 1. They climbed onto Interstate 295 and headed south. The faint sound of a police siren echoed in the distance. He pressed the gas to the floor and the Hummer careened through Yarmouth and Falmouth. The nearer they got to Portland the denser the traffic became and he had to slow down once they reached Tukey's Bridge. He weaved through the congestion as the hot air began to loosen his joints, especially in his hands gripping the wheel. Fez put his head up against the vent and let the air blow through his long, stringy hair. Glancing in the rearview mirror, Tag saw blue lights flashing behind him. He knew it was only a matter of time before they caught up to him on this stretch of Interstate.

The voice on the GPS instructed him to get off at Forrest Avenue, which was only a quarter mile away. He cut hard to the breakdown lane and accelerated past traffic, praying that no cars had broken down along it. Two cop cars sat parked along the off ramp, preventing anyone from exiting. Racing past the blockade, he sped toward the next exit. The voice on the GPS directed him to turn off on Forrest Avenue, but two cop cars had already blocked it off.

"Hold onto your hat, kid."

"You not gonna bust through it, are you?"

"They leave me no other choice."

"This is so cool!"

"It's not cool at all. Now duck your head down and keep your fingers crossed."

41

Tag aimed the front end of the Hummer toward the middle of the two cars, keeping his eyes just over the dashboard. The two officers raised their heads up from behind the hoods and pointed rifles at him. A blast went up and the windshield shattered. A second shot ricocheted off the hood. Tag raised his head up and saw the cops dive out of the way ahead of the collision. The Hummer rammed spectacularly through the barricade and shot down the off ramp.

Two women stepped off the curb as he attempted to merge with traffic. He cut the wheel hard to the right to avoid hitting them and barreled over the guardrail. The Hummer crashed through a chain-link fence and landed hard onto an empty parking lot. Tag hooked left and then right, turning into a narrow alley. He sped through the tight corridor, scraping the walls as he passed and knocking over trash barrels and wooden pallets. To his disappointment he noticed that the alley came to a dead end. A large green dumpster sat pushed up against a brick wall, making it impossible for them to go any further.

An idea popped into his head as a police car turned into the alley. He accelerated rather than slow down and wedged the Hummer between the dumpster and the adjoining wall. Black smoke rose up out of the crumpled hood.

"Come on, Fez," he shouted, unbuckling his seatbelt and hopping out of the Hummer.

"Where we going?"

"Follow me."

Tag jumped up on the hood and grabbed Fez's hand, pulling him up onto the steaming hood. A police car raced down the alley, blue lights flashing and siren blaring.

"What are we going to do?" Fez asked

"Jump over the fence!"

"I can't make it over without a boost."

"By all means let me help you then."

Tag catapulted Fez over the top before clambering over himself. Then he fell into the void below, landing hard on the pavement. It took him a few seconds to realize that there were other people gathered in this alley. Once his eyes adjusted to the dark, he noticed a group of homeless men sitting at the far end and passing a bottle between them. He quickly unzipped the pouch cinched around his waist and felt inside until he pulled out a few crumpled bills. Then he went over to the men and passed the money out.

"There's more where this came from if you keep your mouths shut," Tag said to the men.

"Don't worry, pal. Our lips are sealed," one of the men said as he admired his ten-dollar bill.

He and Fez walked with the men out of the alley and into the glare of the supermarket's parking lot. Four police cars raced toward them. Glancing over at Fez, he realized that the kid looked exactly like a homeless urchin out of a Dickens novel. A cop jumped out of his car and sprinted toward them.

"You fellas see anyone running down this alley?" the cop asked.

"Seen two guys runnin' toward the cove," one of the homeless men replied. "We was drinkin' over there when we heard a loud crash. Then we see two crazy ass niggas running thataway."

"Toward the boulevard?" the cop asked.

"Nah, toward the 295 side."

Tag pretended to be drunk, rolling his eyes and swaying in place. Would they recognize him, despite all the changes to his appearance? He couldn't imagine that anyone had gotten a good look at him from behind the tinted windows of that Hummer. With his long hair and matted beard, he figured that he was probably unrecognizable to himself.

"What did they look like?" the cop asked.

"Black as coal. Niggas be runnin' like they chasin' gazelles," one of the black men said.

"They were black men?" he asked.

"Fresh off the boat, officer. Prolly Somalians."

They stood silently as the cop studied them.

"Get the hell out of here. I don't want to see your faces anywhere near here tonight!"

"Get us a bottle, officer, and then we'll be outta your hair for good," another man said.

Tag shuffled past the procession of cops, hoping that none of them recognized him. He snuck a glance over at the black homeless man for reassurance, and the old guy winked back knowingly. These men had saved their hides, and he felt guilty about all the times he'd callously walked past their outstretched hands. He looked back one last time toward the alley and saw a dozen or so cops scurrying around.

Someday my luck will run out. But not today!

Chapter 5
The Next Day

Once the tour had finished one of the Naval officers escorted Nolette and the others into the makeshift compound that the military had constructed soon after sanitizing the island. A briefing inside the van had informed her that it contained offices on the first floor and dorms upstairs. No other explanation was given for its existence, and so she assumed that its purpose was to facilitate study of the attack while at the same time maintaining security. They had no plans to rebuild or allow the public to roam around this island so soon after the event.

He led them into a small conference room where they sat facing a laptop computer and a whiteboard. On the table sat a large thermos of coffee, some plastic cups, and a box filled with pastries. The four other reporters remained somber and silent, and only Bacon freely helped himself to the amenities.

Nolette could see that the others, like herself, were visibly shaken from what they'd seen and heard on this tour. The deserted island had shaken her confidence in the country's security measures and made her more circumspect about her government. Viewing the depopulated and rolling landscape, the horror of it all seemed to come alive, and she could practically envision the disfigured smallpox victims stumbling around and attacking innocent people. She'd read in medical journals about the sickly sweet odor of their rotting flesh, the odiferous byproduct of the disease.

After ten minutes had passed, Rear Admiral Starbuck walked into the room and stood behind the podium. He smiled with ease, never breaking from his erect military bearing. Aside from his grayish blond hair and tall, lanky frame, she thought he bore a slight resemblance to Colonel Oliver North. The patch of ribbons across his chest reminded her of the prizes given out at country fairs for the best pumpkin pie.

"Before fielding your questions, let me say that while this biological event was a malicious act of terrorism, the United States military successfully quelled this threat and ensured the continued safety of the American people. Thanks to the brave actions of our men and women in uniform, many of whom sacrificed their lives during this event, the virulent strain of smallpox never made it off this island. Colonel Taggert Winters, the architect of this act of terrorism, perished in the inferno, leaving us with many unanswered questions. Now, if there are any questions that you might have, I will address them now." Starbuck waited a few seconds before pointing at a raised hand.

"James Bacon from the Times. Rumor has it that there was a second infection involved in this attack that caused the smallpox victims to become hyper-aggressive. In fact, based on video footage that survived this event, it's believed that the victims here exhibited certain cannibalistic traits."

The admiral laughed. "First let me say that any video footage that exists of this event has either been doctored or manipulated in some way, and I would not trust any of it. There have been so many false rumors going around, Mr. Bacon, that it's hard to keep track of them all. But I can assure you that none of the victims turned into cannibals," Starbuck said, smiling in an almost patronizing manner.

"But we saw specific things on those initial videos, Admiral," Bacon said in disbelief. "We saw murderous acts of taboo that leave no doubt about what happened on this island."

"What you saw was the edited footage created by those individuals who planned this attack. It's pure propaganda with the stated intention of making the situation seem more draconian than it appeared."

Nolette raised her hand but Starbuck picked on someone else.

"Monica Gomez from the Chicago Post. We've heard that the smallpox virus used in this attack was stolen out of a freezer in Corpus 6, Vector in Siberia. Apart from the CDC, is it the only known repository in the world storing this particular strain?"

"That I can't verify or confirm, Ms. Gomez, except to say that this virus was well known to those in the field. And that's a good thing, as far as these things are concerned, because it allows the medical and scientific community to utilize the genetic material to begin developing a vaccine in the event it is ever used again," Starbuck said.

Nolette raised her hand and felt her phone vibrate against her thigh. She pulled it out and saw that she had a text. It said, *Don't believe them. Colonel Winters is still alive!*

"Ms. Swain," Starbuck said, leaning over the table to view her name tag. "Did you have a question?"

Nolette stashed her phone away and looked up at Starbuck.

"I was wondering what evidence you can provide to prove that Colonel Winters perished in that attack?" she asked, feeling her phone vibrating yet again against her thigh.

"It was virtually impossible for anyone to have made it off the island, and only a few lucky ones managed to survive the attack. The island had to be razed in order to completely eradicate the pathogen. Many of the deceased were not accounted for because they hid in tunnels and some out-of-the-way places. Unfortunately, they perished in the sterilization process. But I can assure you that no one could have possibly slipped past that iron-clad quarantine."

"Are you sure about that, Admiral?" she followed up without waiting for permission. "Colonel Winters proved very resourceful in fighting off not only the diseased, but those pursuing him. On top of that, he was able to disable every craft on the island and keep the virus from spreading to the mainland," she said, dying to look at her phone.

"Colonel Tag Winters was once a respectable scientist and a valued member of the military community. But something changed him, for what reason we do not know, and his motives served his own selfish interests. He gave his life trying to destroy this great country and for that I have no sympathy for him," Starbuck said. "As well, he had the requisite skills and technical proficiency to both create and plant this virus."

Nolette could tell that Starbuck would never relent on the matter of Winters' guilt, regardless of what evidence was presented to him. Someone else asked a question about the reconstruction of the island, and in that time Nolette snapped open her phone and stared at the screen.

The government is lying to you, Swain! Colonel Winters is alive and well. And it's not the smallpox you should be worried about anymore. It's EHF.

EHF? What did those initials stand for?

Starbuck wrapped up the Q & A session and then thanked them for their time before walking out of the room. Bacon immediately let out a laugh.

"Does that bellhop actually think we'll buy his bullshit? We all know that those videos weren't edited. This smells like a cover-up to me," Bacon said.

"But why would they cover it up?" another reporter asked.

"Think about it. Would you want to admit to the American public that you allowed this virus to turn its victims into cannibals? Then there's the diplomatic relations with other nations, particularly Russia and China. They have no other choice *but* to cover it up."

"And what if Colonel Winters is alive and well and was indeed responsible for this attack?" Nolette asked.

"I bet they captured the good old colonel and are holding him in protective custody as we speak. Of course no one will ever know about it, and they'd never admit that to us."

One of the Naval officers walked into the room and ordered them back onto the bus. The five of them filed out of the room, and as she climbed the bus's steps, Nolette wondered again what the initials EHF stood for. Once they were all seated, the bus pulled away and traveled down the hill until it stopped at the ferry terminal. They exited the van and immediately boarded the vessel. Nolette sat as far in the back as possible, wincing as Bacon sat down beside her. Did she dare ask him what EHF stood for? No, she didn't feel like talking to anyone, especially him.

Her phone vibrated again with another text message. She flipped it open and read it.

Write the things that thou hast seen, and the things which are, and the things which shall be hereafter. (Rev. 1:19)

Nolette assumed that this was from scripture, and she'd read much of it. But what did it mean?

The craft pulled into the Portland ferry terminal and in minutes Nolette had disembarked and was walking up the ramp toward Commercial Street. She'd nearly made it to the top when her knees buckled at the realization of what those initials stood for. Why hadn't she made that connection earlier? The implication sent a shudder down her spine now that she understood what EHF meant: *Ebola Hemorrhagic Fever!*

Chapter 6

Tag handed the homeless guys two more ten-dollar bills as a token of his thanks before he and Fez took off toward Forrest Avenue. They moved languidly past the police cars, their flashing blue lights practically imprinting on his brain. No one paid any attention to them as they staggered along, hopeless and broken. In fact they fit in so seamlessly into the fabric of Portland's streets as to appear invisible.

They trudged up Brighton Avenue. This route, he knew, would take them into Westbrook center. The chill of autumn hung thick in the air. They came upon a convenience store where they walked inside to warm up. With what little money he had left, Tag purchased two long submarine sandwiches, a bottle of Coke for the kid, and a coffee for himself. It had been so long since he'd had a cup of hot coffee that his mouth watered at the prospect. He glanced around, hoping there might be a table where they could sit and eat, but he saw nothing. Instead, the two of them sat on the edge of curb and ate their sandwiches in silence. An exterior floodlight provided their only source of illumination. Tag brought the cup up to his lips, savoring the roasted flavor. He'd forgotten how good a cup of hot coffee could taste. Even the plastic-wrapped submarine sandwich with its assortment of chilled tomatoes, sliced onions, provolone cheese, deli meats, and salty pickles tasted wonderful. He turned to Fez and watched as the kid devoured his meatball sub. Smears of tomato sauce streaked across his lips and mouth. They hadn't eaten this good in months.

Fez downed his Coke and asked if he could have another. Tag handed him two dollars and watched as he returned with a second bottle. He recalled how he and his wife had forbidden their kids from soda and sweets. But now that restriction seemed silly after all that they'd been through on Cooke's Island. And Fez didn't ask for much. The kid never complained or burdened him with unnecessary complaints. What the hell was another Coke in the larger scope of things.

Once their bellies were full, they started walking up Brighton Avenue. Tag's crotch hurt from the sand in his wet pants, and his eyelids felt like sewer covers. If only he could find a warm bed he might collapse for days in a deep slumber. Fez shuffled next to him, shivering and occasionally sneezing. He knew he had to do something before the kid came down sick. Two dollars and some change jungled in his pocket; not even enough money to get a hotel room or a cab to Westbrook.

He spun around and stuck his thumb out, watching as the first car zoomed past.

"Wha … what are you doing?" Fez asked, his teeth chattering.

"Trying to hitch a ride."

"Aren't you afraid we'll ... we'll get caught?" Fez's asked.

"The longer we stay out in the open the more likely we'll get picked up and identified," Tag said as another vehicle approached.

A pick-up truck screeched to a stop a few feet in front of them. Tag ran over to the passenger window and saw a burly, bald-headed guy at the wheel dressed in a police officer's uniform. The sight of his badge worried him.

"Where you guys headed?" the cop asked.

"Westbrook."

"Little late to be hitching a ride, don't you think?" the cop asked.

Tag remembered that he had Oggy's ID in his pouch. "We're heading to my mother's house."

"I don't usually pick up hitchhikers." The cop leaned over the seat and stared at Fez. "But in this case I'll make an exception. You and the kid get in."

Tag opened the door and sat in the passenger seat and Fez climbed in the back. Despite his trepidation, he had to admit that it felt good to sit down and let the hot air thaw his bones. He held his grimy hands out over the vent to warm them up. He couldn't believe his bad luck. Of all the drivers that could have stopped to help them they had to get picked up by a cop. At least the cop hadn't recognized him—yet.

"You boys look like you've been through a shitstorm," the cop said, looking at Fez through the rearview mirror. "What's your name, son?"

"Fez," Fez said.

"What the hell kind of name is that?"

"It's my nickname."

"That's one helluva nickname."

"What's your name?" Fez asked.

"Officer Thompson. But everyone calls me Dean," the cop replied.

"Thanks for picking us up, Dean," Tag said, trying to change the subject. "My car broke down in town. Figure I'll head back and pick it up tomorrow."

"Hate when that happens." They climbed the bridge and crossed over into Westbrook. The cop glanced over at Tag. "So what's your name, pal?"

Tag hesitated for a second. "Oggy."

"Oggy?" The cop laughed. "I once knew an Oggy. Of course that's when I was a kid."

Tag suddenly realized that he didn't know Oggy's first or last name. While the cop continued to drive, he unzipped the pouch attached to his midsection and, using his fingers, lifted out the ID card. Holding it below his right thigh so that it was out of the cop's sight, he discovered that Oggy's real name was Robert Ogden. Age: 39. Address: 27 Fournier Drive. Oggy was six years younger than himself, but with the long hair and beard their age difference probably didn't matter.

Once he'd memorized all the information he slipped the ID back into the pouch.

"I can drop you off at the house if you want," Dean said.

"Thanks, Officer, but you've done enough for us already. Just let us off at the end of our street and we'll walk the rest of the way."

"For God's sake!" The cop turned to him and smiled. "You really don't remember me?"

Alarms went off in Tag's head. "Sorry, but my mind's been a little hazy lately."

"It's been a few years, Bobby, but you and I grew up together. You mean to say you don't remember your old pal, Deano?" The cop held out his beefy hand.

"Sure, I remember you now." He shook the cop's hand and stared nervously at the road ahead. "Sorry, Dean, but the war really messed with my head."

"Heard those towelheads did a number on you and that you were living on some island." Dean said. "That's pretty fucked up, Bobby."

"Yeah, I guess it is."

The truck cruised through Westbrook Center. All the businesses were closed for the night, and the sidewalks were deserted. The glow of street lamps cast strange shadows over the sidewalks and storefronts.

"We got tattoos our senior year. Remember, Bobby? On the bicep of our right arm?"

"Yeah, I remember," Tag said, hoping the cop wouldn't ask to see his arm. "Guess I'm trying to forget the past,"

"Totally understandable, Bobby. That's cool," the cop said, rolling his sleeve back down.

The cop took a sharp right near the center of town and steered between two dimly lit store fronts. Behind the buildings was an empty parking lot and beyond that was a guard rail. Tag could make out a river flowing just beneath the lot. A set of train tracks ran parallel to the river on the opposite side.

The truck idled next to the guard rail as Tag waited to see what the cop would do next.

"Get out of my truck!" the cop said, pointing his revolver at him. "Hands up over your head where I can see them. And move slowly."

"Whoa! Take it easy, Dean," Tag protested.

"Shut up, asshole and get out."

With his hands raised, Tag backed out of the truck. He could hear the sound of the river rushing over a waterfall a few hundred feet away.

"You're not Oggy, you lying son-of-a-bitch. Everyone in town knows who Oggy is."

"But I have an ID to prove it."

"Then either it's a fake or you stole it, because me and Oggy were never friends at Westbrook High. In fact I kicked his ass once in front of half the school." Dean pointed the gun at his head. "You're a goddamn liar, pal. And I know there's no tattoo over your bicep either because I made that story up."

"Here's the honest-to-god truth, Officer. Oggy let me borrow his ID. Said I could use his car while he was away on that island." Tag looked around for Fez.

"Douchebag! It took me a few seconds to make the connection, but now I know exactly who you are," he said, grinning from ear to ear.

Tag stood perfectly still.

"Hell yeah, I'd recognize that face anywhere. You're Colonel Winters. I don't know how you escaped that island, Colonel, but it's pretty obvious you did. This is going to be the biggest capture since Osama Bin Laden and Al Capone." He shook his head, not quite believing his good fortune.

"You're making a terrible mistake," Tag said.

"I stayed up most nights watching cable news and saw your mug up on that screen so many times that I ended up seeing you in my dreams. I'd recognize you anywhere, Colonel."

"Then why aren't you arresting me?" Tag asked. "Unless you're planning to kill me!"

"Kill you? Are you kidding?" Dean laughed. "You're a helluva lot more valuable to me alive than dead. But if I call this into the station then my asshole of-a-chief will try and take all the credit, leaving me high and dry. But if I play my cards right I'll be set for life. They'll be calling me a hero instead of some small town cop with a chip on his shoulder." The cop walked around the front end of his truck and stood in front of him.

"I didn't attack that island. I was only trying to save those people as well as the people on the mainland," Tag said.

"I don't give a shit about your guilt or innocence, Colonel. This is my one big break in life." He stepped forward. "I hope there's no hard feelings."

Tag coughed. "Aren't you worried about catching this disease?"

"Catching what disease?"

"Smallpox. I'm still a carrier you know. And we did share the same air circulating inside the truck's cabin."

"You're telling me you're still infected?" He looked confused.

"Fortunately, I was one of the lucky ones who lived."

"Bullshit, Colonel. I don't believe you." A look of relief spread over his face. "You don't look too sick to me."

Tag realized that few people knew anything about infectious disease transmission. He also knew that he could use this ignorance to his advantage.

"You don't have to be sick in order to be a carrier of a disease."

"Is that how you infected all those people on the island, Colonel, by running around like a madman and slaughtering all those sick fucks?"

Tag made a show of looking around. "Looks like the kid's run away."

"I couldn't give one shit about that kid. It's you I want." He started punching numbers into his cell phone.

"Who are you calling?"

"The news outlets. And the state police." The cop laughed. "They'll be asking me to sit for interviews and sign autographs come morning. Maybe Brad Pitt will play me in the movie. A lot of people say I kind of look like him, you know."

"Maybe if Brad Pitt was bald and overweight."

The cop grimaced. "Don't matter who plays me."

"Dean, if you want to be a real hero then you'll let me go. I've recently been informed that there's soon to be a much bigger attack on this country."

"Prove it then."

"That's the problem. I can't prove it right now. I need some time."

"You gotta understand. This is my one chance to make a score and take care of my wife and kids."

"This isn't about you, Dean. It's about the fate of the nation and keeping our citizens safe. It's not about you becoming rich and famous."

"What's the big deal? If you're guilty then you'll get what's coming to you. And if you're innocent then they'll set you free."

"I'm afraid it's more complicated than that."

"Not from where I'm standing. Easiest decision I've ever made."

He could now see Fez creeping up behind the cop. "I'm telling you, Dean, another attack is about to hit this country and this one will be much worse than the last. A real hero would do the right thing."

"I guess I ain't cut out to be a hero then. But being interviewed on the Tonight Show ain't a bad alternative."

Fez crept up behind the cop and put a finger to his lips.

"I have to give you props, Colonel," Dean said. "I feel like I'm standing next to a bona fide celebrity."

Fez continued to move toward them.

"Too bad that wife of yours turned against you. And if she thinks you're guilty, Colonel, then you're as good as fucked."

His wife had turned against him? This was the first he'd heard about it. He suddenly felt as if he'd gotten punched in the stomach.

"You mean you didn't know?"

He shook his head, not quite believing this unexpected news.

"And she did it on national TV, in front of millions of people."

Fez sprinted toward the cop. Dean turned at the last second and saw the kid screaming like a feral animal before landing on top of him. The cop fired his gun in the air. Tag delivered a right hook to his kidney and with his left hand grabbed the cop's wrist and squeezed, causing him to drop the gun. Fez sank his teeth into Dean's shoulder and instinctively the cop turned and punched him in the head. Tag scooped the man's revolver up off the ground and pointed it at him.

"Get on your knees," Tag ordered.

"Come on, man, I got a wife and kids." The cop dropped to his knees and put his hands behind his head.

"You okay, Fez?"

Fez stood slowly, rubbing his sore jaw. "Yeah, I think so."

Tag moved behind the cop and kicked him between the shoulder blades. Dean fell to the pavement and landed on his stomach. Tag grabbed his handcuffs off his belt and secured his wrists behind his back. Then he pulled him up to his knees and to his feet. Off in the distance he could hear the faint sound of police sirens. The stupid cop had given away their location! They had only minutes to get the hell out of here before the reporters and state police arrived.

He locked the door after pushing the cop into the backseat. Passing the revolver over to Fez, he climbed into the driver's seat and turned the ignition. Fez kept the gun trained on the cop as Tag steered the truck out of the parking lot. He cruised through the center of town as a Channel 6 news van raced past them on the street. Moments later a Maine State police car sped past. Tag clicked on the GPS system and configured Oggy's address.

Seconds later the voice on the GPS system began to direct him toward his destination.

"Why didn't you just ask me where he lived?" the cop said.

"You're not exactly on my most trusted list these days," Tag replied.

"You're not going to kill me are you, Colonel?"

"I don't see that I have any other choice, *Deano*," he said, hoping to scare him.

"But I have a wife and kids," Dean pleaded.

"I guess you should have thought about that before you started acting like such a greedy shithead," Tag said.

Fez said, "And if you seen what he did on that island, cop, you wouldn't think twice about trying something stupid."

Tag drove cautiously, trying not to draw any attention to their vehicle. The voice on the GPS led him through a labyrinth of tree-lined streets until he arrived at Oggy's address. He parked along the curve and looked up at the run-down house. It was an old Victorian that sat high up on the hill and was fronted by a crumbling stone wall. A long, cracked driveway snaked up to what looked to be a double bay garage set back from the main structure. A light shone from behind the brown curtain of a second floor bedroom. Tag pulled up on the long driveway, noticing that the truck's headlights were illuminating the front doors of the green garage.

He knew he had to park out of view or else they'd be discovered. Soon every police cruiser in town would be on the lookout for the missing cop. He ran out and lifted the garage door. Luckily, there were no cars parked inside. Useless junk sat piled high against the walls: tires, chairs, boxes of clothes, shovels, and brooms. He climbed back behind the wheel and guided the truck inside until it just fit past the doors. Shutting off the engine, he jumped out and pulled down the garage door. Then he went around to the side door and ordered the cop out.

Fez pressed the gun against the cop's back as they exited the side door. The three of them walked up to the back door and climbed the steps. Tag rapped his knuckles against the splintered wood. Then they waited a few minutes before the door opened and an old woman with deep wrinkles appeared. She stood hunched over and enfeebled. A pair of eyeglasses hooked to a silver chain dangled from her neck.

"I don't need whatever it is you people are selling," the old woman said, starting to close the door.

"That's not why we're here, Mrs. Ogden! We're friends with your son, Robert," Tag said.

"My Robby?" She put a wrinkled hand to her mouth. "Is he okay?"

"Yes, he's fine. He's still living on that island."

"Him and that stupid island." She nodded her head and looked at Dean. "What's with the cop?"

"Dean went to high school with your son," Tag said, pinching the skin on the cop's elbow. "Isn't that right, Dean?"

"Yeah, we were best buds back in high school," Dean said.

"That's odd, because my Robby didn't have many friends back in those days." She seemed to think the matter over. "Are you boys hungry?"

"We're starving," Fez said, rubbing his hands together.

"Good. Then I'll whip you boys up something good to eat." She studied them for a second. "I'm Dolores by the way. Come on in."

They followed her into the kitchen. The inside smelled like his grandmother's house, a medicinal odor he fondly recalled from his childhood. As Tag settled down at the kitchen table, he kept his eyes focused on Dean, hoping the cop wouldn't do anything stupid until he could think matters through.

Chapter 7

Hawthorne College sat on a plateau in the valley town of Brookhaven, Maine. From the center of town the man with the hint of acne stopped and stared up at the domed administrative building, admiring the autumnal sun reflecting off the shimmering gold skin. Surrounded by mountains, and with a stately river flowing through the center of town, Brookhaven couldn't have been better suited for what he was about to unleash upon it.

He breathed in the fresh air as he walked down the center of town, taking in the brilliant fall colors on the surrounding mountains. Everyone greeted him with a hello or a friendly gesture, even those who didn't know him. He'd joined the Rotary and Lions Club and took part in every civic activity imaginable. But what he loved most was his time spent volunteering with the local theater company, making costumes and preparing the actors before they went onstage.

Even the small antique store he'd opened was doing surprisingly well. Business had picked up to the point where he had to hire a young woman to work the days he wasn't there, which turned out to be most days of the week. It surprised him that he had any business at all, the store acting as a front, and on his trips throughout New England he found himself buying inventory wherever he could find it.

"Morning, Vernon," a pedestrian called out to him.

"Morning, George," he replied, waving as the person approached.

"How's the show going?"

"Fine, George, just fine."

"I hear you're quite a wiz at making those costumes," the man said.

"I do what I can," he replied, smiling.

If the antique shop gave him respectability in the community then volunteering at the theater company had greatly endeared him to the local townsfolk, many of whom took a fierce public pride in Brookhaven's reputation for fostering the arts.

He neared his car and was about to move to the driver's side when he noticed the poster taped to the coffee shop's window. A smile crossed his lips upon seeing what it was for. Many of the biggest names in infectious diseases and biological security would be attending the conference, which had been assembled in response to the attack on Cooke's Island. That the guest speaker would be none other than Monica Winters only made the irony more delicious. How else could he entice his favorite fugitive-of-the-law, Colonel Winters, to travel up to these parts and witness his brilliance? Especially after his successful experiment in L.A.

He drove out of downtown and guided his hybrid up to the chalet he'd purchased on the hill. Such a beautiful spot. From his living room he had an unobstructed view of the entire valley, including the ivy-strewn campus of Hawthorne College, which also happened to be the host site of the infectious disease conference. At night he often liked to sit on the deck and stare out at the lights twinkling below, and dream about what a normal life would be like here. But it didn't much matter. Once his designer pathogen began to spread, this quaint town would not seem so quaint anymore. He laughed because everyone thought an island of seven thousand people had been a disaster. Wait until they got a load of fifteen thousand human beings turning into viral bombs, replicating Ebola threads at an alarming rate.

The first thing he did upon entering his home was head down to the basement. The first room to the left contained high tech communications equipment used to conduct his surveillance. He punched in the eight-digit password and released the door, flicking the switch as he entered. A row of fluorescent lights lit up across the ceiling. He moved over to the computer and studied the footage on screen. Winters and that kid had made it safely back to Ogden's house. His adversary had proved far more resilient than he'd ever dreamed; the perfect candidate for his future plans. The tracking chip he'd embedded in Winters had paid off handsomely, allowing him to keep track of Winters' every move.

He switched off the lights and exited the room, securing the metal door behind him. Moving to the second room, he punched in the eight-digit code and stood in the staging area guarding the threshold. He pushed the red button on the wall and allowed the ultraviolet to wash over him. It took a minimum of thirty seconds to fully eradicate any residual virus that might corrupt his results. Although he'd vaccinated himself against this particular strain—a nasty process that left him deathly ill for weeks—he'd come out the other side fully protected against exposure. The staging merely prevented him from being a carrier and infecting the town's people before the time was ripe.

He punched in the security code for the second door and entered the room, which was shrouded in darkness. From the opposite corner an animal-like growl rose up. He flicked on the lights and saw the subject fall back against the far wall and cover his eyes. A sheet of blood-smeared Plexiglas separated him from the runaway teenager inside. Light sensitivity seemed to be a common denominator between the smallpox and Ebola virus, and he didn't quite understand why. The homeless kid he'd picked up in Portland had ripped off all of his clothes and tossed them away. Now he lay balled up in a fetal position and trembling with a mixture of fear and rage.

He studied the disease's progression over the boy's body. Sores covered him from head-to-toe and accounted for why he'd ripped off all his clothes. The kid looked up over his blood-stained knees and growled. Blood covered every inch of his body and the whites of his eyes were now a deep ruby. The symptoms indicated to him that the boy had entered the zone of third spacing. The man with the acne walked over to further analyze his test subject, but the kid suddenly leapt up to the glass and slammed his body against it. The sudden move startled him as the boy pounded his fists against the glass and opened his mouth, revealing rows of bloody teeth that resembled the Great White sharks he'd seen on nature shows.

The results here had been the same he'd achieved in L.A. No criminal leads had come of that experiment, and the cops and politicians had been baffled by the charred remains. All the L.A. cops ended up with was a bunch of burnt corpses, three of whom had died from gunshot wounds to the head. He'd kept up on the story in the L.A. Times, delighting in the fact that the investigators had been completely stymied by the murders.

He picked up a clipboard and jotted down his observations on the test subject. The kid pressed his hands and face against the Plexiglas, smearing bloody handprints across the glass. The red spots over his body indicated significant subcutaneous bleeding; more evidence that he'd entered the third spacing of the disease. Squatting down to examine the boy's genitals, he noted the telltale sign of an Ebola infection: grotesquely swelled and reddened testicles and penis. Why the Ebola virus targeted human genitalia and eyes was an intriguing puzzle that he'd not been able to answer. But he wouldn't worry about that now. He only hoped that the rabies virus he'd spliced into the Ebola would produce the targeted cerebral damage necessary to cause hyper-aggression.

"Dude, let me go. I swear I won't tell anyone," the kid pleaded from behind the glass.

He smiled coldly. "Don't worry, young man. Your pain and suffering will soon come to an end."

"You're a fucking monster!"

"No, you're the monster. I'm merely Dr. Frankenstein."

He smiled while jotting down a few more notes. The pounding on the glass became louder as the boy's anguished screams died to a whimper. Reaching inside the mini refrigerator on the workspace, he pulled a sandwich out from between some test tubes of experimental pathogen. Egg salad. Then he removed a bottle of grape juice and an apple. He placed them on a tray and slid it underneath the slit in the door. The boy picked up the tray and studied it for a second before hurling everything against the far wall. The apple split apart upon hitting it. Rivulets of Ebola blood formed a random splash pattern against the glass and across the apple's pink flesh.

Subject's reasoning still intact. Aggression, however, seems to be increasing. Two weeks since incubation and still thriving. No 'crash out' symptoms as of yet. Virus seems to be stabilizing and causing a slow, steady hemorrhage in third spacing phase. Blood clotting in the brain seems to be occurring primarily in the frontal lobe.

After jotting down his observations, he placed the clipboard on the bench and turned toward the door.

"Please don't leave me here!" the kid cried out, pounding the Plexiglas. "Please! Have a heart."

"My heart is most definitely in the right place. And trust me, your suffering will not be in vain."

"Fuck you!"

"There's no need to be crass."

"Fucking homo!"

"Do you know what Homo Sapiens even means? It is Latin for wise man. You, my friend, have not been very wise in your life choices."

"Go to hell!"

He held the kid's gaze for a moment before laughing. It reminded him of all those years he'd spent toiling in the hot lab and dealing with those sorry primates, whose only crime was to be in the wrong place at the wrong time. Many of those primates exhibited a similar, albeit wordless range of emotions once they were subjected to the cruelty of confinement and experimentation. And yet no one gave a shit about them. Why? Because of a presumed absence of soul?

The young man started to howl in protest as he shut the door behind him. Standing in the staging area, he waited patiently as the ultraviolet blue light scanned his body from head-to-toe. Once thoroughly sterilized, he exited the staging area and slammed the door shut behind him, grateful not to hear the boy's bloodcurdling screams anymore.

He took a quick shower and made a pimento cheese sandwich on rye before driving over to the Brookhaven Lyrical Theater. Tonight was the opening night of Grease and the prospect of watching everyone's hard work coming together excited him. A tear formed in his eye just thinking about the theater—his second great love. His passion for it had only grown since his days at Yale, and had it not been for his discovery of infectious diseases he might have stayed working on Broadway for life. But what a loss to humanity that would have been. And yet the only times he'd ever cried in his life was when he'd been sitting in that darkened theater and witnessing the churn of human conflict.

He pulled up to the theater. It had once been a Methodist church that had closed due to low attendance and the abundance of newer, more charismatic churches in the valley. Ten years ago a wealthy philanthropist had purchased the stone building and generously donated it to the Lyrical Theater. The structure had been completely remodeled and was now the town's architectural gem, seating just over a hundred patrons. A small cafe and wine bar had been built into the lobby, allowing the troupe to raise much needed funds. Many people in town considered the theater to be the epicenter of Brookhaven's art community, and since its redesign it had hosted art shows, lectures, and even a few concerts.

Entering through the back door, he made his way to the stage where some of the actors had gathered to sound check the acoustics. Upon seeing him walking toward them, crew and cast greeted him warmly, eager to have him tweak their costumes and touch up their makeup. Many of the actors even came to him for acting advice, sensing that his stage experience extended far beyond the realm of mere community theater.

"Come on, Cathy. Let's get you started, seeing how you're the star of the show," he said, grabbing the girl's hand.

"I'm so nervous that I feel like I'm going to throw up," the pretty blonde said, plunking down in the chair and fluffing up her teased hair.

"A perfectly healthy response to performance anxiety. Being up on stage and performing is when we find out who we truly are and what we are made of." He stood behind the chair and smiled at her reflection in the mirror. Then he pulled out his comb and stressed out her hair. "The key is to control your emotions and not let fear get the best of you. Fear is your worst enemy— but it can also be your best friend too."

"Once I get through that first song I should be okay." She reached back and patted his hand. "Thanks so much, Vernon. I don't know what I'd do without you."

"You're going to make a perfect Sandy Olsson tonight. Just remember that when you're standing in front of all those townspeople, it's you who has the power over them. Have confidence in yourself. Visualize your success."

"I know you're new to town, Vernon, but it seems like you've been living here forever. I seriously hope you stay for a while."

He threw his head back and laughed. His stage was far bigger than this quaint little college town. After penning his own drama, a tragedy that would put Shakespeare's greatest works to shame, he'd be ready to move onto a bigger stage, using the smallest, most primitive life forms to write his script.

He set to work styling her coif in the big-hair style of the fifties before applying her makeup. It reminded him of his most recent role on Cooke's Island where he'd played the role of that widowed old sea hag. He'd put Robin Williams to shame with that performance.

After finishing Cathy, he began working on another cast member until he had them all looking their parts. Then he took up a position alongside the stage and waited for the fun to begin. People began to filter into the seats. The sold-out crowd buzzed with excitement and he could feel goosebumps rising on his arms. He so loved musicals. During one performance of Hair many years ago, he remembered weeping inconsolably at the plight of Claude, whose philosophy of resistance informed his own struggles and provided an aesthetic framework to his unorthodox and radical plan to change the world.

The lights dimmed and the curtain opened, and he quickly lost himself in the drama of the story. The wonderful singing and dancing brought the house down. Cathy looked great and performed even better, hardly the puddle of nerves she feared she would be. It made him temporarily forget that in a few weeks he'd be unleashing a deadly new virus on this quaint New England town, and that most of his fellow actors and crew would succumb to the disease; it was the price to pay for change.

The audience gave a standing ovation once the curtain dropped. Tears streamed down his face he was so moved by the performance. He went backstage and congratulated cast and crew on a job well done. A party was to be held afterward at the director's house and everyone demanded he be in attendance. Unfortunately, he told them, he had a previous business engagement and couldn't be there this evening. Disappointed, they thanked him anyway for his contribution. He left quickly, proud of this little troupe, and fell wearily into his car for the two-hour journey to Portland.

Cathy came running up to his window before he could pull away.

"Are you sure you can't come to the party?" she asked, still chewing her gum.

"I so wish I could." He patted her manicured hand. "You were magnificent onstage, Cathy. You completely owned that crowd with your performance."

"Thanks to you."

"Life is short, Cathy. Oftentimes cruel as well. There are times we must step forward and take control of our destiny. Theater is one of the few ways we can exert such control in our lives. It lifts the human spirit and provides a framework to our chaotic existence. It's why I so love being involved with it."

"Wow, that's some deep shit." She laughed. "To me it's just a lotta fun and hanging with good friends."

He smiled wanly at this shallow bitch. "I must get going now."

"See you when you get back?"

"Oh, you'll see me alright. Maybe more than you care."

He waved goodbye as he pulled away from the curb. If only she knew how much he'd sacrificed in his life to get to this point. If only she knew how much more he had in store for everyone. He'd sworn to give until he couldn't give anymore. Until there was hardly anyone left to give it to.

Chapter 8

Nolette stood at the curb facing Commercial Street, waiting impatiently for traffic to slow so that she could return to the privacy of her hotel room. She needed time to process all the information in her brain and arrive at some meaningful answers. The hateful chants of the Baptists echoed against the brick buildings. The sound of their voices carried over to the waterfront before emptying into the ocean and sinking to the bottom of the bay. Bacon stood alongside her, uninvited, waiting to cross the street as well. Her phone had been buzzing with texts every few seconds since she'd gotten off that boat, and now she couldn't wait to get back to her room and read each one. Maybe she'd be given a clue as to what was to come next. The threat, however, of an Ebola-like outbreak now terrified her.

She took advantage of the break in traffic and raced across Commercial Street, her heels clicking loudly against the pavement and momentarily blocking out the hate-filled words filling the air around her. Bacon ran alongside, trying to keep pace. Once they reached the other side of the street, he grabbed her elbow and tried to keep her from continuing on.

She turned and shot him an angry look. "What the hell are you doing?"

"Look, Swain, I'm staying a few blocks down from here. How about we meet for a drink tonight and talk about this?"

"Let me go!" Nolette jerked back her elbow, releasing his grip. Then she turned and headed toward the lobby.

"Wait," he said, sprinting over and blocking her path.

"Don't you think you've had too much to drink, Bacon?"

"Hell no, I'm just getting started for the night, and there's more on the way."

"I'm not now, nor am I ever, going out for a drink with you. Now would you please get the hell out of my way so I can get some work done."

"There's more to this story than you can even begin to know. I've been covering it from the very beginning and what I've uncovered so far might change your mind."

Nolette hesitated before sidestepping around him. Although she'd been receiving these intriguing text messages, she knew she had little else to go on. She wondered if she could trust Bacon. Of all the reporters covering this story, why had he wanted to reveal this information to her?

"You've got quite a reputation, Bacon. And to think I idolized you at one time and waited in line to meet you back in college."

"You did?" He seemed genuinely taken aback. "Look, Swain, I'm well aware that I have a reputation as a booze hound, but I can assure you that I'm still capable of doing good work. As for sleeping around, I never shit where I eat."

"Oh? That's not what I heard."

"Okay, not as a general rule. But sometimes things happen beyond my control."

"Get out of my way."

He pulled something out and showed it to her. "I've charted every character in this ongoing fiasco and constructed a detailed flow chart of their timelines. I'm not greedy, Swain; this story is big enough for the two of us." His lips were so close to her own that she swore she could practically smell the vodka on his breath.

"What about your reputation for doing anything humanely possible to get a story, including throwing people under the bus."

Bacon looked away and shook his head. "There was a time, when I was younger and hungry, when I was the biggest asshole on the planet. Admittedly, I'd have pushed my own mother out of the way to get a good scoop. But trust me, Swain, I've mellowed as I've gotten older. Gone back to kindergarten class and learned to be nice and share my toys. This story we have on our hands is way too big for just one reporter."

"So what are you offering?"

"We divide the research and writing and share equal billing: Bacon and Swain."

"How about Swain and Bacon?"

"I actually like Bacon and Swain better. It's alphabetized and rolls nicely off the tongue."

"You'll never change." She sidestepped him and walked toward the lobby.

"Okay, you win. Swain and Bacon it is. Just as long as this story gets out," he shouted just as she reached the door.

Nolette pulled the handle and turned to face him. "Well?"

"Well what?"

"Where and what time are we meeting for drinks?"

"You won't regret it! I've got a dinner reservation at Fore Street tonight. Best restaurant in town. A quick nap and I'll meet you there at 8:45. It's just up the street from here."

"I'll find it."

Nolette entered the lobby and headed toward the elevator, eager to read the text messages. The lobby was empty except for the tall girl at the desk. Nolette's two-inch heels echoed loudly against the ornate marble tiles, creating an eerie sound. A glass partition separated the bar from the lobby and she could see a few people sitting on elevated wooden stools and enjoying a drink. Above her hung a massive chandelier glistening with crystals suspended from gold cables.

The elevator's doors parted and she scooted inside, retreating to the privacy of its stainless steel enclosure. A man sprinted through the lobby and toward the open doors. Nolette reached out and held them so that he could enter. Once safely inside, the man turned and faced the control panel. Nolette stood behind him, her back pressed up against the handrail and her mind still reeling from the tour.

The man pressed the eighth floor, one floor above her own, and the elevator began to ascend. She usually took the stairs for exercise, but she was tired now and seven floors was a long way up. She intended to run a five-mile loop around the Old Port this afternoon. After passing the fourth floor, the man turned and smiled. She caught a glimpse of the faint acne scars across his cheeks. For some reason the expression on his face seemed odd. But then again maybe she was projecting her own fears onto the people around her.

Her knees buckled and suddenly she found herself balled up in the corner of her childhood closet. It smelled of dust and cat piss. Shoes lay around her feet, and tattered winter coats and old dresses dangled around her pigtails. It was the middle of summer and the heat inside the closet was unbearable. Her hands stung from the razor blade wounds. Warm blood trickled down from the cuts on her palm. Her mother told her to pray to Jesus and beg for His forgiveness and maybe she'd be redeemed for her sins. The mock crucifix wounds were meant to bring her closer to Christ and His suffering.

Nolette snapped out of her daydream only to realize that the elevator was still ascending. A bead of sweat dripped down her temple. That brief flashback had felt like an eternity. By the time the elevator doors parted she realized that she had a death grip on the handrail. She lifted her hand and noticed that her knuckles had turned white. Staggering forward, she accidentally bumped into the man in front of her. Her knees felt weak and for a second she thought she might faint. Nolette turned toward the man.

"So sorry about that," she said, holding the door.

"No worries. You have a wonderful day." The man smiled before his acned-scarred face disappeared behind the sliding doors.

Nolette ran to her room, still spooked over that painful flashback. She fumbled in her purse for the card key, praying that she hadn't locked herself out of her room. There was no way she could take that elevator back to the first floor to retrieve another key. And who was that creepy guy in front of her? Once she found the card key, she quickly unlocked the door and sprinted inside, engaging the deadbolt behind her.

She collapsed on the leather chair. Then she pulled out her phone and unlocked the screen and saw that she had twenty-one text messages. One by one she opened each one, trying to make sense of the bizarre but terrifying photos: images of Ebola victims deep in the African jungle; smallpox victims; photos of Colonel Winters wading among the infected; the book of Revelation; an aerial view of a large compound. And pictures of ligers. Lots of ligers.

Once she'd gathered her composure, she slipped off her heels and went to the window, sweeping back the curtains. From her vantage she could see the entire waterfront, including Cooke's Island in all its infamous grandeur. Its bare topography looked strange and unsettling sitting in the middle of the blue ocean. Almost like an island of desert rising up from the depths of the Casco Bay. Down below on the waterfront, the Baptists were still preaching to all who would listen.

It was a vile message she'd heard many times as a child: morality wrapped in fear. Every Sunday without fail all the families and the community members would gather together at their dilapidated little church just to listen to the fire-and-brimstone sermon of their minister. Since that time she'd come to learn that the congregation her parents had joined was an exclusionary one, which was the reason she'd never met her grandparents or any of her aunts, uncles, or cousins. Only later had she tried to make contact with them, and explain who she was and why they'd never met.

Her phone buzzed. Another text message. This one was a video from the Channel 4 news. Its logo was displayed in the upper right corner and had run last night. She pressed the play button and watched a brief video of a white Hummer speeding through downtown Portland. She played it again, focusing on the image of the long-haired, bearded man staring out of an open window. Before she had a chance to view it again, the file disappeared only to be replaced by another text message. This one was of a man walking into a living room decorated with floral wallpaper from the fifties. She was struck by his long hair and beard. It took her a few seconds to realize that this was the same man who'd been driving the Hummer. The video zoomed briefly on his face, and she was stunned to realize who she was looking at. She pulled the photograph out of her pocket and compared the two images.

Colonel Winters!

She pressed play and the text exploded. Digital blood sprayed over the screen before fading into black. A reel of grainy footage appeared onscreen of a liger pacing inside a fenced perimeter. What was the deal with ligers? The beast turned its head toward the camera and roared. Then the video was replaced by one of a male Ebola victim lying on a cot, obviously in the last stages of the disease. A pool of black sludge dripped onto the dirt beneath his cot. But it wasn't sludge: the victim had hemorrhaged his inner organs and sloughed off his intestines. The words *Coming Soon Near You!* flashed at the bottom of the video. Nauseous, Nolette slammed her phone shut and tossed it onto the bed as if it had just been infected with the virus.

Chapter 9

She followed the hostess across the crowded dining room and sat across from Bacon at a small table located in the corner of the restaurant. A candle flickered between them, the melted wax smelling like pumpkin pie and forming into hard orange crinkles. Massive windows ran from floor to ceiling giving her a clear view out onto the street.

She'd jogged around the Old Port after she'd gotten back from the tour, and the exercise had helped settle her nerves. Ever since she'd run away from home those many years ago, running had been both a metaphor and an escape valve in her life. It cleared her mind and helped her deal with her 'issues.' Running focused her thoughts on the present instead of the painful past, and the even more frightening future.

Bacon sat in front of her, his long salt and pepper hair gelled perfectly back over his scalp. He looked somewhat somber and sober, which was hard to believe considering all the booze he'd drunk today. The waiter came over and Bacon ordered a single malt Scotch. She ordered a glass of Chablis and studied him out of the corner of her eye. He didn't look too bad for his age, especially over the flickering candlelight. And yet on closer examination his face showed subtle hints of a life filled with fast living. The skin on his cheeks was splotchy and red, and he had that weathered glint in his gray eyes that could only come from a life spent chain smoking.

"So what is all this great information you've been supposedly uncovering?" Nolette asked.

"I thought we might enjoy a nice meal before getting down to business." He held up the tumbler of Scotch just delivered to their table. "Salud."

She refused to toast and instead slipped her fingers around the crystal stem and swirled the wine around. "I was under the impression that we'd be talking business or I might have never agreed to this."

"I figure why let the threat of another smallpox epidemic ruin a good meal." He smiled and pulled something out of his pocket before spreading it out on the table.

"A map?"

"Casco Bay and its satellite islands, all but one of which is uninhabited. I've been thinking about what you were saying about Winters still being alive and so I did a little homework. What if Colonel Winters somehow escaped from that island and merely moved to another. I must have talked to every lobsterman in this area before I discovered that someone was living right here on this one." He jabbed his finger at a small dot on the page.

Nolette leaned over and read the name just above it.

"Rabbit Island! It's the size of postage stamp. No one could survive on that place."

"The fishermen I spoke to told me that a homeless guy lives there during the summer. Sounds ridiculous, but the place was inundated with rabbits. All the lobstermen knew about it and left the guy alone. Sometimes they even gave him a lift to and from the mainland to get some supplies." He jabbed his finger on the map again. "Now bear with me. What if by some miracle Winters made it past that quarantine and ended up on that island? He'd have plenty of food, judging by all the rabbits reproducing on it, as well as shelter and companionship."

"I'm certain the authorities must have checked out every island already."

"Possibly, but what if he built a tree hut or something to hide out in while they passed. Saw them coming and scampered up there to hide."

"I think you're reaching for straws, Bacon."

"I suppose." He downed his Scotch, held the glass up and smiled. "Then again I've been reaching for straws my entire life and I'm not about to stop now."

"Think about it. How would Winters have even known about its existence?" she asked. "Or even that anyone lived on that island."

Bacon shrugged. "He vacationed on Cooke's all those years, maybe he heard rumors about a hermit living there." He tore off the pointed end of a baguette and slathered garlic butter over the crusty layer.

"I'm confused now, Bacon. Despite what the government is saying about his culpability, do you believe that Winters had nothing to do with that attack?"

Bacon waved the buttered baguette in the air. "The government's a lying sack of shit, Swain. I don't trust those assholes as far as I could throw them. Never have. But do you really think it's a mere coincidence that the head of USAMRIID was vacationing on that island when the shit hit the fan?"

"What reason could Winters possibly have for releasing a virus on the same island he and his family were vacationing on?"

"That's not what I'm saying. We both know he had the technical skills and expertise to pull it off; isn't that enough proof? He was one of maybe a handful of scientists in the world who possessed such specialized genetic knowledge. As for motive? Who knows what his motive was. He could have gotten screwed over by someone higher up and decided to get payback. Then there's the offshore bank accounts they found, which on paper looks pretty damning to me. He could have had a martyr complex in the name of some radical religious belief, like them whack jobs protesting along the pier. And yet despite all this overwhelming evidence, I'm starting to believe he had nothing to do with this."

Nolette leaned over the table. "All I know is that whoever committed this act of terror is going to strike again, and very soon."

"Oh?" He leaned back in his chair and smiled, watching as the waiter placed down another expensive Scotch. "Do you have some special access to information that no one else has?"

"This creep has been text messaging me for the last few hours. It's how I came to the realization that Colonel Winters is still alive," she whispered.

The smile faded from his lips. "Prove it."

"If only I could. Whoever sent me these texts configured the software so that each message self-destructs after a certain amount of time has passed. It's why I'm afraid to go to the police with this idea; I have no real evidence. Not to mention the fact that my credibility as a reporter would be ruined if I made such a claim."

"True. Ever since that attack they've been getting thousands of threat calls a day," Bacon said, sipping his Scotch. "Maybe this person is keeping tabs on you as well."

"I never thought about that, but it's entirely possible." She remembered the man in the elevator for some reason.

"Doesn't much matter now, Swain. He's most likely got a good look at you, so you might as well keep taking notes on all these messages he's sending you."

The waitress came over and they immediately stopped talking and ordered off the menu without much forethought. Surf and Turf for Bacon and Lobster Thermidor for her.

He leaned over the table once the waiter left. "Consider yourself a lucky gal tonight, Swain. I'm picking up the tab."

"Thanks, big spender, but I have an expense account too."

"You really know how to emasculate a guy," he said. "So what else did this freak send you?"

She ripped off a small portion of baguette. "Video proof that Winters is still alive. It appears that he's holed up somewhere in the general vicinity."

"He could be anywhere in the country by now," Bacon said, chewing the last morsel of bread.

"I learned that Interstate 295 was closed off last night because of a high speed chase through downtown Portland. I'm almost certain the driver of that car was Colonel Winters. But I'm not sure the police were aware whom they were chasing."

"Maybe the local cops didn't know but I bet you the Feds did."

"They found a white Hummer abandoned over by the Back Cove. With his long hair and beard, he easily could have slipped unknown into the general population. He looks nothing like his former self."

"Are you sure it was him?"

"The vehicle was registered to a William Bethelman of Fryberg, Maine. Because of the storm last night, Bethelman and his wife stayed overnight at his friend's house in Freeport. The house is on the water, five miles northwest from Rabbit Island. The same track as that powerful storm last night. People walking along the beach this morning reported seeing a number of logs washed along the beach, some tied together."

"Fuck me! A raft?"

"The remains of one. Officials eventually shut down air traffic at the Portland Jetport. They said it was because of the storm, but I think the Feds feared he might try and take a flight out of town. I'll bet they're keeping this under wraps from the public."

"They've probably staked out at the bus and train station too. How the hell did he break inside a Hummer? Hotwire the engine?"

"Much easier than that. Bethelman remote-started the vehicle as he was leaving the party. Winters is a smart cookie and must have been waiting nearby. Once he heard the doors click open and the engine start up, he climbed in and took off."

"So if Winters is still alive then who's texting you all these messages?"

She shrugged. "I'm assuming that it's the same person who planted smallpox on that island."

"Okay, let's start with that assumption."

"Whoever is sending me these messages is extremely tech savvy and obviously had access to all those video cameras situated throughout Cooke's Island."

"Those cameras were put there to study some dumb bird."

"A rare tern," she corrected.

"I could give two shits if it's a Dodo bird or an albatross," Bacon said.

Nolette looked around the dim, crowded room, wishing she was anywhere else but here. This conversation was making her queasy and she realized that she wasn't even hungry anymore. Too bad, because she'd been craving a Maine lobster the moment she stepped off the plane.

"For the last two months I've been researching all the people who've dealt with Colonel Winters in an official capacity," she said.

"And what did you find?"

"He was extremely well liked. Unbelievably, I couldn't find anyone who had a bad word to say about him. Only one person seemed somewhat suspicious to me and he disappeared without a trace, presumably in a plane crash over the Atlantic."

"How? When?"

"His name was Remington Guilfoyle and he was a scientist working in the hot lab with Winters. This was the same lab that handled the most lethal pathogens known to mankind. He allegedly piloted an experimental plane into the ocean and his body was never recovered. I checked into his past, although there wasn't much to find. Changed his name from Ernest Drinkwater the summer before he entered Yale. Graduated high school in Oklahoma City in 1995. School records show he attended high school there for only one year. Prior to that I couldn't find any record of an Ernest Drinkwater. Not even a birth record," she said, swirling the wine in her glass.

"Jesus, Swain, don't you see the connection?"

"What connection?"

"This Drinkwater character graduated exactly one month after Timothy McVeigh bombed that federal building in Oklahoma City. Don't you find that an interesting coincidence?"

Nolette stared at the wine in her glass. Why hadn't she made that connection before? Drinkwater had been living in Oklahoma City when Timothy McVeigh parked that truck filled with ammonium nitrate in front of the Alfred P. Murrah Federal Building, blowing it to smithereens. She'd only been eleven at the time, and remembered seeing it on the small black-and-white television located in her church's basement. She had to push her way past the adults to see the aftermath of the carnage onscreen, and she remembered hearing the murmuring of the adults as they discussed the bombing in hushed tones. All the adults agreed that, despite the deaths of innocent women and children, McVeigh's deed had been God's will. Somehow that notion seemed strange to her at the time: Why would God choose to harm innocent people?

She was snapped back to reality by the sound of the waitress placing her plate down on the lacquered wood table. The smell of briny lobster mixed in with brandy nearly made her sick. Looking down at it, she didn't think she had the stomach to eat it. She watched in disgust as Bacon gripped his fork and knife and sawed into his rare filet. Bright streams of blood sluiced out from between the grains of beef. How could he just sit there and eat that massive hunk of protein after all they'd been discussing, especially the possibility of an Ebola attack striking American shores.

"He also texted me the initials EHF. It took me a little while to figure out what this acronym stood for."

"And what is that?"

"Ebola Hemorrhagic Fever."

Bacon suspended his forkful of beef in front of his mouth and stared at her in shock. "There's no known cure for Ebola, Swain. In fact, nine out of ten people who come down with it end up dead."

"That's specific to the Zaire strain, which is now currently spreading across Western Africa."

"Could there be any connection?"

She shrugged. "How familiar are you with ligers?"

He laughed, forking the meat into his mouth. "What the hell is a liger?"

"Obviously you're not that familiar with them." She sighed and stirred her fork through the creamy lobster. "It's a lion bred with a tiger."

"A mythical beast, I assume. Like the unicorn and chupacabra."

"Ligers are a real animal, but only bred in captivity."

"Am I missing something here?" He drained his Scotch and held up his glass for a another.

"The same person who is sending me these text messages has been sending me photos of ligers. I guess I'm not making the connection. Thought you might be able to shed some light on the subject."

"Sorry I couldn't be of any help."

Her stomach turned just watching him eat. She looked around the restaurant and saw diners in discussion and digging into their ridiculously expensive meals. How could they be so happy and spirited when another terrorist attack on America was imminent? Just out in the bay, Cooke's Island lay in ruins, specifically targeted for destruction. She lifted the napkin to her mouth and gagged, trying to conceal the involuntary reflex that she'd struggled with ever since running away from home those many years ago. Smoke continued to coil from the gluey mess congealing in the dish. All she wanted to do was to run out of this clamorous restaurant and return to the privacy of her hotel room.

She started to rise up out of her chair when her phone chirped. She glanced at the screen and saw that it was from her hotel. What did they want, she wondered?

"Ms. Swain?"

"Speaking."

"This is Jennifer at the desk of the Wharf Hotel. Don't be overly alarmed, but you might want to come over here as soon as possible."

"What's wrong?"

"There's been a breach of security here at the hotel and I'm afraid to inform you that someone has broken into your room."

Chapter 10

Tag bolted upright out of bed, sweat pouring from his face. How long had he been asleep since arriving at this house? He stared into the black void, gasping for breath while trying to shake the terrible nightmares that had been haunting him on a nightly basis. In these dreams, the depraved victims of smallpox chased him endlessly: gawping, biting, reaching, and never letting him rest. Their mouths remained perpetually open, dripping with blood and saliva, and their bodies were covered in a litany of fiery red sores.

It took him a few seconds to get his bearings and realize that this was the same house he'd arrived at less than twenty-four hours ago. The same drab bedroom. The same rock-hard mattress with the squeaky springs. But something seemed different. For starters, his head pounded with the worst migraine he'd ever experienced. Even worse than the headache he'd experienced after coming down with smallpox. An oily sweat oozed from every pore on his body. Thick, hot tears cascaded down his face and sluiced between his bearded jowls. He lifted his hands in front of his face, but couldn't see them because of the dark. He felt dizzy, weak. The shades had been drawn and the curtains pulled tight. Something seemed wrong but he had no idea what it was. He lay on his back and stared up at the dark void, listening for any sound. Wind rattled against a window. Tugging at his long beard, he realized that this was no dream.

Did something move? He froze for a second and remained still, sensing someone in the room with him: listening, breathing, watching. Was he imagining this? Had he become paranoid, his myopic brain damaged by the lethal pox vaccine? Other than the ticking clock on the wall, he couldn't hear anything but the ringing in his ears. Fez lay asleep in the other room, safely ensconced under a mound of warm blankets. Before turning in for the night, he'd handcuffed the cop to a cast iron pipe in the basement, taped his mouth shut, and left him there until he could figure out what to do with him.

A dizzying sense of apprehension filled him. What if the cops had tracked him here? He tried to remember how he'd arrived at this house. Then it came to him; Oggy had given him directions just before they departed that island on the raft they'd built. It felt as if his brain had turned to mush and would eventually drip out of his nose and ears like warm oatmeal. Something pressed against his right foot. Reaching down to see what it was, he felt a metallic object encircling his ankle. It took him a second to realize that it was a restraint of some sort. A handcuff?

Blood rushed to his head and for a brief second he felt like his skull might explode. He fell back against the bed, clutching his hot temples and trying hard not to cry despite the tears trailing like lava down his cheeks. He missed his wife and kids more than anything in the world and wondered if he'd ever again see them.

"It's me, Colonel," a voice in the dark said. "I'm your worst nightmare and your only hope."

"Who are you? How did you get in here?"

"I think you know who I am." He thought for a second.

"And I can access just about anywhere I want." He moved closer. "I have to say, Colonel, I'm very impressed how you made it off that island."

"No thanks to you."

"Where's the gratitude, good sir? Didn't I see to it that your wife and daughter made it safely back to the mainland?"

Tag turned and stared into the pitch blackness, trying to see the man's face. The voice sounded vaguely familiar to him. Or maybe he was just imagining it. He tried to sit up but experienced a sharp pain at the base of his neck that caused him to fall back onto the mattress.

"Honestly, I wasn't so sure you'd make it. But boy, did you ever prove me wrong. You are truly a beast, Colonel."

"Who are you? What's your name?"

"Does it really matter who I am? I could be Jimmy, George, or Lenny for all you care. It's hardly relevant to our plight."

"Lenny! Show yourself to me, you coward!"

"Oh no, Colonel. You don't want to see what a boogeyman looks like." The man laughed. "Please, let's not be so petty about our identities, especially considering the importance of our mission."

"You mean *your* mission."

"No, I mean *our* mission. You and I are gifted scientists handing off our knowledge to future generations." The man paused. "Tell me, Colonel. Do you want to save your family or not?"

Tag remained quiet.

"Wonderful then. We're in mutual agreement."

"Are my wife and kids okay?" Tag asked, trying to ignore the excruciating pain at the back of his skull.

"Your other two children I'm not too sure about, but your wife and your daughter seem to be doing fine," he said, pausing to let the words sink in. "You mean you haven't heard the news?"

"I've been marooned on that island for the last few months and haven't heard a thing."

"Yes, of course. How thoughtless of me," the man said. "Then I'm sorry to be the bearer of bad news, Colonel, but that traitorous wife of yours has turned against you."

The cop had been right about Monica, confirming his worst fear. There must have been some kind of a mistake.

"She's convinced that you're responsible for that attack on Cooke's Island. As we speak, she's been making herself available to the national media and making quite a name for herself. Some celebrity she's become, too, profiting from your unfortunate downfall."

"I don't believe Monica is capable of such a thing."

"You'd be surprised how effective our government is at persuading people what the truth is. They're shameless manipulators, as you know. But you have to admit, Colonel, all the evidence has been stacked against you."

"Thanks to you."

"No thanks is necessary. Maybe someday you'll appreciate what I've done for this world."

"Doubtful. Because one day I'll track you down and make you pay for what you've done," Tag growled through clenched teeth.

The man laughed. "It's quite possible you will, Colonel, but not today. And by the time you do, it'll be too late anyway."

"Too late for what?"

"The die will be cast. The world will be inexplicably transformed."

Tag struggled to sit up. "Why do I feel so shitty?"

"It's the vaccine I gave you, Colonel. The Liger's blood."

"Liger's blood." The word 'liger' jolted his memory of those icons he'd seen at the island. "You've given me another vaccine?"

"Yes. Like the one I left for you in your jeep after that infectious conference at Harvard Medical."

"When did you do it?"

"When you were asleep. I had to spike the old lady's tea first to administer it. I gave one to the boy as well. Expect it should take you a day or so to fully recover from its effects, although I'm not sure how long the symptoms from the vaccine will linger."

"How did you find me?"

"You insult my intelligence, Colonel," he said, sounding disappointed. "I left you detailed instructions on the bureau as well. As soon as you're feeling better you're to travel to an upcoming infectious disease conference being held upstate."

"How in the world will I do that? I'm the most recognized man in America, dead or alive."

"You obviously haven't been keeping up on the news," the man said.

"Like I said, I've been out of commission for a while."

"You've been pronounced dead by the government." the man said. "Officially, you no longer exist, which is a shame because no one has any idea what a hero you truly are."

"For doing what anyone else would do?"

"For keeping that virus locked up on the island as I intended. Because if it had reached the mainland—end of game. But don't for a second think that the government actually believes you're dead. No, they need you presumed dead for a multitude of reasons, not the least of which is to prevent international and civil unrest. But they searched every inch of that island to find you before they torched it. Since then things in this country have drastically changed."

Tag let a wave of nausea pass over him before he spoke. "In what way?"

"Intense scrutiny. Checkpoints, drones, the full brunt of the newly revised Patriot Act being used against its citizens. Economic indexes have plunged. These are the worst of times, Colonel, doctored-up through propaganda to be the best of times. Trust me when I tell you that the government will do just about anything to find you. Compared to the way the FBI and Homeland Security would interrogate you, you should be grateful that I found you first."

"Spare me your generosity. I only care that my wife and children are safe!"

"As long as you continue to do as I instruct, your family will be fine," the man said. "But now I'd like to tell you a bedtime story about the fifty villages surrounding the Ebola River. I'm fairly certain you know that story by now, Colonel." The legs of the chair scratched against the oak floor.

The mention of the word Ebola sent a shockwave through Tag's system, and he knew instantly what disease was ailing him.

The Ebola River in Zaire was the site of some of the most horrific viral outbreaks in the history of mankind. Worse, just this spring the disease had been spreading throughout Western Africa, killing nine out of ten people who'd become infected with it. Every scientist working in the hot lab broke out in a cold sweat at the prospect of handling the virulent pathogen. Identified because of the threadlike shape when studied under an electron microscope, it was one of the few microbes that put the fear of God into the scientists working under him.

"You've got my full attention," Tag said, realizing what he was now dealing with—what was making him sick!

"I figured that old river tale might get your attention," the man said. "Do you truly want your family to remain safe, Colonel? Even that traitorous bitch you call your wife?"

"Yes. Just tell me what I need to do."

"You've got to *want* to do it, Colonel. Personally, I don't *need* you to do anything."

"Okay, I really *want* to do it."

"Very good then." The man clapped his hands. "You have a few days to prepare yourself. Enjoy your time with the boy and the senile granny. Then get ready to work."

"Don't hurt the old lady. She's just an innocent bystander in all this."

"No one is an innocent bystander if we're all born with sin."

Tag closed his eyes and thought of his wife and kids, and prayed for their well-being.

"I'll be with you every step of the way, Colonel. You'll never know who I am or where I'll show up, but I'll be rooting for you the whole time." The man laughed. "I may even see you at that infectious disease conference."

"How am I supposed to get ahold of you?"

"No worries, Colonel. I'll be in contact you when the time is right."

Tag lay his head back down on the pillow, trying to regulate the pain.

"You've been given high levels of an Immunoglobulin G vaccine, which has proven 99.8% effective against the Zaire Ebola virus. It is derived from the infected blood of an Ebola victim who has progressed to the third spacing. Of course there is a remote chance that you might fall into the .2% category of those who succumb from the vaccine, but that's the risk one assumes with these sort of agents."

Tag heard footsteps falling away and then heard the door open.

"Best of luck to you," the voice called out. "I look forward to seeing you at that conference, Colonel. I suppose I don't need to warn you about prematurely calling in the Feds. Do so and you put the entire country in jeopardy."

"Of course."

"Then I bid you adieu, Colonel."

He heard the sound of the man approaching the bed. He stopped at the foot of the mattress. Tag reached out and tried to grab his hand but realized that he couldn't extend that far. He heard a distinct click and realized that the man had freed his foot from the restraint. He patted his ankle before moving toward the door. Everything suddenly became still and Tag could hear the wind blowing against the pane of glass just behind his head.

He groaned in agony as an intense wave of pain rippled through his body. So it was Ebola he had to now worry about. How could he do anything to help anyone when he barely possessed enough energy to get out of bed?

Chapter 11

Nolette sprinted out of the restaurant and ran directly to her hotel. The prim and proper girl manning the front desk, dressed in a pressed navy blue uniform, appeared flustered when she announced herself loudly. In hushed tones, she asked that Nolette calmly wait in the lobby until her manager arrived. But she didn't want to wait around knowing that someone had broken into her room and searched through her things.

The manager, a small man with a regal bearing and a French accent, immediately met her in the lobby.

"I'm so sorry, Ms. Swain. I don't understand how this could have happened with all of our security measures. We will get you another room right away and, of course, comp the entire bill," he said. "Follow me and we'll go up to your room so that you can report your losses to the police."

"Did someone have a card key to my room?"

"Every card key has its own security code, even card keys assigned to the same room. Our computer is usually able to identify whose card it was that accessed a particular room. The problem is that we had no warning that your room was being broken into until just now, when our computer security system alerted us to the breach. It is supposed to alert us immediately."

"So who broke into my room?" she asked. "And why the delay?"

"That's the strange thing, Ms. Swain. We don't know. The computer cannot identify whose card was responsible for the breach. Nor do we know why it took so long to notify us."

"That makes no sense. Could it have been one of your staff who entered the room?" she asked.

"Our staff have keys to all the rooms, Ms. Swain. The card key system is the only mechanism we use for gaining access into rooms. A staff member would not be stupid enough to do this. Every room is monitored 24/7 by tracking software and then reviewed by security. We know every time a guest enters a room, when the maid enters, and what maid had access to what room, as well as the specific card key used." The doors opened and he gestured for her to enter the elevator first.

"Then the card that was used to get in my room should come up on your computer's system"

"A scheduled security check of the entry data revealed a numerical omission. As soon as security discovered the breach, they called the police and sealed off the room. Whoever gained access to your room utilized a sophisticated software program to not only bypass security measures, but to manipulate the time of entry."

Nolette felt slightly nauseous at the implication. Some very well-connected people wanted to know what she'd learned. People with sophisticated technology and security expertise. She stepped out of the elevator, guessing it might have been a governmental agency like the CIA or NSA. Or else it might have been the terrorist responsible for the attack on Cooke's Island. Either way, she realized that she needed to tell someone what she knew before something else happened.

She followed the hotel manager down the hall. As soon as they turned the corner she saw two uniformed police officers in front of her room. The manager explained to the officers that she was the occupant of the room, and a detective walked out and greeted her. Nolette glanced inside and saw that it had been turned upside down.

"Detective Brennan, ma'am. I'm sorry about what happened here. When you're ready I'd like you to come inside and catalogue any missing items."

"There was nothing of any value in this room, Detective, so I doubt anything is missing," she said, clutching the bag containing her wallet and iPad. It was all she needed. "The only thing I left in here was a suitcase filled with clothes."

"Well, you might want to take a look anyway," the detective said.

Shaken, Nolette flipped breezily through her clothes and personal items, knowing that nothing of value had been taken. Then again, she hadn't expected burglars to covet her unspectacular wardrobe, much of it purchased from J.C. Penney. It felt strange knowing that someone had rifled through her underwear and garments. It made her sick to her stomach, and reminded her of growing up with that loser stepfather her mother had married. She thought quickly about what to tell the cops so as not to give away what she had discovered.

"You're sure there's nothing missing from your room, Ms. Swain?" the detective asked after she'd looked through the room.

"Positive. Nothing here is missing. I never leave money or jewelry in my hotel room."

"I'm not sure why someone with such technical savvy would want to break into your room. Is there something else you want to tell us, Ms. Swain?"

"What else is there to tell?" She walked around, searching for any sign of who might have broken in. "Maybe they were searching for the person who stayed in here before me. During that attack. Have you considered that?"

"She has a valid point," the hotel manager said. "Since the Cooke's Island tragedy, we've had all sorts of people staying in this hotel: reporters, media types, scientists, government officials, as well as many other persons connected to that attack."

"We've dusted for fingerprints but I doubt we'll find anything. Whoever broke into this hotel room will not have left any evidence of their crime, being the professionals that they are," the detective said.

"Am I free to go then, Detective?" she asked.

"As long as we have all your contact information then you're free to leave," he replied.

"We'll set you up in another room, Ms. Swain, and an executive suite at that. Everything will be comped, from the minibar to the restaurant," the manager said.

"Can you assure me that this hotel will be secure?" she asked, knowing that any security measures the hotel utilized would be useless against this group.

"I guarantee it. The first thing I'm going to do is reconfigure every lock and card key in the facility and reset the passwords," the manager said.

Nolette grabbed the handle and lifted the suitcase off the bed. She had no intention of staying in the executive suite or any other room in this hotel. But she would play along for now. Whoever was looking for her would certainly try it again, but she wouldn't be here when they did. Her best bet would be to find other accommodations tonight and then sneak out first thing in the morning and catch a plane back to D.C.

The hotel manager escorted her back to the desk and wrote out a new registration, assigning her a reconfigured card. In addition, he gave her a debit card for all of the hotel's services. She took the card and escaped into the lounge, taking a table in the back, hidden away from sight. While waiting for the waitress to take her order, she made a reservation at The Fairfield Hotel located just a few blocks away. Then she took out her tablet and started typing down everything she'd learned about Cooke's Island—and what she believed was to come in the future. To ensure that she didn't lose any of the information, she sent versions to her cloud account every ten minutes, making certain that all her notes were properly backed-up.

Once she was done, she logged onto her browser and typed in the name Ernest Drinkwater. After fifteen minutes of searching, some in places she ought not to be, she came up with something she thought interesting. Ernest Drinkwater's school records indicated that his parents were Miriam and John Drinkwater, 27 Bradford Way. Rather than fly back to D.C., she decided instead to make a trip out to Oklahoma City and question the Drinkwaters about their missing son.

The waitress came over and Nolette ordered an appetizer and a Coke. She searched around on the Internet for over an hour before finally shutting down her tablet. After finishing her hummus and grape leaves, she stood to leave. The lounge was now filled to capacity and humming. She took the elevator up to her new suite, wanting to at least see what she would be missing. Sliding the card in the slot, she opened the door and was amazed at what she saw. A grand room with giant floor-to-ceiling windows which provided an amazing view of Casco Bay. She strolled around, marveling at the oversized bedroom and mini kitchen. A grand piano sat on one side of the room and on the other side was a massive flat screen TV. Two mocha-colored leather sofas surrounded the screen. Out in the dark harbor, navy ships circled around Casco Bay and the surrounding islands. Only the military's makeshift command facility continued to glow on that barren stretch of land.

She reached inside the minibar and grabbed a few nips of Chablis and Scotch, stuffing them in her bag. Then she left the room before she changed her mind. The idea of kicking back in this spectacular pad was tempting. Never in her life had she stayed in a hotel room so luxurious and accommodating. But then she thought about her previous room, and what had happened there, and decided she'd better stay elsewhere.

Chapter 12

A frigid wind blew off the bay and chilled her as she humped her suitcase down Commercial Street. The streets were filled with people enjoying the Old Port's night life, and she had to dodge and weave around the crowds milling about on the sidewalk. She heard laughter and loud conversations. It appeared to her as if all eyes were staring at her as she passed. Or was she being paranoid? What bothered her was how quickly life could return to normal after that massacre. And yet she knew that no matter what tragedy happened in this country, life inevitably went on. She heard footsteps running up behind her, and before she could turn and see whom it was she felt something sharp pressing up against her back.

"Keep moving, Ms. Swain, and everything will be fine," a man's deep voice said.

"Is this a hold-up? Because I don't have any money on me, if that's what you're looking for."

The man laughed and she could feel the object, which she assumed was a gun, pressing deeper into the small of her back.

"Why did you break into my room?" she asked.

"I think you know why," he replied.

"Okay, take it easy with that thing," she said, stepping up her pace to keep up with him. "Does this have anything to do with what happened on Cooke's Island?"

"You're a bright girl, Swain. I can see why you've become such a decorated reporter," he said. "The sooner you tell us where Colonel Winters is hiding out the sooner we'll resolve all this."

"What agency are you with? The CIA? Because if you're arresting me on some trumped-up charge then I must insist on calling my lawyer." The man laughed at her brazenness. "Hey, pal, you ever heard of the Constitution? You have no right to detain me like this. I know my rights."

"With all due respect, lady, fuck you and your rights. A new day has dawned in this country because of that attack on Cooke's Island, and the President and Congress have signed off on the revised Patriot Act bill, making my job easier."

She knew he was right. Fearing another attack, the citizens of this country had allowed their Constitutional rights to be chipped away. Most of the governmental abuses, she believed, had been committed under the radar so the public never knew about them. Now she was experiencing these lost liberties up close and personal.

This, she realized, was the end of her investigation; finished before it even got started. It could quite possibly be the end of her career as a reporter as well. She knew she had to at least try and talk her way out of this situation. Up ahead she could see a group of patrons exiting a restaurant. Despite the gun pressing against her back, she assumed that this government agent would not kill her out in the open and front of a crowd. She glanced over her shoulder and to her surprise saw Bacon following them.

"Keep your eyes on the road ahead, Swain," the man said, pushing her forward with the barrel of the gun. "There's a lot of drinking going on here tonight and I wouldn't want anyone to get hurt."

Nolette waited until they reached the group milling about in front of the restaurant. They lingered on the sidewalk, embracing one another before heading back to their cars. She counted to three, drew in some air, and then began to scream at the top of her lungs as if she was being savagely attacked.

"Please, someone help! This man's trying rape me!"

"Shut up!" the man ordered, jabbing the gun in her back.

The pain caused her to stumble forward. But her cry for help had worked, evident by the surprised expression on the people's faces. One of the men standing on the curb stepped forward and tried to confront her kidnapper, but he was quickly pistol-whipped over the head and collapsed to the pavement.

Nolette rammed her suitcase into her kidnapper's shins and he howled in pain. Kicking off her heels, she took off running. She glanced over her shoulder and saw her kidnapper punching another man in the face. The other people along the street backed away in fear after seeing his gun. He took off after her, an evil smile on his chiseled face. A three-inch scar ran vertical on his left cheek. Frightened, Nolette gripped her bag and ran as fast as she could.

"That was not a very wise thing to do, Swain," he said as soon as he'd caught up to her.

"Go to hell, ass wipe!"

"Ass wipe. Very clever."

She spun around and saw Bacon sneaking up behind them. She tried to keep her eyes focused and not give away his position. Bacon swung a bottle into the man's temple, sending him hurtling on top of her. She fell to the pavement, holding onto her kidnapper in order to keep from hitting her head. Bacon discarded the glass crown in his hand and pulled something out of his jacket. Woozy, the kidnapper pushed himself off her and climbed to his knees, turning to identify his attacker. He lifted his gun and with his free hand wiped away the blood dripping into his eyes.

"Fucking asshole!" the man with the scar muttered

"Cover your eyes, Swain!" Bacon shouted.

She pressed her eyes shut and heard Bacon spraying something into the man's face. A gunshot went off and she heard someone cry out. A body fell on top of her. She tried to push herself off of him, but he was so big he failed to move. The man with the scar growled and clawed madly at his eyes. Someone gripped her wrists and she felt herself being dragged backwards. Once freed from his body weight, she jumped to her feet, careful not to step on the broken shards of glass. The kidnapper rose to his feet, arms out and shouting for her to come back. He opened his red-stained eyes and glared in her general direction.

"This man tried to rape her!" Bacon shouted to the crowd gathered. He snatched the man's gun off the pavement. "Hold him down until the cops get here."

"He's lying! I'm a government official. Don't let those two get away!" the man with the scar shouted. Four men standing on the sidewalk jumped on top of him and began to pummel him into submission.

"Jesus Christ, Swain, someone really wants that information you've uncovered," Bacon gasped as they ran down the street.

"He wanted to know about Winters," she said.

"Goddamnit, so they do believe he's alive. And if they think he's still out there then it must be true."

"I told you it was true," she said, her bare feet starting to hurt from running on the cobblestones. "Where do we go now?"

"Follow me."

Bacon turned into one of Portland's many alleys. They descended a set of stairs and entered a dank lounge located below street level. Bacon pulled her down the steep stairs, moving past the boozy crowd until they found a quiet booth in the furthest corner of the room. They collapsed into it, struggling to catch their breath. An acoustic guitar played loudly, making it almost impossible to hold a conversation. The table was littered with dirty dishes, half-empty beer glasses, and balled up napkins soiled with greasy food. In one corner of the room a guy with long hair was singing into a mic and playing 'American Pie' on guitar. The faux brown leather over the booth seats was patched with green duct tape. Bacon slipped the man's gun into his waistband and then covered the weapon over with his jacket. Nolette continued to keep a death grip on her bag, swearing to never let it go.

"Thanks, Bacon. I owe you for this."

"No you don't. We reporters have to stick together, right?"

"Right. So what do we do now?" she asked over the music. "They'll surely be looking for us."

"Wait here a sec. I need to go grab some napkins." He exited the booth.

A waitress rushed over and knelt down next to her table. "Did that guy hit you, hon?"

"Why do you ask?"

"You have a bruise under your eye and some nicks on your face." The waitress sighed. "Come on, hon. You don't have to lie for that asshole. I can call the cops if you want."

"No cops!" she blurted, realizing that she had to convince this waitress to go away. "Please don't make this any harder on me by calling the cops or he'll definitely kill me!"

The waitress smiled sadly and patted her hand. "Sure, sweetie. But you need to leave that asshole as soon as possible or you'll end up dead. And I should know. I've been in the same boat."

"I'm planning on it, believe me. I'm just waiting for the right time to leave him," Nolette said. "Is there another way out of this place in case I need to take off?"

"Sweetie, you sure you don't want me to call the cops for you?"

"This guy is a psycho and by the time the cops arrive he'll have already killed me."

"Fucking asshole!" She shook her head. "Through the kitchen back there. It's just for the staff, so don't tell anybody I told you. Take a left and you'll see a set of stairs in the back. The cooks use that door to throw out the trash."

"He's coming back. Thanks so much for all your help. Could you bring us a couple of Scotches so that he calms down?"

"Sure thing, hon."

"And don't worry, I've got a plan to leave this jerk."

Bacon returned to the table with a stack of napkins and a plastic cup filled with water. After dabbing the napkins in the water, he reached across the table and wiped the blood off her face.

"Here, let me do it," Nolette said, snatching the napkins out of his hand.

"You're missing some spots."

"Relax." She took a small mirror out of her bag and used it to clean off the blood. "Someone broke into my room back at the hotel and tore it apart. That's why I took off out of that restaurant."

"That's a relief. I thought it was me you were running away from," he said. "Whoever broke in there was probably looking for evidence of Winters."

"We can't stay in Portland any longer, Bacon. They'll find us sooner or later," she said.

"Do you know who that giant scarface was?"

"FBI? CIA? Homeland Security? I'm assuming he's from one of those agencies, especially now that they've got carte blanche to do whatever they want thanks to the new Patriot Act." She dabbed the napkin against her bruised eye and felt a stinging sensation.

"Whoever sent you those text messages must have been feeding you some serious shit."

"We need to get the hell out of here and fast," she whispered as the waitress brought over two Scotches. Nolette smiled up at her.

"That asshole should pay for what he did, making me smash an expensive bottle of Merlot over his head," Bacon said, wondering why the waitress was glaring at him. "Is there a problem here?" he asked the waitress.

"No problem, pal. Drinks are on the house," she said bitterly before walking away.

"Forget your goddamn Merlot, Bacon. I need to travel out to Oklahoma City so I can figure out who this Ernest Drinkwater is. Then I need to figure out a way to stop this potential threat."

"I'm coming with you." He downed his Scotch in one gulp. "We're a team, right?"

"Sure we're a team. But there's no way we should board a plane together. They'll grab us both if we try it, and then we'll never find out the truth," she said.

Bacon laughed. "Swain, you obviously don't understand the gravity of the situation. Your name is most certainly on a no-fly list now. You can't travel. Those assholes will certainly be staked out at the airport. Probably at train and bus stations too. We want to go to Oklahoma City, then we're going to have to drive there."

"In what? Neither one of us has a car." She glanced up at the windows positioned at street level. "And we're not safe sitting here for very long. If that thug with the scar has any friends, and I'm sure he does, they'll be scouring every bar in town trying to find us."

"Is that front door the only way out?"

"The waitress told me there's an exit out back that only the cooks use," she said, nodding her head toward the kitchen.

"Finish your drink and we'll head out."

"Let me ask you a hypothetical question," she said, sliding her Scotch over to him.

"Shoot." He downed the Scotch, his hooded eyes just over the rim of the glass.

"Do you think the government is justified in trying to capture us if it's in the name of public safety?" she asked. "Especially if it involves the Ebola virus?"

"That's more of a philosophical inquiry than a hypothetical question." He pondered this for a moment. "If it tramples on our Constitutional rights then no, I don't believe life under a dictatorship is worth the added security even if it is Ebola."

"What defines freedom if people are being ravished by a deadly plague? Because there's no liberty if you're dead."

"We can wax philosophic all we want once we're on the road to Oklahoma."

"You've made my point precisely."

"A minor victory in a larger war."

"Except there's no victories here, especially now that we know what's coming."

Nolette heard brakes screeching and when she looked up she saw the bottom half of a van pulling up on the curb. The doors opened and closed. She knew intuitively that they were here for them. She slid out of the booth slowly so as not to attract attention and Bacon followed her lead. Luckily, the crowd provided ample cover. They'd been lucky to find this basement pub to hide out in. But now they had to go. The front door opened and she heard the sound of heels hitting the wooden stairs. It gave her an idea.

"Fire!" Nolette shouted. "Everyone get out of here!"

The patrons of the bar froze momentarily and then dropped whatever they were holding and began to run en masse toward the stairwell. She prayed that no one would get hurt in the stampede, but she had no other choice. Grabbing Bacon's hand, she led him back toward the kitchen, pushing people out of her way. They ran past all the startled cooks, servers, and dishwashers, and headed toward the back door. She released Bacon's hand and took the concrete steps two at a time. Someone shouted at them to get out but they kept on moving. Pushing through the flimsy screen door, she ran out into a small alley and then headed up toward Fore Street. Three Yellow cabs sat at the curb in front of Gritty's Pub. She opened the back door of the first cab they came across and collapsed inside. Bacon dove in after her, slamming the door shut behind him.

"Go! Go! Go!" she shouted to the driver as Bacon pushed her down onto the seat.

"Where to?" the driver asked.

"Just drive." She reached into her jacket and tossed three twenties over the seat.

She felt the cab begin to move. After waiting a few seconds, she raised her head up and glanced out the rear window. The lights of the Old Port receded from view. They'd made it safely out of there. Now they had to figure out how to get to Oklahoma City in one piece.

Chapter 13

Tag spent the rest of the night tossing and turning. As if the headache and aching weren't enough, the sounds of Fez sobbing in the other room made it worse. He went in every now and then to check in on the kid, gave him some Tylenol and water, but knew he couldn't do much else except let the vaccination run its course. Taking care of Fez reminded him of the days when his own kids were little and had come down sick. He and Monica would take turns tending to them at night and taking their temperatures and giving them medicine.

On top of the dresser he saw the manila envelope that had been left for him. He couldn't bear to open it just yet, especially feeling as rotten as he did. He'd look at it later after he fully assessed the situation. He rose out of bed, blood coursing through his head like the advent of a tsunami rushing toward a small Japanese town in one of those You Tube videos. He felt as if he might vomit at any minute. Stumbling out of the room and into the bathroom, he lowered his head into the toilet bowl but nothing came up. His hands on the white rim were bright red and a trickle of blood ran out his nose and splashed into the toilet water. Another wave of nausea hit him and he dry-heaved, noticing a streak of bloody phlegm floating on the surface. He flushed it away and stood. Frightened, he reached down between his legs and palmed his testicles, realizing they were sore to the touch. They had now swelled to two times their normal size; one of the classic symptoms of the Ebola virus. He went over and examined himself in the mirror, noticing his bloodshot eyes and the broken vessels over his nose and cheeks.

He staggered out of the bathroom and entered Fez's room. The old lady was sitting on the bed and looking after the kid. The room reeked with the stench of illness. He knocked on the frame to announce himself and saw Dolores turn and face him. Fez lay on his back with his head resting on the pillow. Pink tears spilled from his cheeks and onto the white bed sheet. A steady trickle of blood leaked from his nose.

"The boy's running a fever," the old woman said. "Best you take him to the doctor."

"I am a doctor, Mrs. Ogden."

She shook her head and clucked. "You look like no doctor I've ever seen before. Hit on some hard times?"

"Yeah, you could say that." He went over to Fez's side and felt his forehead. The kid was burning up. "Do you have more Tylenol?"

Dolores laughed. "Do I have more Tylenol? Pope Catholic? I should own stock in the company." She struggled to stand. "Wait until you get old someday, young fellow."

"My main ambition in life is to grow old." He laughed bitterly.

"Well, let me warn you. The golden years ain't so golden. Wish I had my Robby here to help me out with things." She picked up her cane and stretched her back. "Everything in me aches and creaks. I sure hope you boys didn't bring that bug into the house. Look at my arm. It's black and blue. Looks like a Tarantula bit me while I was sleeping."

A sinking feeling set in as he passed her a tissue. "Your nose is bleeding, Dolores."

"So it is." She took the tissue from him and wiped away the trickle of blood over her hirsute upper lip. "Seems this old gal is ready for the glue factory."

Tag thought to change the subject. "You must have been a very good mother, judging by the way you've looked after the boy."

105

"Oh, I don't know about that. My Robby was a little different from all the other boys growing up, but he always had a good heart. I tried talking to him but it was like talking to a wall. He just liked to be left alone and do his own thing. After he went into the Army, he only got worse."

"He served in the Iraqi War?"

"Yup. He was patriotic when he first started out and wanted to be the one to kill Osama. When he found out that Bush and his cronies lied about finding all those weapons of mass destruction, my Robby turned hard against his country. Can't say I blame him either. They sent that boy door to door in the worst of those Muslim ghettos, searching for the enemy. Something bad must have happened to him during that time, because it really messed him up."

"I'm very sorry about what happened to your son, Dolores."

She waved her veiny hand in the air. "You're talking like he's already dead. I expect my Robby to walk through that door any day now. He usually leaves the island just before the worst of winter hits. Such a crazy life he lives, if you ask me, but that's the way he wants it. Now you wait here and I'll go get that Tylenol, because you don't look so good either."

Dolores hobbled away and he knew just by observing her that she was manifesting the initial symptoms of the disease. The vaccine was designed to produce quicker results. The introduction of pure Ebola into the human bloodstream would take slightly longer before the expansion of viral replication set in. Bricks of viral material would begin to amass, and it would grow at such a frenetic pace that the victim's tissue and vital organs would literally be consumed by it until finally the bricks exploded out of the victim's body in the massive hemorrhaging that occurred in the third spacing. The hemorrhaging was the virus's final attempt at finding a new host. Although technically a living organism, Ebola was a parasitical eating machine that required a living host in order to subsist. Deep in the African jungle, where the organism prospered in its lush eco-system, it could lay dormant for years until it latched onto its next victim.

Tag leaned over Fez and wiped the damp hair out of his eyes. He pushed the blanket off him and removed the kid's shirt and pants so that he might cool down. His entire body had a red and pinkish hue to it, and he noticed deep red welts over his skin.

"Am I going to die?" Fez asked. "Because I feel like I'm dying."

"Not if I can help it, kid," he said, placing his ear on the boy's chest and listening to his heartbeat. "Heart and lungs sound good. How else are you feeling?"

"My entire body aches."

"This is going to sound creepy, Fez, but I'm going to ask you anyways. How do your balls feel?"

"My balls?"

"Your testicles."

Fez turned his head on the pillow and stared up at him.

"Thought you said you weren't a perv, Tag? Now you want to feel my nuts?"

"Jesus, Fez, I'm a doctor for crying out loud."

The kid broke out laughing. "I'm just messing with you," Fez said, holding his hand up for a high five. "I trust you more than anyone else in this world."

He slapped the kid's hand.

"I didn't want to say anything but my balls are killing me. Feels like someone kneed me in the nuts." He stared up at him with his bloodshot eyes. "You don't look too good neither."

"Don't worry about me. I'm going to get some ice and cool you down," Tag said.

Dolores returned with the Tylenol and passed it over to him. He emptied three tablets into his palm and gave it to the kid along with a glass of water. Fez swallowed all three, pressing his eyes shut to minimize the pain in his throat. Then Fez dropped his head back down on the pillow and took a few breaths. Dolores hobbled out to the living room and collapsed in her armchair. She clicked on the television while Tag retrieved two bags of ice out of the freezer. One bag he put on his forehead and the other he gave to Fez to hold on his swollen testicles. Then he told the kid to rest up before swallowing three Tylenols himself.

He closed the door and sat next to Dolores, who continued to flip through the channels. His head throbbed and his vision became blurry and unfocused. Glancing around the room, he stared at the photographs of Dolores and her family. The three boys appeared clean-cut in many of the pictures, and looked so much alike that Tag had no idea which one was Oggy. Of course Oggy's appearance had changed quite radically since then. He noticed a framed photograph of a young man dressed in an Army uniform and figured that must have been him. Hard to believe that the innocent kid in that picture was the same pot-smoking, fringe lunatic that had befriended him on Rabbit Island.

The sound of the channels changing caused his head to pound and he wished she'd just settle on one show. And she'd turned the volume up so high that he assumed she must have been partially deaf. His own grandfather used to do the same thing in his later years.

She finally settled on one of the cable news channels. Tag was about to go down to the basement and check up on the cop when he heard the sound of a familiar voice speaking. The man's voice coming from the set resonated so strongly with him that he sat back down and kept his eyes riveted on the screen. Suddenly the channel changed, and he glanced over and saw Dolores thumbing the clicker.

"Dolores, could you please change it back to the previous station," he said.

"But The Golden Girls are on."

"Keep going back and I'll tell you when to stop," he said. Dolores reversed channels until she came to the one he wanted. "That's it."

"I'm so sick and tired of hearing about that Cooke's Island ordeal," she said, standing to her feet. "That's all they talked about twenty-four hours a day. Don't get me wrong, I feel sorry for those poor people, but a person can only deal with so much sadness before it starts to get to them."

"Where you going?" he asked.

"The idiot box is all yours, Doctor. I'm going into the kitchen to make some tea."

Dr. Simon Wolfe was dressed in a charcoal grey suit with his signature red bow tie and tortoiseshell glasses. The sight of his old friend almost brought Tag to tears. He desperately felt like calling him up and asking for advice. But in his precarious state, an outlaw and fugitive from the law, he knew that calling any of his contacts would only alert the authorities to his whereabouts.

"There have been rumors and innuendo, and some questionable video, of rampant cannibalism on Cooke's Island during that biological attack. Can you address that medical issue, Dr. Wolfe?" asked Jans Norquist, host of the popular cable news show.

"The rumors, innuendoes, and questionable video footage that were released during the outbreak are all untrue, Jans. They are what we refer to as urban myths. What is true is that we had a particularly virulent and highly unusual case of smallpox that infected those poor people on that island. Although smallpox affects a person's mental and emotional state, there's been no historical or medical evidence of this virus causing such extreme and aggressive behavior. Deadly, yes. But causing rampant hyper-aggression and cannibalism, certainly not."

"What about the video footage from cell phones, and the victims' calls relayed back to the mainland?" Jans asked.

"The mind plays tricks on those who are sick. Look, there is a fine distinction between the desperate will-to-survive versus hyper-aggression. It's why the Grimm brothers' fairy tales were so popular; because they were rooted in well-known tragedies," Dr. Wolfe replied with the certainty of a college professor. "As far as the videos are concerned, I've taken a look at a few of these clips myself and can only conclude that they've been reedited for maximum effect. No doubt the persons responsible for this attack wanted to make this event look as destructive as possible for reasons having to do with propaganda."

"So do you believe another attack is imminent, Doctor?"

"In this day and age, I suppose anything is possible. But I wouldn't expect one so soon after."

"Many people are worried that something like this could hit the mainland and spread like wildfire, especially now that the Ebola virus is spreading across western Africa."

"We live in uncertain times, Jans, so of course that possibility exists. But you must consider a few important things. The smallpox virus that was used in the attack was a well-known agent and was housed exclusively in bio-facilities in the U.S. and Russia. It's a highly fragile and rare strain that needs proper storage and care. And because it is known to us, we have the unique ability to manufacture a vaccine from this particular strain. So I highly doubt that we'll see this agent reproduced again. Secondly, the attack on Cooke's Island was like a shot across the bow; a message, if you will. If the terrorists so desired they could have easily attacked the mainland. As for Ebola, I seriously doubt we'll see that on our shores any time soon. The method of transmission for Ebola is primarily through the passage of bodily fluids, which means it wouldn't spread as easily as the flu. And in my experience, the Ebola virus does not mutate as quickly as other viruses, which is why the flu poses a much greater risk to us."

"Then why is Ebola so prevalent in western Africa?"

"Ebola is a terrifying disease, no doubt. But to get one's hands on Ebola would be ten times harder than possessing smallpox. It's deadlier, yes, much harder to handle because of its instability, and far more difficult to procure. But as I said, it requires the passing of bodily fluids. Unfortunately, the sanitation procedures in western Africa, particularly in caring for the deceased, are far less stringent than in the States."

"One last question, Dr. Wolfe," Jans asked. "What is your take on your old student, Dr. Winters? Is he a terrorist like the government is calling him or a hero like some other people believe."

"Dr. Winters was not only one of my most brilliant students, but certainly one of the most ethical scientists I have ever had the pleasure to know. In fact, we offered him a tenured-track position at Harvard Medical School before this all happened. The man had an intuitive understanding of viral behavior and its method of replication. I was extremely close to him and his wife, and believe that what he did, contrary to what the government believes, constituted a heroic attempt in trying to keep that virus from spreading." Dr. Wolfe shrugged. "But in the end who knows what lives in the hearts of other men? How well do we really know the people we associate with on a regular basis? I personally believe that his actions on Cooke's Island saved the lives of millions of people around the world. It's just a damn shame he's not around to answer the many questions we have for him."

"So you believe he's dead?"

"I'm afraid I do, Jans. There's no way he, or anyone else, could have escaped that island."

"Thank you for your time, Dr. Wolfe," Jans said, turning to the camera. "Our thanks to Dr. Simon Wolfe of Harvard Medical School for coming on the Jans Norquist Show today."

Tag clicked off the TV, not quite believing what he'd just heard. Did he detect the slightest hint of doubt in Simon's voice? He tried to clear his pounding head and think rationally. Wolfe had been effusive in his praise for him. He was right in one regard though; whom could anyone trust these days? He'd put all his trust in that miserable old island hag and the bitch had completely played him for a fool.

The sound of a kettle whistled in his ears. He pushed himself off the armchair and stood, holding onto it for support. The whistling faded once Dolores removed the kettle from the stovetop. Two cups sat on placemats next to a couple of toasted blueberry muffins. He certainly hoped that she wasn't expecting visitors.

111

"Tea?" she asked, pouring the boiling water over her bag. With her free hand she lifted the bag up and down in the steaming brown water.

"I'd love some. Right after I check on our guest downstairs." He opened the door to the basement. "Thank you for taking us in and treating us so well, Dolores."

"Any friend of my Robby's is a friend of mine. I only wish he brought more friends over when he was younger," she said, pouring hot water into his teacup. "Don't be too long down there or your tea will get cold."

Tag headed downstairs, afraid of what he might discover. The burly cop sat against the wall, his one secured wrist bleeding from the handcuff. The masking tape over his mouth had turned red and he was laboring to breathe out of his nose. Tag ripped the tape off his mouth, but not before the cop grabbed his shirt with his free hand and pulled him down towards him. He tried to wrestle the cop away, but he was strong and seemed possessed by some demonic force. His eyes had turned pink and Tag noticed a trickle of blood seeping out of his ear. Was he crashing out? Tag reached for the cop's service revolver, which he'd put on the bench, and struggled to free himself. Once he had the gun in hand, he punched the cop in the head.

"What'd you do that for?" Dean cried.

"Why'd you attack me?"

"Because you stuck me with a needle last night, same way you infected all those people on Cooke's Island."

"Whoever stuck you did the same to me," Tag said, rolling up his sleeve and showing him his own needle mark.

The cop struggled to free himself but the cuff only dug deeper into his wrist.

"What's happening to me, Winters? I feel like shit."

"I'm not sure just yet," Tag lied.

"Please let me go. I'm gonna go crazy if I stay chained up against this fucking pipe all day."

"I'm sorry, Dean, but I can't do that right now."

"Why? I got smallpox or some shit?"

"You know why. You'll turn against me if I let you go."

"Swear to God I won't."

"Sorry, Dean, but I can't trust you."

"I'm gonna make you pay once I get outta these restraints, Winters." He moved his arm up and down, but the cuff merely slid on the rusted pipe. "And I'm gonna cheer like shit when they stick that needle in your arm and put you to sleep."

"Bring your pom poms, Dean."

Tag turned and headed up the stairs, not able to look the man in the eye. The cop started to scream, begging to not be left in the basement and chained to the pipe. Could the neighbors hear him screaming? He had to find a way to keep the cop quiet, and yet he couldn't put tape over his mouth without suffocating him to death. Instead, he headed back down the stairs, pointing the gun at the cop's head. Bloody tears streaked down the man's fluttering cheeks.

"Go ahead and shoot me then, Winters. I can't live like an animal," he cried.

"I need you to shut the hell up for a minute until we figure something out."

"I'll just keep screaming until you release me," he said. "I can't go on living in this fucking basement."

Tag stared at the infected man, feeling sorry for what he was about to say. But if he released this cop he would no doubt turn against him. Worse, he might pass the Ebola virus on to the general public.

"I'm not going to kill you, Dean, but I might just pay a visit to your family if you don't shut the hell up."

The cop glared at him with a look of hate. "You leave my family out of this!"

"Then do as you're told, Dean, and shut the hell up."

"My head feels so fucked up. I don't want to turn into one of those cannibals."

"Everything's going to be fine. You need to rest and keep your voice down and I'll be gone soon. And don't piss me off."

Tag started up the stairs, despising himself for the lie he'd just told.

"At least give me the dignity of the truth, Winters," the cop shouted up to him. "Did you infect all those people?"

Tag stared down at him from the stairs. "I swear to God that I had nothing to do with that attack."

"Okay, Winters, I believe you. I'm just begging you to leave my family out of this."

"You keep your mouth shut and they'll be fine."

Tag bolted up the stairs, feeling terrible about how he'd treated the cop. But he'd learned a valuable lesson on Cooke's Island and that was to save only those who could be saved. Although he felt guilty about not taking Dean to the hospital, he knew that an emergency room would only act as an incubator for the virus, causing it to spread out-of-control. Then there was the hysteria that would ensue once people found out. No, if the cop was infected with the Ebola virus, and not merely the vaccine, then hospitalization would be useless. His odds of surviving were tenuous at best. Death would come swiftly once the symptoms manifested—a matter of days. He'd crash out and then burn, his internal organs turning into gelatinous sludge before sloughing out his body. Once that happened, the house and everything in it would need to be burned to the ground.

He'd forgotten about his tea! Dolores had left the kitchen and was now reclined on the sofa in the living room. Grabbing his cup, he sidled up next to the old lady. Her eyes were glossy, and he noticed blood trickling from the veins protruding across the top of her hands. Beads of sweat bubbled up out of the pores over her scalp and clung to the fine grey hairs. The sound of The Golden Girls arguing was followed by a laugh track.

"How are you feeling?" He knelt next to her.

She looked over at him and smiled, her upper lip quivering and exposing her dentures.

"Did you get your tea? I left it on the table for you." She returned to The Golden Girls.

114

He held up his cup. "Do you have a computer in the house, Dolores?"

She pointed an arthritic finger. "My Robby has one of those things in his room somewhere. But don't ask me how to use it because I know nothing about them."

"Thanks," he said, squatting down next to her. "If there's anything you need, just holler."

She grabbed his wrist and pulled him toward her. He tried to take his hand back but her grip was stronger than expected, and she wouldn't let go. Was this the body's neurological reaction to stress? Surging adrenaline rushes similar to when people lifted cars to save loved ones trapped beneath it? He reached over and pressed his thumb into the soft flesh of her wrist, and the pressure caused her to release her grip.

"Try to rest, Dolores. I'll check in on you later, okay?" he said.

"You're a good boy just like my Robby. I bet your mother is proud of you being a doctor and all."

"Yes, she is."

He recalled his mother's sad, painful death five years ago. She'd been a brave soul, taking her diagnosis in stride, more worried about the rest of her family than herself. And then a few months into her diagnosis her mood abruptly changed and she became surly and unpredictable. His father was a patient man, but clearly troubled by the change in his wife's behavior, knowing this wasn't the woman he'd been married to for forty-five years. But when she turned abusive and violent, lashing out at loved ones for no apparent reason, they had no choice but to admit her into a secure facility. The heavy medication sedated her until she passed quietly with her family around her.

After checking on Fez, now asleep in his room, Tag bolted upstairs and turned on the computer. It was old and took a few minutes to boot up. He typed in the name Dr. Simon Wolfe and came upon his personal website. A list of his public appearances showed up onscreen. Tag noticed that his good friend had been benefitting quite nicely from the disaster on Cooke's Island:

speeches, interviews, public appearances. Considering his own impoverished state, it rankled his nerves that Simon had profited so handsomely from that vicious attack. Scrolling down the screen, he saw something that made his heart gallop. Wolfe would be appearing as a guest speaker at an infectious disease conference in Maine, organized in response to the attack on Cooke's Island. He was stunned to see that the other guest speaker was none other than his wife—Monica Winters!

Chapter 14

Bacon instructed the taxi driver to take the first exit after crossing over the 295 bridge. They traveled a few miles along Route 1 until they found a cheap motel with a blinking red Vacancy sign. The bulb in the "V" had burnt out and there were only two other cars in the lot. Nolette pulled out her wallet and realized she barely had enough cash to tip the driver. The cab stopped and before exiting she handed over the fare, apologizing for the small tip. Then they watched as he sped off into the night, leaving them standing alone in the empty parking lot.

"Wonderful place," she said, thinking about that magnificent penthouse she could have had.

"We book a room for the night and then head out in the morning," Bacon said, walking toward the office.

"Book a room for the night? We need to get out of this state as soon as possible and before they come looking for us!"

"No, tonight we stay here and rest. Tomorrow morning we'll head out. I'm sure there's a car rental agency located somewhere along Route 1."

"This place is a shit hole," she said, staring at the L-shaped, one-story motel. "Be sure to book two rooms."

"It'll look less conspicuous if we book one. If anyone asks, we're a married couple from Wisconsin. Ellen and Jack Pickler."

"Pickler?" Nolette laughed at the absurdity of the name. "At least get us separate beds."

"One bed to be on the safe side. Don't worry, Swain, I'll crash on the floor."

"Can't you at least give me a better name than Ellen Pickler?"

"I left all my possessions back in that hotel, including my computer and clothes. And I gave up an expensive bottle of merlot to save your ass, so you're going to be Ellen Pickler and like it." He smiled.

"Okay, I guess I can be Ellen from Wisconsin for one night."

"A foot rub would be nice once we get in our room, hon."

"Don't push your luck, Bacon," she said once they stopped in front of the office. "Are all your notes back in that hotel room?"

"Yeah, but I always save everything to cloud." He reached inside his pants pocket and pulled out his iPhone. "I have three separate accounts with three different identities and can access everything from one phone." He held it up and showed it to her.

"Why three separate accounts?"

"I opened them on a hunch soon after that disaster on Cooke's Island. Figured the government would be cracking down on reporters searching for the truth. That's why there's three accounts."

They entered the office and Bacon spoke to the Indian girl at the front desk, who looked as if she'd just awoken from a deep sleep. She took his corporate credit card and swiped it through the processing machine. Her teeth were crooked and what was left of them were stained and chipped. The woman handed him an old-fashioned key to the room.

Bacon held up the key once they left the office. "A real key. Made out of metal. This way they can't keep track of us."

"But you paid with your credit card. Can't they track that?"

"It's under a different name and registered to a make-believe employee in one of their umbrella companies. The paper gave it to me in case I found myself in such a situation."

"Smart thinking, Bacon." She studied the key in his hand. "I can't remember the last time I used an actual key in a hotel room."

"That's because a hotshot reporter like you only travels first class. The real muckrakers go undercover and report out of fleabag joints so as not to be discovered."

"You've stayed at dumps like this?"

"Of course I have. It's how it's done by us Pulitzer Prize winners." He smiled knowingly.

Nolette followed him to the third room on the left and watched as he stuck the key in the door and turned the handle. Bacon flicked the lights on and the room came into full view. An old television sat on the dresser in front of a queen bed draped in an emerald comforter. The red shag carpet was stained and looked disgusting. She didn't know whether she wanted to sleep on the floor or the mattress lest she catch bedbugs or worse. She grabbed a pillow and ripped the comforter off the bed and then lay down on the floor.

"I said you can have the bed, Swain."

"I'm not sleeping on that shitty mattress," she said, wrapping the blanket around her body like a burrito.

"Suit yourself." He jumped on the bed, the springs squealing, and quickly clicked off the lamp.

Nolette pulled her iPad out once she was fully enveloped and turned it on. The soft glow lit up her cocoon and she was happy to discover that this dump at least had WiFi. The shag carpet, as disgusting as it looked, actually felt comfortable beneath the comforter. She stared at the screen, noting all the new text messages sent to her. She clicked on the first message and a video of an Ebola victim appeared on screen. The African woman looked to be in the last stages of the disease. She lay on a cot staring glassy-eyed into the lens. The video blurred and moved out of focus. A few seconds passed before the woman moved. In the final throes of the disease, a rush of blood and diarrhea burst out of her backside. It happened so fast that it stunned Nolette, and gave her no time to turn away. Dark, thick blood began to pour out of every orifice on the victim's body. The scene made her nauseous and for a moment she thought she might vomit. She quickly clicked out of the video and onto the next message. A short clip of a gigantic cat playing with its trainer. The cat tackled the trainer to the ground and licked him with his massively long tongue. At first she thought it was a tiger. Then it turned toward the camera and she swore that she was looking at a lion. It took her a moment to connect the dots and realize that this was another one of those ligers.

She skipped to the last one and was stunned to see Colonel Winters sitting down in front of a desk and staring at her. Was he typing something? With his long hair and beard he looked like a homeless person. She recalled his former clean-cut image with the all American good looks of a former athlete. It took her a few seconds to realize that he was sitting in front a desktop computer. She wondered if this video was happening in real time or if it was prerecorded. If only somehow she could communicate with him and relay her worst fears. For a moment she felt like Dorothy watching as Auntie Em called for her in that crystal ball. *Dorothy? Dorothy?* The video abruptly ended and the text messages vanished from the screen.

Shaken, she turned off her tablet and pressed her eyes shut. The idea of an Ebola virus hitting America's shores frightened her. At least she knew that Colonel Winters was alive and well. It was one advantage she had in the battle against this terrorist.

"Hey, Bacon. You asleep yet?"

"I was this close until you started yapping."

"Thank you for saving me back there."

"Go to sleep, Swain. We have a long drive ahead of us tomorrow."

* * *

The next morning they called a cab, stopped to get some cash out of an ATM, and then got dropped off at a car rental in Saco. In less than an hour they were driving on I-95 and headed to Oklahoma City. Bacon drove first while Nolette watched the landscape fly past. They'd agreed beforehand to set the cruise-control to sixty-seven so as not to draw any extra police attention to themselves.

They stopped off at highway exits for lunch and dinner. Equipped with satellite radio, they didn't converse much, instead listening to the news stations for any updates. Bacon surrendered the wheel once darkness fell, allowing to Nolette to drive into the morning. With her eyes on the road, she thought of all the questions she might ask the Drinkwaters once she sat down to interview them.

Bacon fell asleep around ten at night, his head resting against the window of the passenger door. She cruised the deserted highway, letting her mind roam freely and thinking about everything that had transpired in the last twenty-four hours. Around three in the morning she felt herself starting to nod off, and so she switched seats with Bacon and closed her eyes. By the time she opened them the sun was beginning to rise in the horizon. The vast blue sky shone with unusual intensity, and a streak of orange blazed in the distant clouds. The plains spread out around her, endless and expanding. Marveling at the landscape, she felt a twinge of anxiety at entering Oklahoma.

"How far are we from downtown?" she asked

Bacon yawned. "Can't be much longer. I'm guessing maybe fifteen minutes."

"It's way too early to try for an interview."

"True. I suppose we'll be here for a few days interviewing all the people who knew this whack job. I say we start with his parents before we reach out to anyone else." He turned to her. "I'm dying to have one of those big cowboy breakfasts that everyone's always talking about. Steak and eggs, pancakes, biscuits and gravy, pots of hot coffee."

"Ugh. I can't even think about food right now."

"How can you not be hungry after such a long night of driving?"

"Butterflies in my stomach."

"Nervous about this meeting?"

"Not as much as I am about seeing that Oklahoma bombing memorial."

"Oh? I didn't realize that was on our itinerary," Bacon said, turning into the crowded parking lot of a restaurant called The Gravy Train.

"Come all this way, I figure I might as well see it."

"Suppose you're entitled to."

He found a parking space and they entered the restaurant, taking a booth in the back. Every seat in the place was taken. Waitresses in pink uniforms rushed to and fro carrying massive trays of food. Once they were seated, Nolette ordered a coffee and bagel, and Bacon ordered The Gravy Train Special. The waitress, a beefy woman who looked overworked and underpaid, left a pot of steaming coffee on their table.

"Now this is my kind of place," Bacon said, pouring himself a cup.

"You strike me as being more the urbane type rather than a fan of The Gravy Train," she said as she poured herself a cup.

"Give me a place like this any day over Tavern on the Green."

"Coffee's pretty bland," she said after taking a sip. She dumped more cream and sugar into her cup.

"It ain't Starbucks, Swain, but it's hot and there's plenty of it so don't be such a snob."

"At least it's got caffeine in it," she said after taking a second sip. "I've never been to Oklahoma City before."

"Not exactly a vacation destination."

"You've been here?"

He looked up at her and she noticed a subtle change in his expression.

"I didn't want to tell you, Swain, if you didn't know, but I covered the Oklahoma City bombing. That story helped make my bones as a reporter and got me noticed in the profession." He clenched his jaw and seemed momentarily shaken by the memory of that experience.

"You did?"

"Yeah. Covered the trial too. Do you know what it's like to look into the eyes of a man who murdered over a hundred and sixty people and destroyed the lives of many more?"

She shook her head, taken aback by this stunning admission.

"There's no way you could understand the emotional toll it took on me unless you were there. I covered every day of that punk's trial, reporting on it until he was sentenced to hell by lethal injection." He leaned over the Formica table, his eyes moist, and whispered, "I was in the gallery the day they stuck that needle into his arm."

"Jesus, Bacon, I had no idea you reported on that." How did she not know this? And why hadn't he mentioned this before?

"You were probably too young to remember, but you can go back and read all the stories I wrote. I kept wondering at the time what could cause a person to go off the deep end like that. Then during the trial I started to gain a better understanding of his motivation, as crazy as that sounds. He had a bitter, scathing hatred of the federal government. Saw it as an unjust occupier of the American people just as the Nazis occupied Europe. In his heart, McVeigh must have felt as repressed as the Jews did during Kristallnacht."

"Probably how the Cooke's Island terrorist feels about this country."

"Absolutely, except instead of using five thousand pounds of ammonia nitrate fertilizer, nitromethane and diesel fuel, our guy used biological weapons. I have no doubt that if McVeigh could have used a viral bomb he certainly would have."

"We've been together for less than two days, Bacon, and I'm now realizing that I know next to nothing about you," Nolette said, watching as the waitress approached with their food. "I'm afraid that I've terribly misjudged you."

"Don't sweat it. Not the first time and it certainly won't be the last." He downed his coffee and poured himself another. "Sounds like I'm growing on you."

"I brought some fungicide just in case it gets out of hand."

"Come on, Swain, just admit I'm not that bad of a guy. Maybe you even like me a wee bit." He held up his forefinger and thumb.

"If I admit it will you please change the subject?"

"Certainly," he said, sipping his coffee. "Honestly though, I don't give a shit what people think about me, Pulitzer or no Pulitzer. I do whatever the hell I want and when I want."

"What else about you should I know?"

"Two kids and an ex-wife. My son's a freshman at Syracuse and my daughter's a junior in high school. My wife and I divorced when the kids were young, my job as a reporter keeping me away from home quite a bit. Being on the road all the time didn't exactly hone my skills as a husband. But I love my kids more than anything and try to be the best father I can to them, considering the demands of my job."

She sipped her coffee and looked down at the table in chagrin as the waitress set the plates of food down.

"What about a smart babe like you? What's your story?"

"I suppose I haven't met the right person yet. Of course with all the travel I do it makes it difficult to meet anyone," she said, spreading cream cheese lightly over her toasted bagel. "And it wouldn't be fair to have kids while working the crazy hours that I do."

"Where'd you grow up?" he asked, forking slabs of sausage into his mouth. "I know zero about you, Swain. Throw me a friggin' bone, will you?"

She took a bird's bite out of her bagel and stared at him. "So where do you think this terrorist will strike next?"

"Okay, be like that." Bacon jabbed a wedge of syrupy pancake into his mouth. "How the hell should I know where the bastard'll strike next. If I knew that I wouldn't be out here in the middle of fucking Oklahoma eating pig entrails and pancakes."

They ate the rest of their breakfast in silence. Nolette had no interest in opening up about her painful childhood in that repressive religious community. Bacon paid the bill in cash after they'd finished their meal, and once back in the car they headed straight into the city. Bacon couldn't remember how to get to the Oklahoma City Bombing Memorial and so Nolette programmed it into the GPS. Within minutes they were cruising through downtown Oklahoma City. An unsettling feeling settled into the pit of her stomach as Bacon turned onto Fifth Street. Even Bacon seemed unusually somber at the prospect of reliving one of the worst serial killings in the country's history. Contrasted to the thousands of people killed and maimed on Cooke's Island, this tragedy, which had happened over two decades ago, seemed minuscule in comparison.

She suddenly felt an affinity with Bacon and maybe even liked him a little. Behind that gruff and cocky exterior was a highly intelligent and sensitive man. He'd opened up to her, revealing his soft side, and in the process revealed more to her than he'd let on. She could see how women fell for him.

Bacon parked on NW Harvey Avenue and they exited the car and began to hike over to the site. She felt an overwhelming sadness as they approached the Outdoor Symbolic Memorial. She stood in front of the Twin Gates and stared up at the impressive structure. A powerful emotion surged through her. The East Gate represented the moment just before the terrorist attack occurred, and the West Gate represented the moment just after the attack. Tears streamed down her cheeks and her hands began to tremble. She looked over at Bacon and watched as he swept his hair back over his scalp. He looked tired and small, the bags under his eyes weighted down with grief. She had no doubt, from the grave expression settling over his face, that he was reliving his own tormented connection to this tragedy.

"We've got a lot to do today, Swain. You still want to go inside and look around?"

"Yeah. Just for a little bit. That okay?" she asked, wiping her moist eyes.

"Knock yourself out. Never know when you'll ever come here again."

"Thanks."

"Just make it quick. I don't want to start blabbering like a little baby."

Nolette realized that she'd left her bag in the rental car; she wanted to take a few pictures to remember this day. She asked Bacon for the keys so that she could run back and retrieve it.

"Grab my phone while you're at it. I left it in the tray between the seats."

She jogged back to the car and found her bag beneath the passenger seat. Bacon's phone sat in the tray exactly where he'd said it would be. She lifted it off the loose change they'd tossed inside for tolls and coffee. Reaching down for her bag, she pulled out her iPad as well as the vial containing her Valium. Dumping a pill in her palm, she tossed it back, hoping its therapeutic effects would soon take hold so that she didn't turn into a puddle in front of Bacon. Luckily, she hadn't had a big breakfast, which would allow the Valium to enter her bloodstream more quickly.

She was about to exit the car when Bacon's phone buzzed. The screen lit up, asking for his eight-digit password. She'd seen him type it in a number of times, and although she'd not intentionally memorized it, she had the kind of mind that refused to let facts go. Most people would have thought such a memory a gift, but in many ways she thought it a hindrance; except when it came in handy. Her memory was like a pit-bull; once it locked onto its target it refused to let go.

She knew that it was wrong to snoop in his stuff, but curiosity made it impossible *not* to look. What did she really know about Bacon other than what he'd told her? She'd already assumed that much of what he said was bullshit, although she didn't doubt for one moment that he'd been here to report on the Oklahoma bombing. She typed in the eight-digit code and the screen flashed to life. At least twenty text messages waited to be opened. She went to an old message and opened it.

Keep an eye on her.

What the hell did that mean! She opened another.

My story must be told for the world to know.

Then the next one.

126

JOSEPH SOUZA

Try and make it look like an accident.

Make what look like an accident? Nolette felt sick to her stomach as she slipped the phone into her pocket. Had Bacon been collaborating with the terrorist? She leaned over the sidewalk and felt her stomach rumble. Something felt very wrong and she had no idea what to do or where to turn. It now seemed quite a coincidence that he'd saved her from that government agent with the scar. She felt scared and alone. The idea of driving off in this rental car crossed her mind, but if this conspiracy was as big as she believed, then those involved would easily be able to track her down if they wanted. No, she vowed to return to Bacon and keep him in her sights at all times.

The Valium started to kick in. She stood on the sidewalk, gathering her composure and trying not to lose her bearings. Whoever had hired Bacon to keep track of her had obviously planned on the two of them penning a sympathetic story. If she went along with him, and pretended not to know she was being manipulated, maybe they wouldn't harm her. Then she could get to the bottom of this bullshit and report on the *real* story, exposing all the players involved.

She took a deep breath and felt herself becoming more relaxed. Bacon must be getting impatient right about now. She'd given him no reason to believe that she'd memorized his password. With her bag and his cell phone, she jogged back to the Twin Gates and found him standing off to the side, watching in rapt attention as a group of Japanese tourists snapped pictures of the memorial.

"Got it," she said, holding up her iPad.

"What the hell took you so long?" he grumbled, snatching the phone from her hand.

"I saw this guy rolling past me in a wheelchair and I imagined that he'd been in that attack. Guess I got a little emotional."

"Women." He shook his head. "For all you know, Swain, the guy could have been a bum or gotten hit by a bus."

127

"Sure, but that's not the point. Seeing that guy brought all 'this' home to me and made the bombing seem more real."

"You're so weird."

"See! You've finally got me pegged." She faked a laugh. "Come on, Bacon, let's get this over quickly so I never have to see this shit again."

"A woman being quick?" He laughed morosely. "That'll be the day."

She needed to play along until she knew the truth. No matter what happened she would never let him out of her sights. The race to stop this new Ebola attack was now on.

Chapter 15

Vernon woke early that morning, still groggy from his roundtrip journey to Portland. The journey had been a resounding success. He'd infected Winters as well as the other inhabitants of that house, and had stood close enough to that reporter to see the fear in her eyes. All the pieces were in place for this biological masterpiece. Soon enough he would start implementing the next phase of his plan.

With coffee in hand, he walked onto his deck and scanned the valley. A fine mist hovered over the trees tops, and a dusting of powder had whitened the peaks. A majestic waterfall presented itself at the northern rim. He looked down upon the town of Brookhaven with its historic brick buildings and tree-lined streets. The main artery ran north and south through town, cutting through the mountains before exiting out the valley. In the northwest quadrant sat the stately campus of Hawthorne College, slightly elevated from the rest of town. The liberal arts college was renowned for its biology department and esteemed faculty of scientists and professors.

Although it was the weekend, a smattering of students strolled around the campus. Five kids played Hacky Sack in the quad while two others tossed a Frisbee. On the western end of the campus a ground crew mowed the football field in preparation for Hawthorne's upcoming game.

He sipped his coffee and enjoyed the spectacular view. Hard to believe this small New England town would soon be inundated with the horrors of his novel virus.

A busy day lay ahead of him. Tonight there was a meeting for those citizens volunteering for the upcoming disease conference: ushers, drivers, and greeters for all the guests arriving into town.

Above the college stood the Brookhaven Ski Resort. In a few months there'd be enough snow—or they'd make enough snow—to cover every trail that snaked down the mountain. He had no interest in skiing. Or hiking. He turned and looked to his right and saw two towers high above Statler Mountain: a cell tower and transmission tower stood maybe a half a mile apart. In due time he'd handle those minor obstacles as well.

He went inside and walked down to the basement to check in on his subject. A shrill scream went up as soon as he entered the lab. The smell inside was strong and metallic, and had a unique mineral quality to it. The subject was covered in dried blood and was hurling himself into the Plexiglas with a reckless abandon not typically seen in Ebola victims in this stage of the disease. It pleased him to no end to see that the subject's blood had begun to clot at a much slower rate than usual. The boy ran back and forth between the wall and the Plexiglas, bouncing off one to get to the other. He stopped after the third cycle and stared at him through the opaque glass. His gaze seemed unfocused and primitive. The blood clotting, he theorized, had damaged the subject's frontal lobe and had effectively lobotomized his emotional center. All that functioned now were the primitive instincts, the primary one being to eat and kill—and to pass on the virus to another healthy host.

The experiment had run its course; he had no more need for the boy. He went over to his lab desk and pulled out a blowpipe and needle. Removing one of the vials, he filled the syringe with a powerful tranquilizer. He inserted the needle into the blowpipe, making sure to use the safety cap in case some of the liquid flowed back. Once assembled, he walked over to the Plexiglas. As soon as the test subject saw what was happening, he bull-rushed the glass until he fell back against the concrete floor.

It reminded him of the infected primates in the hot lab and how they somehow knew that death was imminent.

Locating the circular hole in the Plexiglas, he inserted the end of the blowpipe into the opening. The victim stood slowly, covered in cuts and bruises, and then charged. It was obvious that his brain's receptors had completely shut down. He aimed the blowpipe at the onrushing subject and blew a short, violent breath. The dart shot forth and penetrated into his chest. The subject hadn't even noticed the dart and kept on charging until his shoulder rammed against the glass. The concussion from the impact of the glass caused the blowpipe to shoot out over Vernon's shoulder and crash along the floor. He stepped back in surprise, the force of the test subject's momentum more powerful than he'd expected. The boy stood in the middle of the room, wobbling and dazed. Then his knees buckled and he collapsed in a puddle of his own blood.

The introduction of the tranquilizer had effectively cut him down. The naked subject lay prostrate with his legs spread-eagled. From his vantage he could see the boy's grotesquely swelled genitals. They were bright red and bursting at the seams with the lava of hot virus.

Before disinfecting the cell with an antiviral solution, he dabbed a tear on a swab and smeared it over a rectangle of glass. He slipped the glass under the scope and examined the infected sample under the electron microscope. The results of the virus never ceased to amaze him, reminding him of the powerful forces of nature that his creator had brought forth from chaos.

Closing one eye, he stared into the scope. Telltale bricks of viral material had stacked up on itself like an Egyptian pyramid. The bricks contained threads—the seeds—of the vaunted Ebola virus. A life force in the way a parasite was a living thing. These were the building blocks of death as well as life. The cause of plagues that both annihilated mankind and had made mankind what it was today. For without viral events throughout history the human brain would have never achieved top status on the evolutionary chain. He truly believed that plagues were God's way of starting over, bringing forth the new, and eventually bringing about the end of times in order to usher forth His Kingdom on earth.

He sprayed the infected surface area of the glass, turned on a nearby valve, and watched as a stream of disinfecting liquid within the confinement area washed the blood down into a floor drain. The solution contained water, bleach, and a powerful antiviral fluid that destroyed the replicating pathogens as they swirled down the pipes.

He was so excited that he couldn't wait to unleash this virus on Brookhaven once the conference got started. He made his way inside the Plexiglas and washed off the tranquilized subject. The boy was unconscious but still breathing. Using a towel, he dried the boy off and then dressed him in a proper wardrobe. Once the boy was fully dressed, he carried him out to his car on a dolly and positioned him in the back seat. He would leave the subject in the poorest section of town where kids played among the rubble and rusted chassis. Rat Town they called it. From there the first stage of the Ebola infection would begin before the lethal chain of transmission rippled throughout the community.

Chapter 16

Tag sat back, amazed that his wife had actually survived that Cooke's Island ordeal. But what happened to Taylor? He had to know if his daughter had survived as well. He couldn't even begin to contemplate the notion that his daughter had succumbed to the smallpox. The last time he saw the two of them together was when Versa had been navigating them out into Casco Bay in that motorized rubber raft. It wasn't until much later that he learned he'd been duped. And to think he'd come to depend on that nagging old bitch. It would have been so much better if he'd put a bullet in her brain right at the beginning.

He searched around on the computer until he found the website for this infectious disease conference. It was to be held at Hawthorne College, a small liberal arts college situated in a town named Brookhaven. He had no idea where Brookhaven was, so he looked it up and discovered that it was located in a mountainous region of Maine only two hours away. It was one of those artsy New England towns that his wife typically loved to visit. Surrounded by mountains, it had a ski resort with over a hundred and seventy trails as well as a thriving theater scene. But what most defined Brookhaven was the presence of Hawthorne College, the elite liberal arts college that sat elevated above the rest of town.

Someone downstairs let out a terrible scream. He pushed the chair out from under him and stood. He'd been so caught up in learning about this conference that he'd momentarily forgotten that he was still infected. His legs felt weak and his vision became blurred. Tag's knees buckled and he collapsed to the floor, unable to move.

The sound of a clock above him ticked loudly as he slipped into unconsciousness. He slept in terrible fits, occasionally lifting his head off the hardwood floor and watching as the room spun around him. Gobs of bloody saliva dripped from his mouth and pooled up along the floor. His head felt heavy like a block of cement. Unable to lift his hands or move his feet, he closed his eyes and slipped back into unconsciousness.

A loud scream pierced his ears and snapped him awake. Slowly, and with the help of the computer desk, he pulled himself up to a standing position. It took him fifteen minutes before he'd propped himself up in the leather chair, where he sat sweating for over an hour. Streaks of blood lay splattered along the floor and he realized he'd pissed his pants. Looking down at his arms, he noticed blood seeping through the bruises forming over his skin. He lifted his hand and brushed back his sweat-dampened hair. His palm was covered in oily blood the color of molasses. And yet his mind now felt clearer than it had in a while. He only hoped that he could recover in time to attend that conference and possibly see his wife.

The computer screen glowed. He tapped a key and the browser appeared. How long had he been unconscious? According to the date on the browser, he'd been on that floor for almost two days. From downstairs, he heard a scream followed by a series of loud, intense banging. He stood uneasily to his feet, holding the desk to keep from falling. As soon as he got his bearings, he made his way downstairs, gripping the bannister for support.

At the bottom of the stairs he saw a horrifying sight. Dolores was propped up against Fez's door, banging her cane against the chipped paint. She'd stripped off all her clothes and stood naked, her wrinkled body slathered in black fluid like a freshly slaughtered pig. He could hear Fez crying out from behind the door, struggling to keep the old lady from breaking in.

"What are you doing, Dolores?"

She spun around and pointed an arthritic finger at him. "You fucking bastard! I wouldn't be sick as a dog if it wasn't for you two leaches."

"Believe me, I didn't mean for this to happen."

"You probably killed my Robby too," she said, limping toward him with the help of her cane. "Probably infected that island too."

Fez shouted through the door, "Is that you, Tag?"

"Yeah, it's me. How you doing in there, kid?"

"There's blood all over the floor and my head still hurts, but I'm feeling a little better. The old lady's trying to kill me."

"Hang tight. I'll get you out of there in a minute."

The volume on the television had been turned up to deafening levels. Tag heard a disturbing report from the local news anchors. A veteran cop in Westbrook had been missing for two days, and no one had any idea what had happened to him. The police were now scouring the city in search of him. Tag turned toward the TV and saw Dean's wife begging for help in finding her husband. By her side were her three boys, and Tag noticed a striking resemblance between the oldest boy and his father. He felt terrible about what he'd been forced to do in the name of public safety. But what else could he have done? He couldn't risk exposing the public to the Ebola virus by releasing Dean back into society.

"Could it be possible that he fled town?" the reporter asked Dean's wife.

"No way he fled town. Dean grew up in Westbrook and loved it here. And he loved his family more than anything else in the world. He coached our kids' little league and hockey team and rarely if ever missed a game. No, something bad happened to him because he would never leave us like that."

"Was he depressed or in any financial trouble?"

"Dean was the most outgoing, happy person I've ever met. No way he was depressed. As far as having money problems, we had no more problems than any other family. Life's hard: mortgage, car payments, braces for the kids. But we were happy and had a comfortable life." She broke down crying. "The kids and I miss him terribly. Please, if anyone out there has any information as to my husband's whereabouts, please call the police."

A sudden, intense pain shot through his left bicep, and for a brief second he thought he might be having a heart attack. But then he felt a sharp pain on his hand and knew it wasn't a heart attack. Dolores had smacked the backside of his hand with her cane. He jumped back in shock as the crook whooshed past his face. He kicked his foot along the floor and tripped the old lady up, causing her to fall back on her behind.

"Fez! Get out here. Now!" he shouted.

The door opened and Fez dragged himself out of the room. He looked pale and withdrawn, like a zombie child. Rivulets of blood sluiced down his sunken cheeks and his hollowed-out eyes scanned the room with a stare so vacant that it frightened Tag.

Dolores groaned and rolled to her stomach. Struggling to rise, she pushed herself up on all fours as the blood dripped off her forehead and stained the floor. She tried to stand but fell back to her knees. Tag slipped his hands under her steaming armpits and lifted her up. She felt light in his hands as he carried her toward the bedroom. He gently heaved her body onto the mattress, but something came loose in his hands as she collapsed onto the bed. It took him a second to realize that a portion of the woman's skin had sloughed off in his hands. To his horror he held up a gelatinous sheet of subcutaneous layer. He quickly threw it down to the floor in disgust as Dolores rose up. She ripped the sheet off the mattress and stood facing him, holding onto the bedframe for support. Tears of black liquid streaked down her eyes like mascara running in a rain storm.

"I don't know what's happening to me. Please don't leave like me this," she pleaded.

"Lay down on the bed and rest, Dolores."

"I feel so angry and I don't know why. And I'm bleeding all over the place," she said, falling back onto the bed. "I'm old and tired and don't have much time left. Don't let me leave this world in such a sorry state."

"I promise you I won't."

"When you see my Robby again, tell him how much I love him."

"I certainly will, Dolores. He told me to tell you how much he loves you as well."

"My Robby is such a good boy."

Tag heard a loud series of bangs against the basement door. But how could that be? He'd handcuffed the cop to a reinforced steel pipe in the basement. Unless, of course, he'd somehow managed to pull the pipe away from its mooring. But those old pipes were practically indestructible and would require heavy equipment to dislodge.

Fez helped him move the old hutch in front of the bedroom door so Dolores couldn't escape. Despite the crippling pain in his joints, they managed to slide it across the oak floor, effectively sealing off the room.

"We need to get out of here as soon as possible," he said, gripping Fez's shoulders.

"I'd never been so sick in my life, Tag."

"I need you by my side. We need to find out who's responsible for these attacks."

"I want my old life back, Tag. I want to see my mom and dad again, and my brothers too. Let's go back to Cooke's Island and see if they're still there."

Tag's heart sank. He felt sorry for the kid. Should he tell him that his family was gone and the island he'd once called home now lay in ruins? No, Fez would soon snap back to reality and realize the error himself.

"Go in the kitchen and search for the keys to Dolores' car. Once you find them, I want you to bring them back to me."

"Sure, Tag. Then maybe we can catch the ferry back to Cooke's?"

"Sure, kid."

Fez stumbled into the kitchen, ignoring the loud banging against the basement door. Dean shouted at the top of his lungs to let him out. Tag grabbed the cop's revolver, which he'd hidden atop the refrigerator, and approached the door with trepidation. Despite chaining Dean to the steel pipe, he'd also secured the dead bolt to be on the safe side. He tiptoed over, careful not get too close in case the cop punched his fist through the thin membrane of wood.

"Relax, Dean. Let's talk about this."

"Fuck you, asshole! I'm done talking. You let me out of here right now!" the cop shouted. He pounded the door three times in rapid succession.

"You're sick and not thinking clearly."

"No shit, Sherlock." He punched his fist so hard against the door that the wood splintered.

Tag knew he couldn't keep the cop locked away for much longer. He'd learned his lesson on Cooke's Island. Dean's bloodied, scarred hand punched through the jagged hole and began to feel around for the deadbolt as if it had a life of its own. Tag raised the gun up and watched as the shards of wood dug into the skin covering Dean's bloody forearm. The green tattoo over it lay obscured and faded. Once he'd unlocked it, he reached down and gripped the door handle. Tag's finger tickled the trigger; would he really kill this cop? A few seconds passed before the door flew open. The cop stood in front of him, his eyes glazed over and his entire body soaked in blood the color of motor oil.

But what shocked him most was the cop's missing right arm. A shard of splintered bone protruded from Dean's severed wrist. The skin surrounding it looked—unbelievably enough— like it had been gnawed off by human teeth. Had Dean chewed off his own arm just so he could slip out of the handcuff? It was too horrible to even contemplate.

"Did you ..." he waved the gun at the cop's missing hand.

"Yeah, I bit my fucking arm off. Told you I couldn't stay down there any longer." The cop brought his mangled arm up to his mouth and tore off a loose chunk of flesh, chomping it with equal parts pleasure and precision. Black sludge oozed from the gaping wound.

"Don't move or I swear I'll shoot, Dean," Tag said, trying to fight off a bout of vertigo.

"I don't give a fuck if you shoot me, dickhead. I'm already dead anyways."

"It doesn't need to be like this."

"Fuck you, asshole. You're the one who chained me to that pipe down there."

"Your wife and kids want you to come home."

"That bitch can go to hell for all I care, the goddamn nag. I'll beat her fucking senseless for all the shit she put me through!"

The cop bull-rushed without warning, forcing Tag to fire two quick shots in rapid succession, both of which struck the cop in the stomach. Surprisingly, neither injury slowed him. The cop tackled him to the floor and Tag struggled to hold onto the gun. Dean sat atop his chest, a disgusting bungee of phlegm, blood, and sweat dripping onto Tag's face. He aimed the gun at Dean's face but the cop swatted it easily out of his hand. His strength seemed superhuman and he gave off that familiar mineral-like odor. Weakened by the vaccine, Tag tried to push the sick bastard off him but the cop wouldn't budge. He called out for Fez to help him.

Dean leaned in and snapped his jaws near Tag's face. His hot breath reeked of death and disease. Tag bobbed his head from side to side to avoid being bitten. Then he reached back to try and grab the gun off the floor but couldn't locate it. Dean raised his injured arm and the jagged splinter of bone dropped toward his face. He turned his head at the last second as the radius bone lodged into the oak floor inches from his eyes. Tag reached back and again searched for the revolver while Dean struggled to pull the sharp bone out of the floor. Moving his hand along the floor, he felt the barrel of the gun, but accidentally punched it out of reach. He looked up in horror as the cop gripped his throat with his good hand while lifting his jagged bone from the floor. Once Dean raised his wrist to eye level, he drove it down toward his face. Tag turned his cheek at the last second, trying to avoid being stabbed, but the man's grip was too strong to resist.

He closed his eyes and prayed to God for mercy, waiting for that sharp bone to plunge into his brain. Instead he heard a loud scream go up just above his head. Opening his eyes, he saw Dean's eyes rolled back in his head as he collapsed on top of him. Tag rolled to his right and pushed the injured cop off him. What the hell just happened?

He tried to sit up but the jagged bone had imbedded a section of his hair into the floor. Fez stood over him, a bloody butcher knife in hand. The kid reached down and grabbed a handful of his hair, then cut away until Tag's head came free. As he stood to his feet, Tag could see Dean's body convulsing in the final throes of death. His eyes gazed up at the ceiling as he struggled to breathe. Blood and brain matter poured out of the gaping wound over his left temple where the knife had plunged.

Tag stared over at Fez in shock and the kid gave him a lifeless stare in return. He dropped the butcher knife to the floor and then collapsed in a state of exhaustion. Tag picked the kid's limp body up and carried him over to the couch. Then he walked back into the kitchen and peered out the rear window. Parked in front of the second garage door was Dolores' old Crown Victoria. He guessed that it was twenty years old and rarely driven.

He ran out to the garage and next to the lawnmower found a container half-filled with gas. Sirens blared in the distance. He sprinted back into the house, knowing he had little time left to act. He picked Fez up and carried him out to the car, setting him across the backseat. Then he ran back inside the house and dragged Dean's body to the middle of the living room. Dolores began to bang against the bedroom door, demanding to be let out. Using all his strength, he pushed the hutch aside and opened the door, watching as Dolores fell face-first to the floor. Tag pulled the gun out of his waistband and pressed the barrel against her wrinkled forehead.

"What are you waiting for, you dumb jerk? Pull the damn trigger," she shrieked. "Either you kill me or I'm going to kill you!"

"God have mercy on me!"

"God doesn't give a shit anymore. Now hurry up and do it."

"Dolores, I'm so sorry for what I'm about to do."

"Go fuck yourself, asshole." She turned and glared up at him with the most horrifying face he'd ever seen.

He closed his eyes and pulled the trigger. As soon as he opened them he saw her body go slack against the floor. At least her suffering was over. After saying a quick prayer, he grabbed the container of fuel and poured it over their infected bodies and then around the house. The fire would destroy the deadly pathogens and eradicate the threat of Ebola from spreading out of this house. He grabbed Dolores' cigarette lighter and set fire to some old newspapers. Tossing them into the middle of the room, he watched as the flames shot up and spread across the floor, rising up toward the ceiling and quickly engulfing the two corpses and everything in the room. He knew that an old, creaky house like this would go up fast.

Checking that his pack was still attached to his waist, he sprinted toward the old Crown Victoria, praying that it would start the first time. The sirens off in the distance seemed to be growing closer. Fez sat up in the backseat and glanced around at his surroundings. Tag turned the key in the ignition and thankfully the engine roared to life. Glancing down at the speedometer, he saw that it had 49,387 miles on it. He shifted into reverse, threw his right arm over the passenger seat, and sped out of the driveway until the back fender scraped against the sidewalk. Shifting into drive, he glanced at the house one last time. Black smoke rose up out of the windows and from under roof tiles. The fire had spread much faster than expected, and he figured that the bodies of Dean and Dolores would be burnt beyond recognition by the time the fire department arrived.

He said a quick prayer for the cop's family as he sped down the dark street. He hadn't meant to involve innocent citizens in this fiasco, but he felt he'd had no other choice; the disease would've spread like wildfire if he hadn't taken action when he did. And yet it didn't ameliorate the intense sadness he felt on account of their deaths. Dolores had been at the end of her life, but Dean now had a widow and three kids that needed looking after. He put the blame squarely on the shoulders of this sociopath terrorizing the nation.

The tires of the Crown Victoria screeched as he turned the corner.

"Slow down, Tag, or you'll get us busted," Fez complained.

He eased off the gas and saw a sign indicating that he was approaching Route 25. He followed it west, passing a fleet of speeding police cars headed in the opposite direction, until he arrived at Route 202. This road would eventually take him to Interstate 89 and that, he knew, would lead him to the northern part of the state.

He started to relax the further he drove, realizing that he was now in the clear. Time to put that all behind him now, he thought. He couldn't undo the past and bring those two back to life. But hopefully he could prevent others from dying.

Chapter 17

Bacon seemed nervous and irritable as they walked into the main entrance of the memorial. They approached the Reflecting Pool and stood side-by-side, staring at it in complete silence. Nolette felt a powerful emotion well up inside her while recalling the attack from her youthful perspective, and because of that she reached up and quickly wiped away a tear. The onyx pond barely rippled, reflecting the clear blue Oklahoma sky. Bacon fidgeted next to her and she got the sense that he wanted to leave this place as soon as possible.

They moved to the Field of Empty Chairs. One hundred and sixty-nine chairs arranged in a row of nine, with the nine rows representing the nine floors of the Alfred P. Murrah building. Each seat had the name of a victim written on it. She tried to hold it together as best she could upon arriving at the nineteen tiny chairs, each bearing the names of the children who had died in the bombing.

But it was the Survivor Tree that pushed her over the edge. She left the park in tears, chagrined that she'd let her guard down in front of Bacon. She jogged back to the car, hearing him call out her name while trying to keep up with her. Upon reaching the car he stood panting against the passenger door, cursing under his breath at having to run all the way back. He lit a cigarette and blew smoke out the side of his mouth.

"You okay?" he finally asked after he'd caught his breath.

"Not really."

"That's tough to look at, I know, especially if you're seeing it for the first time." He took another drag. "It's just tragic."

"Open the stupid door, jerk. I just want to leave now and get the story we came out here for."

"Whoa! Looks like someone's pissed off."

She stared at him, wondering what his level of involvement in all of this was. Maybe he was merely a pawn in the terrorist's scheme. Or maybe he had a more important role. It even crossed her mind that this was all a big misunderstanding. She resolved to keep him in sight at all times so that she could find out the truth.

She configured the GPS to the Drinkwaters' address. Fifteen minutes later they turned onto a quiet, tree-lined street filled with modest ranch houses. It was a beautiful late fall day and the air felt crisp and clean. The voice on the GPS instructed her to drive to the end of the street. Upon arriving she saw a chain link fence separating the dead end from a large public park. They got out of the car and approached the front door of the modest one-story home. A white Chevy Tahoe sat on the black tarred driveway. She rang the doorbell and waited, hoping someone might be home. After a minute the door opened and an elderly woman appeared.

"Can I help you?" the woman asked.

"Mrs. Drinkwater?"

"Yes, that's me."

"My name is Nolette Swain and this is James Bacon. We're news reporters and were wondering if we could ask you and your husband a few questions?" she asked.

"My husband is no longer alive." She crossed her arms in defiance. "What is it you want to ask me?"

"My sincere sympathies about your husband," Nolette said, clearing her throat and preparing for her next sentence. "It's about Ernest."

The woman stared at them for a few seconds, unsure of what to make of this question.

"I haven't heard his name mentioned in years," she said.

"I promise we won't take up much of your time."

"What specifically would you like to know?"

"Could we come inside and speak?"

"I'm not sure that I want to talk to either of you."

"I can't insist that you talk to us, Mrs. Drinkwater, but you need to know that people's lives are at stake." The woman didn't budge, her resolve only seeming to harden. "We just paid a visit to the Oklahoma City Memorial and found it very moving."

"You say lives are at stake? How so?"

"Well," Nolette said, wondering how much to tell her. "You've obviously heard of the attack on Cooke's Island?"

The woman's expression softened after hearing the words "Cooke's Island" and she stepped aside, pointing them to a set of leather sofas. The woman walked over and sat on one of the couches, and Nolette and Bacon sat on the other side. An oak coffee table separated them and was topped with quilting magazines and books. Nolette remembered how her mother was always busy making colorful religious quilts of Jesus, doves, crosses, and other religious symbols. The walls in this woman's house were plastered with family pictures and framed religious quotes. The pictures were of a mother, father, two sons, and a daughter. She wondered which one was Ernest.

"Those are pictures of my family," the woman said, catching her staring at them. "Dick passed away last year, five years after being diagnosed with Alzheimer's. My other children have left Oklahoma for greener pastures."

"Which one is Ernest?" she asked.

She stared at the wall. "He's not in any of them."

"Not one?" James said.

The woman shook her head, her pink lips pressed tight.

"Why would he not be in any of your family photos?" Nolette asked.

The woman leaned forward and whispered, "Because he's not my real son."

"You disowned him? Or had some kind of falling out?" Bacon asked.

"No. We never raised him to begin with."

"I don't understand. If you didn't raise him then who did?" Nolette said.

"I'm an old lady now so this is the first time I've actually admitted this to anybody. We're not his biological parents."

"So where are his real parents?" Nolette asked.

"It's a complicated story. Dick came home one day and told me that Pastor Dempsey of our church needed us to do the Lord's work; he wanted us to take in a sixteen year-old boy who I assumed had no family. He gave us no reason why and I took it to understand that either his parents had died or had subjected him to some sort of abuse. Being devout Christians, we agreed to take him, no-questions-asked, but in hindsight it turned out to be one of the worst decisions we ever made."

"Why?" Bacon asked.

"The boy was extremely intelligent, but there was something about him that just wasn't right." She cocked her head as if to remember. "A certain lack of empathy? A coldness? I'm not quite sure what it was, but we had a difficult time trying to make a connection. It almost seemed as if he was using us until he could finally be independent. Some of this I understood, being separated from his family, or whatever his situation happened to be. But nothing we did seemed to please the boy."

"So you have no idea where he came from?"

"None whatsoever—and we didn't ask. All our kids were in college at the time so we agreed to move from Texas to Oklahoma City in order to give this boy a chance at a new life. Dick worked in the federal court system and was able to transfer here. All the neighbors believed Ernest was our son, and so in that way we were able to conceal the truth of our situation."

"And yet somehow he managed to get a top security clearance in the federal government," Nolette said.

"I honestly never heard from him after he left us," the woman said.

"What else about those years do you remember?" Bacon asked.

"They were extremely difficult on Dick and I. Dick worked a lot at the court, which left me to deal with Ernest. The boy rarely talked and when he did he seemed quite contemptuous, even after all we did for him. It felt strange living with this odd teenager who would barely look at you, and who often took his dinner into his bedroom and never came out. And yet all his teachers told us how brilliant he was and, with some social adjustments, that he could go far in life. But he rarely spoke to us about his future."

"Do you know what happened to him after he graduated?" Nolette asked.

"I didn't ask. By the time his senior year came around I couldn't wait for him to get out of the house. Many nights he sat in his room watching the coverage of the Oklahoma City Bombing. He seemed obsessed with it. At first I chalked it up to a teenager's natural curiosity about death and destruction. Then one day I heard him cheering for McVeigh as that murderer got led to court in shackles. It sent a chill down my spine. When I told Dick about it he just pooh-poohed it, reassuring me that he'd soon be off to college."

"So you and Ernest didn't keep in touch after he left?" Bacon asked.

"Oh, God no. Never heard from him again, and as terrible as that sounds, that was fine by me. Same with Dick. He'd had it. The two never developed a bond. Dick offered to take him to Sooners games, but he laughed it off. No interest in football. At that point I didn't even bother to ask him about his future. Then one day in July, early in the morning, he just packed up his stuff and drove away in the pick-up truck Dick had purchased for him. Not even a thanks or goodbye."

"So he had no hobbies or friends that you know of?" Nolette asked.

"I don't remember him having any friends. As far as hobbies, the only activity he was involved with at school was the drama club."

"I see," Nolette said, hoping for any clue that might help them. "Is there anything else you remember about him that might help us, Mrs. Drinkwater?"

"Other than his fascination with the Oklahoma City bombing, I can't think of anything else that might interest you." She folded her hands over her lap. "Oh, there is one other thing. He had this fascination with some zoo located about an hour away from here, and he would visit it whenever he had the chance. I remember that because he would always bring back these colorful photographs of lions and tigers."

Nolette placed her tablet down on the table and quickly brought up the browser. "Lions and tigers?"

"Yes. The zoo is located about an hour south of here, just off Interstate 35."

Nolette typed in the words zoo and Oklahoma City and what popped up was the Garold Wayne Interactive Zoological Park. A sense of excitement filled her as she clicked on the list of animals on exhibition. She glanced in shock over at Bacon, forgetting momentarily about what she'd seen on his phone.

The zoo contained LIGERS!

"Mrs. Drinkwater, do you know if this pastor is still alive?" she asked.

"He is but he's very old. I know this because I check every day in the newspaper to see if he's passed away, figuring that there'll be something in his obituary that'll explain this mystery away. Then again, sometimes I think I'm just being silly about this period in my life, and that God was merely testing our faith by sending us this troubled boy."

"Did you know that Ernest graduated from Yale?" Bacon asked.

"I had no idea. Good for him." The woman smiled and looked down at her hands. "I honestly wish him no ill will. I hope he's had a successful life despite my feelings for him."

"He ended up earning a Ph.D. in biology and working as a biologist in a military institute."

"Then I'm happy he turned out okay and that maybe we made a small difference in his life. My fears were obviously unjustified."

"They say he passed away about seven years ago while piloting his experimental plane over the ocean, but his body was never found," Nolette said.

"By that point in time he'd changed his name to Remington Guilfoyle," Bacon added.

"Never heard any of that, but I'm sorry to hear he passed away. Of course I never knew about his death."

"Like I said, Mrs. Drinkwater, they never found his body," Nolette said, trying not to infer that he was still alive.

"Such a shame," she said without a hint of sincerity. She stood in order to see them out. "If that's all, I have my book group coming over in twenty minutes."

Nolette and Bacon allowed the woman to open the door for them. Bright autumn sunshine filled the living room and lit up the old family pictures hanging on the wall.

"One last thing," Nolette said, turning. "Where does this pastor live?"

"After he retired from the ministry he moved down to an assisted living facility in Gainesville, Texas. It's a facility that caters to retired church personnel so you should have no problem tracking him down."

"Thanks." She scribbled the information down on the back of a business card. "And his name?"

"Dempsey. LeRoy H. Dempsey."

Nolette reached out and grabbed her hand. "Thank you so much, Mrs. Drinkwater."

"It's Marnie and you're very welcome. Good luck."

The door closed and in minutes they were heading south on the Interstate and heading toward Texas. She hoped this pastor had his wits about him because he was their only link to this mysterious man's past. If she did uncover Ernest Drinkwater's personal history it would make one hell of a story. Ernest Drinkwater, if indeed he was the culprit, was now the worst serial killer in the history of this country. But somehow just writing about him did not seem enough. She felt a larger moral responsibility to stop any future attacks. And what about Winters' remarkable journey of survival? He was out there somewhere, alive and hiding from the authorities. What was his role in all this?

She glanced over at Bacon, clutching the steering wheel, his eyes glued on the long strip of road. She needed to somehow gain his trust if she wanted to ascertain his role in these connected events. More importantly, she had to be ready to defend herself if he ever turned against her.

Bacon turned the radio on, quickly switching from country station to classic rock. 'More Than A Feeling' by Boston played over the speakers. The landscape seemed flat and endless, and she envisioned all the killer tornadoes that had wreaked havoc across this landscape. A green highway sign flew past with the words Gainesville, Texas. Only thirty seven miles to go. She wanted so badly to close her eyes and take a nap, but feared doing so with Bacon driving next to her. And yet forty minutes later she was jarred back to consciousness by the sound of Bacon's voice announcing their arrival. 'Back in Black' by AC/DC blared over the speakers, and Bacon thrummed his thigh to the beat. Nolette shot up in her seat and wiped her bleary eyes, not quite believing that she'd dozed off. Bacon turned off the ramp and headed toward a fast food ghetto below the exit.

"What gives?" she asked.

"You got to sleep, I need to eat. Besides, I have no idea where we're headed. Best we stop and grab some chow. Then we can figure out where this preacher is living out his golden years."

"Can I ask you a personal question, Bacon?"

"Transparency is my middle name, kid." He stuck an unlit cigarette in his mouth.

"Do you believe in God?"

"Been a card-carrying Atheist since I was forced to sit through all those shitty Bible classes as a kid." He looked over at her. "Look at all the problems in this world that have been caused by religions."

She stared out the window.

"And you?"

"Depends on what day it is."

He opened the door and stepped out. "This trip's going to wreak havoc on my cholesterol."

"Could be worse," she said, catching up to him. "You could have the Ebola virus pulsing through your veins."

"Touché."

He wolfed down his cheeseburger and fries as she searched for Pastor Dempsey's address. Twenty minutes later they were on the road again and headed to the facility. She'd found only one home in the Gainsville area that catered to retired clergy; it had to be the same one. They drove for another fifteen minutes before arriving at a modest brick facility located along a barren stretch of land. Bacon pulled up to the circular driveway and parked in one of the lined spaces. A few of the residents sat slumped in wheelchairs and were being pushed around the grounds by black caretakers dressed in white. There were no flowers or bushes to soften the landscape, only flat, parched earth.

"Excuse me, sir," she said, stopping a caretaker who was pushing an elderly woman along the path. "Could you tell us where we could find LeRoy Dempsey?"

He laughed. "You foget to say da H, lady."

"Excuse me?"

"Da H. His name is LeRoy *H.* Dempsey. Mr. Dempsey gets mighty angry if you fogets to say da H."

"Thanks." A crisp breeze blew off the plains.

The caretaker pointed over her shoulder. "LeRoy's sitting ova dere, on a bench by his lonesome. Probably be coming in real soon. Wind be kickin' up something fierce."

"Thank you for your help."

"And don't fogets to say da H. Mr. Dempsey won't even look at you if you fogets to say it."

"I certainly won't forget thanks to you."

151

She waved goodbye to the caretaker and the old woman in the wheelchair fluttered a veiny hand in the air.

Nolette headed toward the old pastor who was sitting on a green bench, his wrinkled hands folded over his lap. He looked nothing like what she had imagined. She'd pictured Dempsey to be one of those tall, imposing figures with a charismatic voice and a stern, narrow face. Instead, as she pulled up in front of him, she saw a tiny, round-faced man wearing wire-rimmed glasses and with ears that stuck out like pancakes. On his head was a black trilby with a feather sticking out of the ribbon.

"Pastor LeRoy *H.* Dempsey?" she asked.

"Thank you," he said in a surprisingly high-pitched voice, smiling as he looked up at her.

"For what? I haven't done anything."

"You said the H."

"That's your name, right?"

"Yes, but most people neglect to say the H. It was my grandfather's name and I loved the man. He practically raised me, you know."

"Then you're very welcome, sir," Nolette said. "But the real reason I came here was to speak to you about Ernest Drinkwater."

He smiled. "I've been expecting a visit like this for quite some time now. Wasn't sure it was ever going to happen."

Nolette glanced over at Bacon, who shrugged and raised an eyebrow. Dempsey said he'd been waiting 'quite a long time now' for this visit. What the hell did that mean, she thought? Had no one ever interviewed him about this mysterious man named Ernest Drinkwater?

* * *

Professor Heinrich Van Huesen stood at the podium inside Taylor Hall, staring down at him and the thirty-odd people who had volunteered for the infectious disease conference. The duties included escorting VIPs around campus and making sure they arrived to the conference on time. Van Huesen, with his gray goatee, appeared stern and officious, and seemed put off by having to give this talk, as if it were beneath him to do it.

"Very shortly there will be over one hundred scientists and guests converging on campus to attend this conference. Our guests will be arriving from all over the world and will come from every major university. I beseech you to treat them with the utmost dignity and respect. Many of these individuals have won major awards for their work, and two have won the Nobel Peace Prize. As the Chair of the Biology Department here at Hawthorne College, I can't emphasize to you how important this event is to the institution. If all goes well, we anticipate this becoming an annual event, bringing revenue and national attention not only to this campus but to the town as well."

Oh, there'll be attention brought to this town alright!

Vernon stared at the tall, gaunt professor wearing his navy blue blazer with Hawthorne's suit of arms affixed to the breast. The look this WASPish professor gave them denoted their second-class status. He felt like walking up there and challenging this pretentious ass to a public debate on infectious pathogens. He'd read all of Van Huesen's work on Signal Transduction Events During Host Pathogen Interactions and had come to the conclusion that his findings were laughable. In his opinion, Van Huesen had wrongly focused on hypersensitive cell death. How could the man not see that virulence gene function was more associated with the suppression of primitive mechanisms of resistance not involving hypersensitive cell death? Then again, Vernon knew that he was one of the few people in the field who held this radical view.

"You've all been given a packet with specific instructions to follow when dealing with conferees. Each of you have been given three VIPs to handle. Please treat them with the utmost care, and above all, respect their privacy. Do not converse with them unless asked to do so. Thank you all for your help. If there are any questions I would ask you to please address them to my secretary, Ms. Jane Perry."

People rose up out of their seats and approached the front of the hall to mingle. Gripping his manila envelope, he marched to the front of the room and headed toward Van Huesen, who stood on stage conversing with one of his colleagues. Van Huesen had his arms crossed and nodded coolly to those who came over to introduce themselves.

"Hello there, Heinrich," Vernon said in a sing-song voice as he climbed halfway up the steps.

Van Huesen shot him a fierce look, obviously displeased that some no-name townie would dare call him by his first name. Van Huesen had no idea that with a snap of his fingers he could activate over a thousand soldiers to do his bidding. And by bidding he meant that he could unleash the most virulent plague on every city in America.

"Heinrich, any interest in grabbing a beer?"

The professor crinkled his eyebrows in dismay and returned to his conversation.

"Because I've got some really good ideas I want to share with you about making this conference more successful."

"It's Dr. Van Huesen, good sir, and any ideas you may have you can write them down and pass them onto my secretary."

"Okay, Doc, but what are you going to do when The Revelation Baptist Ministry shows up here with their signs and end-of-the-world prophecies, and then start screaming bloody murder at your guests?"

A slightly worried look came over Van Huesen's face, and he discreetly excused himself from his colleague and stepped over to engage him.

"What is your name, sir?"

"Vernon. Please to meet you, Professor." He held out his hand and Van Huesen shook it gingerly, as if it was infected with Ebola.

"Now what were you rambling on about?"

"Didn't you hear the news? Those religious lunatics are planning on coming here to protest your conference." He smiled. "They're the same nuts who believed that the Cooke's Island attack was God's way of telling us that we're all sinners. Can you believe such bull crap?"

"Where did you hear this?"

"I read it over the Internet."

"Thank you for that information," Van Huesen said, rudely walking away from him. "We'll alert security immediately."

He laughed aloud at this pretentious asshole.

"Something funny?" Van Huesen said, turning to glare at him.

"Oh, not really. It's just that I've read some of your research in my spare time and found it quite amusing."

"Amusing?" He waved his hand in condescension. "You obviously don't have the necessary education to understand such complicated research. It's highly esoteric and not for the lay person."

"I don't presume to be on your level, Doc, or anywhere near it, but the data you used implies direct activation of triggering receptors expressed in myeloid cells. But filoviruses indicate that neutrophils may play a prominent role in the immune and inflammatory responses to filovirus infections."

A look of bewilderment cam over Van Huesen's face. It took him a few seconds to get his bearings before he lifted his hand as if to rebut. But no words came out of his mouth. Vernon was having so much fun watching this pompous ass sweat that he almost didn't want to leave. Instead, he clambered down the stairs and walked away. His theater background at Yale had served him well, and passing time as the company's costume designer had provided him with a convincing cover in town.

Passing through the crowd, he hoped that his worthy adversary, Colonel Winters, would be able to make it in time for the conference's main event. Winters was a tough bastard and hadn't yet disappointed him. As soon as the news reporter came through with the goods, then he could step up his game and move to the next level of terror.

LETHAL CHAIN

But for now he had other pressing matters. There was an afternoon post-performance briefing with the cast and crew, and he couldn't wait to get to the theater and congratulate them on a job well done. The idea of transforming these local town folks into glamorous, exotic characters thrilled him to no end. And then to see them performing on stage and singing those lovely ballads moved him to tears. He'd taken Shakespeare's quote to heart and took them as words to live by.

All the world's a stage,
And all the men and women merely players.
They have their exits and their entrances,
And one man in his time plays many parts

Chapter 18

Tag kept to a moderate speed along 202, cruising through the Maine countryside. Fez slept in the backseat, every now and then crying out in pain. Although Tag's headache continued to persist, and his entire body still ached, he felt as if the worst of the vaccine's side effects had passed.

He drove past dairy farms and wide fields filled with harvested corn stalks. Gentle mountains rose up and then receded from view. Brilliant blue ponds not yet frozen appeared, followed by long stretches of dense woods. He drove up and down steep hills fronted by granite outcroppings. Every now and then a car would pass, but otherwise the roads were mostly clear.

His overwhelming desire to see his wife made him want to drive faster, and yet he knew he couldn't risk getting pulled over by some bored cop looking to make a name for himself. How would he explain the bloody clothes? Or the smears of blood that had dried over his skin. Oggy's ID remained in his pouch as well as the two thousand dollars in twenties that he'd grabbed from under his mattress.

Fez stirred as he approached the onramp to Interstate 89. Tag glanced in the rearview mirror and saw the kid sitting up in his seat and yawning. His hair was matted down from sleep and dried blood. Fez climbed over the seat and plunked down next to him, leaning his head on the passenger window.

He turned to the kid. "How you feeling?"

"A little better'n before."

"Good. I was getting a little worried about you."

"What happened back at that house, Tag?"

"You don't remember?" He wondered how much he should tell the kid.

Fez shook his head. "I must have really been out of it."

"You were pretty sick."

"What did I catch?"

Tag decided not to hold anything back. "The Ebola virus."

"Bola virus?"

"E. Bola. One word. It's a highly communicable disease from Africa. Someone broke inside the house while we were sleeping and vaccinated us with a hypodermic needle."

"Holy crap. Is this E-bola crap as bad as the pox?" Fez asked, fiddling with the radio tuner.

Tag picked up speed upon turning on 89. "Worse."

Fez found a country western station he liked. "Kenny Chesney."

"Never heard of him." He glanced over at the kid. "I hate country music."

"Give it a listen." He turned up the volume, "Better than disco as my dad used to say."

"Your dad was a smart man."

"So are people going to turn into zombies if they get this E-bola?"

"I can't say for sure." He turned to the kid. "Hey, this Chestnut's not that bad."

"It's Chesney, dummy. Think I'd make you listen to crap?"

He grabbed the kid's neck and playfully squeezed it.

"You know, Tag, I'm getting too old for all this."

Tag burst out laughing. It was the first time he'd laughed in quite some time. The song changed and he listened with pleasure as Fez sang along with Taylor Swift. Swift was beloved by his kids and many a times he'd heard his own Taylor singing along with her celebrity namesake. He glanced down at the speedometer every so often to make sure he wasn't speeding, only to realize that he'd been tapping in rhythm with the tune.

158

Thirty minutes passed before they came across anything resembling a store. A column of white-capped mountains dotted the horizon. He gazed up at the old wooden sign as he pulled into the lot: Wagner's General Store. Removing his bloody shirt and turning it inside out, he threw on his jacket. Then he stuffed the wad of bills in his pocket and made his way inside.

The store was much bigger than he'd expected. Besides the girl at the register, they were the only ones inside. The variety and the amount of products sold here amazed him: everything from electronics to appliances, clothes to food, guns to sporting equipment. Fez wandered over to the toy section and checked out the merchandise, occasionally lifting one of the action figures off the shelf to examine it. It was a reminder that Fez was still a kid, and the horrors he'd witnessed were something no kid should have seen.

He waited a few minutes before calling Fez over, allowing the kid a little time to enjoy himself. They tried on some pants and shirts before finally settling on a pair for each of them. How long had it been since he'd performed the simple act of trying on a pair of pants? Ever since he'd been a little boy he'd hated clothes shopping, but today it felt like an extravagant luxury. He tossed in a button-down shirt and tie in the event he finagled his way into the conference. After adding some socks, t-shirts, and underwear to his cart, he wheeled it over to the cash register to pay. The girl behind the counter held the National Enquirer up to her face. He would have loved one of those Remington 700 series bolt action rifles, but at just over a thousand bucks it was way beyond his budget.

The young girl at the cash register flipped through the tabloid in a bored manner, snapping the bubblegum in her mouth and twirling her hair around her finger. Tag placed the items on the conveyor belt and waited for her to notice him. Fez, his face dirty and his eyes bugging with excitement, stood nearby, gawking at the large selection of candy bars. Pulling a twenty out of his stack, Tag dangled it in front of the kid's face.

"What's this for?" Fez asked.

"Go buy yourself something nice."

"Like what?"

"Anything you want. And don't bring back the change and that's an order."

"For real?"

Tag nodded. "For real."

"Cool! Thanks, Tag."

The kid sprinted down the aisle and disappeared from sight. Once Tag placed all the items on the belt, he stood across from the girl and watched as she continued to flip through the tabloid pages. He cleared his throat and she looked over at him and smiled.

"Sorry about that. I was reading this really interesting article about Lady GaGa." She set down the tabloid. "Find everything okay, hon?"

"Yeah." He had to laugh at this young girl calling him hon. She looked the same age as his Taylor. But then he remembered something: he probably looked to her like a homeless person or worse.

"I'm just waiting for my kid to come back."

"How about I ring up this stuff while he's looking. Not too busy in here as you can see." Her toothy smile made him happy. Teeth as white as marble. The smile—and he laughed at the metaphor—highly infectious.

He grabbed a road map off the shelf and threw it onto the belt.

"Where you guys headed anyway?"

"Brookhaven. You know how much longer it'll take to get there?"

"'It's about a thirty minute ride from here. Just be sure not to go over the speed limit. There's only one way in from here and the cops like to hide out in every nook and cranny and bust tourists. Not much else for the cops to do in these parts except to pull over tourists and lock up the cooks."

"Cooks?"

160

"Meth cooks. There's a lot of demand for that drug in Brookhaven, especially in Rat Town with some of the rich college kids." She registered his confused expression. "Rat Town's the nickname of a neighborhood. Brookhaven, despite its reputation, is not all it's made out to be."

"In what way?"

"Lot of weird shit going on there. Bunch of pretentious assholes at that college too. Lot of rich kids doing drugs and partying, although you'd never know it. They sometimes come in here and think they're all that."

"Thanks for the heads-up," he said while glancing over his shoulder for Fez.

She placed his goods in two paper bags and then stared at him, pink bubblegum snapping between her pouty red lips.

"You look familiar for some reason, mister. Ever been around here before?"

Tag shrugged, wishing Fez would hurry up with his shopping. "Nope. First time ever."

She squinted her eyes and studied him. "Oh well, I could've sworn I've seen you before."

"Is it always this quiet in here?" he asked, changing the subject.

"Weekends get crazy busy, and of course during ski season it's nuts," she said, resuming her hair twirling. "Had a bus load of yahoos in here about an hour ago. Bunch of religious wackos carrying Bibles and preaching that the world's gonna end. Said if I didn't repent I was going to hell." She laughed.

"You know where were they going?"

"Said they was heading into town to protest some big meeting they're having there. Saw a sign on their bus that said The Revelation Baptist Ministry."

He vaguely remembered the group protesting at military funerals and other events at which people were being memorialized.

Fez walked over with his arms filled up to his filthy chin. He dumped it onto the belt and smiled at the girl. Tag counted

161

seven bags of Bugles, a phone charger, two bags of red licorice, and a Transformer Lego action figure.

"Hey, handsome," the girl said, unleashing her killer smile.

"Lady, you have the prettiest white teeth I've ever seen."

"Thanks, sweetie," she said, scanning his items. "Get them bleached every six months."

"And pretty blue eyes too."

"You're smooth as silk, boy. You just may be the cutest little thing I've ever seen." She tossed them in a bag and handed them over. "If only you were ten years older I'd probably eat you right up."

"I guess you really like Bugles, huh?" Tag asked Fez.

"My favorite snack in the world. Used to ride downtown to Cooke's Market every Saturday and buy bags of them after they came in off the ferry," Fez said, studying his toy.

"You got twenty-nine cents left to spend," the girl said to Fez. "And your dad here said you had to spend every penny of it."

"Cool." Fez reached into a cooler and pulled out an orange can. "Take a Moxie. Will that cover it?"

"Not quite," she said, leaning over the belt and smiling. "But for a cute kid like you I'll make it work."

"For real?"

"On the house, handsome."

"Thanks, lady," he said, snapping off the tab and gulping it down. "This stuff is awesome."

"You boys take good care," the girl said.

Tag thanked the girl and made his way back out to the car. He and Fez changed into the new clothes once inside. For the first time in months they looked like semi-respectable citizens. All they needed were fresh haircuts and showers. Of course the haircut would have to wait; people would recognize him if his hair was short. Had it not been for his long hair, beard, and weight loss, the girl at the cash register might have identified him.

Fez split open a bag of Bugles, grabbed a handful of the orange cylinders, and shoved them into his mouth. Crumbs spilled everywhere as a soft moan of pleasure emitted from his lips. Fez held the bag up to him but he politely declined. The smell of MSG overpowered his nose and nearly made him gag. After eating rabbit, fish, and seaweed for the past few months, the odor of processed food still seemed strange and foreign to him. Besides, he barely had an appetite so soon after recovering from his illness.

"I've never tried a Bugle before and I'm not about to start now."

"Once you try one, Tag, you'll be hooked," Fez said, the rim of his mouth covered with orange crumbs. "So where do we go from here?"

"We rent a room in town. Then we take a nice hot shower, watch some crappy TV, and get a good night's rest. Come morning, we'll plan our next move over eggs, bacon, and stacks of pancakes covered with Maine maple syrup."

"Crap, Tag, that sounds delicious." Fez's eyes glazed over as if contemplating such a feast. "Been so long since I had a feast like that. My mom used to cook us a huge breakfast every Sunday morning."

"We're going to eat like kings, kid."

"Good, because just thinking about this E-Bola stuff has suddenly made me hungry."

Tag reached into the bag and pulled out the road map. It was one of those maps that had to be unfolded at least a half dozen times before it could be read. He found the town of Brookhaven on the map and noticed that it was completely surrounded by mountains. There were only two roads in and out. He hastily folded the map into a crumpled mess and stuck it back in the bag. Then he cruised out of the empty parking lot and drove straight toward the mountain range looming ahead of them.

Chapter 19

"Excuse me for asking, Pastor, but how could you have possibly known we were coming when we've never before spoken?"

"Not you two per se, but reporters in general," Dempsey said, chuckling more for his own benefit than theirs.

"So then you know why we're here?" Bacon asked incredulously.

"I believe I do." He stood to his full height, which wasn't very tall at all, and zipped his windbreaker up to his red necktie. "How about we walk around the grounds while we talk. There's not much to see around here, but the exercise will do me good."

Nolette followed the diminutive pastor along the path and toward the rear of the facility. He walked slowly, wobbling as if on bowed legs with the help of his wooden cane, which was shaped like a baseball bat. He said nothing until they rounded the corner and got closer to the facility. Beyond them she saw endless plains; a landscape so different than what she was used to that she found it hard to acclimate. The old man walked over to a park bench and sat down facing the windswept plains. A small tumbleweed rolled past them. She turned and saw Bacon standing against the building twenty yards away, finishing the last dregs of his cigarette.

"We were told that you know something about Ernest Drinkwater," Nolette said.

"I've only met him a few times."

"Pastor, no offense, but I don't understand. Who is Ernest Drinkwater and what's his connection to you?"

"I'm quite curious as to why you need to know?"

"Let's just say that there are lives at stake. We've travelled all the way from Maine to speak to you."

"Oh my, I've never been to Maine." His face crinkled up. "That certainly is a long way to travel. Then again, I suppose it wouldn't be prudent to speak of such matters by phone."

"I'm sure you heard about the attack on Cooke's Island."

He stared at her, his scaly lips slightly ajar. "You think Ernest was somehow involved?"

"We don't know, Pastor. That's why we've come all this way to speak to you."

"His real name is Robert Cooper. I met him only once but his story is quite interesting, what little I know of it. Do you know what ever happened to Ernest?"

"He changed his name one more time and was presumed dead years later in a plane crash," Nolette said.

"I'm sorry to hear that. Such sad news."

Bacon walked over and sat down next to him. "So what's this guy's story, Pastor?"

Dempsey turned and regarded him as if he were an interloper. "Back in 1993, you may recall that the ATF raided the Branch Davidian compound near Waco. What the federal government did during that standoff was a terrible crime committed against those people. After the ATF raided the compound, and murdered a few of their citizens in cold blood, the FBI took over negotiations with the leader of the Branch Davidians."

"They said the sick bastard was piddling with all those little girls," Bacon said. "Koresh was a cult leader who brainwashed his followers."

"It sounds like you're the one who's been brainwashed. That was the biggest lie the government spread in order to justify their criminal actions." Dempsey turned and looked up at Nolette. "I knew David Koresh very well and he was a man of God. While he was a gifted and charismatic speaker, he was certainly no cult leader. As far as brain washing goes, it was quite the opposite;

165

many recall how he would actually order people out of his Bible studies if they lacked the desire to do the work."

"What about being a pedophile?" Bacon asked.

"Another lie the government spread to make him look bad."

"So what's the connection?" Nolette said, eager to learn more.

"Have some patience, young lady, I'm getting to that." Dempsey took out a handkerchief and used it to wipe his chapped lips. He moved in slow motion. "I can attest to the fact that David was an amazing speaker because I heard him preach many times. His primary focus was on the Book of Revelation. It's the final book in the New Testament and in it John is given a revelation by God. The revelation tells what Jesus is going to do in the last days."

"But didn't Koresh see himself as Christ?" Bacon asked.

"Not at all. He saw himself as the lamb opening the Seven Seals." He frowned at Bacon.

"And what happens when they are opened?" Bacon asked.

Nolette knew about the Seven Seals from her own experience in the church but wanted to hear it from Dempsey's mouth.

"The long and short of it is that the lamb opens the seals and reveals the catastrophes that will take place on earth before God reveals himself."

"Like plague and pestilence," Nolette added.

"Yes, although it is not limited to those. But certainly plague and pestilence are two of the catastrophes included in the Book of Revelation," Dempsey said. "During these catastrophes, God will allow women and children to die painful deaths. But in order for that to happen the Seals need to be opened first. John, who is dreaming all of this, is brought to heaven where he believes they will be revealed to him. God says, 'Weep not: behold the lion of the tribe of Judah, the root of David, hath prevailed to open the book, and to loose the Seven Seals thereof.'"

"What the hell does that mean?" Bacon asked.

"After the Seals are opened and the catastrophes take place, his followers are supposed to see 'the son of man coming in the clouds, with great power and glory,' before God would begin establishing His Kingdom." Dempsey turned to address Bacon. "You see, David Koresh believed that he was the prophet who would open the Seven Seals and bring about these catastrophes. Doing this would bring about the coming of the Messiah and thus God's kingdom."

"But he was killed in the raid before he got the chance to deliver them," Nolette said, remembering the chronology of events. She was a young girl at the time and all the adults in her congregation were aghast at how the federal government had treated both the Branch Davidians and the Weavers at Ruby Ridge.

"This is where the story gets interesting. David made a deal with the head FBI negotiator. Once he finished interpreting the Seven Seals, he and his congregation would come out of the compound. Despite agreeing to this arrangement, the attorney general in D.C. reneged on the deal and ordered the FBI to gas the compound. The government went back on their word and because of that hundreds of innocent people were killed. I knew David, and when he gave his word about something he kept it."

"So assuming the government lied, which is nothing new, tell us how that relates to our guy Drinkwater," Bacon said, sounding impatient.

"The government did not live up to its end of the bargain and because of that hundreds of people were murdered in cold blood. But a few people managed to come out of that compound and surrender to the authorities. Most were tried in court and served prison time," Dempsey said, turning from Bacon to Nolette. "Afterwards, there were all kinds of rumors circulating about David having finished his interpretation. Some people claimed that he somehow had them smuggled out of the compound before everything was destroyed. I met Robert soon after the raid. Robert claimed that David handed him the finished

Seven Seals before he crawled through the tunnel and escaped from the FBI."

"Jesus, how far did the kid crawl?" Bacon asked.

"I examined the area sealed off by the FBI and estimated that he must have crawled over a mile before he made it out of that tunnel," Dempsey said.

"What about the Seven Seals? Did you determine if he actually carried them out?"

"Robert claimed that he hid them somewhere, but he wouldn't tell us where. We tried to emphasize the importance of these Seven Seals to the world, and still it did not sway him. Around that time the FBI was beginning to question all the people in town. Maybe they did the math and figured out that someone had escaped that compound. The couple who initially took him in could not properly take care of the boy; they were elderly and enfeebled. So I arranged for my devout friends, the Drinkwaters, to adopt him. Being the good Christians that they were, they agreed to care of the boy for two years until he graduated from high school."

"So the Seven Seals were never found?"

"Not to my knowledge," Dempsey said, using his cane to rise up off the bench. "I'm very tired now. Would you please walk me back to the front door, young lady?"

"Of course."

Nolette and Bacon positioned themselves on either side of the old man. Then the three of them walked slowly back to the front entrance. Once they arrived at the glass door, Dempsey thanked them for their time.

"Now that I've answered all your questions, would you mind telling me why you came to see me?" Dempsey asked.

"We don't think he died in that plane crash, Pastor. We believe that he is still alive and planning another terrorist attack. He went on to earn a Ph.D. in biology and worked for the U.S. Army studying infectious diseases. It's believed that he was responsible for that attack on Cooke's Island."

Pastor Dempsey nodded. "He's trying to bring forth the revelations. Little does he know that only God is able to usher forth these events and not man."

"If that's the case he's one evil son-of-a-bitch," Bacon said. "Sounds like he's doing the work of the devil instead."

"After Robert crawled out of that hole he informed his guardians that he was David's heir apparent."

"Because he believed himself a prophet?" Nolette asked.

"His mother was a fifteen year-old drug addict who abandoned him to abuse drugs and sell her body. After bouncing from foster home to foster home, most of which he ran away from, David brought the boy into the compound and took him under his wing. People who remember him said that he was a brilliant student and could recite biblical passages from memory. David must have recognized the boy's intelligence early on, but he also saw in Robert a burning hatred that he hoped to channel into righteous indignation."

"Thank you for all your help, Pastor."

"I'm an old man now. I've seen enough tragedy to last many lifetimes. I certainly hope you can stop the person responsible for that attack, young lady, and I pray that it's not Robert who's involved," Dempsey said.

The automatic door closed behind him. Nolette watched as Dempsey walked down the drab hallway and past the front desk. She'd recorded their entire conversation on her tablet and would transcribe it later. But first she had to try and figure out how to deal with Bacon.

She walked back to the car, eager to start writing the first part of her investigative series.

"Wait up, Swain," Bacon said, jogging after her. "So what's our plan now?"

"I'm getting a hotel room for the night. In the morning I plan on driving back to D.C. to consult with my editor."

"Those goons will surely be on the lookout for you. You might not even make it back alive, Swain."

Nolette jumped behind the wheel, feeling uneasy about sitting next to him.

"How about we get a hotel for the night and head out first thing in the morning. Besides, you can't take this car. It's registered on my company's expense account."

"One night as long as we leave first thing in the morning."

"Of course. You think I want to stay another day in this crappy place?" he said. "So what did you make of all that? Pretty crazy, huh?"

"Sounded credible to me," Nolette said.

"Do you think Drinkwater's really in possession of those Seven Seals?"

"Does it matter at this point? If he thinks he's the heir to David Koresh then he's going to use that to justify his apocalyptic vision."

"This is going to make one helluva story," Bacon said as he stared out the window. "I hope whatever hotel we stop at has a decent bar because I really need a stiff cocktail right about now."

"Bacon, you always seem to need a stiff cocktail. Ever think you might have a drinking problem?"

"Of course I have a drinking problem. And if I don't get one real soon it'll only get worse."

* * *

They found a hotel a few miles away and booked a single room with two twin beds. Nolette realized that if she used any of her credit cards the Feds would be able to track her movements. Bacon asked her if she wanted to go to the lounge for drinks and appetizers, but that was the last thing she wanted to do. As soon as he left the room she set up her tablet and started furiously writing everything she could remember, using her notes to fill in the blanks. She envisioned this being a multi-part series, and estimated that in less than a week she could turn in the first part of the story to her editor, who would no doubt be eager to run it.

She worked well into the night. Bacon came in a few hours later smelling of whiskey and fried foods. He collapsed on the bed and in a few minutes filled the room with his loud boozy snoring. The sound of it broke her concentration and she realized she couldn't think clearly enough to write.

She closed her tablet and let the battery charge on the night stand. Siting back against the pillows, she watched the late night news, making sure to keep one eye on Bacon. One night was all she had to endure. But he was sound sleep, probably drunk, and no threat to her now. Besides, if he wanted to harm her he'd had plenty of opportunity to do so when she was asleep in the car. So what did he want? Had he been ordered to keep his eye on her? Or was she imagining all this in her head? Her eyelids grew heavy and within a few minutes she had unwillingly surrendered to sleep.

Her tablet beeped in the middle of the night. She shot up in bed and saw the flash of light emanating from the screen. Exhausted, she debated whether she should ignore it or take a quick look. But then the memory of those mysterious messages came back to her and she figured that she should at least take a look before nodding off.

She grabbed her tablet and turned it on. The screen flashed to life. She clicked on the text and read the one line of message.

You have less than two minutes before Bacon is going to try and kill you!

Chapter 20

It was a beautiful fall day and despite the impending doom that was to befall this small town, he couldn't help but be awed by Mother Nature. The crisp autumn air magnified the majesty of the surrounding mountains as well as the lovely river that meandered through town. A dusting of snow had frosted the highest peaks as if sprinkled with powdered sugar. From his balcony he could take in the entire valley, noticing how the clouds blocked the sun and caused shadows to move across the tree-studded landscape. Hawthorne College sat high above the rest of the town, bestowing its self-importance by virtue of its elevated position.

He noticed that the protesters had set up just outside the iron gates facing the admin building. It pleased him to no end to see them gathered there. The conference was swiftly approaching and already the high drama had begun.

He drove downtown and parked across the street from the college. A group of counter protesters had formed across the street, decrying the hate message of the Revelation Ministry. The Brookhaven police had shut the street down and set up a barrier between the two groups. He stood near the back and watched as those in the front led the cheers against hate. A few of the actors in the troupe recognized him and waved him over.

Rather than protesting, he pitched in by passing out coffee and sandwiches to those leading the charge. Many of Hawthorne's undergraduates and professors stopped by to lend their support in vilifying the Baptists.

He watched the group's leader, Reverend Sherman Grout, issue forth passages from the Bible. The man stood on a wooden crate and shouted through a bullhorn, waiting for his flock to call back his words. Grout was tall and gangly, with huge ears protruding out from under a suede cowboy hat. He wore a look of stony disapproval that never seemed to waver; the type of man who would have gladly welcomed the arrival of a plague and then announced it as God's will.

At five o'clock the Baptists abruptly stopped protesting, packed their signs and placards, and departed in an orderly manner. They ignored the counter-protesters' jeers as they formed into a prayer circle. The counter-protesters cheered and sang 'Amazing Grace' in loud cacophony. They continued to sing as the members of the Revelation Ministry broke formation and filed into their bus. Grout paused before boarding and shot them a stern look of reproach. Then he pointed an exceedingly long finger at the crowd and shouted out in a loud, unforgettable voice, "You liberal faggots are going to burn in hell!" The counter-protesters laughed and mocked him, but he'd already disappeared into the safe confines of the bus.

The crowd dispersed once the bus drove off, and he sprinted back to his car and followed the bus to where the Baptists were staying. After ten minutes of driving, the bus turned into the parking lot of a shabby inn located on the outskirts of town. The motel was one of those sad, one-story claptraps that had seen better days. He parked across the street and watched as the congregation filed off the bus and gathered into a prayer circle. They held hands and bowed their heads. Grout lifted his head up as if preaching and raised his Bible in the air. Then, just as quickly, the circle broke and the congregation made their way to their rooms.

Once they'd disappeared, he stripped off his pants and shirt and replaced them with a blue janitor's uniform. Across the left pocket of the shirt he'd sewn the word 'Steve' and on the right 'Mountain View Inn.' He exited the car, tossing the grimy blue windbreaker over his shoulder. Sticking a wad of gum in his mouth, he made his way to the last room on the right and knocked on the door. A few seconds passed before a young couple appeared. They looked surprised, as if they'd been caught doing something they shouldn't have been doing.

"Can I help you?" the man asked in a deep southern drawl.

The man identified as 'Steve' shrugged and made a show of chewing his wad of gum. "Manager told me the heating unit needs adjusting."

"Seems okay to me," the woman said.

He laughed. "You don't know these crappy units like I do, lady," he said in a distinct Maine accent. "It's supposed to get wicked cold tonight and I don't feel like getting a call in the middle of the night to come down and fix it."

"What do you got to do?" the man asked.

"Take it easy, pal. Only take me a few seconds to adjust the thermostat and then I'll be out of your hair," he said.

"Okay, but can you make it quick? We been on our feet all day and are doggone tired," the man said.

"Steve" lifted a screwdriver and pointed it at the man.

"Hey, I seen you on TV protesting in front of that college. Bunch of friggin' spoiled brats if you ask me. About time someone stood up to them friggin' snobs," he said. "Think they're the cat's meow."

"Can you hurry it up, Mister? We gotta get some shuteye so we can preach to them faggots come morning."

"Wasting your breath preaching to them pinkos," he said, shaking his head. "Where you folks from anyway?"

The man looked at his wife and sighed. "Missouri." It came out as Mizz-Or-A.

"Never been that far south," he said as he walked past them. "Heard the barbecue's damn good down there."

He walked across the dingy room with his screwdriver in hand. He turned off the heat and then unscrewed the metal plate, gently placing it on the nightstand. The dark chute appeared before him. He looked over his shoulder and noticed that the husband and wife were conferring near the bed. Positioning himself between him and the couple, he grabbed the vial of powder out of his pants' pocket and poured a speckle onto the flat metal surface. The powder was a mixture of dried Ebola particles combined with silica glass; the first ever dried concoction of Ebola virus. He screwed the panel back onto the wall. Once it was secure, he reset the digital thermometer to seventy degrees to insure it would engage. Tonight's temperature was supposed to drop down to the mid-thirties, insuring that the hot air would circulate the particles throughout the room. Once the dried virus became airborne they'd eventually lodge in the lungs' membrane, and when that happened the end was near.

Tapping the screwdriver against his temple, he thanked the couple and showed himself out. The first thing he saw upon walking outside was their ruddy old bus. He breathed in the cool autumn air, relishing in its vitality and healthful qualities.

Once behind the wheel of his own vehicle, he envisioned the dried Ebola particles circulating in endless loops around the room, searching for a host in which to replicate. It reminded him of those exhilarating moments on Cooke's Island, before all hell broke loose, when that glass liger sculpture had been delivered to Colonel Winters' wife. If only he could have seen the look on Winters' face when she told him about the strange gift she'd received. And how when she pressed the button a mysterious cloud of smoke blew out of its mouth and hovered across the room. The gift had been a viral Trojan horse and stroke of genius that would be hard to surpass.

As he drove back to his chalet, he felt excitement building within him. He couldn't wait to see how fast his new contagion would spread around town. And he had no doubt that the infection had already begun to spread in that rundown section of town known as Rat Town.

* * *

Tag drove cautiously through the pass before cruising into the valley. The town of Brookhaven appeared off in the distance, juxtaposed against the northern mountains. A two-lane road fed into the middle of town. Downtown Brookhaven disappeared from sight once he descended into the valley. An old caboose car appeared on a long stretch of road leading into town. The red neon light over the car advertised it as 'The Brookhaven Diner.' Tag turned into the parking lot and stopped in front of the old rail car.

"Why're we stopping here when we got all these Bugles and licorice?" Fez asked.

"Man cannot live by Bugles and licorice alone, kid. I hear the call of meatloaf with green beans and buttery mashed potatoes smothered in gravy. Chocolate milkshakes and glorious pots of hot coffee. Slices of apple pie topped with scoops of vanilla ice cream." He stepped onto the pavement and noted the eighteen-wheelers parked in the lot; this was a good sign.

"There you go again, Tag, making me hungry all over again."

"After we stuff ourselves we'll find a hotel and fall into a food coma."

"Sounds good to me."

They walked into the caboose and sat down in one of the booths located at the far end of the diner. A line of burly customers sat at the breakfast bar drinking coffee out of bone-white mugs. An elderly waitress wearing a retro blue dress handed them giant menus encased in plastic. Tag started off with a coffee and Fez ordered a root beer float with extra whipped cream and cherries.

"Do you have a phone book we might borrow?" Tag asked the waitress. "We need to book a hotel room for the night."

"Sure we got a phone book, but you boys won't be finding a room in this town anytime soon. There's some fancy pants conference going on at the college and all the hotels have been booked solid for weeks," she said.

"You're saying there's not one place we could stay for the night?"

"You might try the Mountain View Inn. It's about a mile down the road, but I wouldn't advise staying in that roach motel."

Tag smiled and handed her back the menu.

JOSEPH SOUZA

"You boys already to order?"

"Meatloaf with mashed potatoes. And lots of gravy," Tag said.

"Bud makes the best meatloaf in Maine." She turned to Fez. "And you, young fella?"

"Buffalo chicken tenders with cheesy waffle fries. Extra cheese on the fries, please." Fez held up the menu.

"See you boys when I get back."

The piping hot plates arrived ten minutes later. Tag dug into his slab of meatloaf as if his life depended on it, savoring every beefy morsel on his plate. Only his wife's meatloaf had been better. But then again, Monica took a serious interest in the culinary arts and often hosted dinner parties for friends and family. He missed her cooking and the way they would dine by candlelight each night after the kids had shipped off to college.

The apple pie had sold out and so he ordered the coconut cream pie, devouring it in three bites. After they'd finished every crumb on their plates, he left a generous tip for the old waitress and then headed out to his car.

He prayed they could score a room for the night. Worst case scenario, he'd purchase a couple of blankets and they'd sleep in the car. But he hoped it didn't come to that. He'd hoped to sleep in a comfortable bed and then take a nice hot shower come morning.

He drove down the road a way until he noticed the sickly yellow neon sign for the Mountain View Inn. With nothing to lose, he pulled into the lot. A few cars sat in the parking lot. The sun was just beginning to set over the western edge of the mountains, and the eastern peaks glowed a brilliant pink. A long yellow bus was parked in the rear of the lot. On the side it said 'The Revelation Baptist Ministry.'

They made their way into the front office where a middle-aged Punjabi man wearing a turban came out to greet them.

"Can I help you?"

"We're looking to book a room for the night."

"Ah ha! Today is your lucky day. Fortunately for you, one of the parties could not make the trip. I have one room available, but it has only one bed."

"We'll take it!"

"Credit card or cash?"

"Cash."

"That will be two-fifty please."

Tag stared in shock. "Two hundred and fifty dollars?"

"Consider yourself lucky that I even have a room. With this conference in town I can easily find someone else to rent it to." He stared at him. "So do you want it or not?"

Tab gulped at the prospect of spending that much money. "Okay, we'll take it." He paid in cash and the man handed him a gold key.

"Complimentary coffee and pastries in the morning. The breakfast lounge is down the hall to the left. There's a large church group staying here that will be using the conference room from time to time, so please be considerate and stay out of their way. Other than that, I hope you have a wonderful stay at The Mountain View Inn."

He and Fez exited the office and walked down the crumbling concrete path leading to their room. It was the second to last unit. He opened the door and tried not to show his disappointment in front of the kid. Of course it was much better than sleeping in the car. One lumpy bed sat in the middle of the room. It faced a tired dresser with a small flat screen sitting atop it. The tiny bathroom was in the back and had only a shower and no tub. They barely had any space to move around.

Fez grabbed the remote and clicked around until he settled on a cartoon featuring crime-fighting robots who used martial arts to defeat reptilian villains. The sound of the kid's laughter filled the room and made Tag unusually happy. It reminded him of the old days when his kids would sit around on Saturday mornings and watch all those silly cartoons.

Tag ripped open the plastic container that held the phone charger and plugged it into the wall. The lights blinked and the charge took. Exhausted, he fell back on the bed next to Fez and watched as the robots battled the reptiles. Fez held out his bag of licorice and he reached inside and pulled out a ropey twine, twiddling it between his teeth.

Tonight they would rest. Tomorrow he'd find out where this conference was going to be held. Maybe, if luck had it, he could pay a visit to his wife.

He bolted upright sometime in the middle of the night, hearing a strange noise. Fez slept next to him, partially curled up beneath the blankets. The flat screen continued to throw light around the room. Grabbing the remote, he shut the TV off and tried to discern where the noise was coming from. A series of cries came from the adjacent room. *What the hell was that?* He climbed off the bed and cupped his ear against the wall. Again he heard moaning and soft cries. The digital clock said 3:12 A.M. Was the couple in the next room making love at this hour? And yet it didn't sound like love-making, although it had been so long since he'd made love to his wife that he'd almost forgotten what it felt or sounded like. But what else could it be? He looked over at Fez, relieved to see that he was sound asleep on the bed. He pulled the kid's shoes off and covered him with part of the blanket. Then he climbed back in bed and tried to ignore the soft moans coming from the room next door. He soon fell asleep, comforted by the memories of family outings and long, relaxing days at the beach. Then afterwards, going back to the cottage and barbecuing steaks and lobster on the charcoal grill.

Chapter 21

Nolette reread the text message again just to make sure she'd seen it correctly. Was this some sort of joke? She knew that Bacon had been spying on her, but surely he was no killer. Was it possible that he was trying to steal her story and bathe in all the glory? Yes, that had to be it. There could be no argument that he was a gifted journalist who'd won many prestigious awards for his investigative reporting, including a Pulitzer Prize. But maybe on account of his age and his drinking his ethics had been lagging these last few years. Maybe he'd won awards *because* of his diminishing talents. The tablet lit up again and a digital clock appeared under a draining hourglass: two minutes and counting.

This had to be a mistake. No way Bacon would try and harm her. They were a team. She turned toward him and heard the sound of his phone beeping. A wake-up call? He stirred beneath the blanket, his bare feet dangling off the edge of the mattress. Nervous, she opened the nightstand drawer and reached inside for anything she could use to defend herself. Ironically, she took out a leather bound copy of the Bible and slipped it beneath the blanket. Reaching back inside again, she felt around until she happened upon a small metallic object. Upon pulling it out, she realized that someone had left a pair of nail clippers inside. The blade flipped open and she felt its dull edge as well the textured steel on the face used to smooth out cuticles. Peering out from the crumpled blanket, she watched as Bacon's dim form sat up on the bed. He raised his hands in the air as if yawning and then sighed. A few seconds passed before he stood and turned to look at her.

JOSEPH SOUZA

Nolette closed her eyes and pretended to be asleep. To jump up and confront him would be a bad strategy. He outweighed her by forty pounds and could easily bull-rush her if she attempted to take him on. Her pulse beat rapidly and she could hear the blood thumping in her temples. She tried to think about what to do next.

Positioning the file between her fingers so that it protruded like a shiv, she pressed her eyelids together and followed his silhouette. Bacon moved to the other side of the bed and stared at her, convinced that she was asleep. Reaching back to his headboard, he picked up one of the pillows and clasped it between his palms. Was he planning on smothering her? She couldn't believe he could be so cold-blooded, especially after all the time they'd spent together. Her pulse raced with anticipation as he sat down again. He rubbed his eyes with forefinger and thumb and sobbed. But why was he crying?

The darkness of the room made it hard to see. A minute passed before he stopped crying. Then he rose up off the bed and made his way toward her. All those months taking self-defense classes would now be put to use. Slowly, and with much stealth, she slipped her arm out of the blanket and let it dangle over the mattress, careful to conceal the file protruding between her fingers. A few seconds passed before she realized he was standing directly over her. She waited, every tendon in her arm taut, and listened to him breathe. He was working up the courage to kill her. Knowing that she was at a disadvantage, she waited for him to make the first move. It would be her only chance at surviving this fight.

The pillow came down over her face with unexpected force, catching her completely off guard. She could hear him grunting as he leaned into her. Lying on her side had created an air pocket for her to breathe, and so he worked the pillow around so that it fully covered her mouth. She kicked her feet and struggled to free herself, and in her ensuing panic momentarily forgot about the file in her hand. The sudden lack of oxygen induced a terror in her that she'd never before experienced. The

181

prospect of death consumed her every thought and her hand flung open, but by some miracle she was able to hold onto the file.

"I'm sorry about this, Swain. I had no choice in the matter," Bacon groaned while pressing the pillow down over her mouth. "You were such a nice kid, too."

Nolette kicked her feet and felt her toe strike him in the ear, but not hard enough to dislodge him from the bed. Gasping for breath, she managed to compose herself as if she were a child again, diving in the nearby pond where she and her friends use to cool off in the summer. The memory of those days flashed in her head and for a moment she felt a sense of peace and tranquility. But then just as quickly she was jarred back to this fierce struggle, knowing that she had to do something soon or else she'd run out of breath. She clutched the nail clipper until it was wedged into her fist. The full weight of his body sat atop of her chest, pinning her to the mattress. Bacon continued to apologize and by the sound of his voice she could tell that he'd lowered his head against the pillow he was holding. Her head started to spin and she felt almost drunk from the lack of oxygen to her brain.

The sound of his pathetic voice enraged her. Calling forth every last ounce of energy, she gripped the file and threw a roundhouse right at his head. The tip of the steel plunged into his flesh and he cried out in pain. His weight shifted and, after pulling the file out of his head, she jabbed him three more times in the cheek. The weight of his body fell back against her legs and allowed her to breathe.

"You motherfucking bitch!" he cried out.

She bolted upright and gasped for air, nearly falling off the bed. Her lungs seared as the room spun around her. She propped herself up against the nightstand and looked around in the dark. Where was he? She could hear his pathetic whimpering. Sitting up on her haunches, she struggled to get her bearings and locate him. The room went quiet as she tried to get a fix on his position. She reached back to turn on the lamp only to see a shadow lunging at her in the dark. Thinking quickly, she stuck the blade out in front of her and felt it sink into his face. A curdling scream went up as his hands encircled her throat. She pulled the file out and then plunged it deeper into his eye. Warm blood streamed over her hands and wrists. And yet his hands did not let go of her throat but instead seemed to squeeze even harder. The file fell from her hand as she struggled to take in air, and she could feel the fine hairs on his wrist tickling her chin. Sensing an opportunity, she turned her head and chomped down on his wrist. Warm, salty blood gushed into her mouth and over her dry lips. It coated her teeth and trickled down her throat, nearly causing her to gag. But she didn't relent, knowing she was locked in a fight to the death.

She was about to pass out when she felt his resolve loosening. He released his grip and fell away, screaming in agony. Sensing victory, she turned on her side and brought her feet up under the blanket, mule-kicking him to the floor. Bacon crashed between the two mattresses, his body wedged against the beds.

Nolette turned on the lamp and sprang off the mattress, hovering over the bloody reporter. She gritted her teeth in the throes of a murderous rage. Bacon writhed between her ankles, his face and hand sopping in blood. Ooze dripped down his left cheek as he tried to keep the gelatinous mass from escaping his eyelid. The other good eye stared at her in horror. He sobbed uncontrollably, his body convulsing in rhythmic intervals that alternated between fear and merciful pleading. Nolette trembled with rage, unsure what to do next, but knowing that she had to get out of this room as quickly as possible. She wondered if she should kill Bacon or let him live.

"I'm so fucking sorry, Swain," he cried, tears running down his one good eye. "He said if I didn't do it he'd kill my kids, and I believed him."

"Who ordered you to kill me?"

"I don't know his name, but he's the same guy who attacked that island. He tipped me off about the Feds coming after you too." He hyperventilated. "He's the devil incarnate, Swain. You've got to kill this psychopath before he kills more people!"

183

"He wants only one of us to tell his story." She wiped the blood off her face and lips. "The person who survives this fight wins the honor of writing it."

He looked up at her with his one good eye and she noticed a large flap of skin hanging from his cheek.

"You don't have kids, Swain, so you don't understand how desperate I was." He held out his hand as if pleading for forgiveness.

She spit on his hand.

"How did you know I was going to try and kill you?" he asked.

"He sent me a message before he instructed you to kill me."

"That fucking two-faced bitch!" he shouted, banging his hand against the floor. "He said if I failed to kill you then he'd still kill my kids."

"Sorry to say that you failed, Bacon."

His hand shot out and grabbed her ankle. The suddenness of this secondary attack caught her by surprise and she fell back against the bed. He pushed himself off the carpet until he was standing. Nolette swung her feet over the mattress and stood opposite him with only the mattress between them. She positioned herself in a fighting position, knowing that she would now have to kill him in order to survive. Bacon would do virtually anything to save his kids, including killing her—and she didn't blame him!

He stood on the bed and approached her, arms out for balance. Backing up against the wall, she watched as he approached, his gouged eye closed. He'd have a significant weight advantage if it came to hand-to-hand combat. And yet she also knew that he couldn't see out of his left eye. He jumped down off the bed and came toward her. Nolette sidestepped to the right as his hand came down across her forehead. She caught sight of the bloody punctures in his cheek from where she'd stabbed him. They collapsed to the floor in a heap. Bacon's head crashed up against the wall, putting a hole in it before bouncing back toward the bed. Blood dripped down her forehead and onto the bridge of her nose. She sat up and tried to shake off the dizziness that had now taken hold. Bacon started to crawl toward her. He rose up to his knees and punched her in the mouth. The metallic taste of her own blood pooled up on her tongue and collected in the abscesses of her gums. She stuck her forefinger out with its sharp nail and jabbed it in his one good eye. Rather than pulling it out, she shoved her finger deeper into the socket so that it penetrated to the first knuckle.

Bacon fell back, clasping his eyes with his hands and screaming in agony. She kicked him in the stomach several times before grabbing one of the pillows off the bed and pressing it down over his bloodied mouth. He kicked and clawed, but in less than a minute his body went slack and she felt his life slipping away. Sitting back in shock, she struggled to breathe. After a few minutes she removed the pillow from his head and stared down at his lifeless face. His eyelids lay open, revealing two gaping holes.

She collapsed onto the bed, sobbing. It took her a few minutes to collect herself and realize that the people next door might have heard their struggle. Stumbling around the room, she wondered what to do next? Her DNA was everywhere. She walked over to the dresser and stared at herself in the oval mirror. Her eye had swelled and the rest of her face appeared battered and bruised. She touched the purple welt around her eye socket and it pulsed in pain. Blood lay matted over her hair and smeared across her face, a face that looked unrecognizable from a few minutes ago.

Her tablet beeped. Whoever had ordered Bacon to kill her had also saved her life. She grabbed the iPad and frantically read the text.

A rough bout of sex if anyone asks. Shower, dress, and then set fire to the room so that there's no evidence of you having been there. Use the gallon soap container under the sink. Cut the hose attached to the disposable shower and siphon gas out of your rental car to get the fire going. Nice work! I'm watching out for you, sweetheart.

Nolette tossed down the tablet in disgust and ran into the bathroom to vomit. After wiping her mouth, she unscrewed the shower head and then removed the fixture so that it would fit in the car's gas tank.

Holding the flexible tube in her trembling hands, she hesitated for a brief moment to contemplate what she'd just done; she'd killed another human being in self-defense. God had disappeared from her life many years ago after she'd escaped from that religious commune. And yet after killing Bacon she found herself begging for God's forgiveness. She'd killed in self-defense. And yet it was not only her own life that concerned her, but the lives of all those people in jeopardy from this monster as well as Bacon's two kids.

She searched the room, looking for anything that could cut through the rubber material, and all she could find was the nail file. She stuck the pointy end into the thick rubber hose and twisted it around. After a few minutes the sharp end penetrated the exterior. Desperate, she sawed away, making incremental progress. The muscles in her hand ached and she found herself every now and then breaking into fits of hysterical sobbing. She placed the end of the hose under the foot of the bed and pulled with all her might until the fixture became untethered and broke apart. Nolette fell back against the drawer, exhausted. The muscles in her hands had frozen into claws from the exertion. As she stretched them out she heard a knocking at the door.

Thinking on her feet, she jumped onto the bed and began to bounce up and down. "Fuck me!" she screamed at the top of her lungs. Another knock on the door. "Do me harder!" Nolette let out one last scream before jumping down and answering the door.

"What the hell do you want?" she asked, staring through the two-inch crack so as not to be fully seen.

"I'm the night manager of this hotel. Is everything okay in here?"

"Why the fuck you bothering us, dude, when we're getting it on?"

186

"The guests in the other room complained of some loud banging and heard people shouting from your room," he said.

"Is there a law against fucking in a hotel room?"

The manager blushed and glanced at his watch. "Personally, Miss, I don't care what you do in your room as long as it doesn't bother the other guests. But it's almost three-thirty in the morning and the other guests on this floor are trying to sleep. All I'm asking is that you extend some courtesy and keep the noise to a minimum."

"What kind of fucking fleabag joint is this anyway?" Nolette shouted. "See if you get a good review on Yelp from us."

"Just keep the noise down. If I have to come up here again then I'm afraid I'm going to have ask you to leave."

She glared at him. "Chill the fuck out, bro. You totally ruined the mood anyway."

He frowned in embarrassment. "Good night."

Nolette leaned up against the door and exhaled in relief. She'd somehow managed to talk her way out of this jam. She retrieved the hose and removed the fixtures. Moving into the bathroom, she found the plastic gallon container filled with soap. She emptied it into the sink basin and then rinsed out the suds. Once she had the pipe and container ready to go, she grabbed the car keys off the dresser.

She realized that she couldn't go outside with her face looking like such a bloody mess. So she went into the bathroom and stripped off all her clothes and took a hot shower. Blood and strands of her long hair ran down the drain as she compulsively scrubbed herself clean like the victim of rape after the assault.

Drying herself off, she tied her hair up into a bun with one of the towels. The shower felt cleansing and she could have stayed in it for hours. But it did little to soothe her frazzled nerves and myriad of wounds. After towel drying off, she returned back to the room and gazed down at Bacon's lifeless eye sockets staring up at the ceiling. She grabbed one of the clean pillowcases and stuffed the rubber tube, the plastic container, and one of the hand towels inside. Then she slipped out into the bright hallway and made her way down the staircase. Once she reached ground level, she located the exit and slipped outside unseen, making sure to place the rolled-up towel in the door's threshold so that she could slip back inside.

She slid the rubber hose into the gas tank. Pressing her lips against the plastic, she grimaced in anticipation of the bitter taste. It came up faster than expected and she ended up swallowing a mouthful and gagging. Sticking the other end of the hose into the plastic container, she coughed as the gas transferred. When she thought she had enough, she pulled the pipe out and replaced the gas cap. Then she capped the soap container and bolted over to the door.

She scooped up the towel lodged against the door and made her way back upstairs. An industrial hum filled the stairwell as she took them two at a time. Approaching the second level, she heard a door open and saw an elderly Hispanic maid walking toward her with broom and dustpan.

Nolette dropped the container into the pillowcase before the maid noticed her.

"Buenas noches," she said to the maid.

"Buenos noches." The maid appeared startled to see her coming up the stairs, and it took her a second to realize that she was staring at her face.

"Are you okay, Missus?" she asked in a thick Hispanic accent. "Did someone hit you?'

"Oh no, I'm perfectly fine," Nolette said, laughing. She made a fist and held it up to her chin. "I'm a fighter. Have you ever heard of MMA?"

"MMA? No, I never hear."

"Mixed martial arts," she said, hoping the words would resonate with her. "I get paid to fight other women. Unfortunately, this bitch beat the hell out of me tonight."

"I see men fight on TV but I no see women fight like that."

"Great country when us girls can kill each other, huh?" She elbowed the maid playfully.

188

The maid smiled tentatively. "Yes, America is great country."

"Adios," Nolette shouted as she turned to leave.

She sprinted up the stairs and didn't stop until she was back in her room. Leaning against the door, she took a few deep breaths to calm herself. She needed to remain strong if she was to make a clean break from this hotel. Many more lives were at stake.

Her tablet beeped and she went over to read the new message.

Leave nothing behind. Once you've torched the room head directly to Brookhaven, Maine. There's an infectious disease conference in town you'll find quite interesting. I'm sure I'll see you there, although I'm not sure you'll see me.

She removed Bacon's wallet and money and then ripped the sheet off his bed. Dragging him to the center of the room, she poured gas over his body and then wrapped him in the sheet. Once she'd finished she tied off the ends of the sheet and heaved him up onto the bed. She clicked on the television and turned up the volume. Before leaving, she scoured the room, making sure she left no other personal items behind.

The manager would soon be up here. She poured fuel everywhere, making sure to thoroughly dampen the corpse. Snatching up Bacon's cigarette lighter, she grabbed the newspaper and moved toward the door. Then she lit the newspaper and tossed it toward Bacon's lifeless corpse. In seconds, flames engulfed the room.

She sprinted down the hall until she located the fire alarm. Smashing the glass with her fist, she pulled the handle and set it off, hoping that all the guests would get out of there safely. Satisfied that she'd done all she possibly could to ensure the other guests' safety, she took off down the stairwell, taking the steps three at a time.

Her head throbbed as the fire alarm blared in her ears. She exited the back door and jumped in the car, and the engine roared to life. She shifted into reverse and sped out of the parking lot until she turned onto the main road.

Glancing in her rearview mirror as she sped away, she and saw flames pouring out the window of the hotel room. She configured the town of Brookhaven into the car's GPS system and in a matter of seconds a woman's voice was directing her to Maine.

Chapter 22

Tag woke the next morning feeling irritable and cranky. The greasy diner food hadn't sat well in his stomach after weeks of eating rabbit and fish. He'd also not slept soundly because of the commotion in the adjacent room. Rather than try and go back to sleep he took a hot shower, shampooing his thick beard and scraggly hair until he'd covered his entire head in a rich lather. Fez was propped up on the bed when he emerged from the bathroom wrapped in a fresh white towel. Surprisingly, the kid looked bright-eyed and wide awake.

Despite his irritable bowels, he and Fez headed to the diner for breakfast. The sun was just beginning to peek over the mountains. Seven eighteen-wheelers sat parked along the road, three of them hauling massive logs harvested from the northern regions of Maine. The Brookhaven Diner was obviously very popular with truck drivers and he could see why: the food was cheap, hearty, and plentiful. And the service even better.

Every seat in the diner was taken and so they had to wait a few minutes before being seated. A couple of burly guys wearing flannel shirts and baseball caps slid out from their booth. A clean-cut busboy ran out and cleared everything off the Formica table before wiping it down for them. Once Tag was seated, he pulled out the map and began to study the town's street patterns and topography. If Brookhaven was to be hit by a major biological attack, then he needed to know the lay of the land.

The mountains surrounding Brookhaven provided a geographical barrier and in the event of an attack would act as a natural quarantine, assuming that the passes could be closed off to traffic. He traced his finger along Route 87 and noticed that it snaked around Hawthorne College before exiting through the northern edge of the mountains. Route 87 completely bypassed Brookhaven's historic downtown district and to get into town he would need to get off at one of two exits.

"If it isn't my favorite two customers," an elderly woman's voice said.

Tag looked up and saw their waitress from the previous day. Her name tag said Millie.

"Hi, Millie," Fez said.

"You boys manage to find a room last night?" she chirped happily.

"Yeah, and you were right about The Mountain View Inn. It's a real dump," Tag said. "But then again, beggars can't be choosy."

"Ha! I told you so," she said, pouring coffee into his cup.

"Did you sleep here in the diner last night, Millie?" Tag asked, laughing.

"I'm seventy-three and work harder than most twenty-year-olds, smart ass. There's plenty of time for sleep when I croak," she said, holding the coffee pot in hand. She turned to Fez. "Root beer float for you, my dear?"

"How about a chocolate milkshake this morning," Fez said, rubbing his hands together.

"One chocolate milkshake coming right up. Might as well live it up while you're on vacation, right?" She turned to Tag. "You boys be careful out there, okay?"

"In Brookhaven?" Fez said, laughing. "The sign on the road says it's 'The Friendliest Little Town in America.'"

"Sure, we're a friendly little town alright. But tell that to the guy they found down by the tracks this morning. It's all over the radio."

"What guy?" Tag asked.

"You didn't hear about it?" She went back and replaced the coffee pot and returned with napkins, inserting them into the holder. "A man was found dead on the train tracks this morning. Cops said they'd never seen nothing like it. Looked like he was attacked by savage wolves. We don't get much violent crime around these parts, except for the occasional drug dealings down in Rat Town. Whatever you two do, stay out of that neighborhood."

"Where's Rat Town?" Fez asked.

"Down below the train tracks and at the base of Busby Mountain. Real seedy. It sits along the Brooke River. Lots of drinking and drug dealers down there too." She took out her pad and pencil. "So, you boys ready to order? I got other customers waiting."

They ordered and afterward Tag returned to the map. Busby Mountain was located at the far western end of town. Rat Town comprised about twenty streets, although nothing on the map referred to it by that name. Nearby was an abandoned chemical plant. The elevated train tracks ran past the neighborhood before disappearing through one of the tunnels on the northern edge of town.

The food arrived and Tag folded the map up to make room for his toast and Fez's mound of chocolate chip pancakes. The kid proceeded to spread pads of butter between the fluffy layers before pouring Maine maple syrup over the entire stack. Tag nibbled on his toast, washing it down with the coffee while watching the kid put away the stack.

The grisly details of the man's death sounded oddly suspicious to him. Most police were meticulous in their investigative techniques, but if this murder was what he thought it might be, then the police would need to be extra cautious when handling the corpse. It was well documented that the majority of Ebola cases in Africa were spread postmortem and then passed onto the people who'd handled the still-infected corpses.

He'd hoped to drive around town and get a better read on Brookhaven, but that would have to wait. There were only a few days left until the conference began and he had much to do before then. Using the diner's phonebook, he jotted down the name and number of every hotel in town, figuring that his wife had to be booked at one of them.

"Did you boys enjoy your breakfast?" Millie asked.

"Killer pancakes," Fez said, sitting back and patting his bloated belly.

"Glad you liked them," Millie said, her blue eyes twinkling happily. "You boys have a great day in Brookhaven. And don't forget to come back and see me before you leave."

"We sure will," Fez said, waving goodbye. "Best diner food I ever had."

Tag took out a wad of cash and paid the bill, leaving a generous tip. His stack of bills was starting to become thinner.

Once they'd returned to the car, he pulled out the map and studied the grid pattern, circling areas of interest, especially the direction to Rat Town. He navigated his way through the outskirts of town, crossing over hills dense with trees and thick vegetation. He drove for a few miles, surprised at how far away the neighborhood was located from the center of town. Any further away and he'd be driving up the logging road situated at the base of the mountain.

Eventually the road ended and he came to a clearing. Idling at the top of the hill, he noticed the low level fog hovering at the base of the mountain. Off in the distance he could just make out the buildings and tanks that once comprised the abandoned chemical plant. Below were rows of old trailers and dilapidated shotgun homes. Elevated above Rat Town ran two sets of tracks and a working train yard. Three police vehicles sat parked in a row. A couple of evidence techs worked around the body, which was covered over with a white tarp.

"Is that the dead guy?" Fez asked.

"Sure looks like it to me."

"So what are you thinking?"

"I'm not sure what I'm thinking."

"Ebola?"

Tag shifted into drive. "We're going to find out."

"Aren't you afraid they might recognize you?"

"Do I look like anyone you might know?"

Fez laughed. "You look like a homeless dude. Either that or a crazy mountain man."

"Then I seriously doubt they'll recognize me."

Tag drove down the hill and toward the train yard. A few engineers ambled around one of the locomotives. A train slowly clanked past, twenty feet from where the dead man lay. He drove slowly through the gates, but before he could go any further a cop ran over and blocked his path. The young officer strode purposefully toward his door and ordered Tag to roll down his window.

"Where the hell do you think you're going?" the young cop shouted.

"I need to talk to the lead detective in charge of the case."

"Unless you've got some relevant information to pass on, pal, then I'm afraid that's impossible. Now why don't you turn your vehicle around and head on out of here."

"Please, Officer, just let me talk to one of your superiors."

The cop stared at him, unsure of what to make of the two of them. He walked back to the other cops and conversed with them briefly. Fez fiddled with the tuner until he found a song he liked. The sun slipped behind the dark clouds and momentarily turned the landscape into a bleak tract of gray. A dark shadow blanketed the base of the mountain and moved slowly across it like a zeppelin. Then a light rain began to fall. Tag leaned over the dashboard and looked up at the obscured peak high above. Its elevation, according to the map, was just over four thousand feet. Roughly half the peak was covered over by a thick cloud.

A plainclothes detective approached his car. Once she reached his window, she leaned over and stared at them.

"Chuck says you might have some information about this case." She sniffed the air inside the cabin as if detecting an odor. Then she grinned from ear to ear. "Let me guess. You two ate at The Brookhaven Diner this morning."

"How'd you know that?" Fez asked, impressed.

"Super-duper smelling power. Okay, let me take another wild guess." She closed her eyes and inhaled again through her nose. "One of you definitely had the chocolate chip pancakes."

"Crap! That's amazing? She knows what I had for breakfast." Fez turned to the cop. "He had just the toast."

"But I had the meatloaf the time before that and it was delicious," Tag added.

"Bud makes the best meatloaf in Maine." She checked out the car's interior. "Welcome to our little slice of heaven, fellas. Of course this isn't the side of town they advertise in all the fancy travel brochures. This is the other side of the tracks." She stood and stretched, and then leaned back down. "I'm kind of busy here, as you can see. Murder investigation." She winked at them.

"Can I ask you a question, Detective?"

"Hey! I'm the one supposed to be asking all the questions around here." She laughed. "You two look like you've spent the night in a dumpster."

"My name is Dr. Robert Ogden and this is my son, Bobby. I take it that you're aware of the infectious disease conference to be held here this weekend. It's the reason we've come here."

"Then welcome to Brookhaven, Doctor." She yawned. "So what gives? I've got a murder to solve here."

"My specialty is infectious diseases and bioterrorism. After the island attack on Cooke's Island, I received a major government grant to analyze the connection between various social groups and the possible diseases they might be propagating within their community." He was making this up as he went along.

"Okay, whatever." She rolled her eyes.

"From the information I gathered on the radio this morning, this murder appears to share many similarities to some of the victims on Cooke's Island," he lied.

"What the hell are you talking about?" The detective stuck her head through the window, looking angry. "I examined the deceased's body and there was no evidence of smallpox. This was merely a drug deal gone bad. Whoever killed him was sending a violent message of retribution."

"First off, Detective, there doesn't need to be any evidence of smallpox for it to be classified as an infectious disease. Have you discerned if there were any human bite marks over the body?"

She stared at him to determine whether he was serious. "No, but we can't be sure until we get the report back from Forensics. But I suppose we can't rule it out either. Honestly, I've never seen injuries quite like it."

"Any number of virulent brain infections could have caused a person to become hyper-aggressive. I strongly suggest that you and your team protect yourself from the victim's blood. Call in a hazardous waste professional and have them disinfect everything in the vicinity with an industrial strength, anti-viral solution. Do you know the identity of the victim?"

"Yeah, he's a well-known crack addict who lived in one of the trailers at the foot of the mountain. Used to cook, too." She pointed down at the row of trailers. "Rat Town, they call it, but you didn't hear that from me."

"Could I possibly take a look at the body? I might be able to get a better handle on what kind of illness we're dealing with, if indeed it's an illness at all."

She appeared to think the matter over. "Sure, you can take a quick look, Doc, but I doubt it's what you think it is. And you have to promise not to tell anyone that I let you see it. The kid waits in the car."

"Agreed."

"Wait here," Tag ordered Fez.

"Awww!"

He followed the detective across a small lot and then high-stepped it over a set of train tracks that were used for maintenance work. He soon saw the white tarp. The detective introduced him to the other officers as a visiting forensic consultant, but no one seemed to care who he was, and they quickly went back to their jobs collecting evidence. As soon as he stood over the corpse, the woman crouched down and lifted a corner of the tarp. Drops of rain beaded up on the surface and rolled away.

Tag made a show of covering his mouth with his shirt, forgetting momentarily that he'd been vaccinated. He'd never known Ebola to be an airborne virus. Of course, all conventional knowledge about infectious diseases was now up for debate after that attack on Cooke's Island. The dead man lay sprawled on his back, his head bent at an odd angle and his arms down by his sides. His eyes were still open, his expression locked in one of consternation. His shirt and jacket had been ripped open, revealing a brutal gash in his abdomen. Intestines and internal organs lay exposed, inexplicably torn apart and shredded like ground beef. A series of red marks, which Tag theorized came from human teeth, ran up to the man's face and scalp. Seeing all he needed, he stood up and faced her.

"I've never seen injuries quite like that. Could it have been caused by an animal? A wolf or mountain lion maybe?" the detective asked.

He pointed to a bite mark on the deceased's cheek. "The impressions on his body have an elliptical pattern with definite tooth and arch marks unique to human beings."

"Jesus!" She squatted down next to the corpse and stared at the wounds.

"No. Stay back, Detective," Tag whispered, pulling her away with his arm. "The victim's blood may be infected. One hundred million particles of virus can lay waiting in just one drop."

"But why would anyone attack someone with their teeth?"

"A person's personality is obliterated by these thread viruses. The affected person becomes depersonalized and violent. Tiny spots liquefy on the surface of the brain until the higher functions are wiped out and only the primitive functions remain. This explains the psychotic dementia that occurs in the third spacing—the hyper-aggression stage, if you will." He didn't mention that this was most likely a hybrid virus.

"Jesus, you're scaring the hell out of me. And I don't scare easy."

"It's just a theory. Of course, it's way too early to say one way or another until the tests come back, but it's best to take all precautions."

"I didn't introduce myself properly, Doc. I'm Detective Renee Micheau." She held out her hand and he shook it. "So how long can one of these viruses live inside a corpse?"

"Up to three weeks in some cases. The majority of Africans who become infected with the Ebola virus contacted it from handling a corpse."

"Ebola?" She gasped. "I thought that only affected Africa?"

"Nonsense. The human anatomy on this planet has essentially been the same since the Neanderthals asserted their dominance. An Ebola plague could just as easily happen here as over there."

"Then are you saying what I think you're saying?"

"I can't be totally sure without examining the blood under an electron microscope, but the possibility of Ebola striking this town certainly exists."

"If that's even remotely possible then shouldn't we be calling in the Feds and sending in a bio-hazard team to check this out?"

Tag had been afraid this question might come up, and it was a valid one. He knew that if she called in the Feds the terrorist responsible for this attack would unleash an attack on a major city.

He stared down at the tarp-covered corpse, watching as the rain pooled up in the creases of the material. It seemed an unlikely coincidence that the terrorist had chosen Brookhaven as the next town to infect, especially considering that Hawthorne College was to host the largest infectious disease conference in the country. What were the odds? Someone well-connected in the infectious disease community must have had their hands in both spheres.

He remembered the phone call he'd received after speaking at Harvard Medical School. The call had come from inside that room. Most likely an infectious disease scientist, and a talented one at that. And what about the question asked to him by the New York Times reporter about the possibility of creating a lethal hybrid virus? Had that been a coincidence as well? Of course not. Certain events from the past were now coming back to him in bits and pieces. But not enough of them to see the bigger picture.

"You going to stare at that all day, Doc, or are you going to answer my question?" Micheau asked.

"I think you should hold off on calling the Feds for the time being, Detective. If they come barreling in here, believing there's been an outbreak of Ebola, they're likely to raze the entire town."

"Are you serious?"

"Have you seen what they did to Cooke's Island?"

A knowing look came over her face. "So what do you propose we do?"

"Bag the body and leave it in the morgue until we can assess whether it's infected or not. Right now I need to get back to my boy."

Tag turned and walked back to his car, feeling nearly sick to his stomach. It was that same feeling of dread that used to come over him whenever he was about to enter the hot lab to handle the deadliest pathogens on earth. At least in the lab it was controlled, and they had safeguards to prevent it from spreading. But now this virus seemed to have flown the coop.

Whoever attacked this man was still out there and capable of infecting others, their brain irreparably impaired by the frontal hemorrhaging. This reengineered strain targeted specific brain functions just as the smallpox virus did. And he understood implicitly that if word got out that a case of Ebola had been discovered in Brookhaven, chaos would ensue. People from all over town would begin to flee in panic and spread the disease far and wide, defeating the purpose of containment. It was similar to the Black Plague, when people from all over the countryside fled to the city for medical help, further spreading the deadly contagion.

Tag heard footsteps behind him as he walked to his car. He turned to see who it was and saw the detective pointing her Glock at him. The expression on her face was one of heightened anticipation and he could see that her hands were trembling. He glanced down at Fez and then instinctively turned toward her.

"Put your hands in the air, Mister, or I swear I'll shoot!"

"What's the problem, Detective?"

"You think I'm some dumb hick cop. I know damn well who you are. You're Colonel Winters!"

Chapter 23

Nolette drove all night despite the intense rain pounding against her windshield. The wipers arced back and forth and it took every ounce of self-restraint to stay within the speed limits. In her condition she knew it was probably not a good idea to get pulled over, especially after what she'd done in that hotel. Despite having showered and cleaned herself up, she had no doubt that traces of Bacon's blood were still on her.

She still found it hard to fathom that she'd killed James Bacon, one of the most respected journalists in the country. As much of an asshole as he could be at times, she'd never taken him for a killer. She wondered if he'd been actually forced to choose between killing her and keeping his kids alive.

She drove through the night, every muscle in her body crying out in pain. Rain splashed against the windshield in violent jags. She turned on some music to keep her mind occupied: "Every Breath You Take" by Sting. As the sun started to break over the horizon, she felt herself nodding off. A twinge in her stomach reminded her that she hadn't eaten in many hours. She pulled off the exit and ordered a cheeseburger and coffee through the drive-thru of a fast food restaurant. The light of day combined with the caffeine brought her back to life, and once back on the highway she nibbled on the burger every so often for energy.

What did Brookhaven and Cooke's Island have in common? The city of Cleveland came and passed. And why had the Feds not intervened earlier in the Cooke's Island crisis? There were too many unanswered questions to wrap her head around.

Remington Guilfoyle appeared to be the main suspect. Somehow he'd flown under everybody's radar right up until his alleged death in that plane crash. He and Colonel Winters had worked together at USAMRIID and that was the most damning piece of evidence against him. She had no doubt that Guilfoyle had faked his own death and that the tragedies that had occurred in his youth had played a crucial role in his nihilistic quests. But what was his ultimate goal? Was it merely to maim and kill? If so, why hadn't he released the smallpox virus on a heavily populated city rather than on a small island off the coast of Maine?

Cow pastures passed along the road and the closer she got to Maine the more nervous she became. Her mind drifted and she thought back to the small community she'd grown up in in Ohio and the mandatory Bible classes she and all the families were forced to attend. Children were to be seen and not heard, and discipline was harsh and administered on a regular basis. Pastor Kroger had been the spiritual leader of their small community and he'd ruled with impunity. He'd orchestrated everything that went on and decided who received punishment and who received praise. On Sundays he preached to their small congregation for over three hours at a time, often in the sweltering heat of summer.

Rumor had been spreading around that time that Kroger had taken liberty with various women in the community, although she'd never seen any evidence of that as a child. But as she grew older and her body matured, she noticed him showing more interest in her. And the more interest he showed in her the more repulsed she became by his untoward intentions. But his Sunday sermons about the second coming were riveting and utterly persuasive, and she lived in fear of burning in hell and not being able to spend eternity with Jesus in the kingdom of God.

She raced past Syracuse, making good time and not slowing down. At this rate she'd be in Brookhaven before dinner.

Kroger had called her over to his house one day. Although she hadn't wanted to go, her parents insisted she do as instructed. Her mother hadn't seemed the least bit worried about her spending time alone with a man nearly twenty-five years older than her.

Kroger saw himself as a divine prophet delivering God's message, and worthy of the fruits of his status. Her stepfather had been a sorry excuse for a man, subservient to his wife's demands, and out of weakness he ordered Nolette to pray alongside Kroger.

The pastor invited her inside, and she remembered walking past his tight-lipped wife, who was busy sewing a dress in the living room, her nervous eyes following her every step. She followed him down a long set of stairs to the paneled basement and sat down on the plaid couch. Kroger sat next to her, much closer than she'd wanted, cupping his hand over her own. Within minutes he began quoting passages from the Book of Revelation and asked her to pray with him. She already knew the New Testament well, having paid close attention during his sermons. And after service she would often go back home and reread the passages on her own. Jesus, in her childhood theology, was hardly the peace-loving Christ that others portrayed him to be.

She sped past Saratoga and in short time had crossed over into New England and then Maine.

He'd invited her to his house at least a half-dozen times after that first time, until she eventually became more comfortable in his presence. He'd broken her down and won her confidence through attrition. They spoke freely about the Second Coming and other matters, and in particular about the natural disasters that would be inflicted on mankind before Jesus came down to save the righteous. He dazzled her with his intricate knowledge of the New Testament, and in private he displayed a gentle and kind nature that ran counter to his stern role as a preacher. But when he put his arm around her and told her that God wanted them to be closer, a warning bell went off in her head. She held him at bay that last time they'd met, telling him she needed to pray first to see what God wanted her to do. This angered him greatly, she could tell, but he managed to keep calm, not wanting to jeopardize all the time he'd spent grooming her. She promised to return the following week, God willing, and do whatever he asked of her.

Off in the distance, she could see a series of mountains and she knew that Brookhaven was only a short distance away.

Flipping the visor down, she glanced briefly at her face in the mirror and wondered how she could possibly perform her job as a reporter looking like this? Who would speak to her? The terrorist who'd been tracking her every movement would recognize her the moment she arrived in town, having no doubt installed some kind of tracking software in her tablet.

Kroger had called her over to his house a week later. She prepared herself just as she had any other meeting with him. Dressed in her Sunday best, she brushed back her long black hair until it reflected Christ's glory. Then she packed the leatherbound New Testament in her handbag. Before leaving the house, she slipped into her mother's bedroom when she wasn't looking and stole all the money her stepfather had kept hidden in a shoebox. The keys to the pickup truck sat sprawled on the kitchen table. She swiped them covertly into her purse. She didn't say goodbye to her parents, instead slipping quietly out the door. The pickup truck sat in the driveway, unlocked and topped off with gas. She knew this because she'd fueled it up for him just yesterday. Learning to drive at such a very young age had been a godsend. He'd let her drive it around the compound to perform errands for Kroger and the others. She climbed inside the driver's seat, turned the ignition, and then drove off until she found the Interstate. Then she never looked back.

The sign for Brookhaven flew by as she made straight for the pass. The mountains loomed above, encircling the valley in a picturesque manner. Not the massive peaks she'd seen in Colorado and Utah, but beautiful all the same. It wouldn't be long until the snow blanketed the region and covered everything. The largest of the mountains had a chairlift that went straight to the top. She'd never skied before but had always wanted to try it. The first thing she came across upon entering the valley was an old-fashioned diner constructed out of a caboose.

She was starving and it was getting late. The half-eaten cheeseburger sat ossified in its greasy wrapper. Nothing could be done tonight and so she turned around and headed back to the diner. She bypassed an eighteen-wheeler and parked in the back before heading inside. An empty booth at the far end of the caboose beckoned her.

"What happened to the other guy?" the old waitress inquired as she passed her a menu.

"You can't win them all," Nolette replied, smiling.

"What's gotten into you gals these days? Ladies aren't supposed to fight."

"Mixed martial arts. And they pay us girls good money to do it." Nolette glanced at the menu. "I'll have the turkey dinner with all the fixings and a cup of joe."

"Turkey dinner and a cuppa joe." The waitress took back the menu. "So I take it you lost the fight?"

"It doesn't look like it, but I actually knocked him out."

"Thought you said you fought other gals?"

"Yeah, that's what I meant. Knocked the bitch out."

The old waitress eyed her suspiciously before waddling back toward the kitchen. Nolette pulled out her tablet. A text message appeared as soon as it booted up. Why couldn't this asshole give it a rest? She opened the message and read it.

Welcome to Brookhaven, Nolette: the friendliest small town in America.

Chapter 24

Micheau drove back to the police station, determined to lock Winters away before he caused any more damage. The grisly murder of that meth-head had at first glance stumped her and the other cops. She'd never seen injuries quite like the ones he'd received and had been baffled about how he could have gotten them. But with the arrival of Winters, whom she'd recognized the moment he drove up in that old car, a horrible realization set in. Brookhaven was at risk of a deadly epidemic!

She'd overheard all the talk around town about the attack on Cooke's Island, but never really considered the possibility that her cloistered little town could become a target. Although the attack occurred on Maine soil, affluent Cooke's Island seemed a thousand miles away from Brookhaven. And yet who among them hadn't speculated about an attack happening in their own town. The conversation probably took place in every community in America. The common belief among her fellow citizens was that Winters' death had provided the U.S. government with a convenient scapegoat. Hardly anyone believed that he'd acted alone, if indeed he did it. And not a one of them believed that he'd made it off that island alive.

Surprisingly, Winters hadn't put up any resistance to being arrested; he'd surrendered peacefully and had not proclaimed his innocence. The fact that he'd survived *and* made it off the island in one piece impressed her greatly. She realized that his capture could make her famous. Maybe she could even parlay the notoriety into a little money for her kids' college fund.

She'd radioed the coroner's office ahead of time and warned them to attend to the corpse as if it was a potential bio-hazard. She also ordered them not to speak to anyone about the possible cause of death, especially the press. Brookhaven was a small town and people would know immediately who had leaked the information. Winters was right about one thing; the citizens of this town would flee in panic if word got out that a person was loose in town with a deadly contagion.

The sun broke through the clouds as she drove into town. She passed through Main Street, a genteel old road filled with quaint cafes, restaurants, and gift shops. Tourists strolled up and down the sidewalk. The mayor, in his briefing two days ago to the police department, estimated that an additional three hundred people in town might be here for the infectious disease conference. Every hotel room in the vicinity had been booked for months. The only time she'd seen it this busy was during the height of the ski season, and in mid-July when the Brookhaven Lyrical Theater held their annual Shakespeare Festival.

The police station was housed in a 19th-century-era brick building in the center of town and alongside the historic Brookhaven Memorial Library with its stone sculptures and stained glass windows. She parked behind the station before ordering Winters and the kid out and guiding them up the station's steps.

"Hold on a moment, Detective," Winters said as they approached the door.

"Do as you're told, Winters. Don't make me spray you," she said, reaching for her belt.

"You're making a mistake by arresting me. I had nothing to do with that attack on Cooke's Island."

She'd been bracing for this line of reasoning.

"He's right, lady. Tag didn't have nothing to do with it."

"Every shred of evidence pointed to you as the terrorist. Do you really expect me to believe that your arrival here in town is a mere coincidence? Especially now that we have a potential case of Ebola on our hands?"

208

"It's certainly not a coincidence. Whoever attacked Cooke's Island gave me specific instructions to come to Brookhaven."

She nodded to a cop walking past her. "I don't know what your plan is, Winters, but it's going to end right here."

"Your murder victim was attacked by a person infected with the Ebola virus. Left unchecked, Detective, that virus will spread like wildfire throughout this town. If you fail to act, I guarantee you that many more people will die."

"Not if I call the FBI first. They'll have the necessary resources to contain this outbreak before it spreads."

"Don't count on it. Because I know for a fact that this particular strain of Ebola has a super fast incubation period. On top of that, we're looking at a death rate as high as ninety percent."

Winters sounded convincing, but she knew that with his medical background he could talk circles around her. She had to remain firm and not allow him to plant the seed of doubt in her mind.

"What better reason than to call the Feds?"

"The moment you call them they'll have military troops at your doorstep. And this time they won't hesitate to do to Brookhaven what they did to Cooke's Island, which is to level it to the ground."

"You're just trying to scare me!"

"Just telling you the truth, Detective."

"I rather doubt that they'd come in here and destroy our beautiful town. Not after the shit they took for leveling Cooke's Island."

"I have no doubt whatsoever they'll do it. Only this time they'll be more efficient."

"Come on, Winters, you can't expect me to just let you go on some remote chance that we have a case of Ebola in town." She felt confused and unsure about what to do, and she rarely second-guessed herself.

"You better hurry and make up your mind, Detective, because the longer you wait the more likely this contagion will spread."

She paused to think about it. "You have twenty-four hours to convince me of your innocence. Then I call in the Feds."

"My wife is one of the keynote speakers at this conference and I need to speak to her," Winters said.

"Is that the real reason you came here?" She laughed. "Because your wife believes you're guilty?"

"I just know she's being coerced by the government to say that."

"God, you have an excuse for everything," she said, nodding her head. "I'm seriously wondering about your sanity."

"I've never been more sane in my life. This terrorist wants me to save lives by enforcing a quarantine in town."

A frightening thought passed through her mind. "By saving lives are you referring to those people living *outside* the quarantine?"

Winters nodded. "But given the chance I can also help save lives inside the quarantine."

"Assuming you're right, and I'm not saying you are, then why is the government putting all the blame on you?"

"That's what I'd like to know."

She paused before asking her next question. "Did that smallpox outbreak really turn people into killers?"

He nodded.

"Zombies?" she asked as they walked into the station.

"It's more complicated than that. One moment they were killers and the next they were rational beings. Mothers begged me to help them find their kids, and then seconds later lunged at me in a murderous rage. A well-known doctor attacked a young girl and ate her, and then expressed to me deep regret about what he'd done. I've never seen anything like it in my life, Detective, and I don't want to see it happen again."

She stared at him in stunned silence.

210

He wiped his moist eyes. "Our deepest seated emotions like fear and love are stored in the amygdala region of the brain, and it was this region that was targeted by the virus. Triggering this violent behavior were radio frequencies from people's cell phones, which caused micro tumors to form in the amygdala."

"Biology was never my strong suit, Winters, so keep it simple."

"The virus that struck Cooke's Island could only have been made by a handful of people in the world. I doubt that even I could have done it. Despite all our research on viruses, we still have little understanding of what makes these mysterious organisms tick."

"But they said on TV that you're one of the foremost virus experts in the world."

"Yes, it's true. But I have no motive to commit this crimes."

She shrugged. "Maybe it's as simple as creating the perfect killing machine that would make you famous."

"How's that fame thing working for me? And what possible motive could I have for releasing a virus on the very same island where my wife and kid were vacationing? I've taken an oath to save lives, Detective, not take them. My entire career has been spent fighting for public safety and the security of this nation. Why in the world would I want to jeopardize my reputation to become a serial killer?"

"Maybe you wanted to be a martyr for some political cause. Or maybe you didn't want to be burdened by the demands of a wife and family." She unlocked the cell and ordered him inside.

Winters laughed. "Do you seriously believe that I'd poison an entire island so that I could be free from my wife and children?"

She had to admit that it sounded rather lame.

"And if I wanted to be a martyr, don't you think I had the perfect opportunity when I was handling all those lethal viruses in

211

the hot lab? And a martyr for what cause? I haven't voted in the last two elections because I despise politics and politicians."

"Timothy McVeigh despised politics too," she said, knowing that she'd crossed some line with that pronouncement. "Look, I don't know what your motive was or even if you had one, Winters. What I do know is that I'm more confused about all this than ever."

"Whoever is planning to infect this town is playing some sort of cat-and-mouse game with me for reasons I can't fathom. This person may have even worked in the hot lab with me. So I suggest that you think long and hard before you make a rash decision."

"Go grab some sack time, Winters. I need to check out a few things first before I inform the chief."

"Don't take too long, Detective. Every second counts."

"Assuming you're right about this, exactly what is it I'm looking for?"

"People with flu-like symptoms, excessive sweating, headaches, body fatigue, bruises, or bleeding cuts. If there's any evidence of that happening in significant numbers near Rat Town, you'll have your answer. The one telltale sign of an Ebola infection is swelled genitalia, although I'm not sure how you'll be able to check on that."

"Ew, gross! You want me to check out people's privates?"

"I'm just telling you one of the telltale symptoms. The disease adversely affects women's reproductive organs as well. But with men it causes their testicles to swell up like balloons."

"Oh my God, that's disgusting," she said, wrinkling her nose.

"Please hurry." He collapsed on the cot and threw his feet up. "Because I can't go on suffering these nightmares night after night."

"Get some rest," she said, suddenly feeling sorry for him.

She booked him under the alias of Robert Ogden to hide his identity. No one would question her decision. With the infectious disease conference upcoming, the mayor wanted the town to appear spotless, and if that meant temporarily locking away the homeless for a few days then so be it.

It helped that Winters looked the part. She stopped and stared at him. He hardly looked the part of a decorated American soldier. He appeared haggard and old, and with his long hair and beard he might have easily passed himself off as a homeless person. She'd watched the events on Cooke's Island at every opportunity possible, until Winters' face had practically been branded into her memory banks. CNN had been covering the event twenty-four seven, showing clips of the tragedy over and over while experts opined on the unfolding tragedy and the implications for America's future.

The kid complained loudly as she escorted him to the juvenile probation officer. His parents, he said, had died during the attack on Cooke's island, and Winters had taken him under his wing. She felt sorry for him. No kid should ever have to witness such a horrific tragedy. Without family or friends to turn to, all he had left in the world was Winters. And yet despite her sympathy for him, she had no other choice but to incarcerate him until she could assess the situation.

The kid plunked down in a seat just outside the probation officer's office. The door was closed, indicating that Julie was currently in a meeting. Micheau realized that she had no time to waste standing here and waiting for the door to open. If what Winters had said was true, and she wasn't yet convinced it was, she needed to travel down into Rat Town and search around for any signs of an infection. The prospect of an epidemic frightened the shit out of her. She'd seen those news reels from West Africa where the people lay dying in huts and on the streets. Was it possible that she was becoming paranoid? Never in her wildest dreams would she have ever imagined that Ebola would arrive on American shores—in her own town!

She approached the office secretary, who was busy typing away on her computer.

"Can you keep an eye on this kid for me, Nicky? I have something important I need to check on."

"Sure, Renée. What's his name?" the secretary asked.

"All I can get out of him is Fez. Just make sure he keeps his butt in that seat until Julie can see him."

"I've got some lollipops in my drawer. Maybe that will keep him busy."

"Handcuff him to the chair for all I care. Whatever you can do." She walked back to Fez and squatted down next to him. "You need to wait here until Julie can see you, kid. Do you understand me?"

"What's going to happen to Tag?"

"He'll be alright. A little rest will probably do him good."

"You heard him. This town's gonna blow if you don't act fast."

"Take it easy, kid. Everything's going to be alright." She ran her hand through his greasy hair.

"You have no idea what it's like, lady."

"You're right, I don't. But I can assure you that we'll not let that happen here in Brookhaven."

"Do you have a family?"

She nodded.

"I used to have one too, but Tag's all I got now. That's one dude you can trust."

"I'll take that into consideration."

"If you don't let Tag help you, then you're gonna wish you never lived, especially after you seen the terrible things that I seen."

"I'm very sorry that you had to witness all that."

"Lady, you're talking to me like I'm a retard. I seen with my own eyes people walking around with blisters and their skin peeling away from their face. The smell was the worst. Real sweet, but not in a good way. I'll never get that smell out of my nose."

"I gotta go now. Keep your butt in this seat. I'll come back and check on you in a little while."

"Where you going?"

"Rat Town. I'm not supposed to call it that."

214

"Looking to see if anyone has E-bola?"

"Yeah, something like that."

"Seven thousand people were on Cooke's when that smallpox hit. How many people you got living here?"

For some reason the kid's tone alarmed her. "About thirteen thousand citizens, give or take a few hundred."

"It'll be crazy if all them people try to get out of here at the same time."

She left the station before she had to listen to any more of this doomsday talk. As farfetched as the two of them sounded, she was starting to believe that a disaster might be possible. The skinny orphan now seemed much older and world-wary than he'd appeared at first sight.

The sun vanished behind the clouds as she drove toward the outskirts of town. She parked in the train yard, knowing that if she left it in Rat Town there was a good chance it would be vandalized and stripped of all its parts.

A light rain began to fall as she made her way down the hill and into the depths of the neighborhood. A thick grove of trees blocked out most of the sun. Under the shade of the mountain, she could see mossy trees and dreary, rain-spattered lots littered with broken-down vehicles and trash.

She'd been told many times by her parents never to venture down into this part of town. The school kids who'd hailed from this neighborhood had been labeled as losers and loners, their fingernails clotted with grease and their out-of-style clothes always dirty and wrinkled. They usually could be found smoking weed in the woods behind the school. Many of them typically dropped out early to work some menial job or because they were pregnant.

She rested her hand on her revolver, something telling that she was making a big mistake by venturing down here without any backup. But she couldn't tell anyone her real reason for coming down here without giving away her hand.

She prayed that this was all a big mistake. And if the threat was real? She had no idea what she would do then. A

215

sudden thought crossed her mind: maybe she just might need to trust Winters.

Chapter 25

Fez sat with his hands folded over his lap, smiling at the elderly secretary typing on her computer. With her hair wrapped in a bun she looked like the old librarian at his school who used to shush him over her reading glasses. The tapping of the keys was like a drum roll in his head, stirring up all his worst thoughts and fears.

He remembered all the troubled kids on the island who needed to meet with their probation officers. They took the ferry over to the mainland every month with their parents in tow, none of who were too happy to take time out of their busy work schedules. There weren't many delinquents on the island, and the ones that were in the most trouble were usually the fishermen's kids, and even those kids eventually changed their ways once they set out to sea. Most crimes were for petty offenses: stealing, drinking, smoking pot, or skipping school. What else was there to do on that small island but to get in trouble?

He remembered one kid named Jimmy Watson, who was always getting in trouble for a variety of petty crimes. Watson smoked cigarettes and drank beer almost every day. His parents didn't work or discipline him, and Jimmy took it as his God-given right to steal whatever he could. Then one day Jimmy disappeared without a trace. No one knew what happened to him until about a year later when he showed up one day, claiming to have spent the last year in a detention center for stealing a car on the mainland.

Although Fez smoked a few cigarettes every now and then and committed the usual pranks, he never drank beer or stole from the local store. Sure, he'd helped his dad cut the trap lines of thieves trying to move in on their turf. He'd even seen his dad pull out a shotgun one day and threaten the asshole pulling traps in their waters.

The typing of the computer keys filled his head with clatter. The disaster had made him older and wiser, and a lot sadder too. The secretary glanced over at him from time to time, but she mostly stayed focused on her typing. The sound of the probation officer's muffled conversation filtered in through the door and added to the static. He needed to get out of here immediately!

Blood pumped through his head. Only a small trace of that headache remained from the vaccine. His mind was racing and he felt as if he was going crazy. He couldn't sit here and do nothing, knowing that another disaster was about to happen. No, he had to get out of this police station and prove that this threat was for real.

He took off down the hallway. It took a few seconds before the secretary realized he'd taken off, and once she did, she started shouting for him to come back. He bolted down the corridor and past the front desk. Surprisingly, no one stopped him or asked where he was going. But he could hear the secretary's heels racing down the hall and her frantic voice getting louder. He punched through the door and hit the ground running. A light rain was falling. Turning the corner, he ran down the street until he slipped in with the pedestrians window-shopping along Main Street.

He took a left on Broadmoore Avenue and headed south toward the pass. High up on the hill were the decorative iron gates that fronted Hawthorne College. A group of people were holding signs and marching around in a small circle. The mountains rose up behind the college, partially covered by billowing puffs of mist. He didn't have time to walk all the way back to their motel and so he spun around and stuck out his thumb just like Tag had done.

Not a minute passed before a car heading in the opposite direction spun around and stopped in front of him. Fez ran over to the door and hopped inside. He was surprised that he'd gotten picked up so quickly. Glancing over at the woman's battered face, he wondered if he'd made a mistake by getting in her car. She looked frightening. It looked as if someone had repeatedly punched her in the head.

"Thanks," he said as he nervously buckled his seatbelt.

She didn't bother to look at him.

"You can drop me off a few miles up the road, Miss. Me and my dad are staying at the Mountain View Inn."

"I know who you are. You used to live on Cooke's Island."

Had he heard correctly?

"Where's Colonel Winters?"

"Huh?" Fez couldn't believe he'd been recognized out here in the middle of nowhere. "Lady, you got me all wrong. I'm here on vacation."

"Don't lie to me, you little shit!" She turned the wheel hard, skidding to a stop. Grabbing him by the shirt collar, she pulled his face toward her own.

"Where's Colonel Winters, and don't lie to me!"

"I'm telling you the God's honest truth."

"I didn't drive over sixteen hundred miles to deal with your lying little ass. Now you better tell me where he is or I'm going to turn you in to the cops."

"They put him in jail." He pulled away from her grip. "This cop at the crime scene recognized him."

"What crime scene?"

"Murder of some dude. They found him over the train tracks with half his guts hanging out. Looked like someone chewed through his belly."

"Jesus! Was he infected?"

"Don't know. Tag says it might have been an E-bola virus."

"Where's the epicenter of the infection?"

"Epi what?"

"Fuck! Where do they think the virus started?"

"Rat Town. It's this shitty neighborhood just below the train yard. Like a trailer park or something."

"Is that where you were heading?"

"No, I was heading back to the place where we stayed last night. I ran away from the police station before they put me in juvie." Fez turned and stared at this mysterious woman. "Who are you and why is your face all beat up like that?"

"Nolette Swain is my name and I'm a reporter for the Washington Tribune. Someone tried to kill me; that's why I look like this."

"Who? Why?"

"Because he was working for the person responsible for these attacks. It was either I kill him or he would kill me."

The sign for The Mountain View Inn appeared up ahead. She turned into the parking lot where a small group of people stood in front of a motel door, holding hands and looking as if they were praying. They got out of the car and approached the group.

"What's going on?" she asked one of the men.

"Two of our people have come down with the demon's blood," the man said. "They're inside and running a fever and acting very strange."

"Why don't you call 911 and get them some help then?" Swain said.

"We don't believe in traditional medicine," the man replied. "The Reverend's tried casting the devil out of them so it's in God's hands now."

Fez pulled his key out and opened the door to the motel room, calling for Swain to join him. Once inside, she fell back against the bed in exhaustion and began to sob. But why was she crying? She wasn't such a hard ass after all. He went over and tried to console her, placing his hand on her shoulder.

"Are you okay, Miss?"

"I just need a minute."

'Sure, take all the time you need."

"Sorry for swearing at you back there," she said. "My life's been a little crazy lately."

"Lady, you don't even know what crazy is." Fez pulled the blanket up over her shoulder. "Close your eyes and I'll wake you in an hour. Then we can figure out a way to bust Tag out of that jail before this E-bola crap starts to spread."

Chapter 26

Everything was going exactly as planned. In twenty-four hours the guests and lecturers would be arriving and he couldn't wait for the fun to begin. No sense not liking one's work.

He put on his hiking clothes, wool hat, gloves and boots, making sure to secure his thermal jacket for when the winds picked up. It would be cold at that elevation and he didn't want to get caught up there unprepared. He'd filled his backpack the previous night and set out all his gear, checking that he'd put the necessary items inside. Once he had everything in place, he drove to the base of the mountain and parked a half a mile away from the access road. Shouldering his backpack, he hiked the rest of the way until he arrived at the narrow trail that snaked up the mountain.

He began to climb, maintaining a steady pace so as not to wear himself out. The higher he climbed, the colder the temperature. About halfway up the trail his back began to ache so he stopped at a clearing and rested along a granite ledge overlooking the valley. The sun felt nice and the view so spectacular that he felt as if he was out for a picnic. Luckily, he'd seen no other hikers on the winding trail, but just in case he'd donned wraparound glasses and a thick wool cap. After a refreshing drink of water and a granola bar, he shouldered his backpack and started back up the mountain, noticing that he had climbed two-thirds of the way up.

The third half was much steeper and trickier than what preceded it and required more physical endurance. Using his walking stick, he maintained a steady pace. A few sheer cliffs presented themselves and he had to walk around them, hoisting himself up and over in order to reach the connecting trail. Nothing too treacherous, but the climb tested his conditioning. By the time he'd reached the top he was sweating profusely and completely exhausted. He realized that he needed a few minutes to recuperate.

A steady, bitter wind gusted at the top. He waited to catch his breath, needing steady hands for the task at hand. He gazed down at the trail he'd just climbed, seeing how it looped down the mountain until it reached the main road just outside the valley. If he wasn't mistaken it almost resembled a thread virus. It disappeared at intervals within the thick cover of pines. The access road a half a mile away would have been a much easier route to take, but he couldn't chance getting caught on private property and being identified. Come winter, the road would be completely snowed in and the repair crews would need to ride snowmobiles in order to reach the top.

He stared up at the cell tower that stood fifty feet away and connected Brookhaven to the outside world. Five hundred yards to the west of it stood the transmission tower supplying the town's electricity. Now the difficult work would begin. Braving the bitter winds, he walked over and grabbed the steel ladder and began to ascend. From what he'd read, this particular antenna stood five hundred feet tall, although he didn't need to climb that high in order to complete the task.

The winds blew colder the higher he climbed. His back ached and he had to stop momentarily to rest before resuming. Upon reaching his target, he climbed onto the platform and studied the configuration. Numerous antennas facilitated the various wireless carriers, signaling transmission and reception to the mobile devices within Brookhaven. He removed his pack and set it down, instantly feeling relief from the pain. His shoulders burned and he had to rotate his arms in order to loosen his joints.

Reaching inside his pack, he pulled out ten explosives, each weighing two and a half pounds apiece, and laid them on the platform. It may have been overkill, but he wanted to ensure full destruction of this cell tower once the time was right. Inside his pack he'd stored ten more for the transmission tower. The explosives were designed for quarry blasting, but would serve adequately for the task at hand. They'd been easy to acquire and allowed him to use a cast booster. An added plus was that the explosives were water resistant.

He secured them against the antenna so that they were difficult to spot from the ladder, not that he expected anyone to climb the tower in the next few days. He'd gone online and learned the repair schedule. So far every carrier serving Brookhaven had reported optimal cell service. Most repairs, he'd come to learn, had occurred after major wind or snow storms. Since the weather had been milder than expected, he anticipated no change in current operations.

Satisfied that all the cylinders were in place, he climbed back down the tower, careful to crimp the nonel tubes to metal every twenty yards. He jumped to the dirt and unwound the tubes until he could set them inside some bushes. The nonel tubes, coated with a reactive explosive compound, would send a low energy signal to the detonator. The electronic detonator would allow him precise control of the blasting, making sure that all ten of the explosives went off in millisecond increments.

Once he'd rigged the cell tower he went over to the transmission tower and rigged that up as well.

With his work on the mountain complete, he hiked back down the trail. The muscles in his thighs and calves burned from the steep grade, and he could feel it in his knees as well. The hike back down was grueling, but the satisfaction he felt lifted his spirits and swept him to the bottom. Once he'd reached the base he glanced back up at the towers.

The use of old-fashioned explosives brought him back to his adolescent years living in Oklahoma City. The destruction wrought on that federal building had been a revelation to him as a young man. It demonstrated the power of violent protest and engendered a hatred of his government only rivaled by the raid on the Davidian compound. A viral weapon would prove far superior to any explosive devices and would leave deep psychological scars on the American public. An Ebola hybrid, capable of ravishing a human body, couldn't bring down a building or cell tower. But it could bring down society and the powers that be.

He drove home, smiling the entire way. Glancing in the rearview mirror, he gazed upon the adolescent acne spread across his face, a consequence of the lethal gasses fired into his compound. Rarely did he reflect on the tragic consequences of his upbringing and the loss of his father-figure and community. Being orphaned at a young age by his biological parents had been the best thing to have happened to him. Had they not left him in the Davidians' care, he would never have developed into the person he was today.

He ran with renewed vigor into his basement. Once inside the lab, he set about configuring the electronic detonator to his cell phone. That way he'd be able to disable the cell and transmission tower with one button.

Twenty-four hours before the fireworks show. By now the test subject should have passed on his disease to others in that flea bag neighborhood. And once those Baptists became infected, he couldn't predict where the virus would spread from there; most likely near the college where they were protesting. The geographical pattern of transmission would be an interesting academic study if he were back in the rarefied world of epidemiology. Too bad he wouldn't have time to track the lethal chain of transmission. A detailed chart of the generational mutations would prove useful to the field. And yet the discovery of that half-eaten corpse lying along the train tracks indicated to him that the poorest of Brookhaven's residents would be the first to manifest the deadly symptoms.

Chapter 27

A dog barked as Micheau traipsed down the main street that bisected Rat Town. A pulsating mist hovered in the trees. In the shadow of Busby Mountain, this rundown neighborhood rarely basked in the sun. Then winter came, along with the snow, covering the valley in a brilliant white blanket.

Except for the barking dog, the neighborhood was eerily quiet. Typically there were lots of kids playing on the street or riding their bikes along the muddy trails. But today she didn't see a soul. Gripped with fear, she scolded herself for coming down here alone. And yet she had no other choice. She couldn't risk telling a fellow cop about the Ebola threat, because if she was wrong and she told someone, and there was always that chance, then she was finished as a cop.

She stopped at a filthy trailer and knocked on the door. Engine parts, abandoned cars, appliances and piles of junk lay in the front yard. The residents here had no interest in raking their lawns, caring for their homes, or tending to colorful flower beds. A gust of wind blew down the corridor, sending debris swirling through the air. Despite hearing muffled voices behind the door, no one answered. This didn't surprise her. People here had always been distrustful of the police.

A child screamed hysterically as she departed. She climbed the rotting steps of the next house, careful not put her foot through the rotting wood. She was almost afraid to touch anything for fear of contracting germs. Removing her handkerchief from her pocket, she swiped it across her mouth. A

226

pair of pit bulls across the street barked savagely and jerked against their chains. She glanced to her left. Trash lay piled to the porch ceiling. The door opened a crack and the weathered face of a woman appeared. Drugs and alcohol had taken their toll and had aged her well beyond her years. The woman opened her mouth, exposing discolored gums and rotting teeth.

"Yeah?" the woman asked, looking around as if paranoid.

"Detective Micheau," she said, holding up her badge. "Brookhaven Police."

"Why you harassing us. We ain't done nuthin' wrong."

"You're in no trouble, ma'am. There's rumors going around that some kind of virus is spreading through this part of town. You know of anyone that's come down sick?"

"We're all sick of you nosy cops."

"No, I mean physically sick. From a virus."

"Like the flu?"

Micheau shrugged vaguely.

"Heard a lot of shouting and howling last night. Sounded like someone was in a lot of pain. Figured them Statler boys was partying hard like they usually do. They can get pretty crazy when they're hitting the pipe."

"Anyone you know that's come down sick?"

"My girl's under the weather. Got herself a temperature. Didn't go to school today neither."

"Can I come in and see her?"

The woman shrugged before flicking her cigarette butt out the crack. Then she opened the door and gestured for her to come in. The smell inside overwhelmed Micheau and she fought the urge to cover her face. Raising a kid in this household bordered on child abuse, and this was probably one of the best homes in the neighborhood. The living room was filthy and cluttered with bags, plastic bottles, and fast food containers. She followed the woman into the bedroom but couldn't see anything because of the dark. The girl in the room coughed and the sound of wet hacking filled her with terror. She immediately donned the surgical mask that she'd brought with her just in case. Could the Ebola virus be

227

passed along through the air? She wished she'd asked Winters that question before she'd ventured down here, but she was at least glad she'd brought the mask.

"What's your name?" she asked the woman.

"Starleigh. And her name is Amberlyn," the woman replied. "Reason it's so dark in here is because the light hurts my baby's eyes."

"How are you taking care of her?"

"Check her temperature every hour. Bring her food and Sprite from time to time. Tylenol when she's running real high. Figure she needs to sleep this shit off, just like sleeping off a bad hangover, right." She laughed.

"How old is your daughter?"

"Tell the lady how old you are, baby girl," Starleigh said.

"Eleven?" a girl's voice said.

"How you feeling, hon?" Micheau asked.

"Not so good. My head hurts really bad."

Micheau turned to where she thought Starleigh was standing.

"Do you mind if I use my flashlight so I can take a better look at her?"

"Thought you said you was a cop, not a doctor," Starleigh said.

"I've been instructed what symptoms to look for."

"Please don't point the light at me," Amberlyn said. "It hurts my eyes."

"Okay, sweetheart, but I need to ask you a favor. Could you take your pajamas off for me," Micheau said.

"What are you, one of them lesbos?" Starleigh said brusquely.

"Ma'am, I have three kids. I'm just trying to help your daughter," Micheau said.

"Amberlyn ain't wearing no pajamas. She's too damn hot," Starleigh said. "You got any medicine to give her?"

"Not at the moment."

"Hell! Figures as much with you cops."

Micheau gulped at what she had to do next. She could get into big trouble for doing this, but she had no time to waste.

"You're not a doctor?" the girl asked.

"No, honey, I'm a police officer, but I've been told what symptoms to look for." Holding the flashlight aloft, she pointed the beam along the girl's naked body. Amberlyn crisscrossed her skinny arms over her chest and cinched her skinny legs together. She looked scared, malnourished, and dehydrated. Micheau hesitated briefly, apprehensive about conducting this visual exam. "Do you have any idea how you got sick?"

"A lot of kids at school were coughing and sneezing." The girl hacked a few times. "A couple of my friends had bloody noses. The boys were acting mean to each other and so the nurse sent a bunch of us home."

"Oh?"

Micheau turned on the flashlight and saw that the young girl had pulled a stuffed turtle up to her chin. Her damp blonde hair lay over the pillow. The girl closed her eyes as the beam of light scanned her face and exposed rib cage. Thin rivulets of blood trickled down her cheek. Micheau pointed the light at her ears and saw pinpricks of blood pooling inside the cavity and along the fine bones. Blood seeped down her nose and out the corners of her mouth. Terrified, Micheau directed the light down to her abdomen and then pelvic area, and was stunned to see a pink stain along the soiled surface of the mattress. Micheau shook her head in disgust; not even a bedsheet cover for the poor kid. Her worst suspicions confirmed, she shut the flashlight off and watched as the room pitched back into darkness.

"Okay, hon. I'm all done now," she whispered.

"Will I be okay?"

"Of course you will." She felt terrible about lying to this poor girl. "I hope you feel better, sweetheart."

"I ain't feeling too good neither, cop. Might be coming down with the crud myself," the girl's mother said. "Or it could've been the ten Captain Morgan and Cokes I had last night at Evelyn's Lounge."

"Keep taking lots of Tylenol and fluid," Micheau said, wanting to sprint out of this hell hole as fast as possible. "Goodbye, Amberlyn. I hope you feel better."

"Thanks."

"I can see myself out," Micheau said to Starleigh.

"Watch out that you don't knock any of my shit over," Starleigh said.

Clicking on the flashlight, the detective shone the beam around until she located the door and escaped out into the living room. She pressed the mask against her face and sprinted out of the house, slamming the door shut behind her. Her entire body was trembling. She had no doubt now that the little girl in that room had come down with Ebola. She could feel it. That deadly organism was alive and pulsing with life in that house, waiting to infect more people. Removing the mask from her face, she gulped in fresh air and prayed to God that she hadn't inhaled any particles into her lungs.

The pit bulls barked savagely as she staggered up the hill. A strong gust of wind blew through the trees and made an eerie groaning sound that echoed along the base of the mountain. It sounded haunted, as if the wind was telling her to leave here as soon as possible. Maybe her mind was playing tricks on her. At the end of the street she heard it again; a low, guttural undertone from deep within the mountain's belly. She glanced up the steep road leading to the train yard. Metal wheels squealed along tracks as a locomotive chugged across the yard. The engine growled and picked up speed, the rhythmic sound of its wheels beating in unison against the wood slats and providing her with a cadence.

Sweat poured down her face upon reaching the top of the hill. Two mechanics dressed in striped overalls walked past her with tools in hand. She now understood the immense crisis facing her beloved town. The Ebola virus had begun to spread and in short time would pass from child to parent until the entire neighborhood was infected. Sadly, she couldn't advise the girl's mother to take her down to the hospital for fear of it spreading to the general population. For the good of the town—no, for the good of the *nation*—Rat Town needed to be strictly quarantined. It sounded cruel and heartless, but sadly it was the best decision for the community as a whole.

Colonel Winters! She'd nearly forgotten about him wasting away in that jail cell. She needed to spring him out of there as soon as possible! Only he could advise them about what to do next.

She jumped in her car and raced back to town, turning on her lights and siren.

If word got out about this crisis, the citizens of Brookhaven would no doubt panic and attempt to flee in their vehicles. The consequences of an Ebola outbreak outside this valley would be disastrous. Assuming a ninety percent mortality rate, that equated to three hundred million deaths. Three hundred million bleeding, ravished corpses perishing from coast to bloody coast.

She sped through downtown, dodging cars, bicyclists, and pedestrians. Once she'd parked in the station's lot, she sprinted up the stairs and into the station. She shouted to the desk sergeant as she passed, telling him to bring Fez over to her. Pulling up to Winters' cell, she saw him sprawled in a fetal position on the cot, his eyes closed, seeking warmth under a flimsy jail blanket.

"Colonel Winters! Get up!"

He raised his head off the pillow and swung his feet over the mattress. His long hair stuck up in all directions and his beard lay matted down along his jawline. Rubbing the back of his neck, he stumbled over to her.

"You were right, Colonel," she whispered through the bars. "I'm sorry for ever doubting you."

He shook his head. "I was afraid of that!"

"So what do we do now?"

"For starters, you can let me out of this depressing cell."

"Certainly, Colonel," she said, treating him with a newfound respect. She slipped the key in the lock and opened the door. "The Ebola virus appears to be spreading by air. Is that common?"

"Not for Ebola, but it's not out of the realm of possibility." He ran his hand through his gnarly beard. "The CDC discovered an airborne strain of Ebola years ago in a Virginia lab, but luckily it only infected primates. That's not to say it can't happen to our own species."

"I'm scared, Colonel."

A woman entered the room. "I'm sorry, Detective, but the boy is not here."

"I thought I asked you to watch him!" she shouted. "I specifically left him in your supervision."

"He ran off before I could do anything," Kim said.

"Put an APB out for that little shit. He's about twelve-years-old with long, greasy hair and a skinny build. Tell every officer on patrol to be on the lookout for him."

"I've already done that, Renée. I'm really sorry."

"We need to find Fez immediately," Winters said.

"Look, Colonel, I know you're tight with the kid, but don't we have more important fish to fry right now?"

"You don't understand," he said. "Fez and I are the only people in town who can battle this deadly virus without coming down with the disease."

"What the hell are you talking about?"

"The two of us have been vaccinated against this strain of Ebola."

"Vaccinated?" Alarms blared in her head.

"The person who engineered this outbreak lured me to this town, and he did the same on Cooke's Island. It's the only reason I was able to survive that smallpox outbreak without becoming sick. And now he's doing it all over again in Brookhaven."

"Why would he vaccinate you?"

"It's a test of some kind. I believe we worked together years ago, handling lethal viruses in the hot lab. He really doesn't want this plague to spread—not yet anyways. He wants me to set up a quarantine just like he did on Cooke's Island."

"Then you're not really here to save this town, Colonel. If I'm hearing you right, you're only trying to prevent it from spreading outside the valley."

He stated at her with a grim resignation. "I assumed you understood that."

"Goddamn you, Winters!" She slapped his face.

A pained look settled in his eyes.

"That means we're sitting fucking ducks."

"Not quite. We can still try and stop it in its tracks."

"I want so very bad to hate your guts, Colonel, but there's no time for that. Just tell me what we need to do and I'll do it."

He put his hand on her arm. "I'm sorry it has to be like this, but whatever I tell you to do will be in the best interests of this country, not Brookhaven's. Do I make myself clear?"

"Clear as being on death row."

Chapter 28

Now that the theater company's production of Grease had run its course, the old church remained empty until the next production ramped up. He let himself in through the back door and climbed the steps to the dressing room, his garment bag slung over his shoulder. Inside the bag was a beautifully tailored navy blue seersucker blazer and matching pencil skirt. He slipped into the dressing room, stripped off his clothes, and put on the skirt and blazer. Then he stepped into the three-inch heels. Checking himself in the full-length mirror, he marveled at how lovely he looked. Conservative but lovely all the same. He applied his mascara and false eyelashes and then affixed the wig to his head. Finally, he put on his fake nails, taking his time to make sure they looked perfect. The full effect of his gender transition was stunning.

It had been quite easy to gain entrance to this disease conference. He'd filed corporation papers in Alaska and set up the firm under the name of Bonnie Haldeman. As CEO of this fabricated start-up, he'd listed Bonnie's ethnicity as Tlingit, which pretty much assured that she would be accepted into these hallowed halls. The conference itself was not exclusionary. Many graduate students had signed up as associate members. The scientists invited to attend had been asked to give brief seminars or take part in call-for-papers presentations, allowing for some discussion on their most recent findings. He'd created a superbly organized PowerPoint presentation called "Smallpox Vaccines for Biodefense" that presented a technical rehashing of some older, more accepted theories that he himself found rather pedestrian. But it would be enough to pass muster without drawing too much attention to himself or his research—Bonnie's research. He'd named the company Biodefense Constructs and the logo was that of a lion alongside a tiger, ready to merge as one cat before leaping into the future.

More than satisfied with his appearance, he slipped out of the theater and drove to the Castleton Hotel. He'd long ago booked a room under his alias upon learning that Monica Winters would be staying there. A van arrived on the hour to shuttle guests back and forth between the hotel and Hawthorne College. If luck would have it, maybe they'd catch the same bus.

She passed through the rotating doors as Bonnie and walked into the hotel lounge, skillfully balancing herself on the high heels. It had taken many hours of practice to be able to walk on them with grace. The van wouldn't be arriving for another fifteen minutes, which meant that she had some time to kill. And yet as soon as she entered the lounge, leather bag slung fashionably over her padded shoulder, she was shocked to see a familiar face sitting at the far end of the bar. Monica was sitting alone and looked so sad and lonely that she felt compelled to befriend her.

Bonnie sat down two stools away from Winters, trying not to stare at her but finding it hard not to be drawn to her horribly scarred face and hands.

"I'll have what she's having," she said to the bartender, eying the nearly finished Cape Cod in front of Winters. "Make it two."

Winters toasted her as soon as the bartender set the drinks down in front of them.

"Cheers." Bonnie reached over and touched her glass with her own. Over Winters' breast pocket was her name tag identifying her as a guest of Hawthorne College.

Monica Winters bore little resemblance to her former self. Her face and body had swelled considerably from the steroid shots and medications. Hideous scars lined her face and hands, painful reminders of her difficult ordeal on Cooke's Island. She'd obviously had some reconstructive surgery and skin grafts. That she'd survived the infection had been a miracle in itself, although her survival had more to do with whom she was married to rather than anything else.

"I see you're attending the conference this week?" Bonnie said. "Me too."

"Yes, although I'm hardly a scientist." She laughed. "Are you?"

"Oh, I'm a scientist alright. Or at least the last time I checked. I just arrived into town this morning and barely have had time to settle in." Bonnie looked at her. "I'm embarrassed to say that I don't know too many people around here. I've traveled a long way and am feeling a bit jet lagged."

"Where are you from?"

"Alaska," Bonnie said.

"My, that is a long way to come. I've never been to Alaska before, but I hear it's quite beautiful," she said, holding out her discolored hand. "Monica."

"Bonnie. It's a pleasure to meet you, Monica."

"The pleasure is all mine, Bonnie. Welcome to Maine," she said, sipping her drink. "What is it you do?"

"I own a start-up company in Alaska called 'Biodefense Constructs.' We're in the business of researching and developing an array of vaccination products that can used for various platforms."

"Hmm. Sounds interesting."

"It really is interesting and important work, but we have a long way to go before we're making a profit." Bonnie sipped her drink, happy beyond words at this fortunate encounter. "So what do you do, Monica?"

"Do you really not know who I am?" She laughed.

"I'm sorry, but I don't. I spend a lot of time either buried in my lab or stuck in my office doing paperwork."

Monica paused to let her words sink in. "My husband was Colonel Winters."

236

Bonnie put her hands to her mouth. "Oh my God! I'm so sorry. I didn't ..."

"It's okay."

"I recognize you now. From all the news reports. Yes, you really are Colonel Winters' wife. They say he died in that attack."

Monica placed her drink on the bar. "I've got a great idea, Bonnie. Why don't we head to that cocktail reception together. The shuttle leaves in five minutes and I could really use the company. What do you say?"

"I'd be honored to ride to that conference with you."

"And don't worry, I won't hold you back if you need to speak with your fellow scientists." Monica slid her Cape Cod over to Bonnie's side of the bar. "I've already had my one drink minimum."

"One is plenty for me too," Bonnie said, pushing her own glass away. "I shouldn't even be drinking. Not only do I not like the taste of alcohol, but alcoholism runs in my family."

"My mother was a closeted drinker and got nasty when she drank. And my grandfather died from cirrhosis."

"At least we have that in common, as depressing as it is," Bonnie said, laughing.

"We can buy each other cranberry juice all weekend and pretend we're big drinkers."

"Deal. And to think I was so worried about those cocktail reception that I came here to acclimate myself to the taste of it."

This had been far easier than expected. He thought of all those hours he'd spent with Winters and her daughter on Cooke's Island, tending to their illnesses and cleaning off their pockmarked and blistered skin. That disguise had worked like a charm. Maybe it was his acting skills that sold it. Or maybe it had more to do with the incredible costume and makeup job. Despite his chameleon-like talents, he was amazed that she hadn't yet called him out.

The shuttle bus pulled up in front of the hotel and Bonnie walked with Monica through the front door of the hotel, becoming more comfortable in the high heels the more she walked in them.

Four dour-looking scientists sat in the front two seats. Monica headed toward the rear of the van and Bonnie followed her until they had settled in the backseat.

"Do you mind if I ask you a personal question, Monica?" Bonnie waited for her approval. "Are you still having medical procedures done?"

"I'll always have these scars. Sure, they may lessen with time, and the doctors have done wonders to keep me alive, but I finally decided not to have anymore."

"Why?"

"Because these scars are a reminder of that attack. I don't want anyone I come in contact with to forget the horrors that happened out there."

"You had a daughter. What ever happened to her?"

"I haven't spoken to Taylor in months."

"Why not?"

"I suppose you can say we had a disagreement."

"About what?" Bonnie noticed her discomfort at this line of questioning. "God, I'm so nosy sometimes. Please stop me if I'm getting too personal."

Monica stared out the window. "No, your curiosity is perfectly understandable. But I'm not quite ready to talk about it just yet."

"Sure, Monica, I understand," Bonnie said, resting her blood-red nails over the top of her hand. "I'm here for you if you ever want to talk."

"Thanks." Monica smiled. "Can I ask you a favor?"

"Of course." She laughed convincingly, as if that was the least she could do.

"Would you mind staying with me while we mingle at the cocktail reception? I'm not familiar with all that technical mumbo jumbo, despite having lived with my husband for all those years."

Bonnie grabbed her hand and squeezed, feeling the abrasive scar tissue rubbing against her fingers. "Of course I will. There'll be plenty of time for all that technical talk once I present my paper. Tonight the two of us will have fun."

The van cruised through town. Couples strolled along the sidewalk, hand in hand, window shopping as they walked past art galleries, restaurants, and antique stores. For a brief moment he thought he could almost live here in Brookhaven and start a whole new life. The notion of him living here seemed suddenly seemed absurd and he chuckled at the idea. Soon this town would go the way of Cooke's Island. After creating these brilliant killing organisms, he knew he couldn't go back to the farm.

The van cruised up Main Street leading to Hawthorne College. The iron rod gates appeared up ahead, inviting and yet at the same time exclusionary. Across the street, a small cadre of protesters stood, holding signs and chanting.

As much as he despised these Bible thumpers, their prophetic message melded in many ways with his own beliefs. An apocalypse was to come. But there were differences in their theology. For instance, he didn't believe that viruses acted maliciously or were in any way immoral. In fact, he believed quite the opposite: that they were the Creator's tools of the trade. The virus simply followed its own internal compass, its own software, which God in his divine wisdom had designed. The AIDs virus, contrary to what many uninformed people believed, did not target gay men. No, it blindly obeyed the universal rules of blood pathogen transmission. The truth was that the majority of AIDs victims were promiscuous truck drivers delivering goods across the African continent, and thus establishing the lethal chain of transmission.

The van passed through the gates before stopping at Lowry Hall. An official greeter awaited them as they got off the van. The man was tall, patrician, and wore a spotted red bow-tie. It took him a few seconds to realize that this was no ordinary greeter.

"Welcome to Hawthorne College. I'm Dr. Wallace McCallister," he said, extending his long graceful hand. "As president of this college, I speak for both the faculty and staff in extending my warmest thanks for attending our conference."

He laughed as he shook the man's hand. All these Ivy League know-it-alls would soon regret hosting this event. He couldn't wait to see the fear in their eyes when confronted with the horrors of the Ebola virus in their own backyard.

Chapter 29

The mayor of Brookhaven, a successful real estate broker, lived in an old Victorian in a historic part of town. A mountain-fed brook bubbled through the back of his lot, which was shaded by three massive weeping willows. It gurgled and swooned as it made its way through town. A well-dressed man wearing horn-rimmed glasses emerged from the front door as they pulled up to the curb. Following Micheau's lead, Tag got out of the car and walked up to the porch to meet him.

"This better be important, Renée," the mayor said, glancing at his watch. "I'm scheduled to give the opening speech at the disease conference in one hour."

"Is there someplace we can talk in private, Mayor?" Micheau asked.

The mayor eyed Tag up and down as if repulsed by this homeless man showing up at his house. "Who's this?"

"We can talk about it once we're inside," Micheau said.

"Okay, but make it quick," the mayor said, holding the door open for them.

They followed him into a parlor outfitted with antique furniture and some built-in bookshelves constructed out of mahogany. It reminded Tag of his own study back in Maryland. He fingered the rich beaded leather along the armchair and marveled at the handcrafted wood chess table. Closing the double doors behind him, the mayor gestured for them to sit as he eyed him nervously. Tag collapsed in the chair, sinking in its leather cocoon and feeling as if he could sleep for days in its comforting fold.

"Okay, Renée, you're on the clock," the mayor said, tapping his watch.

"Mark, we have a serious problem. There's been a virus unleashed in our town."

He paused for a moment before laughing in astonishment. "What am I being punked? I have no time for such childish pranks."

"Mayor, I'd like to introduce you to Colonel Winters."

The mayor sat up, unable to speak, and turned to him with a look of barely concealed astonishment.

"Colonel Winters has informed me that the murder victim we discovered in the lower part of town may have been infected with the Ebola virus," Micheau said.

"Ebola virus?" He glanced between them. "Is this some kind of joke, Renée, showing up here with this poor homeless fellow by your side?"

"If only it was, Mayor."

"What the hell is going on here?" A stricken look came over his face. "Ebola doesn't happen in this country."

"At first I didn't believe it myself. So I went down into Rat Town—sorry, Mayor, I know you find that name distasteful—and I took a look around."

"Those folks are always sick with one thing or another. If it's not from withdrawal symptoms then its something else," he said dismissively. "And we both know that there's a serious meth problem down there."

"This virus is spreading, I confirmed it myself. According to Colonel Winters' timeline, we have a very short window in which to act. I'm afraid if we wait any longer we'll have a full-fledged crisis on our hands."

The mayor stood and pointed his finger at Tag, his face red with rage. "You fucking bastard! You destroyed Cooke's Island and now you've come here to ruin us? Besides, you're supposed to be dead."

"Obviously, Mayor, I'm not dead."

"I'm calling the police right now." He took out his cell phone.

"Damnit, Mark, I am the police," Micheau said, grabbing the phone out of his hand.

Tag stood out of his chair. "As to your accusations, Mayor, I didn't commit either of these crimes. The person responsible for these attacks is here in town as we speak and most likely attending the infectious disease conference."

"This is outrageous, Renée. I'll have them drag the two of you to prison and throw away the key."

"Shut up and listen, Mark!" Micheau shouted, placing her face up against his. "We're talking about a deadly epidemic here, where thousands of people could become infected. If you fuck around like an asshole politician then many more people are going to die. Now sit the fuck down and listen to the man."

The mayor fell back into his seat in resignation. Tag was impressed with Micheau's assertiveness.

"Okay, Renée, assuming that what you say is true, then shouldn't we call in the Feds?" the mayor said, his tone now subdued.

Tag leaned forward. "With all due respect, Mayor, I wouldn't do that if I were you."

"Give me one good reason why I shouldn't," the mayor said, snatching his phone out of Micheau's hand.

"Because if you call in the Feds then you can say goodbye to this nation as we know it. The terrorist responsible for this attack has promised to release a viral bomb in every major city if we call in the Feds prematurely. In less than a month ninety percent of the population will vanish, including most of your own citizens."

The blood drained from the mayor's face. "So we're supposed to sit here and do nothing?"

"I didn't say we do nothing. I'm just explaining the severity of the situation. There's something else. If you call in the Feds right now they will parade in here and proceed to bomb this valley into submission. Do you really think they're going to sit around until this virus crashes and burns? Hell no. If you don't believe me, Mayor, then take a look at what they did to Cooke's Island."

The mayor shook his head in confusion.

"They burned everything to the ground in order to disinfect that island, and I watched them do it," Tag said.

"How did you manage that?" the mayor asked, obviously confused by this admission. "I watched all those news reports like everyone else. Those military boats circled that island, preventing anyone from escaping."

"Mark, does it really matter now how he escaped? Colonel Winters is alive and here now to help us," Micheau said.

"This guy could be an imposter for all I know."

"I've checked him out and he's the real deal."

"Well, it actually does matter to me how he escaped. I want to know how the great Colonel Winters did it." He turned to Tag. "Go on then, Colonel, convince me."

"We grabbed an old fisherman's raft and managed to slip past the naval quarantine at night. We paddled until we arrived at this tiny island a few miles away. A hermit lived on it and he kept rabbits and caught fish, which we ate along with all the seaweed we harvested. For the next two and half months I watched as the military bombed the shit out of that island. Does that answer your question?"

"Mark, the Feds don't give two shits about our town, and they especially won't care after they find out that Ebola has been spreading amongst its citizens," Micheau said.

"But we can't just sit around and twiddle our thumbs while people fall sick," the mayor said.

"Whoever released this virus is highly skilled at what he does and has the means to experiment in a controlled environment. What he's created is a genetically engineered, hybrid weapon that has dual functions. It combines the symptoms of Ebola with a hyper-aggressive component that is intended to disseminate the pathogen and strike fear in the American public," Tag said.

"He's right, Mark. That murder victim was mutilated like nothing I've ever seen before," Micheau said. "Dare I say, eaten."

"Eaten?" The mayor's face contorted into one of shock. "This is just too unbelievable for me to believe. I'm not going to make any rash decisions without having every option available to me."

"I know this terrorist, Mayor. I know his mindset and I know how he operates," Tag said. "I'm fairly certain that he worked with me at the USAMRIID research facility. If he's who I think he is, the man's a brilliant scientist who's perfected a way to splice viruses and then turn them into monstrous hybrids."

"As if this Ebola virus isn't monstrous enough?" the mayor said.

"Not compared to the Frankenstein organism he's created. He's figured out how to speed up a virus's incubation period so the symptoms manifest much earlier. As we speak, wasting valuable time, more and more people are becoming infected and creating new mutations. It's called amplification, and the amplification of this particular epidemic is scary as hell. Which means that every second we sit here and waste time only increases the likelihood that this disease will spread out of Rat Town and into Brookhaven proper."

The mayor chewed his thumbnail. "We in Brookhaven do not refer to that neighborhood as 'Rat Town,' Colonel."

"Oh, fuck all that political correctness, Mark. Are you going to take Colonel Winters' advice or do I have to make a hard decision?" Micheau asked, hand on her holster.

He thought about it for a few seconds. "Okay, Winters, I'm all ears. What do you propose we do?"

"I've studied a map of Brookhaven and noticed that there's only two ways in and out: the northern and southern passes. Call the police chief and apprise him of the situation and demand that he divulge this information to no one. We'll need to station officers along the pass and have them set up blockades. No one comes or goes, and there's no exceptions," Tag said.

"I'll call him immediately," the mayor groaned.

"What about the rest of Brookhaven?" Micheau asked.

"Call in every officer on the force and order half of them to set up an armed perimeter around Rat Town. Maybe, if we're lucky, we can keep this disease isolated in that one neighborhood."

"I'm almost afraid to ask the next question, Colonel, but I'm going to ask it anyways," the mayor said. "What happens to the people who try and break the quarantine?"

Tag paused for a moment. "Shoot them."

"Shoot-to-kill?" Micheau said, surprised by his harsh response. "Isn't there any other way we can enforce this policy without resorting to killing people?"

"No. If I had followed this policy early on during the attack on Cooke's Island we could have saved a lot more lives. It's efficient and it acts as a warning to others trying to break through. More importantly, it keeps people alive."

"Damn," the mayor said, sighing.

"Many of the victims will be bloodied and discombobulated, greatly increasing the chances that the disease will spread. This particular virus thrives in the human bloodstream. Contact the local hospital and round up as much anti-viral disinfectant solution as you can. Every corpse needs to be treated as an extreme biohazard, which means utilizing bio-suits if you have them."

"I can't believe this is happening in our town," the mayor said, turning to Micheau. "Renée, contact the chief and fill him in on this plan. If he has any qualms, have him call me. If we're going to do this right, it makes sense to put Colonel Winters in charge of the operation."

"Yes, sir," Micheau said. "You're making the right decision, Mark."

"I pray to God that I am." He turned to Tag. "Colonel Winters, I'm not sure what your role in all of this is, but as the mayor of Brookhaven we're entrusting you with our lives."

"I wish I could say something to make you feel better, Mayor, but words mean nothing now. Only action can save this town."

"Get to work then. Contact me if you come across any unforeseen issues," the mayor said. "Godspeed to the both of you."

"Where do we go from here, Colonel?" Micheau asked once they were back inside her car.

"Do you know how to get to The Mountain View Inn?"

"Of course I know how to get that dump."

"I need find the kid before we get started."

"Do we really have time for that?"

"We'll make time. You can make all your calls while we drive over."

He thought about Fez as the landscape flew past, hoping desperately that the kid had returned to the motel as planned. The idea of reliving this nightmare filled him with dread. Trapped in another situation that offered little hope, he steeled himself to making the hard decisions that came with being a leader. People would be sacrificed for the good of the whole. Many would suffer and witness unthinkable savagery and suffering. For the sake of his country and his fellow countrymen, he was once again prepared to put his life on the line to save the nation. But he needed his brave little sidekick with him before he got started.

Micheau's phone rang and she answered it. She turned and stared at him, a look of concern over her face. She mostly listened, nodding her head every so often. Then she hung up.

"Everything okay?" he asked her.

"I'm not sure," she said, stashing her phone away.

Chapter 30

The constant banging and shrill screams coming from the adjacent room made it sound like the people inside were trying to break down the wall. Then a gut-wrenching scream went up. It sounded like someone was in terrible pain. She wiped the tears out of her eyes and glanced up at the kid, who was now sitting on the bed next to her and fiddling with something in his hand. It took her a second to realize that he was channel surfing. He finally settled on a cartoon show and turned up the volume. In it a red robot squared off against what looked to be a mythical winged beast.

She wanted to rest up before she went over to Hawthorne College and checked on that disease conference. But there was no way she was getting any sleep with such a racket going on next door. Raising her head off the pillow, she searched around until she settled on the stained yellow curtains hanging from a twisted rod. The jaundiced water damage along the ceiling resembled the map of China, and the sad shag carpet along the floor looked as if it had been installed in the seventies.

Another loud cry went up followed by a loud pounding. Nolette picked up the phone and called down to the front office to complain, but no one picked up. The dividing wall suddenly shook as if an earthquake had struck. She jumped off the bed angrily and told Fez to wait inside while she went to check on the situation.

Outside the room, a tall, haggard man wearing a cowboy hat stood talking to a smaller man with a wide girth and a bandaged arm. The tall man looked familiar, but she couldn't quite place him in her exhausted state. He peered over his counterpart's shoulder and stared at her with a look of disapproval. She approached them, not in the least bit afraid after her epic struggle with Bacon. The nearer she got to them the more familiar the taller man appeared, particularly when she read the words on the side of the yellow bus parked out front. Reverend Grout!

"Can I help you?" Grout asked in a low raspy voice.

"Is this your room?"

"It's one of ours." He lowered his brow. "What's it to you?"

"What's it to me?" She laughed at the absurdity of this statement as the occupant inside howled. "I was trying to take a nap in my room, but it sounds like someone is being tortured in there. Maybe I should call the cops."

"No cops," the smaller man said. "One of our church members is sick in there and his wife has disappeared."

She stared up at Grout; just the sight of him made her sick. His congregation of religious whack jobs had protested everywhere in the nation, spreading their vile message of hate at military funerals and memorial services for murdered children. Now he was here to protest this disease conference. She remembered seeing him a few days ago on the Portland waterfront. As much as she despised the group's antics, the First Amendment protected them just as much as it protected her own right to free speech. She felt compelled to tell him how much she loathed his beliefs and practices, but what good would it do? He must have heard such complaints at least a million times by now, which only calcified his hatred for those who disagreed with him. Nothing she might say or do would ever change his mind, and whatever statement of protest she might make would only serve to gratify her own ego.

Grout took in his surroundings. "Something ain't right in this town, lady, I can just feel it. The devil's come to Brookhaven."

"What symptoms does he have?" Nolette asked.

"Come out covered in blood," the smaller man said. "I went in there and tried to calm him down, but the son-of-a-bitch nicked me." He lifted his bandaged hand to show her.

"Looks like your friend needs medical help," she said.

"Help for what, lady? Ain't no medicine can cure that ailment except repenting." Grout laughed. "Besides, we don't believe in all that medical bullshit. No, I'll leave that for the queers and niggers."

Nolette was about to let him have it when she heard footsteps coming up behind her. She turned and saw the kid standing there; she didn't want him to hear this racist bastard.

"My folks taught me to never use bad words like that, Mister, and they believed in God just like you."

"Then your parents don't know God like I do," Grout said.

"I read where Jesus taught people to love others, not hate them," the kid said.

"That's why they call it Judgment Day, you little urchin. Without judgment anything goes in this world, and sinners will sin without recourse. When that happens, good becomes indistinguishable from evil, and I don't want to live in no world where Satan's running things."

"So God made you judge and jury?" Fez asked.

"Boy, you're testing my patience. Your parents obviously didn't teach you to respect your elders."

"Respect's got to be earned." He walked up to the pastor. "And you haven't earned that right."

"You're going to burn in hell with the kikes and queers, kid." Grout smiled.

"Guess I'll take my chances then," Fez said. "By the way, it's not the devil that got into your friend. He's got an Ebola."

The man inside the room began to pound his fists against the door.

"Ebola? You're out of your mind. God put that on the earth to smite all them niggers in Africa just like he gave AIDs to the faggots and queers."

"It has nothing to do with God, you asshole," Nolette said, putting her hand on the kid's shoulder. "A virus does not judge or have feelings; it only seeks a host to reproduce."

"Your friend's a dead man," Fez said. He turned to the smaller man and stared at his injured hand. "You say he cut you?"

"Yeah, he done scratched me good. We had to tie him to the bed frame, kicking and screaming, just to keep him from hurting himself," the smaller man said. "He was banging his head against the wall and acting all crazy and stuff. Must have loosed himself free after his ole lady split."

"That means you got the virus from him." Fez stepped back from the man and turned to Groat. "Your friend here is going to die."

The smaller man looked up at Groat with a frightened look.

"How do you know this, boy? You working for Satan?"

"I survived that attack on Cooke's Island when most everyone else died, including my own parents. Mister, I seen the devil up close and personal, and there's no way I'm working for that dude."

"I don't want to die," the smaller man said. "Can I take a pill that will make me better?"

"Shut up and be a man, Dale," the pastor said.

"Maybe I need to go to the emergency room, Reverend," he said.

"You ain't going to no emergency room, Dale. Hospitals are for the heathen."

"Your only hope is to lock yourself in your room and pray to God that you beat this virus," Nolette said. "Then pray to God that He forgives you for all the hate you've spread."

"What's going to happen to me?" the man asked.

"Do you really want to know?"

The man gulped and looked over at Nolette for reassurance

"Your chance at survival is about ten percent," Nolette said. "Eventually you will bleed out of every orifice on your body before your stomach pours out of your asshole."

"Jesus, may God have mercy on me," the man wept.

The pounding from the room continued to get louder. Nolette wondered how a person could endure such prolonged aggression without tiring or hurting themselves. It sounded like he was peeling away the drywall in his attempt to escape his confines. She went over to the door and listened to the savage grunts coming from inside. Had he lost all of his humanity, reduced to a mere killing and infecting machine?

Two right-angle brackets had been nailed from the door to the frame to keep him from escaping. Every window had iron grates over the glass.

A loud crack went up and Nolette heard the kid shouting. She sprinted back inside their room and saw that the man had punched his way through the wall, opening a hole big enough to stick his head through. His scalp was drenched in blood, dust, and splinters. Elongated strips of his skin dangled over his forehead, and a tar-like sludge oozed out of his ears and nose. He glared at her and howled, baring his teeth.

The two men ran inside the room and stood in shock as their friend continued to tear away pieces of drywall and push through the hole. Spatters of blood flew up against the wall and along the floral-patterned blanket. Nolette backed away until she was standing against the far wall, not wanting to get splashed with the man's infected blood. He chewed off a triangle of plaster and spit it onto the shag carpet.

"Satan, release yourself from this man's soul!" Groat shouted as he put his hand over the man's head.

"It's too late for that," Fez shouted. "Your friend's too far gone for help."

"It's never too late," Groat said.

Nolette ran over to the bed and grabbed her bag. Fez pulled her shirt, trying to keep her a safe distance from the crazed man. Droplets of blood flew off his hair and splattered around the

252

room. She knew that one small drop posed the risk of infection. Once she was certain that she had all of her belongings, including her bag, she grabbed Fez's hand and ran out into the parking lot.

"They need to kill him or he'll spread the virus," Fez pleaded.

"Forget them. We need to get the hell out of here."

"We've still got time to do it if they can't."

"No, we need to save our own lives and get out of here."

The pounding and ripping suddenly stopped. Nolette glanced back inside the room and saw the infected man leaning over one of the joists and weeping hysterically. This emotional outburst startled her as she'd believed that his cognitive functioning had been reduced to a primitive state.

"I don't want to kill, Reverend. I'm a good man," the man cried out. "I want to live and rejoice in the Lord."

"Relax, Billy. No harm will come to you while I'm praying with you. I can just feel the devil loosening his grip on your soul," Grout said. "I'm going to cast the beast out of you once and for all, and set you free in the name of Jesus!"

"Thank you so much, Reverend. I'm not worthy of your blessings."

The kid ran over and grabbed Grout's arm. "It's a trick, Mister. He's only acting this way so he can infect someone else."

"Get off me, you little parasite," Grout said, shoving the kid hard to the floor.

Nolette dragged Fez out of the room despite his protests. She looked back one last time and saw Grout with his hand on the head of the infected man. He stopped praying and glanced in her direction.

"The good Lord will watch over and protect us. If God chooses to take us then so be it. Now go on and leave us be."

They sprinted out into the parking lot and into the rental car. Then she did a U-turn and sped toward the mountain pass. It took the kid a few seconds to realize that they were heading out of Brookhaven instead of into the center.

"This is not the way into town," he protested. "You got to turn around and go the other way, lady."

"Relax, kid, I know what I'm doing."

She could see the pass up ahead. The highway sign indicated that she had one mile to go before they made it safely out of town. Her hands were trembling as she held the steering wheel; she'd never seen anything so horrific in her life. It made no sense to stay in this town and risk catching Ebola—or whatever hybrid strain this terrorist had hatched. She and the kid could camp out near the base, just outside of town, and safely report on any developments that occurred. She already had enough information to start writing part one of her story, thanks to all the information she'd gathered during her trip to Oklahoma.

"Turn around!" Fez shouted, pulling her arm from the wheel. "We can't leave Tag behind."

"Colonel Winters is perfectly capable of taking care of himself." She saw a police car parked in the middle of the road.

"Me and Tag are a team. He needs me and I need him!" The kid grabbed the steering wheel and she struggled to take control back.

"Get your hand off the wheel."

"Then stop this car or I swear I'll turn it."

"You better not."

"Oh yes I will."

"Sorry, but I'm not stopping until we drive out of this town."

The kid jerked the wheel hard. She braked and the car decelerated, careening into a tailspin. She struggled to keep it under control. The car swerved as the two of them fought for control. She stomped on the brake and the wheels caught on the pavement. The car suddenly flipped and rolled toward the shoulder. Nolette felt something strike her in the face. It took her a second to realize that her airbags had deployed. The car flipped upside down and slid until it came to a halt. Punching the airbag out of her face, she dangled upside down in her seat, suspended by only the belt strapped across her shoulder.

Nolette struggled to extricate herself from the belt. The thought of burning to death inside this car terrified her, and she writhed in vain to free herself.

"Take it easy, lady. You're only making it worse by moving around like that," the kid said, crawling in through the shattered passenger window.

"Hurry up and get me out of there."

"Just be quiet, lady, and hold still."

"How did you get out of here so fast?"

"There's a lot of things I'm good at."

"You stupid brat! You almost got us killed back there."

"That was your fault, lady. If you had just listened to me we would have been fine." He struggled to free the belt but it wouldn't budge. "I was trying to tell you that there's no way out of this town. The cops have already starting quarantining Brookhaven."

"Hurry up and unbuckle me before this piece of shit blows!" She smelled fuel.

"This buckle's jammed. Must have gotten lodged during the crash." He crawled back out and returned moments later holding a jagged piece of glass. Using the sharp edge, he began to saw through the polyester belt.

"Hurry!" she shouted as smoke filled her nostrils.

"I'm cutting it as fast as I can."

The belt finally split apart, causing Nolette to fall headfirst onto the roof. Her head and shoulder throbbed from the collision. Fez gripped her shirt and dragged her out of the open window. Fragments of glass scraped against her forearms and back and embedded in her skin. She clutched her bag to her chest, refusing to let it go. A sharp pain shot through her left knee as she stood, and her ribcage throbbed from the impact of the air bag. Leaning on Fez, she hobbled over toward the police car for assistance. But instead of running out to help them, the cop pointed his rifle over the hood and shouted for them to stop.

Blood dripped down Nolette's forehead and into her eyes. *What was this cop doing?* Fez reached around her waist and tried to spin her around, but she resisted his help. Every breath she took caused her to wince in pain.

"Don't come any closer. I'm under strict orders to shoot anyone who refuses to submit."

"What is this, a fucking police state?" Nolette shouted. "We're American citizens, pal. We have the right to come and go as we please."

"You're wasting time, lady," Fez muttered.

"Turn around and walk away. You can leave when this all passes."

"Can't you see that I'm injured? How about calling me an ambulance."

"He doesn't give a shit about you," Fez said. "He's afraid we have Ebola."

"Ebola? What is he, nuts?"

"That's why they set up the quarantine. To keep any of the infected people from leaving."

She turned toward the cop and shouted, "We're clean, I swear. We don't have Ebola."

"I don't care if you're fit as a fiddle, lady. You need to turn your ass around and walk back to town. I'll give you to the count of three to get moving."

"Then what?"

"Then I start shooting."

Before she had time to process the cop's words, a loud explosion went up behind her. She turned and saw flames shooting out of Bacon's rental car. Plumes of black smoke rose up and drifter toward the mountains. Two smaller explosions went off in rapid succession, sending car parts raining down over the pavement.

"One ..."

"Turn around and walk or I'm taking off without you," Fez said.

"That stupid son-of-a-bitch!" she screamed.

"Two ..."

"He's only doing what he's been ordered to do," Fez said, spinning her around and pushing her in the opposite direction.

"What the hell are you doing?"

"If you had listened to me in the first place we wouldn't be in this situation."

"Don't you blame me for this mess. You were the one who caused us to crash," she said, limping along.

"You can thank me later, lady. Because he would have shot us if I hadn't dragged you out of there."

"I'm not thanking you for shit. Just shut up and keep moving," she said, vowing to document all this in her story.

Nolette looked back one last time at the fiery blaze. She had a bad feeling that things would only get worse from here. Her knee ached and her ribs hurt with every breath. She knew that she had to get this all down and send it to her editor before something else bad happened. And yet the real story hadn't even begun yet. Whether she liked it or not, she'd be here to witness it all to the bitter end.

Chapter 31

He waited patiently as Monica signed the registry book for the guests attending this conference. Her hands were raw and scarred, and he could tell that even holding a pen was an extremely difficult task. After signing in as Bonnie Halderman, he picked up his welcome kit along with the ornate bag embroidered with the logo of Hawthorne College on it.

Eyes turned in their direction as they walked into the reception hall, and for a brief moment he thought he'd been outed as an imposter. But then he realized that they were staring at Monica and not him, and he realized that no one had any idea who he was or that he was a man dressed in women's apparel.

He studied Monica; she seemed to grow in stature amongst these distinguished scientists, proudly wearing her disfigurement as a badge of honor. He had to admire the woman's resilience as well as her refusal to back down in the face of public scrutiny. Considering the hell he'd put her through, he thought her most deserving of celebrity status. Much more so than these cowardly academics now admiring her, especially after how they'd profited from her pain and suffering. As guest speaker of this conference, she had attained an almost hallowed status within these ivy halls.

The low profile she'd kept since the Cooke's Island event had no doubt added to her allure. She'd not been seen by anyone since the disaster, and the few times that she'd been interviewed on TV she'd appeared with thick bandages wrapped around her face so as to conceal the true extent of her injuries. Stunningly beautiful before the attack, the reconstructive surgeries performed on her fine-boned face had transformed her in an exotic, twisted sort of way. All that natural beauty had been wiped out in less than a week and replaced with a gothic, almost vampish look that was a constant reminder of her struggles. She'd survived a horrific, hybrid biological attack, one of the very few persons on earth to do so, and now she represented the living embodiment of that island disaster. He couldn't help but have a healthy dose of respect for her, despite his own culpability in her tragic transformation.

As they reached their assigned table—their names were handwritten on placards folded over their plates—he had to comport himself in a manner bespeaking a lady, and so he resisted the temptation to pull out Monica's chair for her as she sat. He greeted the other guests at the table before tucking his dress underneath his legs and sitting down. From across the room, he saw a distinguished-looking gentleman waving to them and making a bee-line for their table. It took him a few seconds to realize who this man was.

"Monica! How wonderful it is to see you again," the silver-haired gentleman said, cupping her slender hand in his own. "How long has it been?"

"Before the attack, I believe. We attended that cocktail party you hosted in Cambridge, just after Tag announced his retirement from the Institute."

"Ah, yes, I remember that party. Again, Monica, you have my sincere condolences about Taggert. How could anyone have predicted his involvement in that affair. I'm still not thoroughly convinced of his guilt."

"For months after the incident I too tried to convince myself that he was merely an innocent bystander in all this. But then I just couldn't ignore the overwhelming evidence mounted against him. He had all us all fooled," Monica said.

Simon shook his head. "And to think I offered him our most prestigious professorship." He shook his head in regret. "But that's in the past now. That's why we're gathered here; to prevent another tragedy like that from happening. We must learn from our mistakes and fully prepare in the event that another biological attack threatens our way of life. Because it could very well happen again in the hands of another lunatic hell bent on imposing his will."

"I couldn't agree with you more. It's the main reason we're gathered here, right?"

He smiled and held her hand. "You look so much healthier than the last time I saw you. Even the swelling has gone down some."

"I'll never look as good as I used to. But thanks to the miracles of modern medicine I'm not a hideous monster, either."

"You could never be a monster, Monica. Not in my eyes. You have a beautiful soul," he whispered. "How's Taylor?"

"Still not talking to me." She shrugged. "I'd love to reestablish a relationship with her at some point. But on the other hand, I don't want to stick my head in the sand and deny that Tag had nothing to do with that attack. There's too many facts to ignore. Someday, I pray, she'll see the light."

"It must be hard on her to accept the truth. After all, it is her father."

"Yes, she's not looking very hard for the truth. She's young, Simon. It'll take time for it all to sink in, but she'll eventually come to the same conclusion that I did."

He glanced at his watch. "I must be going now, Monica. They're calling for me up on the podium to introduce you."

Simon darted between the tables, occasionally stopping to shake peoples' hands and chat for a brief moment before moving behind the lectern.

"Is that who I think it is?" Bonnie asked Monica.

"Dr. Simon Wolfe, Chair of the Infectious Disease Department at Harvard. My husband was set to retire from the Army this year and Simon was heavily recruiting him to teach at the medical school."

"I don't mean to pry into your personal life, Monica, but I couldn't help overhearing that part about your daughter. Are you two at odds with each other?"

"Oh look. Simon's about to speak."

He smiled at her and directed his attention up at the podium. The infectious disease conference this past summer had taken place at Harvard Medical School and it was the very first time he'd met Wolfe. And the reporter James Bacon as well. Of course he'd been in disguise that day, wandering the halls in excited bliss. He recalled the remarkable speech Winters had given about bio-defense readiness and national security; the man knew how to grab people's attention. And after the speech he'd called Winters on his cell phone while the two of them were in that reception room. What a pleasure it had been to see Winters' face just before he sprinted out of that conference, terrified for his family's safety. Or even before that, when that booze-hound reporter, Bacon, asked him about the possibility of a lethal hybrid virus hitting American soil.

Bacon was now dead. Only one of those reporters could have walked out of that room alive. And of them, the girl was hungrier and more ambitious than that old booze hound. Bacon had already won his Pulitzer prize and had been for the last decade living almost entirely off his reputation. Like evolutionary biology, only the strongest would survive. He'd picked Swain because of her hardscrabble background, similar to his own, and because she would fight to the death in order to tell his story. Like Winters, she'd proved herself a worthy adversary. Hopefully, she and Winters would arrive just in time for the fireworks.

Wolfe approached the podium, stared out at the crowd, and then began his speech. Bonnie held out her hand and admired her shiny red nails, particularly the color and sheen of them in the overhead light. She had no doubt that this was going to be an interesting night.

Chapter 32

The sun was just starting to set behind the mountains, casting shadows along the valley. They'd been driving around town for thirty minutes and he still hadn't seen any sign of Fez. People walked the streets, unaware of the potential danger facing them. Micheau headed toward the southern pass after pointing toward a plume of black smoke rising up against the mountains. They passed The Mountain View Inn and Tag noticed two men standing in front of his hotel room and arguing. Or at least it appeared that way judging by their body language.

Upon reaching the pass he saw an overturned vehicle on fire a thousand yards away. Flames shot out of the windows and undercarriage. Two figures staggered along the road, the smaller of the two supporting the taller person. The woman's face was scarred and badly bruised, and it took Tag less than a few seconds to realize that it was Fez helping her along. A sense of relief filled him. The kid was alright! But who was the woman?

"Stop!" Tag shouted. "That's Fez!"

"Who's the woman?" Micheau asked.

"I don't know, but she looks pretty banged up."

"I'm going to read that little shit the riot act for taking off on me like that," she said.

"Go easy on him. He's a good kid."

"You talk to him then, because I'm afraid of what I might say."

Micheau hit the brakes and the car swerved until it came to a stop twenty yards away. Tag sprinted over to Fez, smothering him in a bear hug. He couldn't believe how overjoyed he felt at finding him. Placing his arm around the woman's slender waist, he helped her over to the car, where she collapsed in the backseat. Cuts and bruises lay over her face, but they didn't appear to be fresh. It looked like someone had beat the hell out of her.

He shut the woman's door and when he looked up saw two men staggering toward him, their arms out as if begging for alms. They were dressed in ripped flannel shirts and dirty jeans, and appeared lost. One of the men wore a blue baseball cap with a hockey logo over the visor. Behind them flames continued to shoot out of the fiery wreck as if hell itself had risen up out of the valley.

"Can you spare some change, Mister?" one of the men asked, holding out his trembling hand.

"Pass me your Glock, Detective," Tag said, leaning into the car.

"Not if you're going to kill them," Micheau said.

"Shut up and give me your gun, Detective, and don't question my motives."

She reluctantly passed him her revolver. Tag snatched it out of her hand and swiveled to face the men, positioning himself into a shooter's stance. He fired a quick warning shot over their heads and then watched as the two men retracted in fear.

"Are you crazy, Mister! Why you shooting at us like that?" the man wearing the blue cap said. "We didn't do nothing."

"Don't come any closer or the next one won't be a warning," Tag said.

"It's cold out here and we just come from Rat Town. We ain't looking for trouble."

"Why are you out here?"

"Things are crazy down in Rat Town. Crazier than ever. We can't go back there."

"And we're broke," the other guy said. "We was maybe looking for a ride to the shelter downtown."

"What do you mean things are crazy down there?" Tag asked.

"Them dumb ass meth-heads are attacking each other right outside Bingo's Pub, biting and kicking."

"Shit yeah, Mister. I even seen Jackson Tully bite another guy's ear off and spit it clear across the room," Blue Cap said.

"Must be a bad batch of meth or some shit. Those boys are either losing their minds or else hyped up on the pipe," the other guy said.

"So can you give us a lift into town or not?" Blue Cap asked. "It's getting cold out here and it's a long walk to the shelter."

"Sorry, fellas, but there's no room in here. Looks like you're going to have to walk."

The two men grumbled as they staggered past the car.

"How you doing, kid?" Tag asked Fez.

"Much better now," Fez said. "I thought you were still in that jail cell?"

"I managed to convince the detective here about what's at stake."

"A deadly epidemic is enough to persuade me of most anything," Micheau said, staring at the bruised girl in the backseat. "Hey you! What's your name?"

"Nolette Swain," the woman muttered. "I've traveled all this way to see Colonel Winters."

"So you know who I am?"

"Of course I know who you are." She laughed. "I wouldn't be here now if it wasn't for the attack that's going to take place here."

"I take it you're referring to this biological threat," Tag said, turning to face her. "And I assume you think I'm responsible."

"I'm not sure what to believe, Colonel."

"I think you already do if you're here."

"Go on the record then, Colonel, and I'll quote you in my investigative report on the attack."

"I had nothing to do with Cooke's Island, just as I had nothing to do with the events going on here."

264

"I believe you." She reached over the seat and shook his hand. "So am I correct in assuming that an Ebola attack on this town has already happened?"

"Your assumption is correct," he said

"They blocked off the pass so that no one can come in or out. We nearly got shot by the cop stationed there," Fez said.

"You can thank Colonel Winters for that," Micheau said, glancing back. "He ordered the quarantine, which means that he's responsible for nearly getting you killed."

"No, it's this lame lady's fault," Fez said, pointing to Swain. "She tried to drive out of town. Then, after we crashed, the cop told us we had three seconds to walk away or he'd start shooting. But she wanted to stay and argue with him about her constitutional rights."

"Please. You don't seriously believe that cop would have shot us?" Swain said. "He was merely bluffing."

"That's Nick Cook. And trust me, 'By-The-Book-Cook' most definitely would have shot you," Micheau said. "Colonel Winters ordered a shoot-to-kill policy against anyone trying to leave this place."

"See, lady! I told you," Fez said.

Swain frowned at Fez and turned to Tag. "So what do we do now that we're stuck in this shitty town and facing the threat of a lethal virus?"

"Our first priority is to keep it from spreading," Tag said, turning back to the injured reporter. "What paper do you work for?"

"Washington Tribune." She slumped down in her seat, reclining her head back and closing her eyes. "I'm working on an important story about these two events and how they tie together, and you in particular."

Tag laughed. "There's not much to write about me. I'm afraid I'm a pretty boring guy, Swain."

"Oh right, Colonel." She burst out laughing. "You were set to retire from the Army's disease institute, where you worked in the hottest of labs, and have been blamed for infecting an entire island. Somehow you and this wiseass kid managed to escape when everyone else was killed. Then, by some miraculous coincidence, you end up in this fucking valley just as a deadly outbreak of Ebola is set to occur. Now either trouble finds you, Colonel, or you're some kind of evil genius. All in all I'd say you're a pretty boring guy."

"How did you even find me?" he asked.

"Someone has been sending me text messages ever since I toured Cooke's Island," Swain said. "Whoever this person is, he seems to know your every move, Colonel."

"You actually got a tour of Cooke's Island?" Micheau asked, incredulous. "What's it like there?"

"Have you ever seen pictures of the Sahara Desert, Detective? The island has been completely destroyed. Not a single building left standing except for a few makeshift facilities that were put up by the military," Swain said. "They paired me up with James Bacon, the well-known reporter for the New York Times."

"Bacon? Why does that name ring a bell?" Tag said, jogging his memory. "Wait! He's the same reporter who attended the Infectious Disease Conference at Harvard Medical School this summer. I distinctly remember him asking me a question about the production of weaponized hybrid viruses. Thought it a rather odd question at the time. Quite a coincidence, now that I think about it."

"It's no coincidence, Colonel. We'd been collaborating on this story together before I learned that Bacon was working the entire time with the terrorist."

"How did you figure that out?" Micheau asked.

"Bacon tried to kill me in an Oklahoma motel," Swain said. "Unknown to the two of us, this terrorist was pitting us against each other for the exclusive right to tell his story. Still, I can't say I blame Bacon for attempting to kill me."

"Why the hell not?" Micheau asked.

"Because he threatened to kill Bacon's kids if he didn't kill me first."

"Jesus! What an asshole," Micheau said.

"Two minutes before it happened I received a text message. It was early in the morning and we were both asleep in our hotel room."

"You were sleeping in the same room?"

"Same room, two beds. He insisted on it in order to keep our cover. I heard him get out of bed. He thought I was asleep, but actually I was waiting for him with a pair of nail clippers. It was the only thing I could find to defend myself."

"Jesus! Did you kill him?" Micheau asked. "And how?"

"What fucking difference does it make how I killed him. I did what I had to do," she said bitterly. "The point I'm trying to make is that I was tipped off about this conference and about Colonel Winters being here."

"Take it back a step, Swain. Why in the world were you in an Oklahoma hotel to begin with?" Tag asked.

"Research, Colonel. I came across a disgruntled former employee of yours named Remington Guilfoyle. It's my theory that he faked his own death in a plane crash and then somehow reinvented himself. Bacon and I were sharing the research and making good progress. Our biggest lead was in discovering that Guilfoyle was a member of the Waco Branch Davidians."

"The same Branch Davidians who had their compound raided by the FBI?" Tag asked.

"One and the same. He was only a teenager at the time, but we confirmed that he was there the day the ATF attacked that compound. The FBI took over from the ATF and for days after were negotiating with David Koresh on terms of surrender."

"But I thought most of his congregation died in that standoff," Micheau said.

"True, most of those people inside the compound did die in the fire. Only a handful made it out alive, many of whom were badly burned. They were later tried and convicted for committing various crimes against the government."

"How did you find this out?" Tag asked.

"We interviewed an elderly minister who knew him back then. He told us that a boy escaped from the compound that day carrying a document. The boy was eventually adopted by an Oklahoma family and had his name changed to Ernest Drinkwater. Here's the kicker, Colonel; he was adopted and living in Oklahoma City the day Timothy McVeigh bombed that federal building."

"No wonder this lunatic is so pissed off at the government," Micheau said.

"You said he carried out a document," Tag said. "What was the document?"

"The head negotiator of the FBI cut a deal with David Koresh; they agreed that once he interpreted the Seven Seals from the Book of Revelation, he and the rest of his followers would be able to surrender in a peaceful manner. But Janet Reno, the head of the FBI at the time, reneged on the deal soon after. She ordered the FBI to attack the compound two weeks before the agreed-upon deadline expired, thus ensuring the deaths of many innocent people. And the sad part is, they could have taken Koresh any time before the raid as he freely walked unarmed through the downtown streets."

"And you believe this Guilfoyle character escaped with Koresh's unfinished Seven Seals interpretation?" Micheau asked.

Swain shrugged. "Who knows exactly what he carried out, or if he actually carried anything out. The Book of Revelation, which Koresh preached, speaks to the disasters that are to occur before Jesus returns to establish God's kingdom on earth. It goes without saying that plagues and pestilence are two of the more prominent apocalyptic scenarios in it."

"So you think this Guilfoyle character is responsible for these attacks?" Micheau asked.

"I'm almost sure of it. He was the one who led me here, and he was the one who convinced me that you were alive and well, Colonel," Swain said.

"Sounds like something this guy would do. During the attack on Cooke's Island, he disguised himself as a middle-aged woman in order to ingratiate himself into my family and learn every detail about us."

"Then you'll love this, Colonel. Guilfoyle honed his skills at Yale by minoring in theater, and while there learned how to make costumes and apply make-up," Nolette said. "I'll bet you anything that he's attending this conference in disguise, either as a volunteer or a guest."

"There's only one problem. If he's changed his appearance, we'll have no idea what he looks like," Tag said.

"Or even what he'll be disguised as," Swain added. "He could be a waiter for all we know."

"Maybe we should lock down the campus and check out each guest," Micheau said.

"He's too smart for that," Swain said. "He'll see that coming a mile away and make things even worse."

"And you'd cause a major firestorm if you tried to lock down all those scientists, many of whom are foreign nationals," Tag said. "Swain's right, that would piss him off even further and make matters worse."

"Not if we lock it down immediately and make sure no one leaves," Micheau replied.

"I'm afraid that's not an option," Tag said. "If he escaped Cooke's Island then he'll have no problem disappearing from this campus. No doubt he's studied every blueprint of the building and put to memory every possible way out. The best thing right now is to put every available officer on the quarantine and keep an eye out in case something breaks."

"Can you get your hands on the guest list for this conference, Detective? As well as the names of all the employees and volunteers?" Swain asked.

"Sure, I suppose I could get a list together. But why bother with it if you don't even know who you're looking for?" Micheau asked.

"Because I'm willing to bet that our guy's attending this conference under an assumed name. I'll conduct a background

269

check on everyone on the list to see if they're legit. I'll certainly be able to find something."

"Detective, could you possibly get me inside that building for just a few minutes so I can see my wife?" Tag asked.

"The moment you walk into that conference the FBI will be all over you, Colonel."

"The FBI is here?" Swain asked, looking surprised.

"Of course they're here, although they're keeping a low profile. And they're not here in the way you think. Ever since that attack on Cooke's Island they've been keeping a close eye on Hawthorne College, making sure the campus is secure. Some of the professors have been protesting their presence and saying it's harassment and intellectual censorship. The government, on the other hand, claims it's a national security measure. And with the revised Patriot Act they can do just about anything they like."

"I don't care how you get me in there, Detective. Dress me up as a cleaning lady for all I care. I just need to speak to my wife for a brief moment and then I'll leave," Tag said.

"I have a better idea, Colonel," Micheau said. "How about I take you over to her hotel instead. I bet it's a lot quieter over there. And I can guarantee that there'll be no FBI agents."

"Look," Fez shouted as they cruised through the center of town.

Tag looked over and saw a half dozen shadowy figures skulking into a wooded park where a small brook bubbled through the center of town. A wooden bridge arced over it. They could have been teenagers out for a stroll. Or quite possibly the first wave of Ebola victims seeking to spread the virus. He couldn't risk killing innocent civilians at this stage in the crisis, especially young kids hanging out and causing mischief. And yet the prospect of an Ebola virus spreading through town sent chills down his spine. He had a responsibility to save as many lives as possible, but at this point he still needed to proceed with caution.

Micheau pulled into the station's parking lot and bolted inside the back entrance. She came out minutes later holding two Remington LTR rifles and four police radios.

"Okay, Colonel, I've got guns and radios. How should we proceed?" Micheau asked.

"Fez and I are going to stroll on foot through the center of town and assess the situation. I'd like you to take a quick spin over to the campus and see what's happening."

"You guys go on without me. I need to set up somewhere so I can connect to the Internet." Swain turned to Micheau. "Can you have someone at the college email me those lists?"

"I don't see why not," Micheau said.

"Make sure everyone has a radio on them; that way we can stay in contact in case something breaks," Tag said, moving out of the vehicle. "Fez and I will try and make it back to the station as soon as we know more."

He and Fez walked down the street and slipped unnoticed into the shadows. By his own estimation, the center of town was roughly a half a mile north of here. He surveyed his surroundings and noticed that he could barely see the silhouette of mountains. The air was cold and he knew they needed to keep moving in order to stay warm.

Something seemed on the verge of breaking. His intuition was based on years of military training and experience, as well as dealing with the most lethal viruses in the hot lab. Throughout the years, he'd developed almost a seventh sense about these dangerous pathogens, and his sensory acuteness had been finely attuned to any small calibrations. He'd learned to trust his gut and his gut was now churning inside his stomach like taffy being spun on Old Orchard Beach.

They switchbacked through the streets and took a shortcut through someone's yard. Tonight promised to be an interesting night. He prayed to God that this threat would not materialize, but he feared it was too late. They had entered the Ebola Zone and there was no turning back now.

271

Chapter 33

Micheau introduced Swain to the desk sergeant before guiding her down the dim hallway. The station was empty and dark, every cop having been called into duty. Nolette wondered if the officers had even been told about the viral threat, or if they had any idea what they were protecting.

Micheau stopped and pulled out a set of keys, dangling them in front of the lock. She opened the door and flipped the switch. A series of fluorescent lights along the ceiling flickered to life. Inside the drab room were some tan file cabinets and a worn conference table. Somewhere in the station a police radio blared. Nolette plopped her bag down on top of the conference table and sat in front of a police-issued laptop. She removed her tablet, turned it on, and placed it down in front of her.

"Do you have everything you need?" Micheau asked.

"I assume the guest list has already been sent?" she asked.

"I called campus security and told them I needed it over here ASAP. So it should be in the station's inbox."

"Thanks, but I can't access the email without the password," Nolette said, staring at the blank screen

Micheau leaned over the laptop and studied it.

"Sorry, but I didn't have much of a choice coming to your town, Detective."

"We all have choices." Micheau typed something on the keyboard and up popped a list of names. Next to the names was the institution or university the guest was affiliated with, as well as the list of employees and volunteers.

"There now, you should have everything at your disposal," Micheau said as she headed to the door.

Nolette looked around, making sure she had everything she needed before being locked inside. Micheau brought her a cup of coffee with some packets of sugar and cream. Although the Internet connection was slower than she was used to, she'd have to make do.

Once she was alone, Nolette plugged her tablet into the outlet, giving her two computers to use. One hundred and twenty-two names were printed on the guest list. She started with the first name at the top, lifting the steaming cup of coffee to her lips. *Ugh!* She nearly spit out the coffee it tasted so bad. *Instant coffee. It isn't Starbucks but at least it has caffeine.* After grabbing a pad of paper and pen, she settled in for a long night.

* * *

Bonnie glanced at her watch. Nine fifty-five. The cocktail reception would end in ten minutes. By her calculation the first wave of infection should be in full swing by now. The phase of headaches and body fatigue had most likely passed, and the hemorrhaging and violent behavior had begun. Tiny spots on the frontal cortex would now be bleeding into the brain and causing victims to become bloodthirsty and hyper-aggressive.

She stood in a small group, holding her purse while listening to Monica speak about the benefits of the new Patriot Act and the closing off of the country's borders. A few of the guests politely disagreed with her before splitting off from the group. She glanced at her nails and then at her dress. She liked wearing this pretty dress and standing in chic high heels, balancing her weight on one leg. A few of the men smiled at her, but she ignored them, choosing to run her hand flirtatiously through her long hair.

Monica talked about her husband and how he'd betrayed his country for reasons unknown to her. It thrilled Bonnie to hear Monica talk this way about the venerable Colonel Winters. She fingered the silver bracelet around her wrist, rotating it back and forth in nervous anticipation. The evidence against Colonel

Winters had been damning—wholly incorrect, but damning—and she knew that Monica couldn't play the supportive wife after seeing the mounting evidence with her own eyes. And yet she chuckled at Monica's ability to be duped. And now here she was being duped all over again by the brilliant and beautiful Bonnie Haldeman, CEO of the fictional company Biodefense Constructs.

"I'm exhausted," Monica said once she'd answered every question. They walked arm-in-arm away from the crowd.

"I suppose we should be returning to the hotel," Bonnie said. "We have a very busy schedule tomorrow. Full of seminars and schmoozing and fascinating lectures. It's making me tired just thinking about it."

"Thanks again, Bonnie. I've really enjoyed your company this evening. You've made me feel so relaxed around this scientific bunch," she said as they made their way to the elevator. "It's kind of weird, but you remind me of someone."

"Oh? And who might that be?"

"I don't quite know, but someone."

"Hopefully, it's someone glamorous and beautiful. And absolutely brilliant. Maybe a cross between Julia Roberts and Madam Curie?" She laughed, although her laughter was masked by a note of nervous tension.

"Oh, I'm sure it's someone beautiful and exotic—and no doubt with a towering intellect."

They boarded the van and rode in silence back to the hotel. Bonnie reached into her coat pocket and fingered the detonator. First thing tomorrow morning she'd set them off, effectively cutting off all communications into Brookhaven. Hopefully, Colonel Winters had managed to seal off the north and south passes by now. She had no desire for this outbreak to turn pandemic. Not yet anyway. Brookhaven's annihilation would do quite nicely for now, setting in motion the events that would follow.

She'd made meticulous escape plans just in case, knowing that the military would quickly move in. She'd stashed a backpack halfway up one of the southernmost mountains. The backpack contained a tent, plenty of dried food, and the necessary supplies needed to hike out of the wilderness and get back to safety. And that was only one contingency.

She noticed the full moon as she exited the van. This was no coincidence: the gravitational pull of the earth's satellite was known to amplify viral replication and help degrade brain cells in the frontal cortex. They strode into the lobby and past the front desk until they reached the elevator. On the way up, they made small talk until they came to their floor. Their rooms were located on opposite ends of the hall and so they stood in front of the elevator doors, ready to part ways for the evening.

"I guess this is goodnight, Monica. Will you have time to hang out tomorrow?"

"Of course we'll hang out. We're BFFs now, as my daughter used to say all the time."

Bonnie laughed before reaching out and taking Monica's hand. "I don't mean to pry into your family life, Monica, but do you truly believe that your husband unleashed that virus on Cooke's Island?"

"I didn't at first, as God is my witness. But as time passed I became more convinced of his guilt. I truly wish I was wrong, because I loved him with all my heart. But the truth is, he's one of the few people in the world with the means and expertise to create such a deadly weapon."

"How do you live with that burden, knowing you were married to him for so long?"

"It's troubling, I admit. You think you know someone all those years, but in the end what do you really know about anyone? You'd think I would have seen some signs of his behavior over the years. But I didn't see a thing."

"What was it that finally convinced you?"

"When I realized that I'd used a hybrid smallpox virus in one of my glass sculptures. How else would I have known about it if Tag hadn't passed it along to me? He must have done it by accident. At first my heart was broken and I cried for days, but then I realized that I had to stay strong for my kids, and so that I could prevent this from happening again."

"What do your children think about what you're doing?"

"Two of them will not even speak to me because they believe that I betrayed their father. But I have to remain strong, Bonnie, and cling to the truth. Hopefully, they'll realize it one day as well and be able to move on in life."

"You're an amazing woman, Monica, do you know that? You're an inspiration."

"Hey, don't sell yourself short, Bonnie Halderman. You're pretty amazing yourself, starting your own company and all. And in Alaska of all places."

"I feel so lucky to have met you. It's such a bummer the night has to end."

"It doesn't have to. Why don't you freshen up and then us girls can have a hot chocolate nightcap."

Bonnie stole a glimpse at her watch. "It's getting pretty late."

"Oh, just one quick cup. How often do we get to have a night out?"

"Sure, why not. My social life is nonexistent lately. I'm usually at my office or in the lab late into the evening."

"Good. Give me about thirty minutes to freshen up before you come over. I just need to apply some ointment over my skin. Then I'll be ready to party." She laughed.

"Okay, see you in about thirty minutes."

Once back in the room, Bonnie collapsed on the bed. Her feet were killing her from walking on heels all day. Fortunately, she'd packed some female lingerie and a silk night robe for just such an occasion. Exhausted, she wished she could go to sleep and wake up to the prospect of tomorrow's fireworks, but the prospect of a close friendship with Monica Winters made everything all the sweeter. She couldn't believe that everything was going so smoothly. After freshening her make-up, she stepped out of the dress and put on a pair of slippers and then donned the pink satin robe. She felt so comfortable and feminine in the robe that it made her giggle. The silky slippers hugged the contours of her feet and were a welcome relief from the relentless heels. She went over to the balcony and stared out at the small town. Behind the veil of darkness loomed the largest of Maine's mountains. Two lights flashed high above the mountain as a warning to small aircraft entering the valley. Soon it would all come crumbling down, allowing the immense beauty of the Ebola thread virus to shine through. Then Bonnie Halderman could shed her identity and be forever free.

* * *

After a quick reconnaissance around the center of town, and seeing nothing out of the ordinary, Tag radioed Micheau and requested that she meet him in front of the station. Once Fez was safely ensconced inside with the desk sergeant, they made their way to the hotel where Monica was staying.

Tag waited for Micheau to give the go ahead before slipping into the hotel lobby. His entire body was trembling with anticipation. From where she stood, he knew Micheau could see both the desk clerk and the women's bathroom. On her hand signal, he walked briskly across the lobby until he reached the restroom. An intense longing filled him as he bolted inside the shiny, clean toilet and locked himself in one of the stalls. The plan was for Micheau to call Monica down from her room and convince her to go inside.

He gently closed the toilet seat and squatted atop it, keeping perfectly still. A few women came and went without incident. After what seemed like forever, the door finally opened and he heard the sound of Micheau's voice whispering his wife's arrival. A swell of emotion came over him at the prospect of reuniting with his wife of twenty-four years. Tears spilled from his cheeks. He didn't care what she looked like. All he wanted to do was see her face, hold her in his arms again, and persuade her that he had nothing to do with any of this.

"Are you really in there, Tag?" Monica whispered. "That police officer told me you were here."

He tried not to cry. "Can I open the door and see you?"

277

"No! I don't want you to see me like this."

"I don't care what you look like, honey. I love you and will always love you just the way you are."

"Don't you dare open that door, Taggart Winters, or I swear I'll walk out of here and you'll never see me again."

"I know you think I'm guilty, Monica, but I swear to you that I had nothing to do with any of this, no matter what lies the government may have told you."

"I know," she whispered.

Had he heard her right! The tears fell from his eyes and pooled up on the tiled floor. "The government made it all up. They needed to convince the American public and the world of my guilt."

"Shhh! You don't have to say another word."

He buried his hands in his head, overwhelmed that she was convinced of his innocence.

"Listen to me, Tag. This is the price I've had to pay for our children's safety. It's what I have to do until we can clear your name or else the government has promised to make their lives miserable."

"Why did you come here, Monica?"

"The government wanted me to attend the conference. It's nothing more than propaganda for them, showing me off like some prize horse. Besides, I believe that the person or persons who committed that attack are here as we speak."

"Monica, listen to me. What happened on Cooke's Island is about to repeat itself in Brookhaven."

"Are you saying that there's going to be another smallpox attack?"

"Worse," he said, trying to sound evasive.

"Worse?" He could hear the nervousness in her voice. "Oh my God, Tag. How can it get much worse than smallpox?"

"We don't really know," he said, feeling terrible about lying to his wife. And yet he didn't want to frighten her either.

She paused. "Do you and that detective have any idea who might be responsible?"

278

"We think it's a one-time coworker of mine named Remington Guilfoyle. He was presumed to have died in a plane crash while flying his plane over the Atlantic, but his body was never found. You met him once at one of our office parties. He was a brilliant scientist but very quiet and introverted."

"I don't remember him."

"Monica, I've missed you so much."

"Don't make me cry, Tag. The scars hurt when I cry." She sniffled. "Quickly, tell me what else you've learned."

"He was a costume designer in college and then worked a year on Broadway. He's able to masterfully disguise himself and then slip effortlessly into a crowd. Do you remember Versa?"

"Vaguely, but I was so out of it during that time that I don't remember much."

"How are the kids?"

"They're fine right now." She paused for a few seconds. "So do you think this Guilfoyle character is responsible?"

"I'm quite certain of it."

"I want so badly to see you, Tag, but it's quite possible that we may never see each other again. If something should happen to me, please remember that I love all of you and have been doing all this for our family. Taylor and James refuse to speak to me, and I've made my peace with that. I just hope one day they might understand the sacrifice I've made to keep them safe."

"I'm certain we'll see each other again, Monica. Just swear to me that when this epidemic breaks, you'll stay in your room and keep the doors locked tight."

"I have to go, my dear Tag. I'm expecting a visitor to my room in a few minutes. But just know that I love you so much and am sorry for all the pain I've caused you and the children." He heard her footsteps as she walked over to the door. "Remember, I've always believed in you despite what you may have heard."

"I love you, Monica," he said, trying to hold back from bursting out the stall door. He heard the door open and then close, and before he knew it his wife was gone.

He squatted on the toilet seat and sobbed for a few seconds before the bathroom door opened.

"Come on, Colonel, we need to get out of here," Micheau whispered. "I'm getting radio reports of some suspicious crowd formations on the outskirts of town."

He wiped his eyes and tried to gather his composure.

"We need to be certain that these people have come down with the disease before we begin implementing the plan."

"It's nighttime, Colonel. How are we going to know if they're sick?"

"Trust me, all those cops will know as soon as they see it."

"I'm going to try and sneak you out through the back door."

Tag sprinted out of the bathroom and followed Micheau down the long hall and toward one of the rear exit doors. They staggered out into the night; it was so cold Tag could see his breath. He almost wished that snow would fall so that they'd be able to track the infecteds' movements. Then he remembered the disease he was up against and realized he wouldn't need snow for that; the trails of blood would be everywhere.

"Thank you for letting me meet with her, Detective," he said once they were in her car. "I'll never forget what you did for me back there."

"Hey, I got a hubby too." She shrugged. "Were you able to convince her?"

"Surprisingly, she never doubted me."

She turned and stared at him. "Even though she's been denouncing you on every news station?"

"She was forced to by the government."

"Wow, I never knew our government could be such shits," Micheau said, shaking her head. "She was so convincing she even persuaded me of your guilt."

"Please keep this between us, Detective, as it involves the safety of my children."

"Of course," she said. "I got kids too, you know."

280

"Good. Now are you prepared to do what's absolutely necessary to save lives in this town?"

"You know I am, or I wouldn't be here."

"Even to the point of putting your life on the line to prevent this virus from spreading?"

"Jesus, you're scaring the shit out of me, Colonel." She swallowed.

"Are you prepared?"

"Yeah, I'm prepared to do what's necessary."

"Good. Now let's go get Fez. The real fun's about to begin."

Chapter 34

It was just past ten at night and the streets appeared deserted. Winters stared mindlessly out the window, reflecting on the brief rendezvous with his wife as Micheau cruised through town. It seemed too quiet for such a busy weekend, and he couldn't help visualizing this virus as a mysterious alien lurking around every corner. Maybe it was the result of being tired and frightened and not having eaten anything for some time.

Where were all the people? He figured that a conference of this size and prestige should have caused a lot more commercial activity in the pubs and restaurants throughout town. He ordered her to stop the car so that he could grab one of the rifles out of the trunk. Upon retrieving it, he walked toward the nearest storefront.

He stood in front of an Irish pub and stared inside the darkened lounge window. The lights were still on but from his vantage he couldn't see any patrons drinking. Micheau and Fez joined him on the sidewalk to peer inside. Something seemed terribly wrong. A few stools lay overturned and the complimentary pretzels and cheese balls lay scattered along the floor. He opened the door and stuck his head inside. The jukebox was playing 'I'm Shipping Up to Boston' by The Dropkick Murphys. He walked in cautiously and Micheau followed behind. He saw pint glasses of Guinness sitting half drunk on the tables and bar. "Anyone home?" he shouted. Something crashed somewhere in the back. A few seconds passed and all he wanted to do was run out of this place and get some fresh air. He was about to turn around and head back to the car when someone stumbled out of the kitchen and headed toward them. With his free arm, the large man swiped all the glasses off the bar and howled at them.

He'd not seen anyone quite like this guy, even during the worst of the smallpox crisis. The man looked deathly ill, as if in the last throes of a bad heroin addiction. Black sludge oozed out of his eyes and nose and was smeared over his ruddy face. Deep red welts ran up and down his arms. The guy looked to be well over six feet tall and over three hundred pounds.

Tag raised the rifle and pointed at the man's head. Unmoved by the threat, the guy turned toward the mirror along the bar and for a moment seemed to stare at his grotesque image, as if questioning his own identity. Half his ear had been torn off and the lobe dangled like some piece of hipster jewelry. He let out a pig-like grunt, raising his arms up in the air. Tag's finger tickled the trigger in anticipation as he kept his aim trained on him.

"Is it Ebola?" Micheau whispered.

"Sure looks that way," he responded.

The man turned back to them and squealed, swinging both arms in front of him. He looked mentally damaged and emboldened by the rage. Damp clots of blood appeared under his armpits and along his crotch.

"Waste him before he gets any closer," Fez said over the guitar riffs of The Dropkick Murphys.

"I thought I told you to wait in the car." He glanced briefly back at the kid.

"We're a team, Tag. We stay together, right?"

The infected man trained his bloody gaze at Fez and for a moment seemed to morph into another person entirely.

"You look just like my son," the man said, looking remorseful. He switched his gaze to Tag. "Fuck is wrong with me?"

"You've been infected with a virus," Tag said.

"All of sudden I started bleeding," the man cried out as he started to inch forward. Tears of blood dripped down his cheeks.

"Don't come any closer!" Tag ordered, raising his gun. "You're contagious."

"Fuck you! I'll go anywhere I want."

Tag kept his aim trained on him.

"I've never been in so much pain in my life." He reached for the bar with his right hand as if to grab a pint of Guinness. "Why is this happening to me?"

"It's a trick, Tag. Don't let him get any closer," Fez said.

"Shut up, you little bitch." He snatched the pint glass off the bar and hurled it at Fez. Luckily, it sailed over his head.

The man broke out in a dead sprint toward them. Tag lowered his aim and fired a round into the man's leg. His kneecap exploded in a mass of blood and tendons, and he sprawled headfirst to the floor. The section below his knee lay bent at a hideous angle. Despite the crippling injury, the man pulled himself up on his three good limbs, his face engorged with blood, and began to crawl forward while gnashing his teeth together. Tag knelt down on one knee, a good twenty feet from the man, and trained his sights on the man's forehead.

"What's your name?" Tag asked him.

"Dwayne." Tarry blood oozed out of the shredded limb as if industrial sludge. "I'm going to fucking kill you, pal, once I get me hands on you."

"Where does it hurt most, Dwayne?"

"What are you, a doctor or something?"

"In fact I am."

"Then get your shoeshine kit and help me out." His nearly severed leg left a trail of sticky blood along the checkered floor.

"I need to know what your symptoms are."

"My head feels like it's going to explode. And my fucking nuts are killing me. Feels like a mule kicked me down there. They're as big as grapefruits and it feels like someone set them on fire. My entire family got sick too, even worse than me, and so I put them out of their misery." He raised his head up and glared like a madman. "I did the right thing by wasting them, didn't I?"

"It's the Ebola virus that killed them, Dwayne, not you."

"Same shit as them niggers got in Africa?"

"Shut up, you racist bastard!" Micheau shouted, pointing her gun at his head.

"Step back, Micheau. The man's not thinking clearly."

"A lot of my good friends are African-American and I'm not going to sit here and listen to his racist bullshit."

"I told you it's the virus talking, Detective. Now step the hell off," Tag said, blocking her with his arm.

"This scumbag just admitted to murdering his entire family, Colonel," she said. "Besides, I know Big Dwayne. Lives down in Rat Town and has a very long rap sheet."

Tag held his fire and watched as the man pulled himself up to the bar with the help of a stool. He grabbed a glass of booze and tossed it down in one gulp. It took a few seconds for him to swallow it before vomiting over the bar. After wiping his hand over his soiled mouth, he tossed the empty shot glass at Micheau's head. She ducked and the glass hurtled through one of the glass windows, shattering crystals onto the sidewalk. The man let out a terrifying scream as he hopped toward them on one leg, his arms reaching out as if to throttle someone. His beet red face contorted into a mask of rage. Tag brought the rifle scope up to his eyes and pulled the trigger, and almost immediately a black hole appeared between Dwayne's eyes.

A millisecond later his head exploded in a wash of blood and brain matter. It sprayed against the walls and ceiling fan. Spatters of black, infected gunk lay smeared against the bar and mirror. Tag couldn't quite believe the amount of blood the man had lost. A dark red stain began to form along the backside of the man's trousers and pooled up along the floor. Tag turned and pushed Micheau out the front door, knowing that she had no protection against this infection.

He kneeled beside the mortally wounded man and analyzed the disease's progression. It was unreal. The stomach and intestines had not yet liquefied, but he knew they would eventually hemorrhage out the anus, which was the virus's reaction to massive brain trauma. He understood the rest of the

285

story, assuming that the virus followed its usual trajectory. In short time the entire corpse would liquefy. The liquefaction process would give the virus the most optimal chance at jumping onto a new host. The blood contained millions of crystallized viruses that had formed into pyramids of bricks, which then replicated exponentially. This was a dangerous situation for the uninfected to happen upon. Only a powerful virus-killing solution could thoroughly sterilize this room, and the solution would need to be sprayed in every nook and cranny in order to be effective. The other known method was to burn this structure to the ground.

A crash occurred outside. Tag spun around and saw three figures crossing the street toward Micheau. The larger of the three men, wearing a bandanna and leather jacket, picked up a rock and threw it at her. The rock landed with a thud against the windshield, causing cracks to spiderweb outward along the glass. Micheau aimed her gun at the three of them as they approached, warning them to stay back. Tag sprinted toward the street, stopping ten feet from the police car and dropping down behind the hood. The two men and the woman didn't appear to be sick, judging by the fluid way they moved.

"Don't come any closer or I'll shoot," he shouted.

"There's no leaving this fucked-up town," the man said as he limped forward. "We tried to ride out through the southern pass but the pigs have it blocked off. That motherfucker shot one of our crew who tried to blow past."

"Where are your bikes parked?" Tag asked.

"Got swarmed by a mob out by the Interstate. We had to abandon them and set out on foot. The three of us split from the others." He raised his arms and stepped forward. "What the fuck is going on in this town?"

"It's an Ebola outbreak."

"Ebola?" He glanced at his cohorts. "Dude, I thought that shit only happens in the jungles or some shit?"

"You thought wrong. I suggest you three find a safe place and lay low until this blows over."

"Who the hell are you?"

"Watch who you're talking to, asshole," Fez shouted, standing over the hood. "This is Colonel Winters."

Bandana Man rubbed his chin and nodded, a smile slowly forming along his face.

"Yeah, now I recognize you. You're the dude from those videos wasting all those freaks. Very cool," Bandana Man said, nodding appreciatively. "We all thought you bit the bucket, Winters."

"Can't get rid of me that easy. Now I suggest you move along. There's going to be a lot of blood spilled on these streets, and most of it will be infected with Ebola."

"How about we travel with you guys," Bandana Man said, taking another step forward. "We could be a big help to you, Winters. Watch your back and shit."

Tag sighed; would these assholes never take no for an answer. "Not going to happen, pal. Now I suggest you get off these streets and find a place to stay."

Bandana Man laughed. "People been telling me to get off the streets my whole life. Do you really think I'm going to start listening to authorities now?"

"Look," Fez whispered, pointing to an approaching mob. They emitted a low, guttural sound as they approached. Once they appeared under the streetlight it was evident that they were infected.

"Come on, Winters. We can help each other out. I wash your back and you wash mine," Bandana Man said. "Done a lot fighting back in my day and haven't lost my touch yet."

"Then it'll come in handy when you're trying to defend yourselves. But I wouldn't recommend hand-to-hand combat against this bunch. You get blood on you and you're likely to become infected. Now keep moving, fellas. There's a group of them heading this way."

"It ain't a question, Colonel. We're coming with you whether you like it or not," Bandana Man said, walking toward them.

"Please don't make me shoot," Tag sighed, lifting the rifle to eye level. "I really don't want to kill you."

"Doubt you'd kill an unarmed man in cold blood, especially in front of his friends," Bandana Man said, arms raised and moving toward him.

"Dude, you're testing the wrong guy," Fez said, shaking his head in disbelief. "He'll shoot if you don't turn around."

"He ain't gonna shoot a good old boy like me who only wants to help people," the man said.

Tag sighed. "This is your last warning. You're wasting my time."

"Put that weapon down, Colonel, and you and I can talk this out in a peaceful manner."

"Take one more step and you're dead."

"You mean a step like this," the man said, taking an exaggerated step forward.

Tag pulled the trigger and shot him in the knee. Despite all he'd been through, he couldn't deliver the necessary lethal force. Bandana Man collapsed to the ground, screaming in agony. The mob of infected marched into the light and lurched toward where the injured man lay. His two friends rushed over and helped him up. Hoisting him on their shoulders, they carried him down the street. He cried out in agony before they disappeared behind one of the stately brick buildings.

"Get in the car," Tag ordered.

They hustled inside. Micheau revved the engine as the mob surrounded the car and pounded the windows with their fists. Micheau punched the gas and accelerated over two of the infected standing in front of the car. Three others clung to the vehicle as it sped down the street.

"Bolas on the right," Fez shouted, sticking his head between their seats.

"Bolas?"

"Ebola dudes. Got anything better to call them?"

"I guess that's as good as anything else."

The windshield shattered, causing crystalline shards of glass to fall over them. Micheau slammed on the brakes and one of the men flew off the front end. The other two, still holding on, began to pull themselves up over the frame and into the cabin. Five more approached the driver's side window. Tag ordered Fez out of the car as bloody hands reached toward Micheau.

"Watch my back, kid," he said.

Tag walked around the vehicle and coolly shot two of the individuals in the head while Fez kept an eye on the perimeter. Five more converged on the driver's side window. Tag raised the rifle and was about to shoot them dead when Micheau panicked and stepped on the gas. The car rocketed down the street. Tag cut down three more before the rifle clicked and he realized that he'd run out of bullets. Micheau glanced back through the rear window and shifted the car into reverse. But Tag realized that he and Fez wouldn't make it safely now that they were out of ammo. The blasts had saved their lives, but the sound of them had also alerted every Bola in the vicinity, evident by the large numbers now pouring onto the street.

"Go! Go!" he shouted to Micheau, waving his arm. "We'll meet up with you later."

The mob surrounded the vehicle and started to pound on it. She gunned the engine and the car accelerated down the street. The infected flew off it until only two clung to the frame. She punched the brakes and they soared through the air. Then she burned rubber and disappeared down the street.

Tag grabbed Fez and led him down an alley. Glancing over his shoulder, he noticed three people stumbling toward them. By the time he caught up to Fez he realized their mistake. A twenty-foot brick wall stood, impeding their progress. A motion-activated light illuminated the evenly stacked bricks. Against the wall sat a dirty green dumpster. The scent of rotting vegetables punched him in the nose.

Tag gripped his rifle. A quick glance around the alley revealed a stack of two-by-fours lying on the cobblestones. Tag picked one up, fingering the six-inch spikes protruding from the

289

end. Moving toward the corner, he gestured for Fez to follow. Then he lifted the two-by-four off his shoulder like a batter waiting for a fastball.

A snarling woman turned the corner first, her long hair drenched as if dunked in Vaseline. He swung the two-by-four so hard that the spike punched through her temple and came out the other side. He pulled the spike out of her head and watched as the woman staggered backwards. The rusty nail appeared as if it had been dipped in motor oil. A teenage girl came up behind her. She glanced down at the dead woman, and when she did Tag tomahawked the board over the top of her head. It split her skull down the middle. The girl dropped to her knees before falling face down, dead. The last to arrive was an old man, crippled and slow. Taking a deep breath, Tag waited a few seconds before shooting the spike through his left eye. The man collapsed on top of the girl. Tag snuck a quick look around the corner and saw that the alley was now clear. Without warning the light illuminating the alley went out and they were plunged into darkness. In the faint glow of moonlight, Tag turned and saw Fez standing atop the dumpster and unscrewing the motion-activated bulb out of the socket. Once he'd removed it he jumped back down onto the cobblestones.

"Smart thinking, kid."

"My folks didn't raise no dummy."

The streetlights continued to illuminate the downtown district and Tag could see the diseased staggering along the main drag, searching for new people to infect. He wondered if the virus worked on a more complex level. Did it actually manage to convince the sick brain to seek out new hosts?

"The Bolas have no idea we're here, Tag. How long you think we can hang out in this alley?"

He shrugged. "Not very long."

"We're screwed if they find us."

"We've been down this road before." He laughed in bitter resignation.

"Yeah, I guess we're getting good at fighting all these sick puppies."

Tag knelt down and kept his eyes on the street. Some of them stopped at the entrance before moving on. He had no idea how they would escape from this situation or where they would go from here. If a large number of them stumbled down this alley then the two of them would be in big trouble. He had the police radio in his pocket, but he'd turned it off so as not to make any sound. With any luck the infected had developed a sensitivity to the light and would go into hiding once the sun came up.

He ordered Fez to rest; he'd keep watch for a few hours. Fez sat back against the wall and quickly fell asleep with his knees pushed up against his stomach. As Tag watched the procession stagger past, he thought about his wife and kids, praying that they were safe. Just knowing that his wife believed in him had given him hope to continue on. Coerced by the government to cooperate for political expediency, she'd been required to lie for the sake of their children.

Tears formed in his eyes. The events of the last five months had been hard. All his belief systems had been completely undone by the tragedies of the last year. Having been separated from his family, his trust in government and the military shattered, he felt adrift from all the institutions he'd once cherished. But he held out hope that one day he'd see his wife and kids again, and they would reunite as a family.

But then what? His life's work had been for naught, and a career's worth of research down the tubes. How could he and his family pick up where they left off after all that had happened?

Moving over to the far wall, he sat back against the bricks, feeling depressed, and kept his eyes trained on the street. Fez sat sleeping across from him. As his mind began to wander, he thought about all the good times he and his family had enjoyed on Cooke's Island: swimming on the beaches; clambakes over coals at night; cold beers in hand and laughing with friends. All those memories brought a smile to his face. The more he reflected on such blissful days, the more his eyelids began to droop, and before he knew it he fell asleep to the big lie that was his life.

He was shot up out of sleep twenty minutes later by the sound of an explosion off in the distance. What the hell was that? He wiped his eyes and looked around at his dark surroundings, cursing himself for falling asleep. *I could have gotten us killed!* And then the lights on the street flickered and died, plunging the town into darkness. Tag crawled over and nudged Fez awake.

"What?" he moaned sleepily.

"Something has happened. All the power in town is out and we need to move on."

"Aw, Tag. I was having such good dreams too."

"Sorry to ruin your sweet dreams, kid, but it's our signal to move out."

Chapter 35

Nolette had made her way halfway through the list when she stopped to take a break. Fatigue had set in and her vision became blurry. Her head throbbed from all the fast food and coffee she'd consumed in the last few days, not to mention the aftermath of her fierce struggle with Bacon. She walked around the hallway in a daze and took a brief bathroom break, hoping to rejuvenate herself with some cold water splashed in her face.

Her life had inexplicably changed and would never be the same. The trials and tribulations she'd endured would either propel her to celebrity or follow her to the grave. Neither scenario particularly appealed to her. She tried not to think about what might happen in this town, hoping to return to the task at hand. But she couldn't help thinking about what her life might be like if she somehow managed to make it out of this valley alive. Would she ever meet someone and have kids? Oddly, it was the first time she'd ever considered having a family.

A bit of fresh air might help clear her mind, she thought. And yet she was afraid to go outside for fear of what she might find. She made herself another cup of that horrible instant coffee before staring at the names she'd not already crossed off. An old radio sat on one of the bookshelves and so she turned it onto the local college station. 'Gigantic' by The Pixies played. She loved The Pixies.

Returning to the list, she checked off the next name on it. Each person had their own extensive biography as well as current photograph to cross-check it against. Forty-five minutes had passed before she came across the name of Bonnie Haldeman. Seemed innocent enough. Undergraduate and Ph.D. in biology from the University of Alaska. She accessed Hawthorne's database and examined all the required paperwork the woman had sent them. Scrolling down the screen, she made note of Haldeman's degrees and research papers, which were not as extensive as most of the others on the list she'd examined. Her company, Biodefense Constructs, had been registered with Alaska's Department of Commerce and was based out of Anchorage. Being an ethnic Tlingit no doubt helped facilitate her career as a scientist, as did being a woman in a male-dominated field. The photograph on her driver's license matched the photograph on her university guest pass. Everything looked good.

So why did she have a nagging feeling as she moved onto the next name on the list? Haldeman's resume seemed almost too perfect, and at the same time vague enough to pass muster with Hawthorne's officials. Something about it continued to stick in her craw and she didn't know why.

She resumed her background checks, working her way through the list. An hour and half later she completed her search. She'd scribbled five names on a legal pad for further examination. Two were Pakistani nationals; one was a Turkish Ph.D. who'd relocated to Houston; one was an American with nebulous ties to the CIA; and the last was Haldeman.

Exhausted, she walked over to the window and stared out into the darkness. A couple of drunken fools staggered over the grounds, most likely heading home after a long night of drinking. She tried desperately to kickstart her brain into gear, but the combination of fatigue, coffee, and pulsating headache dulled her senses.

Just for kicks, she returned to the laptop and typed in "Biodefense Constructs" and up popped an incredibly complex website with a full menu of options. She clicked through it, impressed with the slick graphics and the company's mission statement. *Vaccines: The Future of National Security.* A number of research papers and development projects were listed on the publication page. But oddly enough there was no list of clients, nor was there mention of any contracts awarded to the company. She guessed that such a list might be proprietary information and not available for security reasons, which made perfect sense. What was it about the woman's name that stuck in her craw? She typed in the name "Bonnie" and was about to add her last name when she heard an explosion go off in the distance. The fluorescent lights along the drop ceiling flickered and then died. She pushed the chair back and stood, frightened, and looked down at the computer screen. Although the laptop was operating on full battery, the wireless Internet connection had disconnected.

She ran out to the front desk and saw the desk sergeant holding a pair of binoculars and staring out the window.

"What just happened?" she asked.

"Don't know. Something exploded up on the mountain and knocked all the power out. Looks like the transmission tower blew a gasket." He turned to her, his face a shadow in the pitch dark room. "I don't like the looks of this, lady. All the phone lines are dead too."

"At least we still have our cell phones," Nolette said.

"Nope." The cop held out his cell phone. "Service is out on those too. Cell tower must have blown as well."

"Shit!"

Nolette stared out at the ball of light pulsing atop the mountain, trying to make sense of everything that was happening. A sudden wave of nausea came over her and she nearly fainted from the notion. Her brain had spit back the name of Bonnie Haldeman with a jarring vengeance, and she now recalled with startling clarity where she'd come across that name. It was during her research of the Branch Davidians that she'd seen it. The realization made her tremble with fear and nearly vomit.

Bonnie Haldeman was the name of David Koresh's *mother!*

Chapter 36

Monica scurried around the room, tidying up before Bonnie
arrived for their nonalcoholic nightcap. The brief meeting with
Tag had buoyed her spirits and motivated her to continue on.
Although she felt terrible about brushing him off, she had no
other choice. For now, it had to be that way. Her kids were at risk
if she came out publicly and defended her husband's integrity.
The security of the nation depended on pinning the blame on him.
Otherwise certain foreign nations would begin to grumble and the
American populace would become highly agitated, possibly
fomenting in revolt. Whatever government official had been in
charge of handling her after the attack on Cooke's Island had
made it abundantly clear that her kids' well-being depended on
how persuasive she could be.

She could see the bigger picture now. These attacks were
the work of a highly organized group, possibly working within the
U.S. government. Because Tag was out of commission, presumed
dead by most people, she felt it was up to her to try and discover
the truth about whom this imposter was. But in order to do that
she would need to do it covertly, without anyone in the
government knowing what she was up to.

The rap on the door snapped her back to reality. She shut
the drawer and took out the bottle of soda she'd placed in the
mini-fridge. Glancing around the room, she was satisfied with the
way it looked. She walked over and opened the door, gesturing
for Bonnie to come inside. Then she grabbed two glasses and
filled them. A feeling of dread came over her; she'd developed

such a healthy distrust of those around her that she wondered if she could ever trust anyone again.

"Cheers," she said, holding her glass up.

"To a new friendship," Bonnie said.

"That was a very impressive paper you wrote. I have to admit that I didn't understand a lot of what I read, but I think I got the gist of it."

"You actually read one of my papers? Well I'll be darned, Monica. Maybe there's hope for you after all."

"Does fifty percent comprehension rate merit any hope?"

"It's a start," Bonnie said, daintily tucking her nightgown under her bottom as she sat on the bed. "I'm afraid that's the nature of the beast with these conferences. Research papers tend to be esoteric and highly technical. But the crux of my work revolves around stopping the virus before it takes over the cell and begins replicating."

"Seems to make total sense to me." She sipped her cola. "I had no idea that Dr. Wolfe co-wrote that research paper with you." She thought she noticed a brief moment of hesitation on Bonnie's face.

"Yes, Dr. Wolfe and I corresponded quite often through email and over the phone. He's been a real mentor to me. His incredible knowledge of immunology has been invaluable to my own work." Bonnie sipped her soda.

"How come he didn't acknowledge you when he came over to speak to me this evening?"

Bonnie stared at her with a chagrined expression. "Because Dr. Wolfe and I haven't actually met in person. Our correspondence has been either by telephone or over the Internet. It's typical in this field, seeing as how most of us scientists are spread out over the country. Besides, you two seemed to be such good friends that I didn't want to ruin the moment. I spoke to him later at the cocktail reception."

Monica held the bottle out. "More soda?"

"Oh no, thank you. I'm quite tired and it's getting late. Besides, I have a seminar to give in the morning based on that paper you read."

"Attempted to read."

"Give yourself an A for effort, Monica," Bonnie said cheerfully. She stood and seemed to momentarily lose her balance. Rubbing her eyes, she fell back against the chair. "I don't know what's wrong with me. Guess I'm a little lightheaded from all the excitement."

"Take it easy."

"I'm okay—I think. Just give me a sec to collect myself."

"I'm afraid you won't have time for that, Bonnie," she said, standing over the chair. "Or whoever you are."

"Monica? What are you doing?"

"I suspected you all along."

The woman tried to lift her arms and legs but realized that she couldn't move. Her eyes rolled in her head and saliva began to dribble down the corners of her mouth. She tried to talk but her words came out slurred and incomprehensible.

Monica pulled a roll of masking tape out of the drawer and wrapped it around Bonnie's wrist so that it remained bound to the arm of the chair.

Bonnie lifted her free hand with considerable effort and reached into her pocket. Monica wondered what she was doing, knowing full well that any weapon would be useless in her weakened grip. Bonnie removed a cell phone out of her pocket and the screen flashed to life.

"What are you doing?" Monica asked.

Bonnie struggled but managed to punch in three digits. Monica ran over and slapped the phone out of her hand, fortunate to have stopped her before she'd dialed the full number. It crashed to the floor, but not before emitting a loud series of beeps. Bonnie laughed drunkenly as Monica picked it up off the carpet and studied it. Fireworks appeared on the screen. A few seconds passed before she heard a muffled boom go off in the distance. She ran over to the window, pulled the curtains aside, and saw two fireballs pulsing atop a mountain peak. The lights in the hotel room blinked and then went out. All over the valley the lights died, leaving a black slate for her to gaze out at. She ran back to Bonnie, now slumped in the chair, and ripped the wig off her head. The man's eyes rolled back in his head.

"What have you done?" she asked, trying to recognize his features in the dark. The mascara painted over his face had further prevented her from identifying him.

The man smiled in a boozy manner.

"Son-of-bitch!" She slapped him hard across the face.

He tried to hold his head up, but couldn't because of his weakened neck muscles.

"You're the one responsible for Cooke's Island, aren't you?"

He smiled at her.

"What have you done here in Brookhaven?"

"Eeeee," he moaned with considerable effort. He lifted his free hand a few inches off the arm of the chair. "Bola."

Monica fell back in shock at the realization. Ebola! It was the worst virus one could imagine, and a horrific way to die. She found her phone but realized she had no cell service. The hotel's WiFi connection had also been disabled. In fact there was not a WiFi connection to be found anywhere. She found her suitcase and emptied the contents onto the bed, searching unsuccessfully for her glasses. Outside the room, she could hear people stampeding through the hallway and trying to escape out of the lobby. She prayed that Tag would be okay until she could meet up with him again. But she was determined not leave here without some answers to her questions.

After grabbing the duct tape, she pulled out her glass bead-making kit and opened the tool belt. Each particular tool had been stored in its assigned pocket. She took this kit everywhere she went so that she could work on her bead art in her spare time. Returning to the bed, she rifled through her junk until she found the propane fuel cylinder. Once she had what she needed, she swiped everything off the bed with her arm.

The fire atop the mountain continued to glow. She went over to the imposter, still sitting semi-conscious in the chair, and cut the tape around his wrist. Then she put his arm over her shoulder and guided him over to the bed. Since the disaster on Cooke's Island, her strength had deteriorated to that of a child. Prior to the attack, she used to run three miles a day and work out with weights in the gym. Her body had been like a machine and she'd fueled it accordingly. Now she felt like an old, wrinkled woman who had lost her youthful vigor. As much as she loved her husband—and she'd never considered herself a shallow person— she felt it unfair to him to be married to such an ugly hag.

She stared down at this man, hating him more than anything else in the world. This monster on the bed had been responsible for all her woes, and now she was going to make him pay. Out of her kit she removed a pair of sharp scissors. She cut away the robe from his body until it fell by his side; he was dressed only in lingerie. Seemed rather odd that he would assume this role so thoroughly, including wearing satin pink panties and matching bra when they would have never been seen.

The drug would soon wear off so she needed to act quickly. Dampening a hand towel, she cleaned off his make-up until his face was scrubbed clean. Although she couldn't quite see all his features in the dark, she knew this was the face of the devil. He gazed up at her, slurring his words and fluttering his eyelids. He would soon find out what horrors she'd inflict on him.

She taped his ankles together and then bound up his wrists, letting them rest over his crotch. Turning him onto his stomach, she noticed the faint outline of a tattoo etched across his back, stretching up over his shoulder blades. Because of her poor vision, she struggled to fully make it out. But upon closer examination she noticed that the design was similar to the imagery left on the wall of her summer home: a liger! Then it occurred to her that he was the one who'd sent her that glass sculpture filled with the smallpox dust.

She put her face a millimeter above his flesh and saw the word "REVELATION" in gothic dark lettering. The artistry of the tattoo amazed her. The giant cat rose up off his flesh, claws raised, as if it might leap off the man's back. It took her a few seconds to realize that the man was gagging, that his airway had been impeded by the mattress. Let him suffer, she thought as she waited a few more agonizing seconds before flipping him over.

"No more," he gasped.

"Fuck you, asshole!"

He groaned as she placed a piece of duct tape over his mouth. She'd make him talk, but only after he suffered. Using a C-clamp, she attached the propane tank to the nightstand and then attached the hothead torch. She kept the spark lighter nearby for when she was ready to begin the session.

Funny how things had changed. Prior to all this, she'd considered herself an advocate of human rights. She'd volunteered at a battered women's shelter. Spent time helping immigrant families adjust to their new lives in America. Ironically, a good portion of her volunteer activities had been spent advocating for C.A.T. (Coalition Against Torture). And now here she was with a blow torch in one hand and a set of torture tools in the other. Her family, as well as her country, was in jeopardy and she'd do anything to protect them; and if that included torching this devil then so be it.

Where should she start? She grabbed the pliers and held them over his eyes. His nostrils fluttered like a hummingbird as he struggled in vain to get in air through his nose. She took one of his toes in the pliers and squeezed as hard as she could until she'd pulled off the nail. His muffled scream let her know that he was now feeling the pain. Blood poured from the gash once she released her grip. But the physical act had taken a lot out of her, and she had to step away and catch her breath. She felt weak and dizzy. She reached in her belt and searched for an easier device; a tool that would cause maximum pain and prolonged agony without much exertion.

Replacing the pliers, she slid the double-ended pick out of the sleeve and pressed the point against her thumb. A trickle of blood bubbled out of it. Satisfied, she jabbed the point into his cheek until it penetrated through the flesh and into the gums. Surprisingly, she felt an immense satisfaction in making him suffer, and this feeling of power both stimulated and confused her. Seeking pleasure from another being's pain felt uncivilized and brutish. And yet she couldn't deny the power that she felt surging through her veins. She brushed off her misgivings, eager to get back to the task at hand. She jabbed the pick into his ear, hoping to shatter the drum. Another muffled scream. Then she went up and down his body, piercing sections of his skin as if he was a pin cushion.

The man beneath her looked as if he might pass out from the pain. His face shone red and she could tell he was in immense pain. She moved to his head and in one motion ripped the duct tape off his mouth. He cried out and gulped in air, his fine-boned chest heaving up and down in violent spasms.

"Who else is involved?"

The man swallowed before regaining his composure. His jaw hung open, slack and glistening with saliva.

"Okay, buster, have it your way," she said, picking up the strip of tape and holding it over his mouth.

"This is bigger than you think," he slurred, his voice starting to return. "You can kill me, Monica, but it still won't change a thing."

"Oh really?" She squeezed the spark lighter and a blue flame danced from the head of the torch. "Let's just see about that."

"You can't hurt me. You're wasting your time."

"Don't worry, I've got a lot of time to waste now that we're stuck here together." She moved toward his feet. Blood dripped over the comforter. "I suppose we'll hang out in this room and waste time together."

"You're not cut out for this, Monica. You're too good of a person to torture me."

"No, I used to be a good person. That part of me has died, thanks to you."

She aimed the flame along the balls of his feet, holding it there until he cried out in pain. By now most of the hotel guests here were either downstairs in the lobby or holed up in their rooms and waiting for the power to return. She knew that no one would dare intercede when they heard his desperate cries for help.

"Please, Monica."

She retracted the flame. "What should I call you while I'm busy torturing you?"

He gasped, saying nothing.

"Okay, asshole, take a deep breath before I go in for more."

"There's no way you're making it out of here alive."

"What's the difference; we're all going to die sooner or later."

"Ebola's a terrible way to die."

"As is being tortured to death."

She positioned the flame under his panties and the satin material blackened and burned away. He let out a terrifying scream once the flame hit his testicles, and when she looked up she could just make out the hint of tears streaming down his bloodied cheeks. Holding the blue flame over his face, she could clearly see traces of his adolescent acne.

"You're going to die a slow and painful death if you don't let me go," he said.

"Oh really?" She laughed. "I was about to say the same thing to you."

"You should be thanking me. I saved your life on that island."

She aimed the flame at his cheek and burned the flesh until it bubbled and crisped. His lips convulsed in pain and she moved around and scorched the other side of his face. He was barely conscious now, and his head rolled to one side. She wanted this bastard to feel all the pain that she had felt.

"Who else is involved in this?"

He spit but it only bubbled over his scaly lips. "You can't hurt me, Monica."

303

She recalled how her own family had suffered as she aimed the flame over his bloodied ear. She was about to move in closer when she heard a knock at the door.

Now who the hell is that?

Another knock. Angry, Monica shut off the blow torch and moved to the door. Peering through the eyehole, she saw nothing but pitch blackness. A woman screamed somewhere down the hallway. It sounded like mayhem out there, but she swore she wouldn't open this door for anyone she didn't know.

"Who is it and what do you want?"

"It's me, Monica. Simon. It's important you let me in."

Simon? What was he doing here?

"Dr. Wolfe?"

"Yes. It's a matter of life and death, Monica."

Relieved at the sound of his voice, she knew he'd understand why she'd done what she did. Simon Wolfe was as fond of Tag as anyone and would be ecstatic to learn that he was still alive. She unlocked the door and released the dead bolt, allowing him to enter.

"Are you okay, dear?" he asked, holding her by the elbows.

"I'm fine, Simon. Thank God you're here." She saw his eyes gravitate to the man on the bed.

"What's that smell? Oh my God, it's repulsive." He slipped past her to better see the man. "Oh, Monica. What have you done?"

"Simon, meet the asshole who released that smallpox virus on Cooke's Island. Of course you would know him as Bonnie Halderman. I stopped him before he could unleash that virus here in Brookhaven."

"Oh no, Monica," he lamented, staring down at the man's mutilated body. "Surely this is not the way to proceed in a civilized society." He turned to her. "You've stooped to their level."

"Who gives a fuck, Simon! This man is guilty of genocide, and we've prevented another attack," she said, angered by his pitiful response. "This son-of-bitch has broken up my family and made my husband a national pariah. So fuck him."

"This has changed you, Monica. You're no longer the peaceful woman I once knew." A look of sorrow passed over his celebrated face, thanks to all his appearances on the cable news outlets.

"Are you being serious, Simon?"

"Both of my parents survived the horror of the Nazi Holocaust. Violence can never be the solution."

"Bullshit! You wouldn't have killed Hitler if you had the chance to save innocent people's lives?"

"You're not the same woman I once knew." He shook his head as if terribly disappointed. "We've gathered here to do good and make the world a better place, Monica. As a doctor, I've taken a sworn oath."

"Fuck your oath then." Why was he saying such things and making her out to be the villain?

He pulled a 12mm out of his coat pocket and pointed it at her.

"Simon?"

"I'm afraid the oath I've taken is much grander than merely saving individual lives, Monica. It's about the future of mankind on this endangered planet, all of which has been prophesied throughout the ages."

"Oh my God, Simon. You've known the entire time, haven't you?"

"There are more people out there just like me willing to stand up and fight for what is good and right. It filters up through the ranks of government and the military." He looked genuinely pained to be doing this. "Now put that torch down, Monica, and back up against the wall."

Confused by this turn of events, she dropped the torch and put her hands up. How many scientists attending this conference were conspiring with him, she wondered. Had the entire conference been merely a front to facilitate these traitorous murderers? She thought of Tag and the kids, wondering if she'd ever see them again. At least he was out still there and still fighting. No one knew Tag like she did; he would do everything in his power to make those responsible pay for their crimes. Her own life would soon end, and she was at peace with that. She only wished she could tell her kids one last time how much she loved them.

Simon walked over to the man with the tattoo and stared at him.

"I hate to inform you, Monica," Simon said, turning to face her, "but your punishment had no effect on him whatsoever. This man is a giant among men."

"You should have been here when he cried like a little bitch."

"Impossible." He looked up at her. "It was all an act, and one for which he should probably win an award for."

She felt momentarily confused, certain that she'd burned and cut his flesh.

"He has Congenital Insensitivity to Pain." He helped the man up to a sitting position, gently removing the tape from his mouth.

"I bend but I don't break." The man grabbed a lighter out of his bag and held the flame to his palm. "But I'm very impressed with your calculated determination, Monica. I think you missed your true calling in life."

Chapter 37

Tag pushed Fez back against the brick wall and pinned him there until he felt they were ready to make a break for it. The diseased shuffled along the street, docile and slow. Limited by their cerebral hemorrhaging, they'd been reduced to autobots, their primary goal being to pass on the virus and keep the chain going. He counted down to three. Then he and Fez bolted down the long, dark alley until they reached the street. They sprinted past the mob, many of who were crossing mindlessly over the median strip. It took them a few seconds before they caught wind of their presence, and once they did the mob turned en masse and started after them. The sound of their cries commingling in the night reminded him of the smallpox victims on Cooke's Island.

Tag grabbed Fez by the collar and directed him over to a nearby sporting goods store. Using the butt of his rifle, he pounded the pane of glass until it smashed apart.

"Why we going in here?" Fez asked.

"Because they're all around us. If we're lucky, maybe they'll have some ammo stocked inside."

He climbed through the window and headed toward the back of the facility. Peering through the warehouse door, he saw four employees sitting on boxes and looking bored. He shook the door, but realized it was locked. Then he banged his fist against it and shouted for them to open, but they merely looked away in shame. Behind him the mob had begun to make their way in through the broken window. He couldn't really blame the employees for refusing to let him in, but he'd be damned if he didn't do all he could to break down this door.

"Open up!" he shouted, ramming the butt of the rifle into the wire-encased glass.

"They're ten feet from us," Fez said, elbowing him in the back.

He battered the door repeatedly. "Open up or we're going to die out here!"

Two diseased guys in railroad uniforms approached twenty feet away along the rack filled with golf clubs. Four others staggered past the fly fishing department.

He continued to batter the window until the glass shattered and the wire mesh split apart. Punching his hand through the shards of glass and twisted wire, he reached down and turned the door handle. A terrible thud sounded behind him and upon turning around he saw Fez swinging a three wood into a guy's head. The young girl inside the storeroom screamed. He grabbed Fez and ushered him through the open door. Then he sprinted behind the kid and into the storeroom, locking the door behind him.

"Why didn't you open the door?" he shouted at the four employees.

"Why the hell do you think?" a young guy said sheepishly. The four employees were still wearing their striped referee shirts and black pants.

"You dumb asses," Fez said, standing in front of the four employees. "You know who this guy is?"

The employees glanced over at him and shook their heads. Tag was getting tired of Fez's introductions, but he knew it was only because the kid idolized him.

"This is Colonel Winters, jackasses. The dude who survived that attack on Cooke's Island," Fez said. "So don't even think about messing with him."

Tag paced back and forth, knowing that he'd be a hypocrite if he chewed these four employees out for not letting him enter.

"Sorry," the teenage kid said, staring over at the infected banging against the locked door, their faces pressed up against the mesh wire.

"Those freaks never would have gotten inside if you guys hadn't smashed through the front door," the pretty blonde girl said. "We had the perfect hiding spot until you came along. Those things out there didn't even know we were here."

"Maybe for a couple of days you might have been okay. Then what?" Tag asked. "You got portable grills back here? You got a storage room filled with food? After a week you all would have ended up dying of starvation."

"A bunch of them are pouring into the store," Fez said, standing on a treadmill box and looking through the broken window.

"Where's the ammo?"

"Guns and ammo are Trevor's department. He called in sick today, the lucky bastard," an older man said.

"Probably not as lucky as you think," Tag said. "Why didn't you guys grab a few rifles and arm yourselves?"

"The guns are locked up behind bars and none of us has a key to it. That's Trevor's job," the guy said, leading Tag over to where the firearms were kept in stock. "There's some ammo out back, but not very much. Trevor says it's been difficult to get his hands on ammo these days because of the new Patriot Act. Says it's all a conspiracy to go around the Second Amendment."

"Two boxes? That's all you keep inventoried?"

"Like I told you, Trevor says that shit's hard to come by."

"Trevor must be stupid or just an incompetent."

"A little of both. But he's been working here for five years now," the older guy said, laughing. "Promote the incompetent is the motto of this company."

"Maybe you should try looking for better help, Marvin," Tag said, eying the man's name tag.

"Good help is hard to come by in this small town. We're lucky to have the crew we got."

"Is there a back door?"

309

"There's a loading dock in the back but it's motorized. No power, no opening the door. And from what I can see the power is out."

Tag grabbed the box of ammo off the stack. The Remington had a five-shot capacity and he figured that he should grab enough to get them safely back to the police station. He picked up a lime green aluminum baseball bat and tossed it to Fez. Fez dropped the three wood and caught the bat by the handle.

Gathering the four frightened store employees around him, Tag ordered them to grab a bat, lacrosse or hockey stick for protection. Once they were armed, he led them toward the door. He waited a few seconds before ramming it open with his shoulder. The infected blocking the door flew back against two mannequins holding tennis rackets and decked out in clothes fit for Wimbledon.

They sprinted through the dark storeroom, knocking over sporting equipment as they passed, making sure to stay clear of the diseased stumbling through the aisles.

They hit the street running. Tag heard some of the victims calling out to them for help. He recalled similar behaviors on Cooke's Island, though not quite the same. The smallpox victims, like the victims here, had retained some of their cognitive functioning while in the midst of their degenerative disease. Of course this articulation happened only in brief moments of clarity when their hyper-aggression had temporarily waned. But soon after the primitive functions took control of their brain and the aggression came roaring back to life.

They ran through the streets, dodging and fighting them off with their weapons. Tag battered those in his way with the butt of his gun, the stock of which was now slick with blood. He shouted for the others to cover their mouths with their shirts, knowing full well that the blood in the air was in the form of a fine mist. They approached a deserted intersection and stopped to catch their breath.

"What's our plan now, Tag?" Fez asked as they stopped in the middle of the junction.

"We need to get back to the police station. Once you guys are safely inside I'll be heading over to the hotel to bring back my wife."

The four employees clutched their knees, trying to catch their breath.

"I'm not sure I can travel any further," Marvin said, laughing hysterically.

"What's so funny?" asked Fez.

"I work in a sports store and I'm so badly out of shape," Marvin said.

"Take another second to catch your breath, Marvin. We'll get you back to the station in one piece," Tag said.

"Don't take too long though, because more of those Bolas are heading toward us," Fez said, turning to see the horde approaching from the end of the street.

"Any of you know the way to the police station?" Tag asked, looking around in confusion.

"It's about six blocks away," the pretty girl named Amber said. "My dad's a cop. We take a left on Franklin and then a right on Pearl, and the station is about a half mile down the road."

"Thanks, Amber," Tag said.

"This sporting goods gig is just a part time job," she said to Fez for no apparent reason. "I'm actually a full-time student at Brookhaven Community College."

"How come you don't go to that fancy college up on that hill?" Fez asked.

Amber laughed. "Are you kidding? On my dad's salary. I couldn't afford sixty-two thousand dollars a year to study French literature. Besides, you need perfect SAT scores to get into that pretentious place, and they hardly ever accept townies anyway. I wouldn't go there even if they did give me a full scholarship "

Tag looked back and saw a horde approaching out of the shadows. By now his eyes had adjusted to the dark and he could see clearly. This was another stroke of luck: the sky was clear and the full moon glowed brightly above. Up ahead he saw a few individuals headed their way. They had no choice but to press ahead.

"Heads up, people. We got some coming our way," Tag said. "We need to stay together. And be careful where you swing those clubs. I don't feel like getting a three iron in the kisser."

They started forward. The shrill sound of a woman screaming bore into his soul, but there was nothing he could do. Such senseless violence saddened him, but he'd grown so accustomed to the sounds of violence by now that he'd become numb to it. That he could not save any of these innocent souls hurt him more than anything else.

The sickly slagged toward them. He rammed the butt into the first one's head and watched it explode on impact. Their infected brains had swelled beyond repair and were now like pressure cookers waiting to go off. Behind him he could hear the swish of golf clubs through the air followed by the grisly thumps as the metal pounded their peach-soft skulls.

A cry went up. Tag cracked one of the infected before turning to see that Marvin had tripped. His face landed in a pool of blood and it splashed up into his eyes and mouth. Instinctively, he smeared it across his face with his forearm, embedding the infection deeper into his pores. He cried out in agony as three of the infected converged on him.

"Get up, Marvin!"

"I can't see anything. It's in my eyes."

He swiped the blood out of his eyes, trying desperately to spit it out of his mouth. Climbing to his knees and temporarily blinded, he stared vacantly down at his spattered hands. The realization of what he'd done caused him to cry out. Tag ran over against his better judgment and tried to help him, but out of nowhere a rabid woman descended upon Marvin like a bloodthirsty eagle and sank her teeth into his neck. Blood spurted out of the wound. The infected woman relaxed her jaw and looked up. Blood dripped from her teeth and glistened in the moonlight. Amber lifted the green metal bat and smashed her head in with one swing. Droplets of blood flew through the air and splattered against their clothing.

Marvin stood uneasily, his neck and zebra uniform drenched in blood. He dropped his Louisville Slugger and looked around uneasily, understanding the severity of his wound. Tag knew instantly that the man was doomed, but he helped him up to his feet nonetheless.

They sprinted away from the intersection and slowed to a brisk walking pace. He saw the entrance to a park across the street. The temperature felt as if it had dipped into the mid-thirties, and yet sweat dripped down his forehead. They walked down the center of the street, using the median line as their guide. Shadows moved in his peripheral vision. Or maybe it was his imagination playing tricks on him. Further up he could see a faint light flickering in the window of the police station. It was comforting to know that someone was still inside and holding down the fort.

"Come on," he said to the group. "Let's hustle."

The six of them broke into a jog just as Marvin collapsed to the ground, sobbing into his hands. Tag noticed that he was sweating profusely. Had the infection already taken hold of him? It appeared that the virus's incubation period progressed at a much faster pace than the traditional strains. Replication seemed to have been almost instantaneous to infection. The scientist in him wondered how a virus of this strain could be manufactured in the lab. Whoever had created it was either extremely lucky or an evil genius on par with Einstein and Salk. The prospect of such viral behavior both intrigued and frightened the shit out of him. How could they ever defend this great nation against such cutting edge science?

He knelt down next to Marvin and waited for him to stop sobbing. What could he say to make him feel better, knowing that he was doomed to die? That he'd soon turn into one of these freaks?

"The disease is in me, Colonel. I can feel it like a worm wriggling through my veins." He glanced up at him, his eyes already turning red. He laughed in resignation.

Tag kept silent; there was nothing he could say to make him feel better.

"Is there a cure for this?" Small red dots began to pop over his cheeks.

"There's always hope," he said, knowing that even in the best of times, with the top doctors in the field, the death rate exceeded eighty percent.

"You're a good liar, Colonel!" He shook his head and laughed.

"Come back with us and we'll see what we can do for you. I'm a medical doctor. We'll put you in quarantine, give you lots of liquid, and then maybe—"

"No!" Marvin shouted. "We both know it's fucking useless. Besides, I could infect the rest of you."

"You should at least try. We can lock you up in one of the cells."

"If that's the best I can expect then I don't want to go on living."

Marvin stood to his feet, his hands forming into fists. Pinpricks of blood trickled from the corners of his eyes. Tag kept perfectly still, fearing that if he made a sudden movement he might incite Marvin to violence. The worm had entered his bloodstream and would soon be weaving quilts in his brain. He kept his eyes trained on the man's face, which appeared unnaturally calm. Then, without warning, Marvin swung a fist at his head. Tag ducked and stepped backward in a fighting stance. "We would have been fine if you assholes didn't break into our store," Marvin shouted. Fez sprinted over with bat in hand and cut him off at the shins. Marvin fell to his knees as Fez delivered a lethal blow to his head, instantly killing him. Blood and brain matter oozed out of the gash at the base of his skull. Tag knelt down and noticed that it was the color and consistency of healthy human blood. The infection had not yet churned it into a toxic viral sludge. Marvin had been pissed-off and wanted to die.

Amber began to cry, and Tag realized that he needed to get them all back to safety before the situation escalated. The other employees seemed too shocked by the killing to say anything or complain. They stared at Fez as if he was a psychopath, the way he'd killed with such immunity. Movement, Tag knew, would keep their minds off the fact that their co-worker had just been slaughtered by a scrawny kid.

They jogged the rest of the way. Once on station grounds, they climbed the granite steps and reached the front door. Tag pounded on it with the butt of his rifle, calling out for someone to let them in. He looked behind him and saw a small crowd of people congregating on the street. Upon seeing them, they turned and stumbled forward. A man's voice called out to them behind the door, asking if any of them had the infection.

"What the fuck do you think!" Amber screamed in hysterics, pounding the door with her fists. "Now let us in, asshole! My father's a cop here!"

Nolette's face appeared behind the mesh-filled window and, after recognizing them, she swung the door open. The five of them rushed inside, collapsing along the marbled floor. Swain quickly slammed the door shut behind her, and in less than a minute the mob had pushed up against it and began to pound on it with their fists. Their battered and beaten faces smashed up against the bars over the window until it dug into their flesh. Tag sat with his back up against the door and closed his eyes. Knowing that he couldn't appear weak in front of the others, he gathered his composure and tried not to dwell on the death and dying.

"Are you alright, Colonel?" Swain asked, squatting down next to him.

"Yeah. I just need a moment."

"I understand completely." She put her hand on his knee. "It may not help at this point, Colonel, but I think I found something that might interest you."

315

He took his face out of his hands and looked at her.

"There's a scientist attending this conference named Bonnie Halderman. For whatever reason her name stuck out in my mind. After conducting further research, I'm fairly confident that she may have played a role in these attacks."

"Bonnie Halderman?" He shook his head. "Never heard of her before."

"You wouldn't have because her name and identity is an alias. Not really an alias, but borrowed from a real life person. She used it to set up a business with the Alaska Department of Commerce called Biodefense Constructs. I did some research and learned that it's not that difficult to set up a corporation in Alaska. Her academic credentials are all from the University of Alaska and she's set up a professional website listing her business as well as all her publications."

"I'm listening."

"We've established the fact that Remington Guilfoyle had been in the Branch Davidian compound when the ATF raided it. And he'd been there when the FBI took over negotiations, reneged on these same negotiations, and then burned the compound to the ground, killing hundreds of people. Vernon Howell. Do you know who that man was, Colonel?"

"No idea." He shook his head.

"It was David Koresh's real name."

"So where we going with all this?"

"Don't you see the connection? Bonnie Halderman was the name of David Koresh's mother."

"His mother?"

"Not only that, Colonel, but the coauthor listed in every single one of her publications is none other than Dr. Simon Wolfe, professor emeritus at Harvard University Medical School and your one-time mentor. And if I remember correctly, my paper ran an investigative report this year about a criminal gang in this country using Eastern European migrants as guinea pigs for their various drug experiments. The criminal mastermind of this gang was an individual with the name of Dragan Vukovich. Just this

316

year, before the attack on Cooke's Island, your beloved Dr. Simon Wolfe made a special business trip to Albania to oversee some medical labs. Seems obvious now that it was all a cover. "

Tag looked up at her battered face and tried to make sense of these words. It couldn't be true. He refused to believe that Simon could have had anything to do with this.

No! It can't be him! Not Simon!

Chapter 38

Wolfe ordered her to stand back against the wall. Gripping the gun in one hand, he reached into his pocket with the other and pulled out a pocket knife. Then he cut the masking tape binding his colleague's arms and ankles. Despite being tortured by the various tools of her trade, he sat up without complaint, no evidence of having suffered. Even in the dark she could see that his face was now a blistering, charred mess. Pus oozed out of the cracks like slugs emerging from the dirt. And yet, despite it all, he smiled, knowing that the power balance had just shifted.

"Very well done, Monica. You may not believe me but I'm very proud of you," the tortured man said.

"Go to hell!"

"My, you're as feisty as that husband of yours." He turned to Wolfe. "Thank you so much, Simon. It's nice to know I can count on you."

"Are you okay?" Simon asked.

"Couldn't be better. Would you mind grabbing me one of her nightgowns?"

Monica couldn't comprehend such insensitivity to pain. Any other person would be crying out in agony and require immediate medical attention. But he just sat there as if nothing had happened. Once he'd slipped on one of her robes, along with the black wig over his scalp, he strolled casually out of the hotel room on blistered feet. Wolfe ordered her to sit on the bed. She noticed that Simon was dressed in his signature charcoal gray suit, the one he wore on all the talk shows. With his horn-rimmed glasses and red bow tie, no one would ever mistake him for a bio-terrorist. He stood a few feet away from her, clutching the gun awkwardly in his hand.

"Why, Simon?" she asked. "Is he paying you a fortune?."

"Admittedly, the money's good, but that's not the primary reason for all this." He strolled over to her. "Have you seen the state of things lately, Monica? The world is falling apart around us. Moral decay is rampant and sinners are emboldened by vice. I've been studying viruses my entire life, wondering about their life cycles and their purpose in nature's scheme of things, especially considering their destructive force and the toll they've wrought on humanity. It never made any sense to me, no matter how hard I tried to intellectualize it. That is until I studied the Book of Revelations. You see, Monica, bringing about the end of times is not just God's will but our moral responsibility to future generations."

"But you've killed and maimed innocent people. You're just as evil and depraved as every other mad butcher in the world, Simon, including the Nazis."

"I'll turn the question around so it makes more sense. Wouldn't *you* have exterminated Hitler and all the people in his regime? It's exactly what I'm doing."

"You've turned that moral question on its head, Simon. It's apples and oranges!"

"Is it? Moral decay is rampant: legalized drug use; the death of innocent children in the womb; men lying down with other men; political corruption the likes we haven't seen before; ongoing wars and international disputes between godless heathens. This is exactly what the Book of Revelations speaks to. Now the planet is dying and it's too late to turn back."

"From what I remember about the Book of Revelations, the end of times will be God's handiwork and not man's," she said, trying to buy herself more time.

"Yes, this is true. But then it mentions wars, which are made by man. It's when I realized that plagues are God's unique creation as well as His divine will. What other purpose do they serve other than to facilitate mass genocide? It's the one and only reason viruses exist; they are a tool given to us by our creator to bring forth eternity. And with global warming on the rise, the severity and frequency of viral outbreaks will be significant."

"You're a man of reason and science, Simon. You can't possibly believe that the destruction of our race is divinely ordained." She felt the propane tank pressing against her calf, and it gave her an idea.

"Oh, but I do, Monica. Why else would these microscopic life forms be programmed to maim and kill, if not for a higher purpose? Mankind has ruined this planet with its addiction to fossil fuels. Unfortunately, being a man of science, the science is telling us that we've reached the point of no return."

She knew she had little time to act if she wanted to save herself from certain death—or worse. Wolfe was in his mid-sixties and wore powerful glasses, but his reactions had no doubt slowed with age. Assessing this weakness, and taking in the fact that his vision must be limited, she decided on a plan of action.

"I don't understand. Why not just infect the entire world rather than these small towns?" she asked.

"Despite the lethal nature of these viruses, Ebola being near the top of the list, there's still not a pathogen capable of wiping out everyone on the planet. My guess is that it will take a rare mutating flu virus to do the trick. Until that time, we need a political solution; a government to oversee events until the climactic changes bring forth this savior. This is what Jesus meant by the Second Coming. It could happen tomorrow, or it could take fifty years. It's why we need to take over the running of this country until that time comes. And the events of these past few months are informing us that there's no better person to represent the people than your husband."

She laughed at the absurdity of this. "Tag would never do such a thing."

"He would if it meant saving his family and insuring the health of millions of Americans. He's a leader, and a morally strong leader at that. The people of this country will accept him with open arms."

She knew he was right about her husband being a great leader, and about accepting the role if it meant saving his family.

"This person has to be authentic, heroic in the Greek myth tradition, and seen as a legitimate hero by the American people. We believe your husband is that person, Monica. When citizens see the lies propagated by their government they'll be sure to flock to him."

She laughed, pressing her calf against the cold cylinder, and fingered the nozzle. "He just won't do it."

Simon shrugged. "That may well be the case. Besides, he has one more hurdle to jump before he proves himself worthy to our cause." He paced nervously back and forth, not used to the role of kidnapper, but comfortable lecturing a captive audience.

"Tag adored you, Simon. He saw you almost as a father figure."

"And I love and admire him dearly," he said, moving closer.

"But Tag's been presumed dead. His name and reputation are in tatters. How would you ever convince the public that he's alive, never mind the one to lead them?"

"People love redemption, Monica, and second acts in life. It's why he's the perfect candidate. The first shall be last and the last shall be first. Once people realize the level of corruption that exists in our government, and the degree to which they polluted our planet, this new leader will rise up from the ashes. They'll embrace him as if he were the prodigal son, which in many ways he is."

"My husband's a good man, but he's still only a man."

"Your husband is a brilliant scientist and a man of impeccable morals. His encyclopedic knowledge of virology and infectious diseases, apart from our friend here, is unrivaled in the field. It's another reason he's the perfect candidate. Despite what you think, the student has far surpassed the teacher, and for that I admire him greatly."

"And yet a man of impeccable morals would never create such a deadly disease," she said, focusing on his unzipped fly. "And he would never ever unleash a lethal contagion on his own citizens."

"And yet God created these viruses for a reason. So why is it you cast no aspersions on Him. Is God not blameless in all this?" He paced the floor in front of her. "Tag had obviously never mentioned to you the covert research he'd been doing on hybrid viruses for the NSA. Yes, we conversed about this work on many occasions, and I advised him as best I could, but I was no match for his intellect, nor did I possess the security clearance to fully discuss such sensitive matters with him. It was his research on these matters that formed the jumping-off platform for our own domestic activities."

"That's not true! Tag would have told me if he'd been working on such a secret project," she said.

"He was forbidden by law to speak to anyone about that research. Not even with his closest family members."

"I know my husband better than anyone and there is no way he would have been developing biological weapons without telling me. He didn't believe in that sort of thing."

"You poor, idealistic thing. He was cataloging and developing hybrids for the specific purpose of developing them into vaccines, not to take them into actual battle. His own understanding of climate change convinced him that there would be a desperate need for these vaccines in the future."

"He'll never go along with your plan."

"He'll have no other option. Hard choices will be made. And with his history of making difficult decisions, he'll have the full support of the American people. Of course you'll have the opportunity to be his beloved first lady, if the opportunity ever presents itself."

She wanted to spit in his face, but kept her composure.

"The sun will be coming up in a few hours and when that happens all the world will see what has happened to this quaint little town."

"Just to let you know, Simon, so that you don't ruin your impeccable image; you're flying low." She nodded toward his crotch.

"Huh?"

She pointed. "Your fly is open."

He craned his neck to see. "So it is."

Simon tucked the gun under his chin and reached down to zip up his fly. Wasting no time, she grabbed hold of the hot head torch and swung the tank at his head. Wolfe glanced up at the last second, but it was too late. The cylinder banged off his temple and he fell back against the wall in a daze. His mangled glasses dangled from the bridge of his nose. He raised the gun toward the ceiling and fired off a round. Dazed but still conscious, he fired a second shot in her general vicinity. Monica felt a stinging pain, and realized to her dismay that the bullet had grazed her shoulder.

She sprinted out of the room before the devil returned. The hallway was pitch black and eerily quiet. She felt her way along the corridor by palming the wallpaper. Once at the elevator, she pounded the button with the heel of her palm, fearful that at any moment she might see him. Why wasn't the elevator door opening? It took her a second to realize that there was no power. She turned the corner and peeled down the stairs.

Gripping the handrail, her footsteps echoed in the stairwell. The pain in her shoulder throbbed red hot. Once she reached the bottom, she felt around in the dark until she located the door. She pushed it open and entered the lobby. The grand window had been smashed, and she saw shadows moving along the floor. What were they doing, she wondered. A flashlight lay near her feet, throwing a beam of light along the marble tiles. The shadows turned and began to move toward her, their faces sticky with a tar-like substance. It took her a second to see that there were bodies sprawled along the floor.

She picked up the flashlight and shone it in their eyes. Almost instantly they brought their arms up to their faces. The walls were splattered with blood and the smell of dead, rotting flesh nearly made her sick. She took off running as a hulking man approached. Streaks of blood streaked across his face. Hearing him hot on her heels, she spun around and cracked the flashlight across his cheek and watched as his nose ripped from its base. The wet sound of his breathing frightened her as she ran through the puddles of blood.

Jagged fragments of glass formed a ring around the broken window frame, and she feared that one of the shards might drop down like a guillotine over her head. She stepped gingerly over a broken piece and heard footsteps coming up behind her. A pug-faced woman wearing Native American jewelry limped toward her, her blood-caked arms reaching out in frantic anticipation. Monica lifted her leg over the opening and slit her calf on the edge of glass. Blood spurted from the six-inch gash, but she was safely on the other side. The infected woman crashed through the glass to grab her, but the wedge of broken glass from above released, instantly decapitating her. Monica stepped back in horror and watched as a molasses-like substance pumped out of her exposed jugular.

A helicopter's rotors chopped in the distance. She spun around and started toward the circular driveway. The faint glow of moonlight illuminated the shadowy figures in the street. The infected appeared everywhere, as if they now owned the town. She glanced back and saw a few of the diseased starting to make their way through the opening in the window.

With nowhere to go and no means to escape, she contemplated her fate. Blood flowed freely out of her calf, gripping her in the throes of excruciating pain. Her shoulder throbbed and she knew she was losing a lot of blood. Shadows closed in around her. She spun a full three-sixty and dropped the flashlight onto the pavement. Falling to her knees, she prayed to God that she'd feel no pain once they descended upon her. She closed her eyes and prepared herself for what was to come next.

Chapter 39

Tag couldn't believe what Swain had just said to him. Dr. Simon Wolfe, his good friend and mentor, had been behind these attacks all along? No, he didn't believe it. It had to be some sort of misunderstanding. No way Simon Wolfe, a prestigious Harvard scientist and professor, would collaborate with these terrorists to implement a biological attack. Whoever this brilliant imposter was, he must have somehow tricked Simon into coauthoring those research papers. If this imposter was brilliant enough to create such lethal hybrid viruses, as well as dupe him on that island, then it would have been easy to convince Simon to sign on as a contributing author. He knew Simon to be a kind and generous mentor, willing to help any young scientist trying to break into the field. And in the rarified world of academia, the Simon Wolfes of the world were hard to come by.

"Riggs," Tag asked the desk cop, "are there any vehicles we can borrow?"

"Usually there's a lot of cop cars parked out in the lot, but with this crazy situation and all, the chief has deployed every one of them out in the field," he said.

Tag stared out the window contemplating his next move. Shadows lurked everywhere. It almost seemed to him as if the virus had hijacked the brain's cognitive functioning in order to facilitate its own narrow goals of reproduction and replication.

"I'm going out there and find my wife," he said, picking up the Remington and stuffing magazines into his pocket. "The rest of you stay here until I get back."

"I'm going with you," Fez said.

"I figured you'd say that, kid. You're like my guardian angel."

"We're a team, right? Where one goes the other follows?"

"Damn straight."

"Colonel, I know you're experienced and all, but you're going to get you and the boy killed if you go out there in these conditions," Officer Riggs said. "You're not the only one with family out there. We all got family members that need help."

"Sorry, but this is something I need to do."

"Best thing is for everyone to calm down and sit tight until daybreak. That way we'll have a better idea about what's going on," Riggs said.

He didn't feel the need to explain himself, considering all he'd been through on Cooke's Island. There were too many complexities involved, not to mention the fact that he was being used as some sort of pawn in a larger puzzle he'd not yet solved. But fuck it—he was going for Monica and wouldn't be persuaded otherwise.

"You just keep everyone here until I get back. This is something I need to do alone—and with the kid."

"Okay, but it's your hide, Colonel," Riggs said.

He was about to open the door when he heard the sound of tires peeling out on the street. Glancing out the window, he saw a Chevy Tahoe plowing up onto the manicured lawn and heading directly toward the door. Once it reached the front of the building, it swerved hard to the left, leaving two skid marks in the grass. The Tahoe skidded to a stop in front of the steps. The driver's side door flew open and he saw Micheau's head pop out over the roof of the driver's side. He opened the station's front door.

"Get in," she shouted.

Tag turned and addressed the others. "It's Detective Micheau. Anyone else want to come with us?"

"No way I'm leaving this fortress to go out there," Riggs said. "Besides, I can't abandon my post, especially with all my fellow officers out there. I need to stay near the radio in case they need me."

"Understood," Tag said. "I suggest the rest of you stay here as well. We'll try and round up some food when we get the chance and bring it back to the station."

Under the circumstances, and considering what they'd already been through, he couldn't say as he blamed Riggs for staying behind. But his experience back at Cooke's Island had informed him otherwise.

He, Swain, and Fez bolted out the front door. Fez and Swain sprinted past him and jumped in the backseat. A blood-drenched teenage girl stepped in front of him as he reached for the door. Tag jabbed the rifle so hard into her face that blood spattered over the back window. He jumped into the front seat and slammed the door shut behind him. The Tahoe accelerated ahead.

"Nice seeing you, Detective. I didn't think you'd make it back here alive."

"Very nearly didn't." She turned to him. "I could say the same about you."

He could see that she'd been crying. "You okay, Micheau?"

"What the fuck do you think, Colonel? Most of my fellow officers are either sick with this shit or dead, and now the town is being wiped out by this virus." She blinked, but more tears spilled out. "Did you see that explosion up on the mountain?"

"No, but we heard it."

"It blew both the cell and transmission towers," she said.

"I need you to head toward the Castleton Hotel, Detective. I need to pick up Monica."

She turned to him. "Then what?"

"I haven't thought that far ahead," he said.

"By the way, Colonel, the Feds have already arrived into town." She pointed up past the moon roof. "See for yourself."

Tag glanced out over the windshield and saw lights moving across the sky in a circular fashion. He rolled down his window and heard the *chop chop chop* sounds of their rotors stirring the air.

"We no longer have control of the passes. They're now under the control of the U.S. Army," Micheau said.

"Shit! Did you see it with your own eyes?" he asked.

"Yes, I saw them through my binoculars. They were setting up heavy equipment and some big guns."

"On both passes?"

"Yup."

She sped through the streets, the Tahoe's headlights providing the only source of light along the hardtop. Occasionally she swerved to avoid hitting a person who staggered out into their path. Tag found it increasingly hard to discern the infected population from those who were merely trying to flee their desperate situation. Every so often he noticed a group of people congregating in front of a house or storefront, and he wondered whether they were sick or merely banding together to keep themselves safe.

Unlike the epidemic on Cooke's Island, this disease didn't require cellular HF waves to facilitate the brain impairment; the elements of the two diseases had been self-contained in one spliced pathogen. This was a significant development, and he knew that it was the kind of genetic engineering most people feared. Consequently, the virus incorporated the two hybrid pathogens within the same genetic material. Whoever created this agent had not only improved on current splicing techniques, but had come to some fundamental understanding about viral behavior that he only hoped to one day understand.

Micheau switched on the Tahoe's high beams and the downtown area came into view. Hundreds of infected people wandered the streets, entering and exiting businesses in the search for virgin hosts. The virus had reprogrammed the brains to infect first and foremost, not necessarily to kill. He thought it similar to an ant colony where the individual was subservient to the colony.

They cruised down Main Street. Litter and trash lay everywhere, as if a riot had broken out and the stores had all been looted. The shadow of the Carleton Hotel appeared a half a mile up the road, swathed in darkness. A chopper flew overhead, and Tag guessed the pilot was tracking their path. Someone was obviously keeping an eye out on Brookhaven. He wondered how long it would be before the Feds set about to destroy this town and eradicate the threat posed to the rest of the world. But stuck in this toxic fish bowl, with no way out, all he could think about was grabbing his wife and planning their escape.

He wondered how the Feds had learned of their situation.

The Feds wouldn't waste another second once they determined the threat facing them. They'd send in a bio-hazard team to gather blood and tissue samples, maybe even capture a few of the infected for further study. Then they'd conduct intensive brain and genetic testing like they had on the Cooke's Island survivors. Subject them to intensive neurological and psychological testing. From those few samples, a vaccine would be created that would protect them against future attacks. One hoped!

A pounding on the passenger door jolted him back to reality. Before he knew it the Tahoe began to rock back and forth. He looked out the window and saw that a mob had formed and was now trying to overturn their vehicle. But why wasn't the Tahoe moving? And then he saw why. Because a large crowd had gathered in front the police car, blocking their path.

"Punch it in reverse!" he shouted.

Micheau panicked and momentarily froze. Tag reached over and shifted the gear into reverse, and the Tahoe backed over the crowd. The jolt seemed to snap Micheau back to reality. She took back control of the vehicle and, glancing behind her, gunned it down the street. The dashboard had a video screen built into the console so Tag could make out the road behind them. People staggered into their path and either disappeared beneath the tires or bounced off the vehicle like a bowling pin. The thump of their bodies against the chassis made a sickening sound.

The Tahoe plowed into a moving vehicle once it crossed the main intersection. The collision rocked the cabin. Smoke rose out from the other car's hood and within seconds the diseased had converged on the driver's side door. The mob dragged the poor guy out onto the street and he disappeared beneath their bodies. Sitting in the passenger seat and watching as they savagely attacked the driver, Tag felt helpless.

The Tahoe shot forward, turning right at the intersection before speeding north on a stretch of open road. Having regained her composure, Micheau gripped the wheel with a steely determination. Rather than continue on the street, she cut hard to the left and accelerated down one of the many alleys that cut through the downtown section. The cobblestones caused the police vehicle to shake violently, but surprisingly none of the diseased crossed their path. Upon exiting the alley, she cut hard left and then right before guiding the vehicle down the yellow median strip.

A large crowd appeared up ahead. To Tag's eye they seemed to be moving toward something. But what? Micheau plowed over some stragglers before turning into the circular driveway, which was fronted by a multi-story building. She nudged the infected off the pavement with the front end of the Tahoe. As soon as they reached the lobby door, Tag was shocked to see his wife kneeling on the sidewalk with her hands folded in prayer. Even disfigured and sporting horrific scars, he recognized her instantly.

She opened her eyes and looked over at him in surprise. Wasting no time, Tag jumped out of the vehicle and embraced her.

"I love you," he whispered.

"I didn't think you'd arrive to save me this time."

He helped her up and into the backseat as the mob closed in. Then he climbed in beside her and caressed her face.

"Now you know what I look like, hon. Pretty hideous, right?'" she said.

"No, babe, quite the opposite. You're even more beautiful than ever."

"You deserve better than this," she said.

"You're more beautiful than on the day I met you, Monica. It's me who doesn't deserve you."

He kissed her on the lips and felt her pull back.

"Simon is working with them," she said.

"So I've been told. But that's a discussion we can have later."

He introduced her to the others inside as the dark landscape flew past. He had no idea where they were heading. To the south he could see the pink glow of the sun beginning to rise up over the mountaintops.

Micheau's radio garbled. He'd forgotten about the old-fashioned two-way radio. It operated on a designated radio frequency channel and didn't require electricity or cellular towers. A UHF television station located sixty miles away, and transmitting 3,000 watts on a lower channel, could easily find its way through the mountain passes and reach Brookhaven. He wondered if Micheau had been using it to communicate with any of the surviving cops still holding out somewhere.

Flecks of light began to illuminate the clouds overhead. Where was she taking them? He leaned between the bucket seats and poked his head through the opening.

"Where you taking us, Detective?"

She pointed toward the mountain. "See that house up there? I know that it's vacant. It'll give us time to regroup and think about our next move."

He could see where the road snaked up the mountain, almost like the shape of a thread virus.

"Don't worry, Colonel. I know what I'm doing."

"I certainly hope so, Detective."

Tag looked up and noticed that the chopper had stopped following them. The Tahoe sped down the empty dirt road until it arrived at the base of the mountain. Micheau turned onto a secondary dirt road and they started climbing the hill. Tree branches and bushes brushed up against the side of the police vehicle. Tag glanced behind him and watched as the dark town receded from view. From his vantage, he could see more than a few fires raging throughout the valley. Pebbles and stones flew up under the chassis and pounded against the undercarriage. The Tahoe's engine labored as the hill got steeper. After fifteen minutes had passed, Micheau turned the wheel hard and parked in a small driveway. Behind it stood a tiny house. More like a chalet. Tag jumped out of the car and gazed up at the dark mountain looming behind him, wondering how far up it rose. He helped Monica out of the Tahoe and then followed Micheau inside.

Monica collapsed on the couch once they entered the chalet. He got her a glass of water before joining Micheau and Fez on the deck and gazing in silence at Brookhaven, which lay in ruins. The sun peeked over the valley, shooting rays over the peaks. The light revealed what the night had wrought, and he suddenly felt a wave of exhaustion fall over him like a warm blanket. How much more of this death and mayhem could he take? What he wouldn't give to lay down on one of the chalet's beds and fall asleep for days.

He wiped his blurry eyes and glanced back at Brookhaven. It looked eerily serene in the morning light, and yet he could see the crowds wandering about and looking for fresh hosts. Three helicopters circled downtown. On one of the eastern mountain slopes a helicopter hovered over the trees as troops laddered down. Seeing this depressed him and he knew the endgame was near. He went back inside and plopped down next to his wife. She laid her head down on his chest and closed her eyes. It was then that he noticed a bloodstain on her shirt.

"What happened to your shoulder?"

"I'm fine, hon. Let's just hold each other for a few moments."

He found a towel, rinsed it in water, and cleaned the gunshot wound on her shoulder and the laceration on her calf. Then he cut strips from a bedsheet and wrapped it around the wounds to staunch the bleeding. It would do the trick for now, he thought. Wrapping his arm around her, he gently pulled her in. Swain removed her tablet and began to tap furiously on the glass screen, and he assumed she'd resumed her writing. A few feet in front of him sat a flat screen TV on its stand. Hanging on the wall above it was a framed picture of a ...

No, it couldn't be!

A LIGER!

Chapter 40

Micheau stood in front of the sliding glass doors and next to the 40-inch flat screen television, chewing her upper lip as she watched Colonel Winters attend to his wife's injuries. Behind her the rays of the morning sun filtered into the living room, the walls of which were covered with lacquered oak paneling. Reluctantly, she pulled her service revolver out of its holster and aimed it at her fellow survivors, ordering them all to sit and remain quiet.

"What are you doing, Detective?" Tag asked, shocked at such betrayal.

"Sorry, Colonel, but I have no other choice."

"Of course you have a choice." He sat up, exasperated. "Why are you doing this?"

She shook her head sadly. "Brookhaven never stood a chance." She walked over to the leather recliner and plopped down in it. "My one and only responsibility was to deliver you here."

"In exchange for what?" he asked.

"The hell with it! Nothing matters anymore."

She reached over and placed her gun on the coffee table. Tag wondered why she would do such a stupid thing as to give up her weapon. He leapt off the couch and snatched it, but she seemed not the least bit concerned about her safety. Instead, she sat back in the chair and crossed her legs.

"I'm supposed to keep you all here, but my job is now finished, Colonel. Do as you will with me."

"What's going on?" Nolette asked, looking confused. "Is this another part of the game, Detective?"

"Trust me, this is no game," Micheau sighed.

"I could kill you right now," Tag said.

"You could kill me if you wanted, Colonel, but what good would it do? You and the others will never make it off this mountain alive if you don't do as I say."

"We don't need you! We'll hike to the top and then climb down the other side," Tag said. "Once we make it into back country, they'll never find us."

"Ha!" Micheau said. "If it were only that simple. Look around this valley, Colonel. Special Forces are being placed strategically along the mountain peaks surrounding Brookhaven. Do you really believe that the U.S. government is willing to take any chance that this plague will spread?" She threw her head back and laughed. "They're not fucking idiots! No, there's only one way out of this valley and right now I'm your only hope."

"Jesus, Detective, why are you doing this? I thought we'd established a mutual trust," Tag said

"Don't give me that bullshit, Colonel. I'm doing this for the exact same reason you are: to protect my family. They kidnapped my husband and kids and threatened to expose them to this virus if I didn't do exactly as instructed. I'm not taking any chances. I saw what happened to Cooke's Island, and once I made your identity I swore that I would do everything in my power to protect them, knowing full well that the wheels of destruction had already been set in motion."

"When did they contact you?"

"Right about the time those towers blew. By that time I knew it was already too late, and that I had to save my family."

Tag placed the revolver on the coffee table and walked onto the deck, reeling from this new development. The sun's brilliant rays illuminated a good part of the valley. He could now see the mayhem taking place far below. Mobs roamed the streets, breaking into houses, buildings, cars, and pickup trucks. Some survivors made it to their cars and took off along the Interstate only to be machine-gunned down by the Army troops manning the passes. Military bulldozers pushed the ambushed vehicles off the road and piled them along the shoulder. Three Army helicopters hovered over the mountain tops, dropping troops off before moving on to the next strategic site. Both the northern and southern passes had been barricaded. No humanitarian aid would be arriving to help these people. To his surprise, the ski lift had been activated and chairs rotated up and down the mountain carrying armed troops. He wondered if the next step would be to send in Special Forces trained in biological warfare. The likelihood of a pandemic was too great to chance, and the reward of a quarantine a calculated political risk. One thing he was sure of: no one would come out of this valley alive to tell what happened—except maybe the five of them.

He returned to the living room and saw everyone looking glum. Only Fez appeared animated as he sat there staring at the Glock on the coffee table. Time was running out and their options were limited. Hiking up the mountain now seemed out of the question, especially considering that armed troops were patrolling every peak. And heading back down into the valley was certain suicide.

"You brought us up here, Detective. So what do we do now?" Tag asked.

"We sit here and wait for someone to arrive."

"Wait for someone to arrive?" Monica cried out, leaning forward in her chair. "The U.S. government is about to obliterate this entire valley and we're supposed to sit here and wait? If we'd sat around Cooke's Island picking our asses we wouldn't even be here right now."

"Look, Mrs. Winters, do you think I like waiting any more than you do?" Micheau said. "Now sit the hell back down and wait patiently like everyone else."

Nolette stood. "I'm with Monica. We're sitting ducks if we stay here any longer!"

"I've spoken face to face with this terrorist and am convinced that this is all part of some larger conspiracy to take over our country. There must be others involved if Simon has joined forces with them," Monica said.

"How did you end up meeting him?" Nolette asked.

"He befriended me at the conference disguised as a female scientist from Alaska," Monica said.

"Let me guess: Bonnie Haldeman," Nolette said, snapping her fingers.

"Yes. But how did you know?"

"I did an extensive background checks on all the individuals who were invited to that conference," Nolette said. "Haldeman's resume had red flags written all over it. But it was only when I noticed who coauthored all of her papers that it sank in: Dr. Simon Wolfe, your husband's old mentor."

"Simon must have been working with him all along," Tag said. "In fact he was the one who probably called me that day at Harvard Medical School, just before the outbreak on Cooke's Island."

"I bet he's not the only scientist involved in these attacks," Nolette said.

"We should all rest until the time comes to leave this place. I'll take the first watch," Tag said. "It looks like we'll be in for a long day."

***

Fez found a deck of cards in one of the drawers and began playing with Swain. Tag stood on the deck and kept his eyes on the mountain below. Not much had changed. Military recon choppers continued to buzz over the valley while packs roamed the streets, attacking anything they came across. Downtown Brookhaven lay in ruins. The infected staggered over Hawthorne's pristine campus, freely making their way up into the dorms and admin buildings.

The infection rate of this strain was staggering, as was the incubation period. It seemed to him as if their numbers were growing exponentially. Occasionally, he would see a car speeding in one of the outlying areas, and he knew that there must have been many survivors hiding out and struggling to stay alive. But with all communications disabled, these same drivers had no way of knowing that the passes had been sealed off and manned with armed troops. He couldn't see anyone surviving this onslaught.

They took turns napping on the couch. By late afternoon the sun began to set over the northern edge of the mountains, creating an aura of both beauty and horror. Lovely pink ribbons drifted on puffs of air. The temperature had dropped by at least twenty degrees in the last few hours and he could tell that winter would be arriving any day now, filling the valley with snow.

Tag joined the card game and studied his hand. He was about to discard two cards when he heard a series of loud explosions far below.

He ran over to the deck and saw three Blackhawks circling over Brookhaven and shooting Hellfire missiles into a row of buildings just outside the downtown area. One of them exploded, bricks shooting high into the air. A few of the others gathered around him to witness the destruction. A missile landed amongst a small group of people. Body parts flew up and were now unrecognizable as human life forms. A second Blackhawk fired a missile down on Hawthorne College. The explosion caused the front exterior of the admin building to cave in. Five seemingly healthy students sprinted out of the dorm they'd been hunkering down in, but they were soon chased down and attacked by the bloodthirsty mob.

Despite all the horrors he'd seen in battle and on Cooke's Island, Tag still couldn't believe what he'd been witnessing. It saddened him to see how shortsighted his government was behaving; rather than trying to rescue these people, they'd chosen political expediency. He'd witnessed it on Cooke's Island, but on a far smaller scale. At least in that situation the government had tried to save lives rather than kill witnesses. The actions in Brookhaven spoke of a calculated political strategy designed to cover their asses, both in the U.S. and internationally.

Tag knew they didn't have much time. Once those Blackhawks finished leveling downtown, they'd focus their attention on the outlying areas, including all the rural homes and mountain chalets. They needed to get out of this house as soon as possible. But even assuming someone came to help them, how would they ever get out of this valley? There was no foreseeable way in or out, or any that he could see.

They continued to play cards and nap for the rest of the early evening, although the loud explosions made it difficult to sleep. The sun began to set over the valley as the bombing continued unabated. The whirring blades of the Blackhawks filled the air, followed by the intermittent explosions of the Hellfire missiles. Fez leaned over the railing and watched the slaughter in silence. Tag wondered what the boy was thinking. From where they stood on the deck, it almost resembled the fireworks display on the 4th of July.

And then he noticed a speck barreling up the hill leading to this cabin. Through the pine branches he could make out a green Jeep kicking up dirt and dust behind it. Tag grabbed the Glock off the coffee table, bolted out onto the driveway and waited for it to arrive. The Jeep crested a hill and skidded to a halt alongside the chalet. Waving the dust from his face, Tag approached the vehicle. A soldier dressed in khakis and full combat gear jumped out of the Jeep and ran over to him. He wore a combat helmet and carried an M16 on his back, and his face was painted over with thick camouflage paint.

"Hurry up and get your stuff, Colonel. We don't have much time," the soldier shouted in a deep Southern accent.

"What's your name?" Tag asked, highly suspicious.

"Sergeant First Class Claymore." He snapped into a salute.

"How did you know I was up here, soldier?" Tag asked.

"Sir, I was given direct orders by my superior to escort you and the others to safety. Judging from the map of this mountain, I anticipate that we'll be in for quite a hike."

"Don't bullshit me!" Tag said. "I know who you are!"

"Sergeant First Class Claymore, sir." He pulled out his military ID and showed it to him.

"That ID means nothing to me!"

Claymore didn't back down from his glare, but instead returned it with a vengeance.

"Are you working for the people responsible for this?"

"Sir, I work for the United States Army. Now you can stand here and accuse me of all the bullshit you want, or you and your people can follow me out of this hell hole."

Tag scowled at the man, unable to decide if he was the enemy or actually here to assist them. Did it matter at this point? They had to depend on this soldier to get them to safety. To his credit, the soldier refused to back down, and he had the battle-hardened stare of a world-weary combat veteran, many of whom he'd come across in his years in the Army.

"Do you know who we are?" Fez asked the soldier.

"Kid, I don't give a rat's ass if you're the Queen of England or the Pope. All I know is that I've been given a direct order to escort you all to safety. Now you either gather your shit and follow me up this damn mountain, or you stay here and get blown to pieces."

"What's your full name, soldier, and where are you from?" Tag asked.

"Colonel, do we really have time for this bullshit?"

"Answer my question, First Sergeant, and that's a direct order."

The soldier sighed. "Jimmy Ray Claymore from Biloxi, Mississippi. Never been married, but engaged once to Dixie Lee Turner before breaking it off because of certain infidelities. My daddy, Marshall, is a black jack dealer in the Beau Rivage Casino, and my mama, Paula, works in the high school cafeteria dishing out the worst slop you can imagine. They got two hounds named Outlaw and Skinny. I got twin sisters and a retarded brother named LeRoy that lives with my folks. Got himself a bike that he pedals around town, collecting cans and various shit. Anything else you wanna know about me, Colonel?" A large explosion sounded in the background.

"We have three more people inside that are coming with us."

"Then you better get them a'moving, sir. We've lost valuable time already."

Tag ordered Fez to go back and retrieve the others. Moments later they came running out of the chalet. A Blackhawk hovered over the city and then fired a missile at an unseen target. The Blackhawk spun violently before heading in their direction. Had the pilot spotted them?

Claymore bellowed something before starting up the trail and disappearing behind some dense vegetation. Tag waited until everyone moved ahead of him before following up in the rear. He glanced back and saw the Blackhawk soaring toward the chalet. Climbing higher up the path, he gripped some tree branches to keep himself steady. A loud explosion went off directly behind him. The reverberation from the blast shook the mountainside and, except for Claymore, they all fell back against the trail. Sprawled on his back, he pushed aside a branch and saw that the small chalet was now engulfed in flames. He couldn't believe how fortunate they'd been to have narrowly escaped when they did. Had they remained in that house another minute longer, they would all have been killed.

By the glint of moonlight, and the intermittent glow caused by the explosions rocking the valley, Tag and the others made their way up the trail. Monica struggled and he had to occasionally stop and help her up the trail. Prior to her injuries, she'd been an avid hiker, often scheduling family vacations in order to hike up the Olympic Mountains, Grand Canyon, or through Joshua Tree National Park. But now, in her weakened state, she was a shadow of her former self. He vowed to carry her up this mountain if that's what it took to keep her alive.

They stopped at a clearing halfway up the mountain and huddled beneath a boulder. It was near freezing up here and he could hear Monica shivering. He put his arm around her and stared over the tree tops. Massive flood lights scanned the slopes, searching for anyone who might be trying to escape. It was clear to him that the powers-that-be would go to any length to prevent the news of this atrocity from reaching the outside world.

341

A beam of light swept through the pine trees just below them. Huddled under the ledge, they appeared out of harm's way—for now. The beam scanned the switchback they'd just climbed. He moved closer to his wife to transfer some of his body heat to her. The endless sound of her clattering teeth worried him, and he was scared that she might be coming down with a fever.

The explosions continued to rock the valley as they sat huddled under the rock. Blackhawks circled the mountains in concentric patterns, working their way toward the outlying areas. It was a clean and efficient sweep designated to achieve a one hundred percent kill rate. No living organism would survive this brutal assault, particularly the Ebola virus.

Tag looked to his right and saw the soldier hunched over the map and pointing a small flashlight on it. He'd kept the light concealed in his palms so as not to give away their position. At this time of night, any minor source of illumination could be a virtual death sentence.

"What do we do now, Sergeant?" Tag asked.

"The spot I'm looking for is about a quarter mile up this trail. Having been briefed, I know the coordinates of every platoon stationed atop these peaks. But with the floodlights engaged, I'm afraid that we won't be able to leave here until morning."

"Morning?" Nolette said, her teeth chattering. "We'll freeze to death if we stay out here all night."

"It's either that or we die by fire, ma'am, and I ain't ready to cash in my chips just yet." He sat up and climbed to his knees, passing his jacket over to her. "Here, lady, take this."

"Give it to Monica instead," Nolette said. "She needs it more than me."

"Thank you," Monica said, taking the jacket and slipping it over her shoulders.

"Everyone huddle together for warmth," Claymore said.

"When will it be safe for us to move?" Tag asked.

"I figure we can move out at the break of dawn. There's going to be a brief transition when the Blackhawks cease attacking and return to fuel up. At that point, a squadron of recon choppers will move in to assess the damage. The plan is for the 48th Chemical Brigade to put boots on the ground come morning and neutralize any and every biological threat."

"Which translated means that they will kill every living thing in this valley," Tag said.

"Bingo!" Claymore replied.

"But primarily the Ebola virus."

"Kill whatever is here, Colonel," Claymore said. "It also means that anyone who witnessed this attack is a threat to the government, and that includes you, me, and every other soldier involved in this massacre. So even if you make it out of here alive, it'll be your word against Uncle Sam's, and you ain't winning that fight. Your best bet will be to get the hell out of the country and never look back. They'll think y'all is dead anyways."

"Except for you and a few higher ups."

"Very true, Colonel. And if they give me orders to hunt you down and put an end to your miserable lives then you can bet your buttons that's what I'll do: follow orders."

"Who are these people giving you orders?"

Claymore laughed and fell back on his haunches. "Now that's for me to know, Colonel, isn't it? So don't concern yourself with that."

Tag wrapped the jacket around Monica's body and pulled her into him. The temperature was dropping and the bitter winds had picked up.

They huddled together, the occasional explosion resounding in their ears. Tag leaned back against the jagged ledge and huddled up against his wife. His eyelids felt heavy. The fires below burned bright, illuminating the valley. Black smoke rose up out of the ashes of the ruined homes and buildings.

Tag tried to will himself to sleep but found it elusive. Rubbing his hands together for warmth, he prayed that one day he might see his kids again.

343

Chapter 41

A massive explosion went up, jolting all of them out of their sleep. He wiped his blurry eyes and tried to acclimate himself to his conscious state. The smell of petroleum hung thick in the air and he could practically taste the tang of fuel on his tongue. Almost instantly he sensed that a petroleum bomb had been used: weaponized Napalm. He didn't think that napalm was still being used, but then again there were probably a lot of secret weapons being used by the military that he had no idea about.

He observed the flames burning bright across the valley. Being hit with Napalm meant instantaneous death: the lot of them would be vaporized in a flash. Fortunately, they had luck on their side. The military had started bombing along the southern range, and a large swatch along that mountain sizzled and snapped. He sniffed the air, now thick with styrene, knowing to inhale such toxic fumes was dangerous. But the toxicity would pale in comparison to the inferno they faced if caught in the pyre's five-thousand-degree hell.

Claymore shouted at them to move and they fell into formation. The sun shone over the brilliant white light of the napalm strikes, bleaching out the valley. Tag waited until everyone started up the trail before falling in behind his wife. While ascending, he began to see the rusted remains of machinery and heavy equipment along the trail. What in the world was all this, he wondered. They reached a narrow section of trail that had been washed out by floods and neglect. A part of it had collapsed down the side of the mountain, leaving only a narrow footpath to cross, which ran alongside a sheer wall of granite. One by one they made their way along it, backs pressed against the ledge for support. At its widest point, the trail extended two feet over the precipitous drop. Tag held Monica's hand as they shuffled across. He glanced down midway and estimated the drop to be about five hundred feet.

Claymore hadn't waited for the rest of them to catch up, continuing to scramble up the switchback as fast as he could. Tag called out for him but heard no reply. Monica collapsed to the ground after making it safely over to the other side.

"I don't think I can go any further," she said.

"You have to keep moving, hon. I'm not leaving this mountain without you."

"That pox damaged my lungs. Please, go on without me, Tag, for the sake of the kids."

"Those kids need their mom and their dad. Now get up."

He scooped her into his arms. Then he began to climb methodically up the trail, careful not to go too fast and wear himself out. He gazed up, but the others were nowhere in sight. The odor of styrene was becoming stronger and he knew that if they were exposed to it for much longer they would begin to experience neurological side effects. Monica felt light in his arms as he tried to ignore the pain in his legs and lungs.

More rusted machinery appeared along the trail and he carefully stepped over the debris so as not to trip. He puzzled over why there would be mechanical equipment up here. The ski lifts were at least a few miles away. Sweat poured down his face despite the fact that the temperature had not risen much above freezing. Dark clouds loomed on the horizon, which could only mean snow. But not even snow would douse the petroleum inferno now scorching the valley.

His thighs were burning by the time he reached the next clearing. Black whorls of smoke rose up everywhere. He gently placed Monica down on a flat rock and then collapsed next to her, trying to suck oxygen into his lungs. Instead, he gulped in mouthfuls of petroleum fumes. Monica coughed sporadically, the styrene compromising her damaged lungs and suppressed immune system. They had to get out of this toxic environment as soon as possible, but he had no idea where to go or where the others had disappeared to.

Scooping his wife into his arms, he trudged a short distance only to arrive at a much larger clearing. Along the ground sat a rusted old steam boiler and a large industrial wheel enclosed inside one of the many dilapidated cabins that had been stripped to studs. Judging from the remnants, he guessed that this had at one time been a working outpost of some kind. Massive walls of granite rippled at least a hundred vertical feet up the mountain. A Blackhawk flew overhead, causing him to duck low into some nearby bushes. Seconds later a massive explosion occurred below. The mountain rumbled violently and rocks and debris showered down over him. The winds from the fiery blast rippled past, singing the fine hairs over his skin. The blast of heat was followed by the overwhelming stench of styrene. His vision blurred and for a brief moment he thought he might pass out. Had the napalm strike been any closer, the blast would have killed them.

But the trail stopped at this clearing. He glanced around in every direction, searching for the others. Where had they gone? He'd nearly given up hope when he heard a familiar voice. *Claymore!* He staggered around, his eyes burning from the fumes. The sun popped out of the clouds and temporarily blinded him. Through a slurry of tears, he caught sight of an arm stirring from beneath a pile rocks.

"You fucking crazy standing out in the open like that?" Claymore shouted. "Get your ass over here!"

"I can't see you."

"Grab the missus and move toward me, Colonel, or you'll both be goners."

"The fumes are making me dizzy."

"These fumes will be nothing compared to the hell's bells that's about to git you."

Mustering all his energy, he picked his wife up and carried her to where he thought he saw Claymore's arm. Once he'd made it over to the pile of rocks, someone took Monica off his shoulder and dragged her through a gaping hole in the granite. A second explosion went off, this one even closer than the last. The mountain shook for ten long seconds before he could regain his balance. Something above cracked, and a cloud of dust and pebbles rained down upon him. The next sound he heard reminded him of an approaching train, and when he looked up he saw a house-sized block of granite hurtling toward him. Tag struggled to breathe as he climbed the series of small rocks. With the encouragement of Claymore, he dove inside the hole. Someone grabbed his hands and pulled, and he felt himself falling headfirst until he crash landed along the cave floor. He gazed up and saw an irregular splotch of light disappearing into the darkness.

He sat staring at it, mesmerized, as the light reduced to a pinprick. It took him a second to realize that the others were piling rocks up against the entrance to try and seal off the hole. He jumped up, snapping out of his daze, and passed over a medium-sized rock. Claymore turned on his flashlight and found some pieces of smooth shale. Breaking them over some rocks, he then skillfully wedged the fragments between the crevices to form an ultra-tight bond.

"That's the best we can do, people. Now let's get a move on," Claymore said, pointing the light into a wall of blackness.

"But we're safe right here, Sarge," Fez said. "Can't we just stay and rest for a while?"

"Kid, if that fuel ignites a pocket of methane gas in this cave we're gonna blow sky high."

"Methane gas?"

"Canary in a cave? That's not to mention all the explosives buried in here from the days they used to mine for gold. Did I also mention the rock slides, unstable shafts, rats, and sink holes?"

"Okay, you convinced me," Fez said.

Tag followed the soldier's beam of light. The further they traveled, the rougher the terrain became. Another loud explosion shook the mountain and stone dust and debris rained down over them. Tag looked up into the nothingness and prayed that a boulder didn't break off and come crashing down upon them. The cave continued to shake for over thirty seconds before the tremors lessened to a deathly stillness. Once it stopped, he heard a deafening clap behind him. Turning, he felt a vacuum of air pulling him in. "What the hell was that?" he said, his voice bouncing off the nearby walls. Claymore pointed the flashlight back toward the entrance to the cave. The entire front end had collapsed, completely sealing them off from the valley. The slide had effectively punched their one-way ticket.

"Okay, folks, the good news is that we'll be spared death by napalm. The bad news; I ain't exactly positive this cave has a way out."

"You're not positive it has a way out?" Nolette said, her voice echoing throughout the cave. "What the hell kind of plan is that?"

"Well, sugar, it depends upon which miner's map you want to believe," Claymore said, moving deeper into the belly of the mountain.

"What was this cave used for anyways?" Nolette asked.

"Ore and gold mining back in the late 1880s, from what I can gather. Not many people know about it because the officials don't want people wandering up here and getting themselves killed. The old miners wanted an easy route out of this cave so that they could transfer their minerals to the market. A few of the accounts said they never totally blasted through, while some others claimed that they did. Hell, I'm trying to stay optimistic, but even if they did blast through to the other side, who's to say that a rock slide hadn't collapsed it."

They pushed ahead, their progress slowed by the rocks and debris along the cave floor. A series of flapping wings could be heard from time to time. Water dripped from every crack and fissure as if providing them a cadence by which to walk. Tag

348

reached out and held Monica's hand, guiding her along. He knew the odds were long that they'd make it out of this cave alive, but at least they had no other choice now.

Chapter 42

Being inside this cave reminded him of the expedition he'd once journeyed on a long time ago, deep in the heart of Africa. The hike into Uganda's Kitum Cave had been one of the most surreal experiences of his life. They'd dressed in biohazard suits, knowing that some of the most lethal viruses to mankind resided in that cave. Believed to have harbored the first strains of the Ebola and AIDs virus, Kitum was a like primitive stew of up-and-coming pathogens. Equipped with powerful lamps, he'd seen the most spectacular waterfalls, rock pillars drenched in guano, thousands upon thousands of bats hanging upside down, as well as a range of exotic insects that he'd never before seen, including the Strebelid fly, which many scientists believed was a natural carrier of Ebola. He'd crawled through narrow passages that would have caused most people nightmares. And all the time they'd been traveling through it he'd been collecting samples to see if they could identify and categorize any new or existing viral strains. Although they hadn't discovered anything during the expedition, it ranked as one of the most remarkable trips he'd ever taken.

The cave he was now passing through seemed to exhale and inhale. By this point in time he figured that every tree along these mountains must have been obliterated. Assuming he and the others did make it out safely, who was to say that there weren't troops stationed around the valley's perimeter, making sure that this hemorrhagic fever did not spread. Too late now to second guess. Their fate had been sealed.

After an hour passed, Monica begged Claymore to let them sit down and take a quick break. Reluctantly, he agreed. The cave continued to shake and tremble every so often, but much less so now that they were deep inside the mountain's core. Tag figured that they must have been halfway through it by now. Somewhere nearby he could hear water falling over rocks. Claymore shut off the flashlight to reserve the battery, pitching them into a black void. No one spoke, and only the sound of the waterfall echoed in the darkness. Tag reached out and squeezed his wife's hand.

"What are you going to do after this is all over, Detective?" Nolette whispered to Micheau.

"Now that this town is gone, I don't know what I'll do," Micheau said. "What about you?"

"I'm going to do everything in my power to make sure this story gets told to the public," she said. "This government's got to pay for what it's done."

"Good luck with that," Claymore said, chuckling. "After that island fiasco, I'll bet anything that most Americans will be happy they prevented this shit from spreading into their communities."

"It's possible," Swain said. "Of course the next time it could be their own town destroyed in the name of public safety. Where does it all end? Once the entire country becomes infected?"

Everyone remained quiet for a few moments, letting her words linger in the air.

"How about you, Sergeant?"

"Go back to my unit. After twenty years of service, there ain't no turning back now. Besides, I learned a long time ago never to ask questions but to do what I'm told."

"That's how the Nazis rationalized their behavior," Tag said.

"Hell, I saved y'all's asses, so I don't want to hear no more bitching," Claymore said. "Show me who the bad guy is in all this and I'll gladly fight him. I'm up against a terrorist, a virus, and the U.S. government. So who's the real enemy?"

"That's the irony of these attacks; it's turning people into enemy and victim," Tag said.

"With all due respect, Colonel, you're the one people blame for that island attack. How do we know you ain't the enemy?"

"Don't blame Tag," Fez blurted. "I been with him ever since we got attacked on Cooke's Island and there ain't no better person."

"You're nothing but a snotty-nosed kid. What the hell do you know about life?" Claymore replied.

"I may be a kid but I know Tag's innocent."

"It don't matter to me one way or another, kid. I'm just paid to do my job, and that job right now is to get you all the hell out of here. Fortunately for you, Colonel, someone up there believes in you."

The cave shook again and in a matter of seconds the air began to heat up. Tag wiped his forehead and realized he was sweating. Claymore flicked on the flashlight, shining the beam down the corridor they'd be traveling through. They could hear rats scurrying below their feet and through the puddles.

"We need to get moving," Claymore said. "The heat given off by those napalm strikes is working its way through the mountain. That shit hits methane and BOOM!"

Claymore aimed the beam ahead as they continued single file down the narrow tunnel. In a matter of minutes the cave felt like the hottest sauna Tag had ever been in. Luckily, warm droplets of water filled the air and moistened his skin. He squatted down and dipped his hand in a pool, splashing it over his face and neck.

The cave began to get narrower, evident by the walls closing in, and they had to walk hunched over in order not to hit their heads on the jagged rock above. This would be a terrible place to die, Tag thought. Water trickled from the roof until it had risen up to their ankles.

The tunnel narrowed to where they had to crawl on their hands and knees. Someone ahead of him started to weep, but he couldn't tell who it was. Tag looked up, unable to see anything except the faint beam of light dancing along the wall of the cave. He prayed the batteries in Claymore's flashlight would not die now. Soon they were slithering on their bellies. He called out for Monica, but she grunted something unintelligible in reply. Suddenly everyone in front of him stopped.

"I can't go any further," Micheau sobbed. "There are rats crawling all around me and I'm starting to freak out."

"There's no turning back now," Claymore replied. "Best you compose yourself and keep on moving or else you'll hold the others back."

"I'm fucking freaking out here, asshole."

"Get over yourself, lady, because we're all freaking out. Now get moving."

"I can't."

"Think of your kids, Detective," Tag shouted. "They're depending on you. Now close your eyes and move one leg at a time."

"Okay, Colonel," Micheau said, "I'm thinking about my kids now and not these disgusting rats crawling around me."

"Good! Now move because I want to see my kids too."

They continued to slither along on their bellies, splashing through the pools of water. Tag could feel the patter of little feet scurrying across his back and neck. It seemed as if he'd travelled on his stomach for hours, but in reality they'd probably traveled only a hundred yards. And yet something felt different. Tag stopped for a moment, his elbows bruised and sore, and raised his head up. Surprisingly, it didn't bounce off the roof. It took him a second to realize that the hole was growing larger. The further they crawled the wider the cave became, until finally they could stand hunched over.

Water gushed down the side of the cave walls. He reached out and let it run down his hand, cool and refreshing. Despite the blanket of heat inside the cave, the water streaming down the wall was surprising cold. Had they reached the other side? He splashed some in his face, reveling in its rejuvenating powers. He didn't care now about the bacterial and viral hazards it might pose due to the proliferation of bat and rat shit.

The mountain suddenly shook, causing him to stop and hold onto the walls for support. Debris rained down as the shaking continued. After all they'd been through, he prayed this narrow tunnel would not collapse on them now. Instinctively, like Hercules holding the pillars, he pressed his palms against the ceiling and held on. But then the shaking abruptly stopped. He craned his neck over Monica's shoulder and saw the flashlight's beam pointing down the hole. A series of white dots appeared in his vision. The nearer they got to the constellation the brighter the stars became until he realized that they had reached the other side. He couldn't quite believe it. Micheau whooped happily as they made their way toward the pinpricks of light.

They reached the end and embraced each other, not quite believing their good fortune. And yet he knew they weren't out of the woods yet. They could remove all the rocks only to realize they were on the precipice of a sheer cliff. Micheau wasted no time, frantically clearing away the rocks and tossing them aside. The others lent a hand until sunlight began to pour in and illuminate the cave. Before long, they'd uncovered a two-by-three foot opening. A cold breeze filled the cave as Tag breathed in some fresh air. Micheau crawled out first, followed by the others. Tag waited until Monica had passed through before making his way out into the bright autumn sun. The chilled air tasted wonderful on his tongue. He stared out at the landscape below, waiting for his eyes to adjust to the sunlight.

The panoramic view slowly came into focus. A narrow stream flowed far below along the mountain range. Taking in his surroundings, Tag noticed that they were standing on a wide ridge that sloped off to the southeast. He looked over at his fellow survivors and saw that every one of them was covered head-to-toe in soot.

"Where to?" Swain asked.

Claymore turned and stared at them. His face was still painted black and green, but dirt clung to his sweaty face. His camouflaged helmet lay low over his sunken eyes as he took in his surroundings.

"My job was to get you guys out of that valley, and that's what I did. You're on your own now."

"So we wing it?" Swain asked.

"Creative improvising, I like to call it," Claymore replied.

"Look over there!" Fez shouted.

Tag walked over to where Fez stood. "What are you looking at?"

"There's something painted on that boulder down there."

Tag scanned the horizon. Then he saw the large boulder at the base of a clearing splashed with bright colors.

"You carrying binoculars, Sergeant?"

Claymore reached down to his belt and unclipped the pouch, pulling out a small pair of tactical binoculars.

"There you go, sir," Claymore said, handing them over.

He lifted the glasses to his eyes and studied the colorful image until it came into focus. What he saw both chilled him and confirmed his worst fear.

"What is it, Tag?" Fez asked

"See for yourself." He passed them over to the kid.

"Holy crap! A liger!" Fez handed back the glasses. "Guess we shouldn't be too surprised."

"I should have expected something like that." He grabbed Monica's hand and turned to the others. "Everyone, follow me."

He hiked down the steep trail until they arrived at the painted boulder. They all stopped and stood staring up at the painting. The depth and detail were impressive, and he studied it closely, mesmerized by the vividness of the colors. It had obviously been painted by hand, and under the bright autumn sun the colors appeared almost one with the landscape. Underneath the image it said: *"Congratulations!"* Beneath those words, he'd spray painted a black arrow pointing down the trail.

355

The trail got steeper the further they hiked, forcing them to hold onto branches and rock ledges in order to keep from falling. Tag knew that they had to be careful because a broken leg could be catastrophic, especially with the temperatures hovering around freezing.

Every hundred yards or so a smaller liger icon had been painted on one of the rocks. As long as they followed the arrow, he believed they would arrive where they were supposed to be. But where was that? They reached a thirty-foot sheer cliff and Tag noticed that someone had fastened a rope to a tall pine tree. He glanced down over the outcropping and saw that it dangled to the bottom. He decided to go first so he could steady the line for the others. Then Monica followed, with Claymore behind her. Near the bottom, Tag gazed up at the picturesque mountain. Thick plumes of black smoke flew up behind it as if it was a volcano. The smoke floated east thanks to the prevailing winds.

The trail flattened the lower they descended. They switchbacked down until they reached level ground. An arrow at the base of a large rock pointed them toward the nearby woods, and they trekked along the trail until they disappeared into the thick pines. The liger images now appeared every hundred yards, spray painted on the peeling bark of white birch trees that lined the trail. Fresh fallen leaves covered the forest floor. Monica lagged back from the others, so he picked her up and carried her over the terrain.

After miles of walking they came upon a clearing. A log cabin looked out over a picturesque pond. Mountains appeared off in the distance. A lone, massive pine tree stood a few feet from the cabin. Tag stared up at it, estimating it to be sixty feet high. At the top of the canopy a satellite dish faced the western sky. He walked over to the thick trunk and fingered the black wire leading into the cabin. Next to the house sat two propane tanks.

They gathered on the porch, looking haggard and spent. Tag took the initiative and knocked on the door, but no one answered. He turned the handle and the door easily swung open.

A plain-looking living room appeared before him, boxed in by the lacquered logs.

"Maybe this cabin's a trap," Swain said.

"Why would the person who led us here leave a trap when they could have killed us at any time?" Tag said.

"Well, we've come this far, we might as well go inside," Swain said.

Claymore stuck his hand out. "My job's done here, people. Need to get my ass back to the unit before they try me for desertion." He pulled out a cigarette and lit it.

"Don't you want to stop and rest for a bit, Sarge?" Fez asked.

"Rest is for dead people." He sucked in a cloud of nicotine. "Better I git going now while it's still light out."

"Thank you for helping us," Monica said, reaching out with both arms to embrace him.

Claymore braced himself with his hands by his side as she reached around his thick torso and hugged him. He looked extremely uncomfortable by such a generous show of affection. Tag's eyes locked onto Claymore's as he waited for his wife to release her embrace. Monica let go and stepped back. But instead of returning to Tag's side, she pointed his revolver at the sergeant.

"What in good God's name are you doing stealing my weapon like that, woman?" he said.

"Strip off your shirt."

"It's butt ass cold out here. I ain't taking off my dang shirt for no one," he said, taking another drag on his cigarette.

"What are you doing, Monica?" Tag asked.

"It's him, Tag. It's the terrorist," she said, gripping the gun in her hands. "I've had an odd feeling about this son-of-bitch all along."

"This is the thanks I get for bailing you all out?" Claymore protested.

"How could you tell?" Tag asked, moving to his wife's side.

357

"I can prove it. The terrorist has a tattoo of a liger etched across his back."

"You're fucking crazy, lady!" Claymore said. "There's no way I'm taking off my shirt for you."

Tag kicked him in the balls and Claymore fell to his knees. His face reddened and his eyeballs looked as if they might explode out of his head.

"Sorry about that, Sarge, but if you're who you say you are then it'll only take us a few moments to find out," Tag said.

"Jesus H. Christ!" he groaned.

Tag moved behind Claymore and pushed him face first to the ground. He patted him down, removing the man's pocket knife. Claymore pushed himself up off the ground until he was on his knees.

"Get your rocks off, Colonel?" Claymore said bitterly.

"Unbutton your shirt or I cut it off your back," Tag said.

"Fuck it! I'll do it only because I gotta get back to my unit." He quickly unbuttoned his shirt and then set it on the ground. His tee-shirt came off next. "Ungrateful motherfuckers!"

"There's nothing there," Tag said to his wife.

She walked behind the soldier and saw for herself; his back was a blank canvas.

"Convinced now?" Claymore said.

"No." She turned to Tag. "Make him take off his pants."

"Hon! There's no tattoo on him."

"Please trust me on this, Tag."

Tag tapped his shoe between Claymore's shoulder blades. "You heard her. Drop trou, Sergeant."

"Fuck y'all! There ain't no way I'm dropping trou, especially when there's ladies and children present."

Before Tag could respond, Monica struck Claymore in the head with the butt of the gun. As petite and sickly as she looked, the blow was enough to knock him nearly unconscious. She stood with her hands on her knees, trying to catch her breath. Shocked at his wife's newfound aggression, Tag stood over the groggy soldier.

358

"Monica! What's gotten into you?"

"Don't you start, Tag. Now pull down his trousers before he wakes up."

Tag stared at her in stunned silence. "What are we looking for?"

Monica turned to the others. "Go inside and shut the door." They did as instructed.

"Now you want to tell me what we're looking for?" he asked once the door had closed.

"It's him, Tag, I don't care if there's no tattoo on his back."

"What are we looking for?"

"I used a blow torch on his feet and testicles, and I cut the flesh along his stomach and cheeks."

"What?" Tag couldn't believe his once-sweet wife had turned into such a hardened badass, and it saddened him.

"I wanted to get some information from him, but Simon broke in and interrupted me."

"So you want me to look at his genitals and see if they're burned?" He stared at his wife. "He wouldn't have been able to travel this far with those kinds of injuries."

"You better hurry before I hit him again," she said, nodding toward Claymore.

Tag pulled off the man's socks and shoes. What he saw beneath them caused him to rock back on his heels. The soles of the man's feet were covered in blistering red pustules: second degree burns. How had the soldier walked on such painful injuries? He must have slathered his feet in ointment to help soothe the blisters and prevent an infection. The pain must have been excruciating, and Claymore's threshold for pain super-human.

"It's him," he said.

"Fucking bastard. We should kill him right now before he takes more lives." Monica said, trembling with rage.

He looked up at her. Was this his wife talking? "I need to speak to him first."

Claymore groaned and opened his eyes, sitting up on his haunches.

"How does it feel to know that you're about to die?" Monica said, holding the gun up against his head.

"How does it feel knowing *you're* about to die?" He laughed. "Because when you come right down to it, the study of viruses is essentially the study of death."

Tag stood over him. "That's where you're wrong. It's about the study of life, and if there's anything viruses have taught me it's that we might not have developed a higher consciousness without them." He could barely control his rage. "Of course some people have yet to develop one."

"How noble, Colonel. And then you'll tell me that the cosmos will implode and it will result in universal death." He shrugged. "Well, what are you prepared to do about it?"

"Tell me. How did you manage to travel this far with such extensive burns?" Tag asked.

"A sociopath feels no pain," he said, laughing. "It's an extremely rare condition I suffer."

"It doesn't really matter. You're going to die with or without suffering from pain," Monica said, the gun trembling in her hand.

"I respectfully beg to differ," he said, glancing at his wristwatch. "If I don't return to the mothership soon, those children of yours will be feeling the first symptoms of the infection in about twenty-four hours."

"What the hell are you talking about?" Monica asked.

"I'm talking about little packets of sunshine located in strategic metropolitan areas."

"You're bluffing," she said.

He laughed. "Oh, dear, bluffing's the last thing I would do. I do hope your children have been vaccinated for Marburg's Disease."

"Marburg's," she said, glancing at Tag. "You son-of-bitch! Why don't you leave my kids out of this!"

"I so badly want to leave them out of this, Monica, but you're making it exceedingly difficult for me to do," he said. "The decision is entirely up to you."

"You're the devil incarnate," she said.

"I'm the prophet sent to save people's souls. So what's it going to be, my dear? Me or your precious lambs?"

Monica looked over at Tag for reassurance. As ruthless as she'd become, he knew that she'd put their children above all else. She stepped forward, spit in the man's face, and then walked back inside the cabin.

The imposter held out his hand, but Tag refused to shake.

"Go to hell!"

"I've been to hell and back, Colonel, and it's called the level four hot lab." He turned and walked off.

"What did I do to offend you, Remington?"

He spun around. "Don't ever call me that again if you want to see your children alive!"

"You've made your point, Mister. You don't need to set off another attack to prove to the world how brilliant you are."

"Colonel, your life is about to change in a most drastic way. The government is about to collapse because of what happened here, and you'll be the final straw that brings them down." The imposter dressed as a soldier picked up his helmet and started down the trail.

Tag called out for an explanation, but the man kept on walking. It made no sense to chase him down. His only regret was that he didn't get to see the man's face. Once back in the cabin, he put his arm around his wife, but she shrugged it off and walked away. The abrupt change in his wife's attitude startled him. If only his life could return to the way it was before these tragedies. But he knew it couldn't. Or wouldn't. His life would never again return to any semblance of normality.

Chapter 43

The door opened and footsteps moved toward him. Tag turned and saw Micheau standing on the porch steps.

"Can I come with you, Sarge?" Micheau shouted.

The imposter turned and waved his arm for her to join up with him.

"Do you really want to travel with that guy, Detective?" Tag said.

"I don't care how I get out of here, Colonel. I need to meet up with my husband and kids and make sure they're safe. The man said he'd release them if I did as I was told."

"Be careful out there."

She embraced him, tears pouring from her eyes.

"Don't ever come back here again, if you want your family to stay safe," Tag whispered. "Take your family as far away from this valley as possible."

"My husband used to be stationed in Alaska when he was in the Coast Guard. Said it was the most beautiful place on earth. He's been trying to get me to move there for the last five years, Colonel. Looks like he'll now get the chance."

"Best of luck!" Tag said.

"You too, Colonel. I hope you one day find your kids as well as peace in your life." She turned to Fez and ran her hand through his mop of dirty hair. "Same with you, little man." Then she leaped off the porch and sprinted until she caught up with the imposter.

Once they were out of sight, Tag and Fez moved inside the cabin. He collapsed on the sofa next to his wife, barely able to comprehend the turn of events. Swain sat on one end of it while Fez reclined on the Lazy Boy. Tag stared at the blank flat screen on the wall. Upon locating the remote, he pressed the power button and the screen flashed to life. A rectangular bar popped up on the bottom. The word 'downloading' appeared beneath it. The box began to quickly fill with green space. Once it hit a hundred percent, a video began to play. The person had walked around Brookhaven with a digital camera, filming activity on the streets. Tag saw Micheau sitting in a cafe and sipping from a white mug. She smiled awkwardly at the camera and then, after being directed, she waved self-consciously into the lens. Did she know the person filming this video, he wondered? Footage appeared of his wife giving a speech in front of a logo for Hawthorne College, then standing next to a well-dressed woman wearing wire-rimmed glasses. "That's Bonnie," Monica blurted, pointing at the screen. There was footage of Tag and Fez walking out of the Mountain View Inn. A cast and crew appeared onstage, bowing and dressed as if they were back in the fifties. After a few seconds the screen went blank only to be replaced by footage of the outbreak.

He quickly shut off the TV, not able to watch this clip while the horror of that attack was still fresh in his mind. But he realized something startling: they now had video evidence of the tragedy that had unfolded in Brookhaven.

"Turn it back on, Colonel," Swain ordered. "This is something we need to see."

"I can't watch it right now."

"Fine, then leave the room. I'll watch it myself," she said, walking over to the flat screen and turning it on. She lifted a wire attached to the screen. "Oh my God!"

"What?"

She took her phone out and connected the USB into the port. "I can download this video on my phone. This is our proof— our insurance policy."

"There may be things on that tape you may not want to see," Tag said.

"No more than the horrors I've already seen firsthand."

"You don't know what this guy has in store for us, Swain," Tag said.

"If I'm going to write the story of this attack, then I need to know everything that happened."

Tag sat back down and prepared himself for the succession of horrors he might see on film. The flat screen came to life and a grainy, black and white video played. Tag watched in silence, barely able to understand what he was seeing. A small girl stood in a dilapidated old church surrounded by a congregation of devoted followers. It was the kind of place one might see at a tent revival in the Deep South. The girl received a hug from the pastor and then accepted a kiss on her lips that seemed entirely inappropriate. When Tag looked over at Swain, he saw tears running down her eyes. What was going on here? But what followed next surprised him even more, and he shot up out of the chair in morbid fascination. Even the normally unflappable Fez had a grimace over his face.

***

Watching the old clip of that pastor kissing her on the lips brought back a flood of dark memories that she'd been trying to repress. *That fucking bastard!* She had no idea that those reels even existed. But what came next nearly made her sick to her stomach. The terrorist had planted a camera in the hotel room and had taped her struggle with Bacon, and then had the nerve to send the clip to an Oklahoma news station. How odd was it to learn that she was wanted for questioning in the death of the news reporter? Watching the struggle play out on the flat screen brought back the experience in horrific detail. She hoped to never revisit that day again. Nor had she wanted to recall those dark days holed up with that perverted preacher. How close she had come to being violated by him?

More grainy home footage of her as a young child, running around the compound and looking happy and innocent.

But that was the furthest thing from the truth. Her hippie mother and dopey stepfather appeared, smiling nervously into the camera and waving. She hadn't seen her parents in over twenty years and had no idea if they were even still alive. They had moved out of the compound at some point and never had the decency to tell her where they'd ended up. No great loss. And yet seeing them again brought back a whole host of painful memories that she thought she'd expunged from her mind.

Once the download was complete, Nolette pressed the send button and emailed the video to every address on her contact list, hoping that it might help to vindicate them.

"How long do we stay in this cabin?" she asked, not telling them what she'd done.

"We can't stay in this cabin very long. Sooner or later the authorities will find us, and when they do it won't be pretty."

"Then I need to hurry up and finish the first part of this story before it's too late," Nolette said.

"Do you have much more to write?" he asked.

"A couple of hours at most," she replied.

"We'll wait for you to finish," Tag said. "Then we'll head out."

She paused before saying, "Do you believe that I killed him in self-defense?"

"That video backs your assertion," Tag said.

"But after that, how will you ever return to being a reporter again?" Monica asked.

"I'm not sure, but there's people at the paper who will help me find a safe haven while I finish up writing the entire story. I might need to leave the country, but that's the price I'll have to pay."

Monica said, "The best thing I can do is turn myself into the authorities. It will take the spotlight off our kids while everything settles out."

"There has to be another way," Tag said.

"I've thought about this long and hard, my dear Tag, and there really is no other way. It's you they want. This entire time they were only using me to get to you."

"I can't bear to be away from you again."

"Whatever happened between us, you must know that I never once doubted your integrity."

He wrapped his arms around her. "I always knew you believed in me, Monica. That I never doubted."

"Don't worry, hon, we'll be together again very soon." She kissed him on the lips.

"You and the kids are the only thing in my life that matters."

"Hey, what about me?" Fez said.

Tag turned to him and laughed. "Yeah, kid, you too."

"That's more like it," Fez said.

He kissed her again, savoring this moment with the woman he loved and would always love, knowing that their brief reunion was about to end.

Chapter 44

They slept in the cabin that night, the four of them retiring early due to exhaustion. Upon waking the next morning, he fixed breakfast from the cans of black beans and corned beef hash he'd found in the cupboard. Fez happened upon a box of Frosted Flakes, and although there was no milk, he ate it dry, relishing the sugary wafers. Tag discovered a tin of coffee and some sugar, and using a percolator brewed up a fresh pot.

They sat around the kitchen table, eating quietly, a general sense of unease in the air. Only Nolette kept busy, feverishly tapping on her tablet in an attempt to get down as much information down as possible. Her long hair was still wet from rinsing it under the faucet and the bruises on her face had only started to scab over. Tag could see that prior to the attack, she'd been a very attractive woman.

"Oh my God!" Nolette said, pushing her chair out and standing.

"What is it?" Monica asked.

"You're not going to believe this." Nolette looked over at Tag and cracked a smile. "Last night, without telling any of you, I mass emailed that video to every one of my contacts. Overnight it's gone viral."

"Why didn't you tell us you sent that video?" Tag said.

"Sorry, Colonel, but I had to make an executive decision. I wasn't about to let any of you talk me out of it," she said, holding her cell phone up to his face. "Look, it's already got over twenty million hits."

"What are they saying on social media?" Monica asked, coming over to view the screen.

"The President has gone into seclusion and people all over are calling for his impeachment. Congress is in disarray and has been locked out of the Capitol by the Executive Branch. Every news outlet is pleading with you to come out of hiding and help bring this corrupt government down." She looked up, the hint of a smile over her normally passive face.

"How do they know I'm still alive?" he asked.

Swain shrugged.

"It pains me to see what has happened to this country," Tag said.

"There's protests in every major city," Nolette said, studying her screen. "Ground troops are being called in to help maintain order. Many opposition groups from both sides of the political spectrum are calling for you to come forth and lead the protest against the current administration."

"This is a sign, Tag," Monica said. "It's our chance to vindicate ourselves and be reunited with the kids."

"The video is having international repercussions as well. Israel is under attack from both Iran and Syria, sensing weakness in our government's political will. China and Russia are grumbling, too," Nolette said, scrolling down the screen.

"Damnit! I don't want to lead any protests," Tag said, pacing the floor. "All I want to do is return to my old way of life."

"Wake the hell up, Colonel, and look around you. There is no more everyday life to return to," Monica scolded him. "Your nation needs you, which means you have a moral obligation to help this country in its darkest hour."

"You'd be a wicked awesome president, Tag," Fez said. "Always wanted to go inside the White House and check it out."

Tag laughed. "Don't get your hopes up, kid. There's no chance in hell I'll be in the White House anytime soon, unless it's as a tourist."

Swain tapped her phone a few times. "I'm looking at a map of this area and can see that Route 212 is fifteen miles south of here. I just texted my news editor and he's willing to pick us up and drive us back to the city."

"He'll pick us up? All the way out here?" Monica asked.

"Oh, he'll do it alright. He's just asking for one favor."

"And what's that?" Monica asked.

"He wants first shot at interviewing the two of you."

"Fine. Just tell him to get over here before we get blown to pieces," Tag said.

Nolette snapped her phone shut. "He's on the road as we speak. Should be at our designated meeting place in nine or ten hours."

***

After breakfast they gathered up some food and headed out on the trail. Thick plumes of black smoke continued to rise up out of the valley. The going was slow because of the terrain and the various obstacles they had to overcome: fallen trees, ponds, hills and large boulders to traverse. They stopped for a brief lunch of beans, canned brown bread, and water. Eight hours later they emerged from the woods and found themselves on a barren stretch of road in the middle of nowhere.

They walked onto the pavement and glanced both ways. Not a car coming or going. They moved to the far right-hand lane and started off toward the gravel pit where they were to rendezvous with Swain's editor. Fifteen minutes passed before Fez started jumping up and down and shouting. From the south a large caravan of military vehicles were approaching. They ran off the road and hid in the woods until they passed.

After more than an hour of walking, the sign for the gravel pit came into view. Once safely inside, they collapsed on a pile of rocks and waited for Swain's editor to arrive. They bundled together to keep warm. After about two hours passed, a Cadillac Escalade pulled into the gravel pit and stopped next to them. A tall, patrician man with perfectly combed silver hair exited the car and walked over to them.

"Sorry, I drove here as fast as humanly possible." He smiled and took them in. "Had to do a lot of creative rerouting in order to get here. The Army has set up a roadblock at the entrance of 212." He walked over and shook Swain's hand. "You don't look so good, Nolette."

"I'm not going to lie to you, Forrest, it's been a rough few weeks." She pointed to Tag. "There's the real person you want to talk to."

The news editor moved over to Tag and shook his hand. "It's an honor to meet you, Colonel Winters. Forrest Powers, executive editor of the Washington Tribune."

"The pleasure is all mine." He shook the man's hand. "Is it safe for us to return home?"

"Not unless you've got a battalion of armed guards surrounding your house."

"What are you talking about?"

"You're currently the most popular man in America. People are scared as hell and have lost all faith in their leaders to protect them from these outbreaks. If you want my advice, Colonel, I'd recommend that you address the public right away and tell your story to them. Once they see that you are alive and well, and that you're an honest man who's been wronged, there's no way the government can come after you."

"Things are that bad out there?" Monica asked.

"It's worse than you can know. The only good thing to happen from all this is that people are finally united in their desire to get rid of both political parties and chart a new course."

"Why the hell not!" Tag laughed. "Now that I'm retired, I have a lot of time on my hands."

"Good, because you're going to need every second of it." He waved his arm. "Get in, everyone. I'm taking all of you directly to a protest march in D.C. tomorrow. We'll get you cleaned up, maybe a few hours rest, and then the four of you will appear onstage at a rally being held at the Lincoln Memorial."

"Lincoln Memorial." Fez whistled. "There going to be a lot of people there, Mister?"

"A lot of people?" Forrest laughed. "They're expecting the biggest crowd in the history of the Lincoln Memorial."

JOSEPH SOUZA

"What do they want me to say?" Tag asked.

"Quite frankly, Colonel, what they need right now is a hero, not a politician; a person they can trust and who is so above the political fray as not to have their integrity questioned. In that regard, I suggest you just speak from the heart."

"You're going to be famous, Tag," Fez said.

Tag ran his hand through Fez's hair. "Okay, let's get this over with. I think I have an idea what I'm going to talk about."

"And what is that, Colonel?"

"I'm going to deliver a eulogy to all the innocent people who died in these unjustified attacks."

***

Tag peeked out from behind the stage, staring at the crowd which stretched for as far as the eye could see. It was estimated that well over a million people had gathered here to protest what they believed was a corrupt and incompetent federal government. People in the crowd held signs and chanted slogans, and were comprised of all political parties and races.

Behind him stood his wife, Fez, and Swain. Helicopters circled above the District, keeping tabs on the massive crowd that had gathered. It was a beautiful day in the nation's Capital and the temperature hovered in the mid-fifties. A palpable but nervous tension hung in the air as a man dressed in traditional Indian garb spoke to the crowd about individual liberties and human rights. With his bald head and glasses he bore a slight resemblance to Gandhi. The crowd erupted with applause at his denunciation of the government's genocidal response to the epidemics. Near the end his speech, he requested a moment of silence for the victims of these two attacks.

Tag felt numb. He'd barely had time for a nap and shower. The fresh clothes on his body he'd borrowed from Forrest, and he'd tied his long hair into a ponytail, giving him the look of an aging hippie. Famous actors and rock stars had come backstage to thank him for his service to nation and to acknowledge his acts of heroics. Exhausted and mentally fatigued, he wanted nothing more than to spend time with his family. His kids had not made the trip to D.C., but all three promised to catch the next flight out.

He heard his name over the loudspeakers and realized that the Indian man was waving him over to the lectern. The crowd erupted into applause; like nothing he'd ever heard before. Walking onstage, he felt a rush of adrenaline pass through him upon hearing the crowd's cacophonous roar.

Tag reached the lectern and stuck out his hand, and the Indian man clasped it tightly before walking off the stage. Tag looked down at his hand and noticed that the man had placed a piece of paper in his hand. He gazed out upon the sea of people waving signs and flags, jumping up and down and blowing whistles and horns. Every square inch of real estate had been occupied by the protesters. For a second it frightened him, and, oddly enough, the first thing that came to mind was how quickly a virus could spread in such a scenario.

The crowd began to chant his name as a volunteer rushed onstage and raised the microphone to his lips. Jolted back to reality, Tag unfolded the sheet of paper on the lectern, waiting for what seemed like forever for the applause to stop. The words on the paper looked garbled, as if he was suffering from dyslexia. Had those petroleum fumes affected his cognitive skills? He finally managed to focus his gaze on the sheet, and somehow the words rearranged themselves and became legible. Below the words he noticed a pencil drawing of a ... a liger!

Congratulations, Colonel. I knew you could do it. If you will, envision a scenario where a highly contagious virus begins to spread amongst this crowd. H5N1 or maybe a case of Dengue fever. Could be anything actually. A simple organism of immense, mind-blowing beauty. What would you do then, Colonel? What happens when humanity becomes the virus that is sickening the planet? But fear not, Colonel. It's not the end of the world. Not yet anyways. Now it will be up to you to make the hard decisions facing this country.

Until we meet again,
Your friend

Shocked, Tag searched around for the Indian man, but he was nowhere to be found. He'd no doubt slipped back into the crowd by now and would be impossible to find. He noticed that his hands holding the paper were trembling. Staring up at the crowd, he saw that they had stopped chanting his name and were waiting in hushed silence for him to speak. He couldn't believe how quiet they'd become. Tears spilled down his cheeks thinking about all the people who had perished in these terrorist attacks. The words came slowly at first, but soon enough he had the crowd's undivided attention.

This is just the beginning of our national crisis and not the end. Because the danger is all around us now and not merely some abstract threat that happens on foreign shores. And if you think this can't happen in your own community then ...

ABOUT THE AUTHOR

Joseph Souza's award-winning short stories have been published in various literary journals throughout the country. Winner of the 2004 Andre Dubus Award for short fiction, he also won Honorable Mention for the Al Blanchard award in crime fiction. His novel The Reawakening was the 2013 Maine Literary Award for Speculative Fiction. He currently lives near Portland, Maine with his wife and kids. Visit http://www.josephsouza.net for more information.

Joseph Souza
Facebook: https://www.facebook.com/joseph.souza.7
Twitter: @josephsouza3
http://www.josephsouza.net/

Made in the USA
Monee, IL
18 November 2019